Susan Carlisle's love affair with books began when she made a bad grade in mathematics. Not allowed to watch TV until the grade had improved, she filled her time with books. Turning her love of reading into a love for writing romance, she now pens hot Medicals. She loves castles, travelling, afternoon tea, reading voraciously and hearing from her readers. Join her newsletter at SusanCarlisle.com.

Rachel Dove is a tutor and romance/romcom author from West Yorkshire in the UK. She lives with her husband and two sons, and dreams of a life where housework is done by fairies and she can have as many pets as she wants. When she's not writing or reading she can be found walking her American cocker spaniel, Oliver, in the great outdoors, or dreaming of her next research trip away with the family.

Withdr

Dubli

D0550621

Leabharlanna Taistil
Mobile Libraries
Tel: 8691415

Also by Susan Carlisle

A Daddy Sent by Santa
Nurse to Forever Mum
The Sheikh Doc's Marriage Bargain
Highland Doc's Christmas Rescue
Firefighter's Unexpected Fling
The Neonatal Doc's Baby Surprise

Fighting for the Trauma Doc's Heart

is **Rachel Dove**'s debut title

Look out for more books from Rachel Dove
coming soon

Discover more at millsandboon.co.uk.

Withdrawn From Stock
Dublin Public Libraries

Leabharlanna Taistil
Mobile Libraries
Tel: 8691415

PACIFIC PARADISE, SECOND CHANCE

SUSAN CARLISLE

FIGHTING FOR THE TRAUMA DOC'S HEART

RACHEL DOVE

Leabharlanna Taistil
Mobile Libraries
Tel: 8691415

MILLS & BOON

All rights reserved including the right of reproduction
in whole or in part in any form. This edition is published
by arrangement with Harlequin Books S.A.

This is a work of fiction. Names, characters, places, locations
and incidents are purely fictional and bear no relationship to
any real life individuals, living or dead, or to any actual places,
business establishments, locations, events or incidents.
Any resemblance is entirely coincidental.

This book is sold subject to the condition that it shall not,
by way of trade or otherwise, be lent, resold, hired out
or otherwise circulated without the prior consent of the publisher
in any form of binding or cover other than that in which it is published
and without a similar condition including this condition
being imposed on the subsequent purchaser.

® and TM are trademarks owned and used by the trademark owner
and/or its licensee. Trademarks marked with ® are registered with the
United Kingdom Patent Office and/or the Office for Harmonisation
in the Internal Market and in other countries.

First Published in Great Britain 2020
by Mills & Boon, an imprint of HarperCollins*Publishers*
1 London Bridge Street, London, SE1 9GF

Pacific Paradise, Second Chance © 2020 Susan Carlisle

Fighting for the Trauma Doc's Heart © 2020 Rachel Dove

ISBN: 978-0-263-27979-5

MIX
Paper from
responsible sources
FSC® C007454

This book is produced from independently certified FSC™ paper
to ensure responsible forest management.
For more information visit www.harpercollins.co.uk/green.

Printed and bound in Spain
by CPI, Barcelona

PACIFIC PARADISE, SECOND CHANCE

SUSAN CARLISLE

MILLS & BOON

To Colton

CHAPTER ONE

LANDON COCHRAN, MD, scrolled through the pages of the file on his tablet again. He studied the name in black on the screen: *Macie Beck*. Surely it wasn't the same woman. There must be any number of Macie Becks in the world. What were the chances that the one he had known was currently in the Northern Mariana Islands? Even slimmer the chance that she'd be on the small island of Saipan? It couldn't be her.

As the one-hundred-and-fifty-passenger plane circled the twelve-mile-long lush green island below, Landon looked out the window. Though it was an American territory, Saipan was closer to China than to Hawaii.

The plane lined up for its approach along the single landing strip of the airport, which was built on top of a mountain. This was nothing like the busy airports he was used to. There was none of the hustle and bustle, not even another plane in sight.

He gathered his satchel and hoped his larger bag had made it onto the airplane. In this part of the world, weight was carefully considered on flights. Often bags would be left behind to show up on the next plane, which might be the next day. It had happened to him only once, but ever since, he carried a change of clothes in his smaller bag just in case.

Soon, the plane landed and passengers were disembarking. As Landon stepped out and walked down the metal stairway that had been rolled to the plane, he looked at the lush vines and vegetation all around the area. This part of the world was hot, muggy and rainy. *Welcome to the tropics*, he thought. He followed the other passengers across the tarmac to the low gray terminal.

Landon entered the cool building and waited for his luggage. Twenty minutes later, with his rolling bag in hand, he headed out the glass doors to the parking lot, where the late afternoon heat was offset by a slight ocean breeze. Across the street stood the abandoned cement bones of a chain hotel, left unfinished.

He located a man who held a card with his name on it.

"I'm Dr. Cochran."

"Welcome to Saipan." The man gave him a toothy grin and took his large bag, then led Landon toward a car. "I am Mario," he said with a slight accent.

While Mario put his bag in the trunk, Landon chose to sit in the front so he could check out the area. He wasn't here to be pampered. He had a tough job ahead, and he needed to familiarize himself with the people and the island as quickly as possible.

As Mario drove down the winding road toward the coast, they passed small square houses made of cement blocks. Many had grassy yards while others were surrounded by dirt spaces filled with chickens. They turned south up a wider two-lane road that skirted the coastline. Businesses lined the sides of the road, many with palm trees in front that swirled in the wind. To Landon's amazement, cars filled the roadway.

For someone who had grown up in the American Midwest, this was a completely different environment. When he was in the navy, he'd been deployed as far west as

Hawaii, where he had loved the heat, breeze and ocean. Apparently, he would get plenty of that here. That was, if he had a chance to get out of the hospital long enough to appreciate it. He'd come to evaluate the Saipan Hospital and ensure that it received the updates necessary to give the people of Saipan and the surrounding islands the best healthcare possible.

Soon, a white building with windows running across the front came into view. Mario steered the car into the circular drive and stopped under the brick porte cochere.

"Here we are." Mario gave Landon another grin before getting out. Landon followed suit and met him at the rear of the car to pick up his luggage.

"Thank you," he said to the man, then took the handle of his luggage and rolled it behind him through the glass-door entrance.

Inside, the building was cool. A long tile corridor lay before him, and he searched for a sign that would direct him to the administration office. The pharmacy was located to his left and the emergency waiting room entrance to his right, yet he didn't see any directions to Administration, so he continued down the hallway cross an intersection of a hall and continued on. At the end of the long hall he took a chance and turned left. There he found the office.

After opening the single glass door, he spoke to the thirtysomething, slim, local woman behind the desk. "I'm Dr. Landon Cochran of the World Health Organization. Macie Beck should be expecting me."

Once more, the idea that it might be the same Macie he had known sent a jolt of apprehension through him. Their final parting wasn't one he was proud of. He'd left her in her bed after a night of passion with the promise to call her when he got off his shift at the hospital, but that hadn't happened.

The receptionist glanced toward a closed door. "Macie isn't here right now."

"I assume she is expecting me?"

"She was…uh…is, but they were short of help in the ER and she's down there." The woman looked unsure as she picked up the phone. "I'll let her know you're here."

Landon shook his head. "Don't interrupt her if she's working."

Relief replaced the worry in the receptionist's expression. She stood and came around the desk. "Your office is this way." She led him to a doorway across the waiting room area. "Please make yourself at home." She then left Landon to himself.

Landon grabbed his luggage and entered the room. It was a small space by usual office standards, but it suited him. His work as interim administrator of the Saipan Hospital didn't require a grand office. A bookcase with a few items on it filled the wall behind a very basic desk and chair that faced the door. Windows flanked it on both sides. A couple of chairs that didn't look comfortable sat in front of the desk. A small door off to the side led, Landon assumed, to the restroom.

The receptionist returned shortly and said, "I spoke to Macie. She said she would be here as soon as she could get away and for me to help you in any way I can."

"Okay, then let's start with your name." Landon parked his suitcase beside the desk and walked behind it.

"I'm Tatiana Yuka."

He smiled and the woman visibly relaxed. "It's nice to meet you."

"You too, sir. Would you like me to show you around?" Rolling his chair out, he took his suit jacket off and hung it over the back. "I think I'd like to see the policy-and-procedures manual first."

"You'll find it right there." She pointed to a thick white notebook on the shelf behind the desk.

He pulled it off the shelf and had a seat. "Thanks. Please let me know when Ms. Beck arrives."

"Yes, sir."

Landon got to work. If all went well with this assignment, that promotion he had been working toward for years would be his. He glanced up to see a couple of hours had passed and still no Macie Beck. It was time to go after her. People didn't usually leave him hanging when he wanted to see them. He stepped out of the office. "Tatiana?"

"Sir?"

"If I'm needed, I'll be in the ER."

Concern washed over her face. "Yes, sir. You know where it is?"

"I do. I saw the sign on the way in." Landon turned right and soon reached the intersection and started up the long hall toward the front of the hospital. This time he observed the areas that made up the hospital more closely. He walked by rooms on each side of the hall. Those appeared to hold general medicine patients. He nodded to staff and people he passed. They all gave him a curious look.

Returning to the first intersection where a similar hall crossed, he stopped and looked down each one. The signs indicated the left hall was the pediatric unit and the other side the geriatric unit. He continued on until he saw the double sliding doors of the emergency room waiting area. As he did, the wail of an ambulance in the distance caught his ear.

He entered the waiting area and spoke to the man behind the registration desk. "Please point me in the direction of Macie Beck?"

The staff member looked uncertain. "Uh, she's busy right now."

Landon's patience had become short. After all, Macie had known when he was arriving at Saipan, and it had been over two hours since she'd been informed that he'd wanted to see her. It was time to search her out. "I think she can take a moment for me. I'm the interim administrator, Dr. Cochran."

The man's eyes widened and he pointed behind him. "Uh…hello, sir. Let me walk back there with you." Landon followed the man through the doors into a large space subdivided into smaller areas by curtains. A circular desk was in the center of the room. In front of it stood a petite woman wearing the same light green scrubs as the rest of the staff. Her back was to him and he could see that her dark brown hair had been pulled back at the nape of her neck.

His heart thumped against his chest wall. He recognized those fine feminine curves. It was *his* Macie Beck.

She turned and her gaze met his.

Of all the islands in all the world, this was the one he'd been assigned to. Now he knew how Rick felt in *Casablanca* when Ilsa showed up in his bar.

Well, well, well. If it wasn't *the* Landon Cochran.

The one who had left her high and dry all those years ago when she'd been working in Hawaii at the Veterans' Hospital. Even a Dear John would have been better than the nothing she got after their one and only night together. Landon had not just ignored her, he had left the island. He'd stamped her "men can't be trusted" card and then disappeared.

To make the situation worse, she had been vulnerable after what had happened with her father, and Landon's defection had devastated her. Her fragile pride had taken another hit. It had taken weeks of them working together for her to start trusting Landon. She didn't have any faith in her judgment regarding people, but Landon had managed to get around that. When he had left, she'd been confident he'd found out what her father had done and wanted nothing more to do with her. Landon wouldn't have been the first person. She had hoped Hawaii would have been far enough away to get out from under her father's criminal shadow.

But that had all been eight years ago. Mercy, Landon still looked good. Handsome as ever. He'd filled out some from the lean young man he had once been. His shoulders seemed broader and his body sturdier. Yet there was something granite hard about him, as if he'd seen some tough times. His hair, a tawny color, still had a touch of the unruly waves she remembered well.

He brushed a hand through it. That was the same gentle hand she had seen in action with patients and had experienced directly when it cupped her cheek just before he'd kissed her. And then had done more. Those thoughts were better off not being revisited.

The siren grew louder, cutting her Landon-induced stupor short. She shook her head. There wasn't time for those memories. "Dr. Cochran, I hope you haven't forgotten your medical skills while pushing papers. We could use them now. Auto accident. Three casualties, one a child."

Macie hurried toward the ER entrance. She didn't have time to worry about Landon. There were patients coming in. As she passed the supply cart, she snatched up a mask and nitrile gloves. She handed Landon a gown and left him to get the other supplies he needed.

"Put the boy in exam room two and the man in three. The woman in six." She followed the gurney with the boy on it.

Macie carried out the processes to hook the boy up to the monitors. A deep voice she had heard for months, maybe even years, after her heart had been broken said, "What do we have here?"

"Eight-year-old boy with lacerations to his leg, face and hand."

Landon stood beside her. Too close. "Before I start stitching, I need X-rays to check for broken bones. Start an IV of fluids and give pain meds as needed. A little something to calm him as well."

"He'll need to go down to X-Ray." Macie punched buttons, getting the monitors set.

Landon asked over his shoulder as he stepped out of the way. "Where's the portable one?"

She hated to admit this. "We don't have one."

"Just see it's done while I check to see if the ER doctor needs help with the other two patients." Landon left her.

Macie saw to the medicines Landon had ordered all the while reassuring the boy that his mother was fine. She then started cleaning around his injuries Landon returned fifteen minutes later.

"Has he been to X-Ray yet?"

"No. They're backed up." Macie continued her work.

Landon's lips thinned into a tight line. "Unhook him. Grab the end of his bed and the IV pole."

"What're we doing?" Macie demanded as she obeyed.

"We're taking him there ourselves."

She couldn't agree with him more. As a nurse practitioner she had authority, but she couldn't override procedure like Landon was doing. "Yes, sir."

She remembered his curt decisiveness from long ago. Time hadn't softened that part of his personality. She had appreciated it back then and did now as well. So why hadn't he said goodbye to her all those years ago? That seemed so out of character for him.

Together they rolled the boy out of the department and into the hallway.

"Which way?" Landon asked over his shoulder as he pulled the gurney ahead of her.

"Right," she called. "Down the hall on the right."

Moments later they wheeled the boy into X-Ray.

Landon spoke to the woman behind the desk. "This patient needs X-rays right now."

The woman blinked and stood. "You can't come in here—"

Oh, no. This wasn't going to go well. Landon was about to butt heads with Yuri, the most formidable woman at the hospital. Macie shook her head from where she stood behind Landon.

"I'm Dr. Cochran. This child needs X-rays before I can stitch him up. He needs them now."

"Yuri?" Macie gained the woman's attention. "Dr. Cochran is our new administrator."

Her eyes widened. "Come on through. A clerk was just on his way to get the boy."

"We have saved him the trouble," Landon said on their way past her desk. "Macie and I can handle everything."

Minutes later they had the boy on the X-ray table. Macie stayed with the child as Landon saw to taking the pictures. When they finished, he studied the film for a few minutes.

He rejoined them at the gurney and smiled, cheerfully informing the boy, "It looks like there are no broken bones."

"That's good news." Macie patted the boy's shoulder.

"Now we can get you back to the ER. Then you can check on your mother."

The boy nodded, tears welling in his eyes.

Macie pulled the gurney and Landon pushed. "Don't worry, honey. Dr. Cochran is going to take good care of you." She glanced up to see Landon watching them before he looked away to navigate the hallway. She'd forgotten how good he was with people. His smooth charm had certainly gotten to her. Maybe it was because he had recognized the pain in her like he did in his patients.

She'd been a mess back then. The year before, she had learned that her father, whom she had idolized, was a crook. She had lived a charmed life. The big house, the best schools, her first car a sports car. Her family had traveled. Her mother had been on a number of fundraising committees, and she and her brother and sister had run with the "in crowd." Life had been all she could have dreamed of until…it wasn't. It had all been a lie. Her father had built it all on nothing real. When her world had imploded, it had been public and in royal fashion. Her pain had been raw. If Landon hadn't seen it, maybe he had sensed it.

Back at the exam room, she and Landon situated the boy in the right spot.

"I'm going to start with your leg." He spoke to her and the boy. "Then do your head and then your hand. None of this will hurt, I promise. But I'm going to need you to be very still."

The boy nodded as his eyes closed. The pain medicines were taking effect.

"I need a suture kit over here," Landon called to no one in particular as he pulled a stool up next to the bed.

Macie had already anticipated what he would need and had pulled it off the supply cart. Landon began his careful work.

Half an hour later, Macie regarded Landon's patient. "I see you haven't lost your skills."

Landon pushed back from the gurney. He arched his back, stretching. It pulled his dress shirt tight across his chest. The muscles beneath the thin material showed clearly. He straightened and stood, moving to the boy's head. "Let's see about that when I'm completely done here. One down and two to go. At least this one will be in his hairline. He won't have to worry about a scar."

Macie had already cleaned up the last suture kit and replaced it with a new one.

"And I see that you're still as efficient as ever," Landon said.

"I wasn't sure you remembered me." She sucked in a breath, horrified. "I can't believe I just said that. This isn't the time or the place."

"Macie—"

Thankfully, one of the nurses stuck her head inside the room. "Macie, the mother is asking after her son."

Grateful for a reason to escape Landon, Macie said, "Liz, assist Dr. Cochran while I go talk to her."

It was an hour later before she saw Landon again. She'd just hung up the phone after making sure the rooms for the car-accident patients were ready. Her hands shook as he stepped to her.

"If everything is under control here, Macie, we still need to talk."

"Talk?" The word came out as a squawk. She didn't

want to talk about what had happened between them years ago.

"Yes, about the hospital. You are head of Nursing and I'm the interim administrator." He watched her as if he wasn't sure she was understanding him.

Relief settled over her. She could handle business talk. Staying away from the personal was her plan, despite her one little slipup. Still, she couldn't help but want to know why he'd left her like he had. She'd believed that he had enjoyed their night together as much as she had. She had thought they'd had something special. At least, it had been special to her. Even now he made her blood flow faster. She needed a calm head before she discussed anything—including business—with him.

"I've been on for over sixteen hours. What I need right now is a little R & R. Surely our talk can wait until tomorrow. I still need to show you where you're staying while you're here."

"Okay, we'll let the discussion wait. For now. I could use some rest as well."

"Then I'll drive you to your house and we'll meet tomorrow. I have to go by my office, and I can meet you at the front door in ten minutes." That would give her a few more minutes to gather her thoughts.

"I need to get my suitcase. It's in my office. I'll walk with you."

It looked like she wouldn't be getting those sorely needed few minutes alone. As they headed for Landon's office, she nodded back the way they had come. "Thanks for stepping in back there."

His pace matched hers. "Not a problem. I haven't felt that adrenaline rush in a long time."

"How long have you been working for World Health?"

Landon looked at her. "I was given the opportunity about four years ago. And I'm not a paper pusher."

"Hatchet man?"

His brows drew together. "No. Why would you think that?"

"Isn't that what you do? Close hospitals?" She tried to keep her tone light but missed the mark.

"Again, no. I'm here to evaluate the Saipan Hospital. Review what needs to be done to make it better. See what I can do to move it forward. Closing it has never been on the table."

At least that sounded positive. Macie had come to love this island and its people, and she wouldn't let anything hurt them if she could help it. Landon had said all the right things. She hoped he was being honest rather than diplomatic.

"You do know we've had four administrators in as many years."

"I do. I plan to position the hospital and get it the funding it needs, so that a permanent administrator will want to come and stay."

"So, you're swooping in like Superman to make it all better." Now her bitterness had started to show. That wouldn't be the best way to influence Landon.

They had arrived at their offices. "Why, Macie, I never imagined you'd become a cynic. I'm sorry to hear that. I'm not Superman, but I was assigned this job because the World Health board believed I could do some good here."

"I'm not cynical. I'm practical. I'll meet you at the front door." She left him for the safety of her office, where she closed the door.

Thirty minutes later, with Landon in the passenger seat of her car, she drove along the winding road on the opposite side of the island from the hospital. This area wasn't nearly as populated and the road rose high above the water.

Abruptly, he confessed, "I wondered if it was you when I saw your name in the hospital files. I'll admit I'm surprised to find you still this far from the mainland."

Macie glanced at Landon. She'd guessed he had been as surprised to see her as she had been to see him. In a tight tone she answered, "And I imagine you never planned on seeing me again anywhere."

"That's not what I meant. I realize I left in the wrong way." He shifted his long legs in the cramped car.

His discomfort made her smile with satisfaction. Yeah, he'd left in the wrong way. To promise to call a woman you just bedded and not to do so made him the lowest form of male. Even lower than her father had been. She should've known better than to trust the charming Dr. Cochran. That was what her father had done to all those people he'd stolen from. He'd charmed them out of their money like Landon had charmed her into giving herself to him. Back then she'd been too weak to recognize she was being used.

Things were different now. She'd been hurt and had recovered, had learned her lesson. It was time to move on, just like she had worked to do where her father was concerned. "We both have a job to oversee here. Let's focus on that."

"Agreed." He twisted in the seat again. "I think I would've been better off riding strapped to the top. Is this the smallest car ever made?"

Macie chuckled without sympathy. "Pretty much. Keep in mind this is an island and everything must be shipped in. Size matters."

"Got it. No big SUVs."

"A few, but mostly for the tourists." To her great relief his bungalow came into sight. She pulled the car into a short drive and stopped behind another small car. This house had one of the best views on the entire island. It was home for all the hospital administrators, permanent or interim. She'd been there more than once for a social gathering. The porch, with its white wicker rockers and swing, was her favorite. She'd always thought it would be a wonderful spot to sleep on a rainy night. No doubt that would be lost on Landon. He was here for business and nothing more.

The house was situated on a cliff and built out of cinder block like so many of the other homes on Saipan. Coming from a wood-and-brick world, the construction was unusual to her, but she'd soon learned that with the tropical weather and salt water, it was more practical. Surrounding the house was a small grassy yard and on either side of the front door were flowerpots with bright yellow bougainvillea.

She climbed out. Landon did as well with a groan. "Thanks for the torture-chamber ride."

"Would you have rather walked?" she asked too sweetly.

"No. I was thinking more about calling Mario."

Closing the door of the car, she headed toward the house. "You'd still be waiting on him. It's dinner time and he's with his family. Come on, I'll show you around, then I must get going."

He pulled his bag from the back seat. "Where do you live?"

"Close to the hospital." Macie fished for the key to the place in her scrubs pocket and unlocked the door. Pushing it open, she flipped on the overhead light and moved on into the living area, which ran the length of the back of the house. Thankfully, it was maintained and kept furnished in readiness all the time.

Landon put his bag and satchel inside the door and followed her.

"The bedrooms are through there." She pointed down a short hall. "And the kitchen is over this way." She walked to the black-and-white tiled floor. The house was clearly meant for a family.

"This is far more than I need."

Macie agreed with him. "Perhaps, but this is where the administrators live. They hold a certain position on the island. Need to entertain." She moved to the French doors that opened off the living room and stepped out onto the screened porch. Taking a deep breath, she looked out over the rocky cliffs at the bright, lush vegetation to the blue-green ocean beyond. The sight always awed her, making her problems feel small.

She felt more than saw Landon come to stand beside her.

"This is magnificent."

It was nice to hear that he appreciated it. "I couldn't agree more. When someone asks why I live so far from civilization, I describe this view."

"Why *do* you live so far from civilization?"

Macie had no interest in talking with him or with anyone else about why she had run away to the islands. She wanted to forget that time. That was her secret to carry. She had no desire to relive those days. Seeing him again was enough emotional upheaval for one day.

Landon shifted beside her. "Sorry. That's really not my business."

On that they could agree. She turned and started toward the door. "I'll see you tomorrow, Dr. Cochran. The keys to your car are on the hook by the door. If you need anything, call the hospital. They can get in touch with me. I'll send someone."

He muttered a bewildered "Okay."

It wasn't until she'd backed out of the drive and headed down the road that she took a few deep breaths and settled her racing mind. As if it wasn't bad enough to have Landon back in her life, he'd done the double whammy by bringing up thoughts of her father. Somehow, every truly painful event in her life had been crammed into today.

CHAPTER TWO

LANDON HAD BEEN behind his desk working for a couple of hours when he glanced up to see Macie headed for her office. He looked at his watch. Seven o'clock. She hadn't slept in either.

He needed to move this review along. If he could implement some big-impact, low-cost innovations, that would secure him the job he really wanted— Director of the World Health Organization. His focus was improving medical conditions in underprivileged and sparsely populated areas. He could proudly say he had been successful. The Saipan Hospital shouldn't be any different.

He walked over to Macie's door and leaned his shoulder against the frame.

She looked up. He hadn't forgotten just how attractive she was. When they had first met at the hospital where they'd worked on the same floor, she had struck him has a pretty woman, but she'd had such sad eyes.

After working together for a few weeks, they both happened to attend the party of a coworker where they had gravitated toward each other, spending most of their time in a corner talking. Since the party had been held in the apartment complex where they both lived, he had walked her home.

On an impulse, he had asked her out and they'd dated

over the next month as their schedules had allowed. One thing had led to another and she had invited him into her bedroom. With Macie he had always felt a special spark. That hadn't gone away.

Landon looked at her closer. That sadness she'd once had in her eyes was gone now. Was it defiance, determination or maybe unease that had replaced it? The last bothered him more than he liked.

She cleared her throat.

He blinked and straightened. "Do you mind if we have our talk over some food? I'm hungry."

That didn't seem to reassure her. "Shouldn't we do it privately?"

"I don't think what we say at this point will be so sensitive we need to worry. We aren't going to get into a public brawl, are we?"

"I don't know. I've not heard what you have to say yet."

He liked this frank Macie. She'd been so meek and unsure when he'd first met her that she would have never spoken to him like that. Maybe he needed to ease his way in more, get her on his side. "I'm more interested in what you think needs to be done."

Her eyes widened. "I do have some ideas."

"I thought you might." He nodded.

She leveled a look at him. "You don't know me well enough now to know what I'd think."

"Touché. And that may be so, but I saw your determination in the ER and your face when you had to tell me there was no portable X-ray machine. I'm making an educated guess that you have some thoughts on what could improve care around here."

Her lips thinned in thought.

He waved a hand encouraging her in his direction. "Come on, live dangerously and have breakfast with me."

She hesitated a moment before she pushed the chair back and stood. He didn't let the satisfaction show on his face for fear she would change her mind. Macie would be a key component in the success of his job here. Somehow, he had to win her over.

Macie led the way out of her office, turned left down the hall and headed through a breezeway. "I see you found your way to the hospital this morning."

He matched his strides to her shorter ones. "I did. I made a couple of wrong turns but I managed."

"The nice thing about living on an island is if you keep going in one direction you'll eventually end up where you need to be." She opened a door and they entered another building, which held the cafeteria.

There they went through the line and chose their food. Macie directed him into a courtyard filled with palm trees and cement tables with benches.

Landon set his tray on the table. "This is nice. I don't usually get to eat a meal in such nice weather."

She sat down across from him. "One of the perks of living so close to the equator. It's warm year-round. We have the steadiest temperature in the world, I've been told."

They ate for a few minutes before Macie said, "So what're you wanting to do here, Landon? Save us from ourselves?"

He gave her a level look. "I don't think you're coming into this with the right attitude."

"The only attitude I have is one of skepticism. I've seen administrators come in here and think they can change the world, then they leave. 'Fix-it guys' don't last. No one ever stays long enough to see through even one change. What this hospital needs is someone who'll stay for the long haul. Those of us left behind just keep on doing what we can, doing what we know is best for our patients."

"I get it. We need to make it attractive for an administrator to stay. I'll put that at the top of the list."

She put her fork down and leaned forward. "If you're making a list—"

"I can assure you I am." He forked up some eggs and looked at her.

"Then we need equipment. More specifically, money for it." She almost spat the words.

"Okay. I'll add that to the list." He continued to watch her. That was something he had always enjoyed doing. Her face was so expressive. Especially that moment when he had entered her. After all these years he could remember it clearly. Landon shook his head, clearing it of those types of thoughts.

"And we need doctors who specialize but who are also willing to do general medicine." Macie's words came faster.

"Okay."

She leaned toward him in her eagerness. "There need to be incentives so that they stay for an extended length of time."

"Anything more?"

Macie pursed her lips and leaned back. "I think that's it for right now."

He nodded. "Feel better?"

She smiled. "As a matter of fact, I do."

Landon continued, "I've been reviewing protocols, staff positions and the number of employees. I believe there are areas that can be improved. I'd like us to sit down and evaluate each department individually. I'd also like your insights on each of them."

"Okay. And when do you expect me to do my job?"

"Don't you have someone you can call on to help?" She wasn't going to make this easy on him. He didn't want to have to pull rank to get her cooperation.

"I might, but they have their jobs as well." She pushed her tray away and folded her arms on the table, pinning him with a look. She should have asked this yesterday in the ER. "You do have a current medical license?"

"I do."

"Then I'll tell you what. Why don't you take a few days to work in every department and get some first-hand knowledge instead of looking through the numbers? Then you might really get to know what's going on. We're short on help and you could do something that would actually matter while you're here."

Apparently, the soft-spoken woman he remembered was long gone. Macie wanted to play hardball. She continued to watch him intently. He had never felt more like a nasty germ under a microscope. "You know, that's not a bad idea. But only if you're working right beside me."

She blinked. Her mouth opened and closed. "Why do I need to do that?"

"Because you know everyone, and they'll be less on their guard around me with you putting them at ease."

That determined look had turned to one of anxiousness. "But I can't—"

"Sure you can. Plan our schedule." He checked his watch. Standing, he picked up his tray and hers as well. "I'll be ready to start tomorrow. Have a good day, Macie."

Landon turned his back to her with the sting of daggers hitting him between the shoulder blades. He didn't have to see Macie to know she wasn't happy with him.

Macie watched Landon stroll off like his demands hadn't twisted her world into a knot. He'd called her bluff and now she'd be stuck working closely with him for the foreseeable future. This wasn't what she wanted. All that planning she'd done the night before to stay as far away from him as possible had just gone up like steam after a rain.

She wanted the best for the hospital, and was willing to do what she could to help that happen, but working every minute with Landon might be more than she could endure. The hospital board had requested she be the point person between the hospital and the World Health Organization when the Board had asked for help in developing a strategy. When she agreed to the role, she'd had no idea Landon would be the person she'd have to work with.

For her, their past was just too tender. She would have said that she was over it until Landon had shown up. His arrival had brought all those emotions rushing back.

Only a few months before she'd first met Landon, she had joined a traveling nurses program to get away from the media, who were hounding her about her father's Ponzi scheme bilking millions of people out of their savings. Her family had lived in luxury while others were being cheated. To think about it even now made her sick.

Being on the other side of the world had been the perfect way to get out of the spotlight. The Veterans' Hospital in Hawaii had been her first assignment. She hadn't trusted anyone, yet the new navy doctor, Landon Cochran, had gotten past her defenses—at least those around her heart. She had started to trust again. Not enough to share everything about her past but enough to enjoy his warmth. She had started to believe there could be something real and lasting between them.

Then when he hadn't called, when he'd just disappeared, she'd felt used. Just like when her father had demanded she attend his trial and stand behind him at all the media events. It wasn't surprising Landon's actions had knocked her feet out from under her again. She was obviously a poor judge of character. Never again would she put herself in the position to let someone do that to her.

It wasn't until she had been assigned to Saipan that she had started rebuilding her life. When it had been time to move on to a new location, she had decided to leave the traveling nurses program and had stayed in Saipan. Here she could make a difference, and no one knew who her father was. Her work became her life. There had been a man here and there but nothing that meant anything.

Macie slowly walked back to her office. The hallways were busier than they had been an hour earlier. She stopped a couple of times to answer people's questions. When she finally arrived at Administration, Landon's door was closed. Was he out somewhere checking on things or cloistered with his papers? It didn't matter. She had to figure out their schedule, including making arrangements with the other departments for them to fill in. Then she had to find someone to cover her job. Easier said than done. Her guess was that she'd be putting in extra hours for the next few weeks.

As she came in and out of her office throughout the day, Landon's door remained closed. Before she left for the evening, she knocked on it.

"Enter." Landon's deep voice came from the other side. She'd secretly hoped that he wouldn't answer and she could just leave the scrubs she'd brought on his desk.

She opened the door to find him sitting behind the desk with notebooks and papers spread out all over it. Landon looked up. He wore black-rimmed glasses that should have distracted from his looks; instead, they made him appear super sexy. She stared.

"Hey, what's up?"

Her attention went to his dress shirt sleeves, which were once again rolled up to reveal tan forearms. His hair looked as if he'd been running his hands through it.

"Macie?"

"Oh, I brought you some scrubs. You might want to wear them. You stand out like a flower in the desert in your dress clothes. If you haven't noticed, we're more causal on the island."

"Like a flower in the desert, huh? A flower on a cactus, I'd guess."

"You said that, not me." She grinned and stepped closer to the desk, holding up the garments.

"Why just green scrubs?"

"I don't know. It's what they were wearing when I first came to the hospital. I think everyone sees it as a team uniform."

"A team? Interesting. I can use that to my advantage."

Macie didn't like his look or his statement. She was tempted to snatch the clothing back. "What do you mean by that?"

He stretched his arms over his shoulders. "Just that I've learned that my job doesn't encourage people to open up, and I need them to."

She watched his shirt tighten across his chest. He'd taken care of himself through the years. "I don't imagine it does. Do you mind that?"

He shrugged. "It's more like, I accept it comes with the territory."

"Then why do what you do?"

He crossed his arms on his desk. "Because it needs to be done and I'm good at it."

"You like being a hatchet man?" She couldn't keep her distaste out of her words.

"I'm not a hatchet man." He enunciated each word. "I'd like you to quit looking at me like that. Because it isn't true. I'm good at ferreting out problems and offering solutions."

"And you like that better than caring for people?" Disbelief rang clear in her voice.

"I am still caring for people. Just not one at a time."

She shoved the scrubs at him. "Speaking of one at a time, we're expected on the floor at seven a.m."

Landon's voice followed her to the door. "I'll be ready to get started when you are."

How sad was it that she liked that deep throaty sound of his voice as much as she had before?

The next morning, Macie looked up to see Landon standing in her doorway wearing the scrubs. He made the less than attractive clothes look dashing and, worse than that, the color of them brought out the green in his eyes. She had to figure out some way to wall off the pull he had on her if she were to survive his stay. His hopefully short-lived stay.

"I'm ready." She stood and came around the desk, picking up her phone as she went.

"So where are we headed?" Landon asked as she joined him.

"We'll be spending the next two days in the geriatric unit."

He waved an arm toward the door. "Great. Lead on."

To her amazement, he didn't seem deterred. All he did was wrap the stethoscope he had been holding around his neck and head toward the door. She hadn't expected enthusiasm.

Macie led the way to their assigned area. Stopping at the nurses' desk, she checked in and introduced Landon to the two nurses there. Taking the handle of the chart cart, she pushed it toward the closest patient room.

"What're you doing?"

"Making rounds."

"With that?" He waved a hand toward the cart. "I've not seen a chart cart except in pictures. Don't you have a tablet to do charting on?"

She shook her head. "They are on the wish list but there hasn't been enough money to make that happen."

He shook his head but didn't say anything more as they stopped outside a patient's room.

Macie pulled a chart out of the rack and flipped it open.

"So tell me about our first patient."

"This is Mrs. Neeboo. She's eighty-four years old. Has COPD. She had a heart attack twenty years ago but has done well since. I think at last count she has ten grandchildren and eight great-grandchildren."

Landon's brow wrinkled and he stepped closer, looking over her shoulder at the chart. His scent filled her nose. He smelled of citrus and something else she knew all too well was special to him. Macie still liked it. Too much.

"Is that thing about her grandchildren written on the chart?"

She grinned. "No. I just know that. A couple of her children and three of her grandchildren work here at the hospital."

His lips thinned into a tight smile. "Funny. I was wondering what was being required for your records."

"This hospital is very much a family affair. Many families depend on it not only for their medical care but also for their livelihood."

"Point taken, Macie." He took the chart from her.

Macie knocked on the door, then pushed it open. She went to the end of the bed and Landon joined her. From there the aging woman could clearly see them.

"Good morning, Mrs. Neeboo," Macie said. "How're you feeling today?"

"Much better. I'm ready to go home. My family is expecting me to cook Sunday dinner."

Macie glanced at Landon, who was reading the chart. "Mrs. Neeboo, this is Dr. Cochran. He'll be taking care of you today."

The older woman gave him her attention. A suspicious look filled her eyes. The island people were friendly, but they also guarded themselves until they knew people well.

Landon handed the chart back to Macie and stepped to the side of the bed. In a gentle voice he said, "Mrs. Neeboo, it's nice to meet you. Please call me Landon. I'd like your permission to examine you. I promise to be gentle."

Macie moved so she stood across from him.

"Now, I'm going to have to shine a light in your eyes."

Landon pulled a penlight out of his pocket. He had come prepared. I know it's irritating but it gives me an idea of how you're doing. I'd like you to look up at the TV and keep looking that way." He shone the light in both her eyes. "Good, good." He flipped off the light and slipped it back into his pocket. "Now I'd like you to watch my finger." He moved it back and forth.

Mrs. Neeboo did as he asked with great concentration.

"Good. This might tickle a little bit, but I'm going to check your ears."

He pulled an otoscope out of his pocket and placed it in the woman's ears.

"Please put your head back."

Mrs. Neeboo did as he asked and Landon looked up her nostrils.

"Perfect."

He pulled his stethoscope from around his neck, put the ear pieces in and placed the bell on the woman's chest. "I need to give your heart a good listen."

Macie watched Landon's face as he focused on what he heard. His gaze flickered to hers. That hot awareness she remembered from before zipped through her.

Landon said to Mrs. Neeboo, "Wonderful. Could I get you to sit forward a little?"

He slipped his arm in behind her to help. Macie supported her as well.

"Breathe deeply for me." Landon moved the bell to the patient's back.

The old woman did as he asked.

"One more time please." He paused, then said, "Very nice." His arm brushed Macie's as he eased it out and Mrs. Neeboo lay back.

Even such a small touch was like hot lava against her skin. She couldn't afford to have that type of reaction where Landon was concerned.

"I'm going to do some poking and prodding. Just let me know if anything hurts." Landon started at her neck and worked over her shoulders. "Now I'm going to have to push on your abdomen, so bear with me."

Macie slowly lowered the bed so the older woman was lying flat.

"Tell me about the people in all these pictures." Landon glanced at the frames lining the counter under the window.

"My grandchildren." There was a proud note in her voice. "They are blessings from God. Do you have any children, Dr. Cochran?"

Landon continued to work as he answered, "No. Not even a wife."

Why did that bit of knowledge make Macie's heart skip?

Mrs. Neeboo patted Landon's forearm. "Life is too short to live it alone."

"Maybe one day…" Landon sounded as if he were placating the woman, trying to get out of the discussion.

Macie would have found it humorous if she hadn't been so interested in his answers. Which she shouldn't be. Why hadn't he married?

"All is well. Next, I'd like to have a little peek at your legs and feet." Instead of flipping the sheet down, he carefully pushed it up from her feet. He then gently ran his hands up her calves. Smiling, he placed the sheet back. "You seem to be in good form."

Mrs. Neeboo looked at Landon as if he were a piece of candy. He'd charmed the old woman, just like he'd once charmed Macie. But that wouldn't happen again. Macie adjusted the blanket over the patient.

"I think, the rate you're going, you should be home for that Sunday dinner." He patted her hand. "But I don't want you doing the cooking. Take a few days to be waited on. It was nice to meet you. I look forward to seeing you outside the hospital instead of in it. I'm going to write up your discharge order soon. One of the nurses will be in to see about getting you out of here."

"Thank you, doctor."

Landon patted her leg. "You're welcome."

Once again in the hall, he turned to Macie and put out his hand. "Next."

Macie handed him another chart then followed him to the next patient's door. She couldn't deny that Landon had done a fine job with Mrs. Neeboo. Everything about his interactions with their patient had been genuinely caring and concerned. Macie wasn't surprised, but it would have been nice if she could have found some fault in him. He was almost too good to be true.

Landon had forgotten what it was like to work on a hospital floor. It had taken him hours of examinations to finish these rounds. He'd become rusty. Now he still had more hours of dictation to update the charts. As he and Macie had seen patients, he had noticed the other nurses going in and out of the rooms. He'd been impressed with the staff in the geriatric ward by the end of the day.

The only thing he found lacking was electronic records. He didn't like admitting it, but Macie's demand that he work on the floors was starting to pay off in a huge way. Nowhere in the paperwork of the hospital had he read that there was a need for electronic records. How the last administrator had failed to place them in the budget he had no idea. Was that because it was so far down on the list of needs that it hadn't made it on to the list?

For the rest of the week, his days continued much like the first one. He found he actually looked forward to the weekend. At least he could sleep in. Yet there would be still more paperwork to review.

When he left the hospital on Friday night, Macie wasn't in her office. He assumed she had already gone for the day. While they were seeing patients, she had also been on the phone handling any problems that had arisen. He'd not seen her lose her temper even once, and he was impressed.

With his bag filled with papers he planned to review over the weekend, he exited the hospital. The smell of rain hung heavy in the air. This was the tropics after all.

Showers were part of everyday life. They came and went just as quickly; few lingered for any length of time.

He'd be glad to get home to put his feet up. He'd been on them far more than he was used to. Still, it had been a rewarding week. Getting out from behind a desk and using his knowledge and skills had felt good. He and Macie had made a great team.

After pulling the small car, which was thankfully larger than Macie's, into the carport beside his house, he climbed out. He couldn't think of the last time he'd had a real home. Maybe before his father had left. After that it had been apartments, military housing and hotels—nothing permanent. He found he rather liked coming home to his bungalow on the cliff. He particularly enjoyed the porch. If he wasn't careful, he'd burn hours watching the ocean roll in as the sun reflected across the water.

Saturday midmorning he drove to the hospital to pick up more material to review. A number of staff spoke to him as he walked down the hall. He had no doubt that was because they had seen him with Macie during the week. She'd given him the seal of acceptance.

He entered the administration area and noticed Macie's office door was open. She sat behind her desk, her attention on something in front of her.

"What're you doing here?" Landon hadn't meant for the question to sound like an accusation. He was just surprised to see her. He went to stand in her doorway.

Macie's head jerked up. "I could ask you the same question."

He shrugged. "I have work to do. I was out of the office all week."

"Me too." *Because of you.* Her unspoken comment hung in the air between them.

"I didn't realize what a hardship I was putting on you by requesting that you work with me. I'll handle it from here on out by myself."

Macie shook her head. "No, we made a bargain. I have someone starting Monday who will help me out."

Landon kept his voice businesslike. "Great. Sometimes I don't think, and I make mistakes."

Shadows filled her eyes. Was she thinking of their past relationship? He hoped that wasn't the case.

Macie's work was top quality, as it had been when they'd worked together before. He'd quickly learned they still made a good team. Well-respected, she'd made it easy for him to make inroads into learning the beat of the Saipan Hospital. He wasn't surprised she had achieved such a position of responsibility here.

He stepped into her office. "You need to go home. Take some time off. Everyone needs that."

"Like you?" Macie tapped a pen against the desk. "And aren't you the pot calling the kettle black?"

"At least I'm doing some of it outside this place."

She shrugged. "This can only be done here. I'm almost finished."

"I'll let you get back to work then. See you later." He went to his office and closed the door.

Much later, he gathered what he needed to take home. By the time he left, Macie was no longer in her office. He was glad she had gone home. But then, as he left the hospital, he glanced through the ER department door and saw Macie standing beside the nurses' desk talking to one of the staff. Clearly, Macie was still working. She seemed determined not to take his advice.

The next week followed much as the one before had as he and Macie continued to work together. Monday and

Tuesday they spent in the surgical ward, Wednesday and Thursday with the children, and Friday they worked on the cancer wing.

He'd quickly learned he missed working with patients. He'd gone into medicine because he liked helping people but also because it was a means to help provide for his mother along with Adam, his younger brother and Nancy, his sister. After his parents' horrible divorce, both he and his mother had had to work in order to pay the bills. When he joined the military out of high school his check had continued to help. As the years went by even while the navy sent him to medical school, he continued to send money home. It had been even more necessary when his mother started drinking heavily and became ill. Even his current job he had taken out of financial need after he'd left the navy. He'd had to give up clinical work to look after his family. It had only been in last few years that his help had no longer been needed. The last week had confirmed how much he loved working with patients and how much he missed it. Still, by Friday evening he was ready to get out of the building.

Tatiana had already left for the day when he stopped by Macie's office. He stood in her doorway. "I'm hungry and I know you must be too. Come on. You pick the restaurant and I'll buy."

"I have to admit that those couple of crackers and the soda I had earlier are long gone." She sounded as tired as he felt.

Landon nodded his head toward the exit. "Then let's get some dinner."

She gave him a hesitant look as if she were considering turning him down.

He stepped inside her office. "I tell you what, we'll

make it a working meal. We can talk about some of the needs we've seen over the last few days."

"Okay," Macie agreed.

For some reason he didn't like the fact that she wouldn't eat with him unless it had to do with work.

He wanted her to have dinner with him because he'd asked her.

CHAPTER THREE

A QUARTER OF an hour later, Landon walked beside Macie into the parking lot. "By the way, we're taking my car."

Macie grinned. "I rather enjoyed watching you squeezing into mine. Seeing your legs touching your nose had its satisfaction."

"So, you were laughing at me?"

She lifted her shoulder and dropped it. "Well, maybe just a little bit."

Landon didn't miss the twinkle in her eyes. He rather liked the idea that he'd put it there, even at the expense of his knees.

He was ready to drive out of the parking lot when Macie said, "Turn left. We're going to the next small town."

"I didn't know there was one."

"*Village* is a more accurate description. It's a family-owned place. It might not look like much, but the food is excellent."

"I'll trust your judgment on that."

He wasn't as sure ten minutes later when he drove the car into a gravel lot beside a building that was little more than a shack.

Inside, they sat at a small wooden table. As it was still early for dinner, very few people were there, which gave them some privacy. An older heavyset woman with an unfriendly look came to take their drink orders and then strolled back to the kitchen area.

He leaned back in his chair, leveling a look at Macie. "For a moment there I thought you were going to turn down my invitation to dinner."

"I gave it serious thought." She fingered her fork.

"Macie, I know you're angry with me over the way I left you in Hawaii, but I'd like us to at least try to be friends. I can explain what happened. I know it won't make it any better, but I had a good reason. I am sorry you got hurt. That wasn't my intention."

She studied him. Long enough that he started to squirm. "I can't imagine you having a good enough explanation that'll make up for what you did, but I would sure as hell like to hear it."

Her words were tight and sharp. He had hurt her deeply, far more deeply than he had realized. They'd had a good time back then, but he had no idea she had held on to it for this long. Could it be that he hadn't wanted to know? Because he had no intention of making it permanent, no matter how good they were together? He wasn't planning on doing that with anyone. His parents' marriage—or lack of one—had shaped his life, and he wouldn't willingly enter into that stranglehold. Love meant pain, and he'd had enough of that.

Still, maybe he should have done more to find Macie when he'd returned to Hawaii. "There was a family emergency."

She huffed and raised her hands. "That's the best you've got?"

It wasn't, but he didn't want to go into the details. That would lead to talking about stuff he really wanted to avoid…like how his father had left his family for another woman, his mother had drunk herself into financial ruin and poor health, and how Landon had been left to take care of his young brother and sister. Nope, he wasn't going to say all that. "Yes."

"Thanks for nothing. I think we're back to where we were when we came in here."

"Every time I say something you act as if you're second-guessing it. You can trust me."

Macie studied him again. She picked up a paper napkin and twisted it. "Let's just say that, based on history, I need to be careful. How do I know there won't be another—" she made air quotes with her fingers above her shoulders "—'family emergency.' Let's keep it business, Dr. Cochran. That way neither of us will expect anything and neither of us will be disappointed."

Landon winced. Something about how she said it made him think he might not have been the only person to disappoint her. He hated that he'd helped make her so cynical about people. Or was it just men?

The waitress returned with their drinks and took their order. With a scowl on her face, she nodded and walked away.

"Does she ever smile?" Landon asked in a stage whisper.

"Only when she's had too much to drink," Macie announced without lowering her voice.

Landon continued to study the menu even though he had already ordered. "Does every meal come with rice?"

"I'm afraid so. You know, we're closer to China than we are to mainland America, even though we're an American territory. All our supplies come in by boat, and I guess rice travels well."

"I guess so." He paused. "I have to admit that when I accepted your challenge to work with you, I didn't think it would be such a big deal. But it has been harder than I anticipated. I've really enjoyed being in the trenches again."

"What made you stop?"

She made it sound like he'd defected. It had been his best decision at the time. He leaned back in his chair, trying to appear more at ease than he felt. "After I was discharged from the navy, the World Health Organization made me an offer. The money was good and that was important at the time. I found I liked helping improve hospitals. Now I have a chance to head the entire organization. If I can make strides here, the job should be mine."

Her color paled for a second. "I see."

He shifted in his chair. Macie made it sound as if she might see more than he wanted her to. "Sometimes things happen in life that make us take a different path than we originally planned."

She looked up to meet his gaze. "Well, I have to admit that you're still good with a patient. Actually, one of the best I've ever seen."

Landon nodded. "Thank you. I consider that high praise."

Macie's smile sobered. Had she become uncomfortable with the direction of their conversation?

She crossed her arms over her chest. Her eyes turned thoughtful. "You said we were going to discuss your ideas for the hospital. What do you have in mind?"

Apparently, she *was* ready for a subject change. "First, let's talk about what we've learned over the last week or so."

"I can't say that I've really learned anything." She gave him a sweet smile that didn't reach her eyes.

"Okay, then I'll talk about what I've learned." He cleared his throat. "The hospital staff is a caring group. They really want to help the patients."

Macie nodded. "I couldn't agree with you more."

"But…"

Macie's brow rose.

"They're overworked," he finished.

"I agree."

"The problem areas that stand out are the lack of updated equipment, like a portable X-ray machine, but we both already know that. I'd also like to see an MRI machine installed. Electronic charting is a must."

"That sounds wonderful to me." Excitement filled her words. "But still not new news."

"There's a lack of physicians. There's a lack of staff in a few other areas as well. Too many of the staff are working double shifts, which can lead to poor patient care and creates staff health issues. Lack of funding is a major problem. All that said, I know a number of hospitals that aren't running as efficiently as this one."

Macie blinked and sat forward. "That's good news. So, when and where does the white knight ride up with the bags of money?"

Landon didn't like that picture. He wasn't anyone's knight. Didn't want to be. "I think Pediatrics needs a complete overhaul. As does General Surgery. A number of areas need streamlining."

The eagerness in Macie's face disappeared. She sighed. "That all sounds fabulous to me, but the question still remains—where is the money going to come from? The economy here can't handle a raise in rate. And we need incentives just to get doctors to come here."

"My thought is to offer scholarships to locals to become doctors and nurses so that they will return to the island. It doesn't solve the immediate problem, but if we can show that there's a plan for the future, then there might be more help for the here and now."

This time excitement clearly showed in Macie's eyes. "That's a wonderful idea. Maybe you do wear white armor after all. That's an innovative way of thinking. One that I can get behind."

Maybe the white knight thing wasn't so bad. He rather liked the notion that Macie found him and his idea brilliant. It shouldn't matter as much as it did. Could it be because he had disappointed her all those years ago?

"It would not only help the hospital but the island as a whole. The hospital is one of the largest employers."

Landon held up a hand. "Don't get too excited. There'll be large hurdles to get over. It's just an idea."

"But it's a good one," she insisted.

"Apparently, you didn't think I could have one."

She crossed her arms on the table and leaned forward. "What I thought was you'd want to cut a department, fire people."

"You don't have too high an opinion of me." That knowledge hurt.

She grinned. "Would it help to know that it's improving?"

"It would." He wanted to thump his chest.

Thankfully, their waitress returned with their meals in no better humor. They ate in silence for a few minutes before Landon said, "How about telling me a little bit about this island? I've not even had a chance to see it." For some reason he wanted to know about the place she seemed to love so much.

"Would you like me to show you around tomorrow?"

The shock on her face caused him to chuckle. She hadn't planned to ask that. He purposely made a show of answering her. The look of distress on her face—and could it also be anticipation?—intrigued him. "Well, that would be nice. I'd appreciate it."

She straightened. That determination he'd seen while working with her returned. "I'll pick you up tomorrow around ten."

Macie would be keeping it strictly business if she could. "No. I'll pick you up. My car is bigger, remember?"

Macie had no idea what had possessed her to ask Landon if he wanted her to show him around. The moment the words were out of her mouth she questioned her sanity. Maybe it was that she knew how hard he'd worked the last week and a half or that there was no one else to do it. After all, she was the only person he really knew on the island. Or it could have been that she just liked him and wanted to spend more time with him. Either way, she had to honor her offer.

Against her better judgment she had slowly moved into an area where she didn't want to go. One where she became more familiar with Landon. Learning to like him, appreciate his skills as a doctor and as an administrator. Heaven help her, she was attracted to him. She didn't need any more disappointments in her life. He'd done it before. Her father had done it. What if it happened again? Could she protect herself against it?

She was ready and waiting when Landon arrived the next morning. The day before she'd given him some brief directions for finding her place. Somehow letting Landon know where she lived felt like he was invading her personal space. She couldn't complain since she was the one who had offered to show him around. Maybe he wouldn't be that interested in the island and she'd be with him for only an hour or so... She didn't think that would be the case, from what she knew about him. He'd shown an interest in every detail of the hospital. She'd be surprised if that wasn't the same regarding the island.

The second she saw Landon's car pull up in front of her place she went out to greet him.

"You do know I would've come to the door." He sounded put out.

"It wasn't necessary." She climbed into the car.

"I guess you're ready to go."

"Head along the coast road toward the hospital. We're going north."

"So tell me about Saipan," Landon said as he drove by the hospital.

"You know you can get all that from the internet." She studied him. Landon really was a good-looking man. His hair made her want to run her fingers through it. Even as he drove, his strong jaw reflected what she knew about his personality—solid, dependable and interesting. There were small creases around his eyes that implied he smiled often.

"I can, but I'm interested in hearing it from you. You've been here long enough to know what isn't in the official guide books."

"All right, I'll tell you what I know. This island was ruled by Germany until after World War One when it was turned over to Japan. During the Second World War it was stategic because of the airstrip. When the Americans arrived, there was a battle. Close to where the hospital is now is where the troops first came onshore. You can still see equipment that was left."

"Really?"

"Yep. There are small one-man tanks here and there out in the water. In one of the parks is a cement gun emplacement. In fact, they're all over the place. You just have to know what you're looking at. I'll point out one on our way to the other end of the island. Up near the airport is a large cement armory area where the headquarters were after the Americans took the island. Do you really want all this history?"

He glanced at her and smiled. "Sure, I do. I think it's interesting. Don't you?"

"I do. I like history. Okay. I'm going to leave the war for a little while. I'll tell you more when we get to where we're going."

They headed out of the well-populated area along the coast. The road rose above the ocean as they traveled. When it ended, Landon pulled into a small parking lot. "What're we going to see here?"

"From here we get a great view of the ocean and the waves washing against the rocks."

They walked over to the edge and looked down. The waves beat against the wall of stone, throwing water up at them.

When she stepped closer, Landon grabbed her arm and brought her back against his chest. Macie glanced over her shoulder at him.

"I don't want you to go over. It would look bad for me to lose my tour guide."

She liked being against his warm, strong body. There was safety and security there. Something she'd not had in a long, long time. Yet she'd been fooled before by that feeling. She'd once felt it strongly under her father's care and had come to find out that it was just an illusion; nothing had been real. She stayed a moment longer then stepped away. "When I come here it always makes me feel small. It reminds me of how little my problems are in the big scheme of things."

"That's an intriguing statement. Care to elaborate?"

"Not really." The past wasn't something she wished to revisit. She had moved beyond that time and rebuilt her life on firm ground, something real.

A few minutes later they walked back to the car.

Landon looked over the hood at her as they were getting in. "Macie, why are you out here?"

"Out here?"

His gaze met hers. "Yeah. On Saipan. So far from home."

She didn't want to get into that. No matter how much she thought she'd left what her father had done behind the old insecurity still lingered. "Because this is where I'm needed."

"Surely you could be needed closer to malls, nightclubs, friends and family." He got into the car.

She followed suit. "I've been happy here."

"Still, when was the last time you were on the mainland?" He backed out of the parking lot and headed down the road they had come in on.

Looking out the window, she said softly, "Seven and a half years."

"That long! Don't you miss civilization?"

For her, life had been made of cotton candy that had swirled down to a glob on a stick. Saipan had given her stability. She felt him watching her. "I have everything I want here, and this is where I'm needed."

Finally, he concentrated on his driving. She breathed a sigh of relief. The air had taken on that uncertain feel between them once more. Macie watched the ocean for a few minutes. Usually, she found it soothing, but for some reason it wasn't anymore. Macie didn't like the tension between them. She'd grown to appreciate their camaraderie. It would be nice to have that back.

Landon broke the silence as they headed toward town again. "Tell me about all these abandoned buildings. The ones overgrown with vines. They're everywhere."

Thank goodness he said something, Macie thought.

"About twenty years ago there was a lot of manufacturing being done here. Then the laws were changed and we started allowing manufacturing to be done outside the US where it was cheaper, and most of it went to China. Sadly, Saipan's economy suffered. Buildings were just left behind."

"Like the hotel building at the airport?"

"Yes. That's a prime example. The island was positioning itself as a tourist spot. It still is but not at the rate it once was. It was cheaper to leave it as is than to tear it down. Look down there." She pointed to a long three-story building that had obviously been a nice hotel at one time. "That was a resort. Now it's just part of the jungle."

"That's sad."

"It is. On the other side of town, we'll pass a place that looks much the same but was a shopping center. I guess the only thing visiting now are snakes and bugs. We get most of our supplies from China now. We have to place orders for the hospital at least a month ahead. I wish Washington could do more to help build industry here, but these people are resistant."

The road now ran parallel with the beach. Landon looked at the waves brushing the shore. "A lot of people seem to live the same way here, in small homes built out of cinder block. And they have chickens."

Macie chuckled. "There are a lot of chickens. I'd have a few if I had a place to house them."

"What do you like the most about island life?" Landon sounded as if he really wanted to know instead of just making conversation.

She didn't have to think about it. "The people. They're friendly and open. I also like the dress code—none of that fancy overdressed stuff is necessary."

"I can see the appeal." He patted his cargo shorts.

Landon had lightened up on his dress. Today he wore a T-shirt and khaki shorts with sandals, and he was just as impressive in those as he was in his suit. He had an air of authority about him no matter what he wore.

"You said something about tourism. Are tourists coming from the mainland?"

"Oh, no. Fifty percent of the population at any time is made up of Chinese, Japanese and Korean visitors. The other half is locals. You and I are the ones who stand out."

Landon chuckled. "I have noticed that I'm not as tan as some and much taller."

"I think you would stand out wherever you were." That slipped out before she realized she had said it.

A sexy grin covered his mouth as he looked at her. "You think so?"

She did, but she wouldn't flatter him more by answering.

His attention returned to the road. "Not going to answer, huh? Then how about this. Why don't we stop and eat somewhere before we continue the tour?"

Macie was happy with that idea since right now she just needed to get out of this small enclosed space and put some distance between them. "Okay. There's a resort down here on the left. They have a nice buffet with a Western food bar so you can get more than rice there."

"Now, that sounds nice." Happy anticipation filled his voice.

She looked at the road ahead. "I figured by now you'd want something that didn't include rice."

"You know me so well."

"Not really." She glanced at him, not missing the slight tightening of his jaw. "I have to admit, I had to get used to having rice all the time. Now I would miss it if I didn't have it. The next entrance on the left is the one you want."

* * *

Landon followed Macie to a table next to a picture window where they could look out over a lawn to the ocean beyond. They were in a large room with numerous buffet lines featuring all types of food. He'd gone for a burger and fries while Macie had chosen baked chicken, rice and a salad.

She placed her tray on the table and looked at his plate. "No rice for you, I see."

"No, I'm going for beef today. As a good Midwesterner it's required that we have it at least once a week."

Macie laughed and settled across from him. He liked the sound of her laugh. *She should do it more often*, he thought. Macie was far too serious.

They passed the time while eating talking about what they had seen that morning.

Landon had almost finished with his meal when Macie asked, "Have you ever thought about going back into practice? Start seeing patients again?"

He looked at her over his glass. "Macie, why are you pushing so hard for me to change jobs? I'm good at the one I have. If I don't do it, someone else will."

She didn't say anything for a moment. "I guess it's better having the devil you know."

His eyes narrowed. "I don't like that you think of me as the devil."

"I don't really think of you as the devil. More as an inconvenience."

"Ouch. I'm not sure that's much better." He met her look. "I'm here to help. Really."

Macie didn't appear convinced. "I'm ready to go when you are."

Soon, they were heading down the road again.

"Where to now?" Landon asked.

"We're on our way to another World War II site." She pointed out in the water. "Look there. That's one of those small one-man tanks. You can see about half of it when the tide is out."

"Why didn't they remove them?"

"I guess it was just easier to leave them. And they're a reminder of the island's history. That time was sad—I can only imagine the helplessness the locals felt."

"It was an awful time for the world in general, and to come to this small outlying island…"

"Saipan wasn't the only one affected. The tiny island just south of this one is Tinian. It's where the planes that carried the atomic bombs took off from. For a time, it was the busiest airport in the world." She chuckled. "It's even smaller than Saipan."

"Does anyone live over there?"

"They do. There's a resort that's popular as well. You have to take a single-engine plane to get there." She'd been only once.

"Sounds like an adventure."

She grinned. "The flight alone is an experience. This next place we're going is a particularly sad one."

"Sad?" He glanced at her.

"Yeah. I have a hard time thinking about it, but it's part of the island's history. You need to go at least once."

"Every place and everyone has a sad history." He knew that better than most. His mother and father had given him that. "What's this place about?"

"We're going to Suicide Cliff."

"I've heard of it. It's where the mothers threw their children off the cliff because they were afraid of what the Americans would do to them. They believed the Japanese propaganda."

"That's right. There's a small park there with a remembrance plaque telling the story of what happened." Macie pointed. "Turn up here to the right."

The road twisted up the hill and ended in a parking lot, and Landon pulled in to a spot. They walked the winding paved path beneath trees to the top of the ridge. There they stood behind a rock wall looking at the jagged cliffs below and the waves slapping against the rocky coastline.

Macie spoke as if to herself. "The beauty of the scenery is in direct opposition to the horrors that happened here. No matter how many paper fliers the Americans dropped telling the people they would not be hurt, they didn't believe it. Even the navy fired rounds against the cliff trying to get the mothers to stop. They wouldn't. They were so afraid for the future of their children they would rather have them die at their hands than chance what they had been told was coming. A mother's love, even misguided, can be astounding. Can you imagine a mother fearing for their child's future so much she'd be willing to do that?"

"I can't imagine a mother caring that much," Landon murmured.

She studied him. "That's dark."

There was an underlying question in her remark. One he didn't wish to answer. But he had opened the door and now he had to deal with the consequences. "My mother didn't care about anyone but herself. That's not true. She loved my father so much she smothered him to the point he left us all." Landon took long strides down the path in the direction of the parking lot. He didn't want to answer the question he knew Macie would have after those statements.

Macie caught up with him. "Would you like to talk about it? It might help."

And there was Macie's soft heart. Where someone else

might not want to hear his story, Macie would listen. He liked that about her. For some reason he couldn't name, he realized he wanted her to know about his family. He wanted to give her a chance to understand him. A chance to forgive him for leaving like he did.

"I can't remember a time that my mom and dad didn't fight. Loud and long. They split up when I was a junior in high school after my father found someone else. My mother started drinking. I have a younger brother and sister, who I pretty much had to raise because Mom was out of it most of the time. She started having trouble getting to work on time, then she started losing jobs. More than once we came home to find her passed out on the couch. Dad was no help. He had pretty much washed his hands of us and moved on."

"I'm sorry."

He shrugged. "Yeah, so am I. Anyway, I had good grades. I had always dreamed of being a doctor. I worked and went to the community college until my brother and sister were old enough to take care of themselves. I joined the navy with the promise of help to go to medical school. I sent all the money I could home to my family. But I still felt guilty about leaving my siblings in the situation they were in."

"You were doing what you could to make it better," Macie said softly.

He couldn't look at her. "Maybe so, but I still wasn't there for the day in, day out. We managed to convince Mom to get some help, and things did get better. My brother and sister have good brains and got scholarships to school. It took us all longer than most to get our education, but we all did it. They're both married and have babies."

Macie took his hand. "You should be proud."

He slowed his pace. "I am. My job with the World Health Organization helped make it possible."

"But what about you? You've never married and you don't have any children. Don't you want what your siblings have?"

"No."

She missed a step for a second and tugged on his hand before she rejoined his pace.

"Why not?"

"Because I grew up in the middle of an ugly marriage and saw what professing to be in love can do to someone. I never want to put another person through that or be on the receiving end of it either."

"But you would know what not to do." There was a note of earnestness in her voice.

"Maybe so, but I'm not sure I know what that kind of love really is. I certainly haven't seen it firsthand."

Macie didn't say anything more for a few minutes, but then she asked, "How is your mother now?"

Landon's chest tightened. "She passed away years ago. She developed liver cancer and only lasted six weeks after the diagnosis. I found out the morning after we spent the night together."

Macie's hiss of awareness circled around them. She let go of his hand and went still.

"I was on a plane twenty-four hours later. I wasn't thinking straight and when I returned, you were gone. I tried to find out where you were. I even asked personnel. But nothing. I'm sorry I hurt you. I never intended to. I liked you. Still do."

Macie met his look. "I'm sorry about your mother. And I'm sorry I haven't been fair to you."

"You didn't know. How could you? I wouldn't have

liked me either if I had left you like that. What I'd like to know now… Is it possible for us to be friends again?"

Macie studied him for long enough that he feared she might say no. "Yes, we can be friends."

Landon let out the breath he had been holding. He took her hand again and Macie tangled her fingers in his. It wasn't a sexual touch but one of reassurance, concern. Her eyes held shadows of pity and he didn't want that. "I didn't mean to dump all that garbage on you. I just wanted you to know why I left like I did."

"Sometimes it's just good to get it out." She squeezed his hand. "I'm glad you explained."

They continued like that as they walked to the car. Somehow, having Macie beside him eased his bitterness. His admission had changed something between them. The electricity was still there but now it was more like a steady stream instead of a spark. As if his confession had created a bond between them. The idea appealed to him.

As Landon drove back into town, he asked her, "So what do you do for fun?"

"I don't know. Read, go to the movies, swim to Bird Island, get together with friends. You know, the usual. Take a left up here."

He did as she directed. They started up a hill.

"We're on our way up Capitol Hill, the capital of the island—hence the name. No tour is complete until you have seen a capital. My parents took us to all of them in every state we visited." She paused and said quietly, "I've not thought of that in a long time."

Landon glanced at her. "Is that so?"

"Pull over here. We need to get out. We're high enough for you to see the area."

He parked, they climbed out and went to the front of the car.

"That is Tainan over there." She pointed off in one direction. "There's the hospital down there. You can see the port as well."

They stood there a few moments in silence.

"The white building behind us is the Municipal Building. It was built after the war by the US Army to use as a headquarters, and they gave it to the island years later when they no longer needed it. I figure you've already seen your side of the island, so that concludes your tour."

Landon faced her. "Thank you for taking your day off to show me around."

She wrinkled her nose. "I'm not really off today. I agreed to fill in this evening in the ER."

"And here I am taking up your time when you could be sleeping. You should've said something."

"It's no big deal. I had a good time. I haven't visited those places in a while. It was nice to see it though fresh eyes. But I really should be getting home."

When they arrived at her place, he stepped out of the car with Macie and walked her the short distance to the door.

"Thanks again for showing me around."

"You're welcome." She looked at the ground.

"Also, thanks for listening earlier. I'm sorry about what happened in Hawaii."

"And I'm sorry I didn't give you the benefit of the doubt. Let's start over." She stuck out her hand for a shake. "Friends?"

Macie wanted friendship, but he was thinking about something more. Were her kisses as sweet as he remembered? Taking her hand, he tugged her closer then leaned in. She didn't step back. Instead, she just watched him. Encouraged, he continued until his lips found hers.

He kept the kiss easy despite his desire to pull her even

closer. Regardless of the years that had passed, Macie's lips were as luscious and plump as they ever had been. Nothing had changed. Just that small touch made him want more. The spark between them hadn't lessened—if anything, it had grown hotter. His mouth moved toward hers again.

Macie's hands came to his chest, stopping him.

Disappointment washed through him, but maybe it was for the best. He wouldn't be staying here forever, and he had no intention of making her long-term promises. Avoiding such promises assured him that neither one of them would get hurt.

Yet they were adults. They were older and wiser and she certainly seemed like a strong woman now. What if they set ground rules? Couldn't they enjoy each other while it lasted? Explore this attraction?

That idea ended the moment Macie spoke. "Let's not do this. I think it's best not to complicate things. I'll see you on Monday."

Before Landon could disagree, she had closed the door between them.

He stood there looking at the door, and somehow it seemed more like a brick wall.

And he hated that it existed.

If only he could have one more kiss…

CHAPTER FOUR

MACIE WENT TO WORK on Monday with thoughts of Landon's kiss swimming in her head. She had almost floated though the evening shift in the ER thinking about him. More than one person had asked her if she was okay.

She'd enjoyed her day with Landon...too much. Even their short kiss had been enough to excite her body and let her know that those feelings she'd had for him years ago hadn't changed. If anything, they had intensified. Just another reason she had to put some space between them, to keep their interactions business only. Her heart could so easily be hurt by him. He'd even told her clearly, in his own words, that he wasn't looking for anything lasting. But she had lived through a pretend childhood, and real and forever was what she was looking for.

Even if she wanted more, her life was on this island and his was elsewhere. Landon was just passing through. It would be like Hawaii all over again, except without the misunderstanding. She wasn't putting her heart out there again, at least not with Landon. It would be too risky; there would be too great a chance of pain, and she couldn't invite more of that into her life. There had already been enough. His effect on her was no different than it had been years ago. Even though she now understood what had happened, still she couldn't take that chance. Couldn't trust…

She could still feel his pain from when he had told her about his family and the hardships he had endured. More than that, she had been impressed with the type of young man he had been when it came to taking care of his brother and sister. She'd believed her life had been difficult, but compared to his, hers had been charmed— even though it had been financed by stolen money, which spoiled the memory of it.

Still, their kiss had been nice. Better than nice. In truth, she wanted more of it. She wanted more of Landon, of everything. But she couldn't have him. He couldn't give her what she needed, and therefore the kissing had to stop.

Regardless of her feelings one way or the other, she and Landon had to work together. The sooner he had what he had come for, the faster he would be gone. And there would be less chance of her heart being broken. With Landon gone, her life would return to normal. She had to keep things between them limited to their work at the hospital and make every effort to spend no more time with him than was necessary.

That was easier said than done since they had another three days together working on the floors, and by the time Wednesday rolled around, Macie was emotionally exhausted. More than once, Landon had caught her looking at him. A spark flickered in his eyes as his lips turned up slightly. He knew too well what he did to her. To say she had been looking forward to a few days of space between them was an understatement.

With that in mind she almost skipped into work on Thursday. All went well until Tatiana came to Macie's office door. "Landon asked me to see if you could come to his office at ten this morning."

"Landon?"

She smiled. "That's what he said to call him."

Another example of Landon working his magic. "Please tell him I'll be there. Did he want me to bring anything in particular?"

"Didn't say so." Tatiana moved to leave then turned back. "He's different than the others. I like him."

All the enthusiasm Macie had started the day with disappeared. Once again, they'd be too close for her comfort. His office was the largest in the hospital but would become tiny with the two of them closed up in it. Any time she was with Landon, the world narrowed down to just him.

"Good morning, Macie," he said as she entered. He stood and, with a well-manicured hand, indicated a chair. "Please have a seat."

She took a moment to really look at him, which she hadn't dared to do in days. Landon appeared tired. His hair was mussed; stubble covered his jawline. It made him even sexier—something she shouldn't take notice of. There were smudges under his eyes. Had he not been sleeping?

"Okay. Is this something I should be worried about?" She sank into the chair.

"Not really."

Macie studied him closer. "Have you been here since we finished rounds yesterday?"

He rolled his shoulders forward then back and stretched. "Most of the time. I too had work that wasn't getting done while we were seeing patients."

Fascinated by his movements, Macie just stared. "And the idea was to catch up on everything in one night?"

He smirked. "I did go home for a few hours."

"What's keeping you awake and at this desk now?"

His brows rose with a "you have to ask that?" look. Macie's skin heated and her mouth went dry.

Landon cleared his throat, glanced down then back at her. "I wanted to discuss my findings with you."

This wasn't going to be fun. "And those are?"

"There's a lot of great care going on here, but it's hindered by the lack of staff, equipment and modernization."

"Haven't we already discussed that?" She wasn't sure she was going to like where this would lead.

"We have, but what we haven't done is figure out what we're going to do about it." Firmness filled his voice.

She crossed her arms and legs in a defensive manner. "And have you?"

"I have a few ideas jotted down. I want to run them by you and see if you have others." He folded his arms on the desk. "But your body language suggests you are not receptive to new ideas."

Macie unfolded her arms and placed them along the arms of the chair. "Is this better?"

A grin formed on his lips. Her stomach fluttered. "Much better. Please try to keep an open mind."

"Okay." She drew the word out. "What do you have in mind?"

Landon watched her closely for a moment. She shifted in the chair under his scrutiny. "I'd like to meet with each of the department leaders. Talk to them about what we saw and didn't see. Then I'd like to hear what they would like to have in an ideal world."

She nodded. So far his idea was sound.

"Then I want to meet the leadership of the island to see where they can help, what support we can count on.

Then we'll go to the staff and share our plans and ask for suggestions."

The more he spoke, the more excited she became about the ideas. She liked his use of *we*. It wouldn't be all about what *he* wanted or thought. Landon was asking for input from top to bottom. He appeared interested and concerned about all the parties and wanted their opinions. Unlike the interims who had come shouting about how they were going to improve the hospital on their own, Landon seemed like he wanted it to be a team effort.

"Your overall plan sounds good."

He smiled. "I'm glad you approve, but I hear a note of skepticism in your voice."

"I guess it's hard for me to trust after I've been burned so many times before." In all areas of her life she was careful.

Landon leaned in farther, holding her gaze. "I won't disappoint you again. I promise."

Her heart tapped a dance. She wanted to believe him. "Good."

"After we have all the information, we'll form a plan of action that I can present to my board, which will include a bid for financial help."

Macie scooted to the edge of her seat with excitement. "You'll really do that?"

"Of course I will. It's my job to make things better."

Was he doing that for the hospital or for himself? Hadn't he said this was a stepping stone to a promotion? No matter the reason, if all went as he had mapped out, then it would be to everyone's advantage.

"What do you need from me?"

"I need you to help me figure out how to approach the community leaders." He stood and paced the room. He had delivered the statement matter-of-factly and with authority. Landon had officially become the all-business administrator. Before her was a man who had formed a plan and was confident he could carry it out. For once she felt like someone might actually bring about positive change.

No longer dressed so formally, Landon was more in sync with the community. And she liked this Landon far too much.

"Any ideas?" He turned and pierced her with a look.

"I don't know… You could always just ask them for a meeting. But it would be better to meet each one casually first. Let them get to know you some. They already know about you being here because news travels fast on the island, but if they could first see you in a social setting…" She snapped her fingers as she shot out of her seat. "I know! The hash. Most of them should be there."

"What's that?"

"It's where someone cuts a path through the jungle and people follow it." She moved her hand in a hacking motion.

His face twisted up. "Huh?"

Tatiana tapped on the door and they both turned. "Sorry to bother you, but you're needed in the ER, Macie."

"Okay." She turned back to Landon. "Pick me up on Saturday afternoon at three. I'll explain it all then. Leave anything I need to know on my desk and I'll review it. Got to go."

Landon wasn't sure what he had agreed to, but he arrived at Macie's at the assigned time on Saturday afternoon. He hadn't seen her except in passing since she'd left his office two days earlier. He'd missed her. Far more than he wanted to admit.

Most of the time he'd been confined to his office working on reports and revising his ideas. His best guess was that Macie had spent the days continuing to smooth out problems within the hospital. He'd quickly learned that she had a real talent for doing so. She was good at getting people to do what she needed.

He hadn't known what to wear to a *hash* so he'd gone with T-shirt, cargo shorts and tennis shoes, figuring that since it was a Saturday afternoon the event must be casual. He knocked on her door and when she opened it, he decided he'd made the right choice because Macie was dressed much the same way.

She wore a tight faded baby blue T-shirt that showed off her curves—ones that he had a difficult time not staring at—and that had Saipan stamped across the front. Her cut-off denim shorts showed enough leg that he had a chance to appreciate each bend and dip of her skin and she too wore sport shoes. Her hair was pulled back by a band and a ball cap sat on her head, making her look much younger than she was.

Her lips were glossy pink, as if she had applied something to them. His first instinct was to kiss her to find out, but he resisted his urge, supposing she wouldn't appreciate that. After his last attempt he needed to take things slowly. He would but he still wanted to kiss her again. If she agreed he would.

Everything about Macie called to him. Why couldn't they have some fun together while he was on the island? What could it hurt? They were both adults with natural impulses.

"Hey. Come in. I'll just be a minute. I have to finish up the cookies. I was asked to bring a dessert."

"Should I have brought something?" Landon followed her through the small living area to the even tinier kitchen, which smelled like cinnamon and sugar. He looked over Macie's shoulder at the golden-brown circles. Reaching around her, he snagged one and took a bite. "Mmm…"

"Hey! Stop that. I have to have enough."

For once her voice held a playful note. Maybe them having some space from each other for a few days had been a good thing. He couldn't believe how glad he was to see her. Unable to help himself, he brought his nose close to her neck. "You smell like a cookie. Really sweet."

She straightened causing his lips to touch skin. The tip of his tongue darted out.

Macie hissed.

He stepped away, not wanting to put her on the defensive. "What can I do to help?"

"There are some uh…"

Self-satisfaction washed through him. Macie wasn't as immune to him as she wanted to act.

She cleared her throat and started again, this time sounding more in control. "I have to get these in a container. While I'm doing that, you can put the blanket and the backpack in the car."

"Consider it done." By the time he'd returned, she had a plastic container filled with cookies in her hand and was headed toward the door.

"I'm ready." She pulled the door closed behind her.

They were in the car when he asked, "Which way?"

"Back the way you came. We're going out past your place." She balanced the cookies on her lap.

"Will do. How about telling me what we're going to?" He backed out of the drive.

"Someone—or most times more than one person—cuts a path through the jungle. The rest of us follow, trying to catch them. It's a bit like a fox-and-hounds game.

The fox is the person doing the cutting and the hounds are those coming behind. Some people run while others just walk. The idea is to enjoy being out with friends. More times than not we end up at the beach where there's a big bonfire and food. A hash happens almost every weekend somewhere on the island. This particular one is being hosted by one of the mayors, so the people we want to talk to should be there."

"Good timing." He winked at her.

She grinned and nodded. "Yep."

He shouldn't be flirting with Macie. She'd made it clear where she wanted their relationship to remain, but their kiss had said something different. There was an electric attraction he couldn't resist exploring—for the short-term.

He wasn't ever going to offer her a happily-ever-after. Hell, he didn't even know what that was. He'd certainly not seen it in his parents' marriage. Their relationship left nothing but death and destruction—not something he wanted to bring into his life by choice. A relationship would never work between him and Macie anyway. She seemed planted here, while he was after a job in Washington, DC. A long-distance relationship would be an understatement in their case. Impossible.

"So what happens when you catch up with the fox, as it were? Tie them up?"

Macie giggled. He liked the sound. It was like a warm drink on a cold day.

"No, nothing like that. We don't even touch them and call 'it.'" She poked his upper arm.

"I have to say, this hash thing sounds like fun."

"If nothing else, it's unique." There was a note of pride in her voice.

He made a right turn. "I'll give you that."

They had passed his place when Macie said, "Take the next right and park wherever you can."

Landon did as he was told turning into an obviously recently cleared area creating a makeshift parking lot. They bumped over the uneven ground until he pulled next to another car and stopped. Other vehicles continued to enter the area.

"Okay. We get out and walk from here," Macie announced as she climbed out of the car. "We'll need the backpack and blanket."

"Got them." He slung the backpack strap over one shoulder and put the blanket under his arm.

Macie, with the cookies in hand, said, "This way."

The path into the jungle foliage was obvious. As they entered, the sunlight dimmed but enough remained for them to see. People overtook them as they walked but none seemed in a hurry. As they went by, many of them greeted Macie.

"If you do this all the time, why don't I see paths everywhere?"

She carefully balanced the cookies in her hands. "The vines grow so fast this path will be covered in weeks."

Macie tripped. Landon grabbed her arm to steady her. He liked touching her. Liked knowing that despite how together she acted, sometimes she needed help. "Can't we put these cookies in the backpack? At least you'd have your arms free to catch yourself if you fall."

She gave him an unsure look. "I don't want them to get crushed."

"So you'd rather fall on your face?" He looked at her with disbelief.

Macie glared at him.

Landon rolled his eyes toward the sky. "Oh, I get it. It's kind of like wearing high heels because they look good instead of your feet feeling good. You'll suffer in order to ensure your cookies arrive in perfect condition."

Macie pinned him with a look. "And you have all this wisdom about high heels from experience?"

He pulled a face and shook his head. "Heavens no. What I am is a student of human nature."

"Gotcha. As much as I hate to admit it, you might be right."

Landon took the bag off his shoulder and placed it on the ground. "Give those to me."

With obvious reluctance, Macie handed over the container of cookies. "They'd better not be in crumbs when we get to the beach."

"I promise to carry them like a baby." He wrapped the cookies in the blanket and carefully secured them in the backpack.

"I won't even ask what you know about carrying babies." She made a careful step over the rough terrain then looked at him.

He huffed. "I have handled babies before. Even delivered a few."

"I assume, with your stance on marriage, that you've never thought about having any babies of your own."

Landon wasn't sure if Macie was just making conversation or fishing for information about him. Either way, it made him nervous, as if his answer held some kind of importance to her. "I've already told you that my parents set a poor example, but living by a military schedule and then having a job where I travel all the time doesn't help when a woman wants commitment. I'm not long-term relationship material anyway."

Macie watched him as if she expected him to say more.

If he told the truth, he wasn't sure he'd be good husband or father material. It was best to stay away from the idea entirely. Plus, he'd never been with a woman long enough to take that kind of chance on her.

Her eyes narrowed. "Then you really are a 'love them and leave them guy'?"

"That's not what happened in Hawaii. I explained that."

"Got it." She started off again.

Landon pulled the backpack on. He didn't appreciate her tone of voice. It implied she didn't think much of how he handled his personal life. He caught up with her and they continued to walk in silence.

After a distance, they came to the edge of a ridge. Landon stopped. Before him lay the breadth of the island, luscious, green and humanless as far as he could see. The blue green of the Pacific met the white ribbon of sand that lined the coast. An occasional bird, a dark curve of wings, flew far below him. The handful of white fluffy clouds in the sky only added to the magnitude.

Macie hiked a few paces beyond him. She looked back. "What's wrong?"

"How can you see this view and not stop and admire it? It's amazing."

She backtracked and joined him, standing by his side.

"When I look at this, I understand why you love living here," he said as much to himself as to her. "I feel like we're the only two people in the world."

"It's beautiful. Makes me feel like my problems are small."

He glanced at her. What problems could she possibly have? "This is almost as nice as the view from my porch. It's gorgeous as well. It's my favorite spot. I love the view."

"I agree. I've had a chance to enjoy it a couple of

times when I've been to the house for a party," Macie said softly.

Landon continued looking off into the distance. "You're welcome to come by anytime. I'm more than happy to share."

"You know, Dr. Cochran, I think you might be a bit of a romantic."

He wasn't sure if that was a compliment or not. "Because I can appreciate an amazing view?"

Macie considered him for a moment, as if she had discovered something important about him. "Many people don't take the time to do even that."

Her eyes had turned warm. The temptation to kiss her almost overcame him.

Thankfully, she stepped away. "We'd better get going so we're at the beach before dark. I can assure you we don't want to be on the path after the sun goes down." She started off.

They were now going down a slope. The walking became much more difficult, but they remained side by side.

"What's the plan to get us back to the car?" He hoped it wasn't wandering through the jungle again.

"We'll catch a ride with somebody to the car park." She reached for his arm as she took a step down then quickly released it.

A small group overtook them and one of the men said, "Hi, Macie. I'm glad to see you could make it."

"Hey, Luc. It's good to see you. Thanks for the invitation. Hashes are always good exercise."

The rest of the group moved on ahead of them and waited while Luc spoke to him and Macie. "That they are." The man glanced at Landon.

Macie put her hand on Landon's bicep briefly. "Luc, this is Dr. Landon Cochran. He's the interim administrator for the hospital. I brought him along. I thought I'd give him a real taste of island life."

The local man of medium height, thick shoulders and brown skin chuckled, "A hash will do that."

Landon took the opening Macie offered and extended his hand. "Nice to meet you, Luc."

Luc gave Landon a toothy grin. "You too."

"I'm interested to see what this—" Landon waved his arms "—is all about."

"The best is yet to come. I promise. In fact, I need to get going if I'm going to oversee things." He waved and rejoined his group.

When the man was out of sight Macie said, "He's the mayor of one of the larger villages. One we should talk to."

"He didn't give us much chance to talk business," Landon commented.

"Right now isn't when you want to do that. We'll call for an appointment later. After meeting you tonight they can put a face to the name. They'll remember you and give you some time."

"I see."

They continued around a large boulder that they had to hold on to. Soon, they were out of the foliage, then they had to climb down over rock to reach the sand. Closer to the water a bonfire burned and people stood in clusters around it. Off to one side a couple of long tables had been set up. Food filled both of them.

Landon followed Macie as she made her way toward the tables. Once again, a number of people called out her name then waved. He'd never in his adult life stayed in one place long enough to build those types of relationships. What would it be like to have friendships like that?

"I hope my cookies made it," Macie murmured.

He did too. If he weren't larger than Macie, he might have feared for his life. At the table he lowered the pack and unzipped it. Gently, he removed the blanket then the container and handed the cookies to her.

Macie opened it carefully. With a proud lift of her chin, she placed the cookies on the table with the other desserts.

Landon breathed a sigh of relief. All the cookies had arrived intact, and she beamed up at him. A ripple of warmth washed through him, making him feel like a hero. He grinned. Macie was anxious where her cookies were concerned. He leaned in close and whispered for her ears only, "I'm sure everyone will love them."

Even in the darkening light he could see her blush. She smiled and his heart almost jumped out of his chest.

"Stop teasing me and let's find a place to sit." She started toward the fire.

They found a spot among the other blankets and Landon spread theirs out. Macie took the backpack from him, sat it on the blanket and started removing items they would need to dine. One she was done, she looked around.

"Now, let's go see and be seen."

Over the next half hour she introduced him to a number of the guests. A few were influential people from the villages, including another mayor. Landon was careful not to mention the business of the hospital, despite his first inclination to do so. He and Macie were in the middle of a discussion that included a great deal of laughter when Luc, the man they had met on the path, called for everyone's attention.

"Welcome. Thanks for joining us. We hope you enjoyed the trail down today. Now help yourself to something to eat and stay as long as you wish."

Landon tugged her hand. "Let's go get some of that food. I'm hungry after that walk, and I'm eager to try another one of your cookies."

Macie said over her shoulder, "I hope you aren't disappointed."

They stopped by the blanket and picked up their plates.

"I'm not sure I could ever be disappointed in anything you do."

Her brows drew together with doubt. "I think you might be trying too hard to flatter me. It's not necessary."

"I'd never say what I don't mean."

She smirked at him. "People do it all the time."

Landon wondered who had hidden something from her. Someone she really cared about? An old boyfriend? The idea of her caring about another man somehow bothered him. He held no claim on her, now or years ago. And he had no intention of doing so either.

They joined the buffet line. Famished after their trek, he didn't hesitate to pile his plate full of food. Macie was a little more subdued, but she had covered all the space on her plate as well.

He reached out his hand. "Give me your plate to hold and you can fix us a dessert plate to share. Be sure to put a couple of your cookies on it."

Macie lifted her chin and gave him a defiant look. Landon needed to learn that he couldn't order her around outside the usual chain of command in a medical situation. "Giving orders, Doctor?"

He smiled. "Merely making a suggestion."

She removed the extra plate she'd put under her other one and handed him her food. "Any other type of dessert you'd like?"

"I trust your judgment." The words were thrown over his shoulder as he walked away.

Macie filled the plate with sweets and returned to their blanket. It suddenly occurred to her that she and Landon sharing a blanket might send the wrong message. She looked at the desserts. The two of them sharing a plate of food was even worse.

Landon waited, sitting cross-legged on the blanket. He'd even gone to the open cooler and picked them up iced drinks. Reaching for the plate she held, he took it from her. She exhaled and sank to the blanket.

"What's the sigh for?"

Great. She hadn't planned to do that out loud. "Nothing."

He watched her for a second, then picked up his plate and began eating. She joined him.

"This is all delicious. I'm not sure if it's because I'm so hungry or because everyone is such a good cook." Landon forked a bit of barbequed meat.

"Probably a little bit of both. Eating outside always makes the food taste better."

It didn't take Landon long to clean his plate. He went back for more.

Macie put her plate to the side when she'd finished, and smiled when she saw Landon returning with his plate overflowing again.

"Don't wait on me to start on your dessert," he said.

She placed her hands in her lap. "I don't think I'll have any."

He studied her. "What? If I remember correctly, you used to have a sweet tooth."

He remembered her well. She thought he'd completely forgotten her after he'd left her in Hawaii. She had no idea she'd made that much of an impression on him.

"Come on. You can share, can't you? Except the cookies are all mine." He grinned as he handed her a clean fork.

"I can share." She feared he might charm her into sharing too much with him. Like a kiss, or…more.

When they finished their dessert, Landon set the plate off to the side then leaned back on a bent arm and crossed his ankles. He appeared relaxed. Even in the low light of the fire she saw him studying her. "That might have been the finest meal I've ever eaten. And your cookies are to die for."

She couldn't help but smile, tickled he liked them so much. "Now you're making fun of me."

"No, I'm not. They were great. I'm just sorry there weren't any more to be had."

"Okay, you don't have to go overboard. You can stop now."

Landon's look turned serious. "Only if you promise to make me a plate of my very own some time."

Macie raised a hand. "All right, you win."

He looked around at the other people for a moment. "Is there anyone else that I need to meet tonight?"

She shook her head, a little out of sorts with his scrutiny. "No, we did better than I expected. On Monday I'll have Tatiana start making calls for appointments."

"You know, the military could use your drive and organizational skill when they plan their missions."

She grinned, sitting a little straighter. "I'll take that as a compliment."

"It was meant that way," he said softly.

They both were quiet for a few minutes. She was enjoying the warmth of the fire, the slight breeze off the water and the fact Landon was near.

"Macie, I still don't understand why you're really in

this far-flung place." His voice was low enough that it could have been her subconscious whispering to her.

She'd not expected his question. The truth, even so many years later, was still too raw to share. "I'm making a living."

"You could be doing that anywhere. Why here? Why would a young, attractive, determined, vivacious woman, who could be enjoying parties, movies and having a love life, want to live so far away from the bright lights?"

"Who said I don't have a love life?"

He raised a brow. "Do you?"

"No."

"Why, Macie?" His voice soothed and begged at the same time.

What will it take to get him to stop pushing? "I told you how I came to work here."

"Yes, you did. But not why or what has kept you here. Don't you miss your family, friends, shopping?"

"I talk to a few friends when I can. One has come to visit for a week." She lifted her shoulders proudly. She wasn't as pitiful as he was making her out to be. But the friend who had come to visit was someone she had met in Hawaii, not a childhood friend. She hadn't kept in touch with any of those because her father had stolen from some of their parents.

He gave that a moment of thought. "Seems a long way to come for such a short visit."

"It was. I appreciated her coming. It was great to see her." The truth was she been thrilled and surprised.

"What about your family?"

He needed to stop. She didn't want to talk about the real why. Didn't want to go to that dark place. She rarely shared the true reason. More like *never* shared. But Landon had told her about his parents, his life growing up. Didn't he deserve the same consideration from her? What could it hurt? She lived halfway around the world now. Cameras and journalists would never be in her face again as long as no one knew who she was.

"Okay, since you seem to want to know so badly, then I'll give you the dirty details. I came for the reason I have already told you. I was assigned here and I've stayed here because I'm needed."

"But there's more."

She took a deep breath. It was time. "Yes. My father is Jason Beck. He was head of Limited Investments. Does that ring any bells?" Macie glared at him. She hated talking about this.

Landon sat up and turned toward her. "It sounds familiar, but I'm not sure why."

"It's because he—my family—was on TV and in newspapers for months. My father bilked people out of their money, took all their retirement savings."

"Oh, I remember now."

It sounded as if Landon had started to get it. "My father had been running a Ponzi scheme for years. He destroyed a lot of people's lives. I'd grown up living a life of luxury while my father had been busy stealing from people. I had just finished nursing school when it all exploded. To help my father, the lawyers said the family needed to stand beside him. We needed to appear as a united force, regardless of what we might have thought. I worshipped my father. I was his little princess. But everything in my life had been a lie. When the trial was over, I had to get away. Go somewhere where I wasn't recognized, so I joined the traveling nurses and ended up here."

"I understand now. But that was years ago, wasn't it? Haven't you ever wanted to go back?" His hand came to rest over hers. There was something reassuring and comforting about it.

"Occasionally, but Saipan feels like home now. I'm needed here. I'm not in the spotlight, and that suits me just fine."

Before she could say more or Landon could comment, out of the dark a voice yelled urgently, "Macie? Where are you?"

CHAPTER FIVE

LANDON'S HEAD JERKED AROUND at Macie's name.

She called back, "Over here, Joe."

A man came running toward them. Landon stood and helped Macie to rise.

"You're needed." Joe pulled in a deep breath. "There's been an accident on one of the tankers. A man has fallen through the cargo opening into the hold."

Macie set off toward Joe before he'd finished speaking. The stricken look on her face had told Landon this wasn't good and the adrenaline started pumping immediately. Landon didn't know if the call for help included him, but Macie wasn't leaving without him. He jogged after her.

Shouting off rapid-fire questions, Macie moved into a lope. She asked Joe, "You have a vehicle?"

"Yeah."

"Let's go." She joined the man, and Landon came alongside her. "Where's the ship worker?"

"He hit a container and then went down between them. Worse, it's the ship's medical man."

"Great," Macie mumbled. She didn't slow as she followed Joe. "He's alive?"

"They heard him make some noise right after he fell." Joe kept pushing their pace forward.

"They haven't tried to move him, have they?" Concern wrapped Macie's words.

"The dispatcher told them not to," Joe said.

"Good."

They soon reached parking area, and Joe indicated to a Jeep. Macie climbed in the front passenger seat and gave Landon a startled look when he jumped in behind her. Had she been so focused on what was ahead that she had forgotten about him?

"When did the call come in?" She returned to asking Joe questions.

"Fifteen minutes ago." Joe put the vehicle in gear and made a turn in the sand, slinging it in a wide arc. They quickly hit the pavement and were barreling down the road with the emergency lights flashing. "The ambulance team is out on a run. That's why I came after you. They'll get there behind us. Hopefully, only five or ten minutes."

Macie braced herself against the dashboard. "Yet every minute counts. Is a boat waiting for us at the dock?"

"Yes."

Boat? Landon hadn't thought that far. They were going to have to take a boat to the ship? It wasn't at the dock?

Joe glanced back at him with a questioning look. Macie said, "You haven't met Dr. Cochran yet, have you? He's our interim administrator."

Joe nodded. "Yeah. I heard about him." That didn't sound like a positive thing to Landon's ears. In his type of work, he wasn't always popular. For some reason, this time, he wished it were different.

"Joe's one of our EMTs. He's supposed to be off tonight too." Macie sounded accepting as if it happened often to lose her leisure time. They pulled up in a parking lot near a long, wide industrial pier. He'd previously seen it only from a distance when Macie had been giving him the tour of the island.

"Pete's waiting to take us out to the ship," Joe said as they started down the pier.

"Pete?" Landon asked.

"Yeah. Local guy we call on sometimes," Macie offered.

Waiting near the end of the pier was a speedboat. The three of them ran toward it and climbed in. Pete had the boat running, and as soon as they were seated, he took off.

The sky was inky black. The only lights were those coming from the huge tanker ahead of them.

As Macie held her hair out of her face, she leaned in close to Landon and said, "The reef won't allow the ships to come in any closer. They anchor offshore and everything must come in by smaller boats."

Moments later, Pete backed off the gas and they slowly traveled over the reef. Beyond it, he gave the boat gas again and they thumped and bumped across the wavy water to the oceangoing tanker. Macie grabbed Landon's leg to steady herself over one particularly rough dip and rise. Clouds drifted over the moon and visibility decreased.

Landon glanced back. The lights of the coast were tiny in the distance.

Not quickly enough for Landon, Pete pulled alongside the ship. A large door stood open a few feet above the waterline and a metal ladder hung down over the side. Joe reached for the ladder and started up it. Once Joe stepped inside, Macie didn't hesitate to do the same. But Landon wasn't as enthusiastic. He held out his hands in case he needed to assist her or catch her if she fell, but neither happened. When his turn arrived, he followed suit, leaving the rocking boat behind. Soon, they were all standing in a wide space that ran the width of the belly of the tanker.

Macie spoke to a man whose accent told Landon English wasn't his first language. His short stature and straight black hair showed his Asian descent. Bringing a radio to his mouth, he talked rapidly into it, and someone answered him in Chinese. The group moved farther into the center of the ship and stepped into a large freight elevator. They then exited high above where they had entered the ship, and after going down a short passage, they went through a door onto the outside deck.

Landon looked around. The lights blared and everything around them was huge, intimidating. The entire experience would be surreal if he had been allowed to dwell on where he was and what he was doing. He was out of his element. Macie seemed to take it all in stride. Apparently, she had been on one of these hulking ships before.

They continued across the floodlit riveted metal floor to a gigantic hole surrounded by rails: the cargo hold. Their party joined a group wearing hardhats, standing nearby. Macie spoke to the man with the radio, and he pointed down into the darkness in the center of the ship.

Landon had tried to imagine what Joe and Macie had been discussing on their drive, but this situation was far beyond any scenario he had pictured. In his opinion, it was past the skills of he and Macie. Yet he knew something must be done for the injured man. Hopefully, they wouldn't be too late.

"I need to get down there," Macie said.

"The only way down is by crane." The crew member indicated with a hand the large piece of equipment mounted on the deck.

"Can't we go in from the floor we were just on?" Landon asked, standing beside Macie.

The man shook his head. "No. The man is between shipping containers. This is the only way to reach him."

"Okay, then get me down there," Macie stated.

"If anyone is going in there, it's going to be me," Landon announced.

"You're not—"

Landon gave her a stern look. "We're wasting time. You can better help organize things up here. I'll assess what's needed and let you know." He asked the man, "Do you have radios that we can use?"

The man with the radio nodded then said something to another sailor. He hurried off. "We already have a couple of men down there waiting to help."

Macie remained silent so long that Landon feared she would disagree with his plan, but she finally gave him a firm nod.

"Okay," he said to the man with the radio, "send me down."

The sailor returned with the radios and handed one to each of them.

"You'll need to ride in the harness seat." The man started toward the crane and the cables dangling from it.

Landon moved to follow but a hand on his arm stopped him.

Macie gave him an earnest look. "Be careful."

He gave her a wry smile. "I will."

Not a fan of heights, all too soon Landon found himself sitting in a metal seat slowly being lowered into the center of a huge hole. Using a headlight Macie had handed him from somewhere, as well as the handheld flashlight that a crew member had shoved into his hand at the last second, he searched the area and saw two men waiting on top of a container.

It took longer than he would have wished before his feet touched a steel floor. Landon used the radio to let Macie know he had arrived. She sounded relieved. Soon, the crane operator pulled the basket up again.

"Do either of you speak English?"

"Little," one of them said.

Landon was glad to hear that. "Show me where the injured man is."

The sailor nodded and pointed down. "Watch step."

He was right—the rough and ridged surface was a tripping hazard. Landon stepped over the lip running the width of the container.

The man pointed between two stacks of oceangoing boxes.

A couple of thick ropes were coiled nearby. He and the sailors needed to be tied off so they wouldn't fall as well. Landon found an end and secured it around his waist, then looped it through a metal ring welded to the container. Secured, he went down on his belly and looked into the narrow space between the boxes.

Finally, he saw a flash. He focused the beam of light in that direction again. It was the reflective tape on the man's orange work coveralls. Landon radioed, "I see him."

"His position?" It was Macie speaking.

"About eight feet down. No movement. One leg is in an odd position. Best guess is it's broken. We need more rope. The emergency basket, neck brace, leg brace and some manpower."

"Ten-four."

Landon called down to the man. "Can you hear me? We're here to help. Hang on."

The man who spoke English lay on his stomach beside Landon, looking over the lip.

"Tell him in Chinese we are coming after him," Landon instructed.

The man nodded and spoke. Still no noise or movement from the injured man.

Landon hoped they were not too late. Until he had the medical supplies, there wasn't much more he could do. Soon, the basket was being lowered again. This time it was with Macie in it, her lap full of supplies.

Landon took the large bag from her, then helped her out of the seat. He then radioed up that the contraption could be raised.

"Where's the man?" Macie asked, starting to cross the container.

"Hook yourself up first. I can't have you going over." Landon attached the other rope to the same hook he was using and tied her off. While he worked, he told her, "Don't take any chances."

Her chin jutted out. "I won't."

"This way." Landon led the way to the side. He wouldn't have her getting hurt. For some reason he felt responsible for her.

As they looked over the edge, Macie asked, "Have you formed a plan?"

He had, but he didn't particularly like it—but then he didn't think they had a choice. "We're going to have to go down and get him. Bring him up here before getting him into the emergency basket. We'll have to pull him up here manually since there's so little space."

"Joe's on his way down, along with a few other men for man power. I'll go down to the injured man. I'm the smallest and he'll need a neck brace at minimum. There's no way he doesn't have head trauma. To make matters worse, a storm is coming. The wind is picking up. We need to get this guy out of here and to shore."

Landon didn't like the proposal, but he had to agree with her. The space was so narrow he wouldn't even get close to the man before getting stuck.

Joe arrived with more equipment and the seat went back up. Joe tied himself off with a rope he'd brought down as Macie explained the plan.

Landon hated the idea of her being the one to go down, but outside of his personal issues with it, he couldn't think of a reason to stop her.

He helped her get into a harness that the ship had provided while Joe fastened the rope. Landon then found the neck brace and gave it to her. But figuring she couldn't hold it and see about protecting herself, he took it back from her and secured it to another rope. He would lower it down to her when she was ready.

He placed his hands on her upper arms, holding her in place, and looked into her eyes. "You ready for this?"

"I don't really have a choice, do I?" She wore a resigned but determined look.

"No, not really. I'll be right here when you come up. Don't take any chances." He gave her a quick kiss on the lips and squeezed her arms. "I wouldn't want to lose you now that I have found you again. Now, let's save this man."

Macie's mouth formed a firm line before she went to her knees and then her belly. Rolling over, she slid over the side feetfirst. He and Joe slowly let out the rope holding her.

"Hold right there. I've reached him," Macie called, not using the radio.

She must be afraid she might drop it. Landon could hear his heart beating in his ears.

"He's alive. Barely. Leg is a compound fracture. Bleeding but not pouring. Head trauma."

"Can you put on the neck brace?" Landon yelled.

"No. Send me another rope. I need to secure him then have you bring him up some before I try to put on the brace."

"I've got her." Landon sat and braced his feet against the small ledge running the length of the container.

Joe grunted and hurried to the pile of supplies.

Thankfully, one of the crew took over Joe's position, easing the strain on Landon. Joe threw the line over the side.

Minutes went by and he heard nothing from Macie. He could stand it no longer. "Macie?"

"I'm working here. Almost done."

More long moments stretched out, then she called, "Pull up gently on his line."

Joe and one of the others did so.

"Okay. Now mine."

Landon pulled hand over hand, slowly bringing her up.

"Stop there. Send down the brace," Macie called.

Joe put it over the side.

"I'm getting it into place," Macie called up.

Landon felt Macie's movement through the rope.

"Macie?" he called.

"Almost have it in place."

He was ready to have her back up with him safe and sound. Was there a hand squeezing his heart? He'd never felt like this about another person before. Fear was like a real thing eating at him.

Finally, she called, "Okay. Slowly pull him up."

Again, her movements came through the rope. He couldn't stand not being able to see her. It was time to get her out.

"Stop, stop."

Landon held his breath until Macie called, "Okay, but super slow. Landon, start pulling me up as well."

Using all his strength, he pulled the rope through his hands. The muscles in his thighs quivered and those on his back ached with his effort. Time ticked by slowly.

"Hold me right here. Ease the patient up and over while I steady his legs. Watch the left one."

"Give me a second." Landon looked at the only man left who wasn't doing something and indicated with his head for him to take Landon's place. He hated to leave Macie, but he would be needed immediately to work on the injured man. He handed over the rope and stood. His legs were cramped, but he shook them out.

"Okay. I'm ready." Landon went down on his hands and knees so he could see over the side.

Macie looked up at him. All he wanted to do was haul her into his arms and make sure she was safe, but he had work to do. He gave her his best reassuring smile.

"Okay, guys, pull him up slowly." Landon reached for the patient as soon as he could grasp him and eased him up by placing his hands under his arms. Landon made every effort at gentleness. As the man's hips came over the side, Landon's focus went to seeing to the leg. He held it steady as he was brought onto the container to lie unconscious on his back.

"Get Macie up," he barked at Joe.

On the radio, he heard that the emergency staff were leaving the hospital and heading toward the pier. At least there would be more medical help coming. For now, it was him, Macie and Joe. Landon glanced over to where the men worked Macie's line. He could just now see the top of her head.

"Joe, I need an IV started STAT. The man has a head

injury as well. I've not had time to check for further injuries, but I'm starting now."

Macie had heard Landon's demand as she was being hauled up. Glad she now sat on top of the container and was out of the narrow space hanging by a rope, she took a deep breath. She'd trusted Landon to take care of her, but that didn't mean she had liked being squeezed in between two pieces of metal, unable to see the bottom—not that she'd wanted to.

To her knowledge, Landon had never encountered an emergency like this before, yet he'd been impressive in his command of the situation despite no longer regularly working on the frontline of emergency medicine.

Nursing school hadn't trained her to carry out a roped rescue. All she knew was that a man would die if she didn't do something, terrified or not. Standing, she paused a moment to gather her wits and take another deep breath to settle her pounding heart.

"We need more light here," Landon said.

The man who spoke English translated for the crew members, who then pointed their flashlights over the patient.

Landon slowly worked his fingers over the man's head. She'd seen the large gash on the patient's forehead, but in the poor lighting she'd not been able to determine if he had additional injuries.

"I'll do the vitals." Macie went to the bag and pulled out the stethoscope and blood pressure cuff.

Landon's gaze met hers. An intensity filled his eyes she'd not seen before. "Nice to have you back."

She smiled. It felt good to have someone concerned about her. It had been a long time. Since she had left her family, in fact. She'd heard Landon demand that she be taken care of, the worry in his voice evident. "Nice to be up here again."

His hands were now working their way over the patient's shoulders and down his rib cage.

"BP ninety over fifty, heart rate one ten and thready. He's lost a good deal of blood. We'll need to start plasma and plan for a blood transfusion ASAP. Where are those emergency guys?"

Just then the radio squawked. "The EMTs are at the pier, just waiting on the boat to come get them."

She reached for the radio. "Can you patch me through to them?"

"Yes."

A few seconds later she heard the voice of one of the EMTs.

"This is Macie. Stay where you are. We're coming to you. Tell the ER to have whole blood waiting. Also, call Guam and have them on standby to send the jet. This case is more than our ICU can handle."

"Ten-four" came back through the radio.

"We have a head injury, open wound. Compound break of the femur. Patient is unconscious. Eyes are…"

Landon lifted the man's eyelids. "Fixed and dilated."

She relayed the information and then gave the rest of the vitals. "We'll be on our way as soon as we have him in the basket and out of this hole. When we're on the transfer boat I'll radio again."

The patient barely clung to life. One thing at a time. They had to keep him alive long enough to have surgery and receive more intensive care.

A big fat drop of rain hit Macie's arm. She looked up. Through the deck floodlights she could see the rain falling. Now they would have to contend with the weather.

"It's starting to rain. The water will be getting rough. Let's get him in the basket and up on deck."

"Macie, you go up first and organize things. I'll come up behind the patient."

A man quickly attached the crane seat to the cables and Macie soon rose in the air on the way to the deck. On this ride she spent some time looking around. She couldn't believe she'd been inside a tanker, much less sandwiched between two metal boxes.

At the top she conferred with the lead man about using the ship's wider, flatter and slower ferryboat to get the injured man to land. Someone handed her a well-used yellow slicker, which she gratefully pulled on. The rain had picked up and the deck was slippery. She waited impatiently for the crane to lift her patient out.

When he arrived, she quickly checked his vitals and made sure he had been secured for the trip across the water. She then supervised him being carried to the elevator. On the way she glanced at the dark hole, hoping Landon would soon appear. He would have to catch up since there was no time to wait on him.

She saw to securing the patient in a boat belonging to the ship used to transport small cargo and men. It was wider and more stable than the speedboat. The captain was ready to cast off when Landon came running out the doorway. He scrambled in, flopping into the nearest seat, still in only the clothes he'd been wearing when he'd boarded the ship.

As they took off, she called, "You good?"

He did a thumbs-up.

The rain beat down on them, but the boat kept moving. She pulled off the slicker, sat in the bottom of the boat and held it over the patient's face. Looking up, she saw Landon grimacing as he braced against the rain and wind.

The flat-bottomed boat made for a bumpy and slow trip. Shivering and soaked through, she tried not to think about it. Their patient needed the attention. He wasn't at the hospital nor out of trouble yet.

By the time the boat reached the dock, the wind had increased and the rain beat down harder than ever. The bad weather had turned into a storm. Getting close enough to the cement pier without smashing into it and then not dropping the patient into the water as they got him out would be a challenge, but it must be done. They were still fighting against the clock. It had been too long since the call had first come in.

It required some maneuvering on the captain's part to bring the craft alongside the pier. Thankfully, there were enough people in the boat and waiting on the dock to lift the litter. As quickly as possible, and between swells in the water, they removed the patient without too much difficulty. With heads down against the pouring rain, they hurried to the waiting ambulance.

It was a relief to hand the patient over to the EMTs. Because there wasn't enough room in the ambulance, one of the police officers offered her and Landon a ride to the hospital. Landon put an arm around her shoulders, shielding her against the pounding rain and offering his warmth, as they hurried to the car. They piled into the back seat.

Landon huffed and scooted next to her. "To be out of the weather feels great."

She shivered. "Better than great. Do you think this guy is gonna make it?" She was in need of reassurance that all their efforts wouldn't have been for nothing.

He squeezed her hand. "I don't know, but I do know we gave it our best effort."

Far too often she'd given her best effort and still it

hadn't made a difference. Like when she had stood beside her father and he had still gone to jail. Or when she'd demanded they do something for the people he had hurt, the lawyers had just laughed at her. She'd been as helpless then as she was now. Nothing about being at other people's mercy appealed to her.

At the hospital the officer pulled his car up behind the ambulance, which now stood empty with its back doors wide open. She and Landon hurried inside the hospital and headed straight to the area where the staff huddled around their patient.

"What can I do?" Macie asked.

Landon took her elbow. When she tried to pull away, his grip tightened and he gently drew her out of the room.

"We both need dry clothes and to take a moment to regroup. Our patient is in good hands. We'll ask what we can do after we take care of ourselves."

She jerked her arm, but he tightened his grip. "But—"

"Macie, you can't be everything to everybody all the time. You have to let go sometimes."

She screwed up her face and gave him an unhappy glare. "I call the shower first."

He barked a dry laugh. "Okay. Where's the on-call room?"

"This way." She led him down the hall to a door on the right. Knocking, and not receiving a response, she entered. Hating to admit it, Macie had to allow that Landon was right. Her teeth had started to chatter; she was cold, wet and uncomfortable. Coming into an air-conditioned building hadn't helped. A shower and dry clothes would be heavenly. After she took care of herself, she'd be in a position to help again.

"If we're not careful we'll have hypothermia." Landon stepped into the bathroom and turned the shower on. Still standing in the sleeping area Macie heard the water running.

"In the tropics?" she asked.

"It can happen. In truth I was getting worried you might be in shock back there in the boat." Landon came to stand in the bathroom doorway.

She started kicking off her soggy shoes. "No. Not shock. Just exhaustion."

"And coming down off an adrenaline high. I know the feeling. I bet Joe does too. I'll check on him when he arrives."

"Now, into the shower." Landon stood out of the way and motioned for Macie to enter.

She stepped forward and by him, still wearing her clothes.

"Don't take too long or all the hot water will be gone," Landon said. "If I think that's happening, I'll join you."

Something about the determined look in his eyes made her think he meant it.

Macie swung around and glared at him. "You wouldn't dare!"

Landon's eyes narrowed, his look meeting hers. "Stay too long and just see what I do. I'm cold and miserable and more than ready to get out of these clothes. Now, get busy."

He wasn't kidding. She had better get moving. With a gulp, Macie closed the door between them. After stripping off her damp clinging clothes, she stood under the water. She sighed with pleasure. What if Landon did do as he threatened? A tingle of awareness rippled through her. She might like it. Too much.

Lifting her face to the spray, Macie couldn't help but enjoy the feel of the water flowing over her. Her thoughts went to the events of the last few hours. She'd been hanging from a rope. Everything about the experience had been dangerous. Suddenly, she doubled over sobbing. The tears poured down with the water. What was wrong with her? She never cried. Certainly not for herself. Not since her father's trial.

"Macie, honey, what's wrong? I knocked and you didn't answer."

Landon was there. He turned her in his arms and brought her against his broad bare chest, cupping her head as he held her against him. The sound of his steady heartbeat somehow comforted and excited her at the same time. Despite her tumultuous emotions following their experience that night, her blood zipped through her veins in reaction to being so close to a bare-chested Landon. He wore only his shorts.

She wrapped her arms around his waist. He felt so strong and reassuring, so right.

After a few minutes, his voice filled with concern, he asked, "Are you hurt?"

"No." The word was accompanied by a sniffle.

"Then what's going on?" She felt his compassion in his embrace yet there was also a hum of sexual consciousness between them. Landon held her gently, tenderly, but she had the sensation he was holding himself back.

She mumbled against his neck, "I was so scared."

"I know, honey. I'm glad I wasn't the only one." He kissed the top of her head.

"Mmm." Macie ran a hand over the muscles of his lower back and snuggled closer. Landon felt so good. Why couldn't she let go just once? Let Landon show her how alive she could feel.

Landon felt Macie's smile against his skin. Her hand moving over his back sent heat shooting throughout his body. He was hyperaware of every move she made. He'd stepped into the shower to comfort her and now his body ached to consume her. Between them, he had grown hard with desire. If their embrace didn't end soon he would be asking for more than she might be willing to give.

Macie looked at him with wide eyes. "You were afraid too? It didn't show."

It might not have shown, but he'd felt it all the way to his bones. He had no wish to repeat any of it, especially the part where Macie had hung by a rope.

"That doesn't mean I wasn't worried." He cupped her cheek and lowered his mouth to hers. She tasted so sweet. All he intended to do was reassure himself that she was there, safe and sound. Yet her lips were plump, damp from the water and salty from her tears. She felt like heaven. He kept the kiss gentle, comforting, despite his desire to do more and his control that had become razor thin.

It felt good to be alive. Macie made him feel that way.

She moaned, and her arms came up around his neck as her perfect velvety smooth body leaned into his.

Landon ran a hand down the length of her damp back, stopping himself just short of going too far out of bounds. This wasn't, shouldn't be, about sex but about comfort. But his body begged for the former. Regardless of the fact that he held a naked Macie—which he'd dreamed of doing every night since arriving on Saipan—he couldn't, wouldn't, take advantage of her. If the circumstances were different, would she be letting him hold her like this?

They had to stop now. This wasn't the time or the place. He wouldn't take the chance that she might resent him or regret being with him.

Stepping away from her and breaking the kiss, he

turned her and pulled the shower curtain back. With his palm on her lower back, he gave her a gentle push. "Dry off and get dressed. I put some clean scrubs on the counter."

She stepped out, and he firmly drew the curtain between them, grateful the water had cooled. It saved him from having to turn it to cold.

Macie had left by the time he came out of the bathroom. He was glad, since he had no idea what her reaction would be after she'd had time to think about those moments in the shower. Putting his feet back into his wet shoes, he headed to where he'd last seen their patient.

On arriving, he saw Macie standing at the unit desk holding the phone. "We need the plane here ASAP."

He stopped beside her. Macie glanced up then away as if she didn't want to make eye contact. Was she embarrassed by her actions in the shower? He was hoping she would want to repeat them when her mind had cleared. His body still begged for her to do so.

Macie's attention returned to the phone, "The patient has head trauma. He needs Level One trauma care. He has to come to Guam and then go on to another hospital to get it." There was a pause. "I know there's a storm. I've been out in it trying to save this man's life." Another pause. "Okay, okay, I understand. Just send it when you can." Macie dropped the phone on the hook.

"I'm guessing the plane from Guam can't make it until the storm breaks."

"Correct. The CT scan shows a swelling of the brain. All we can do right now is take him to ICU and wait until he can be flown to Guam. Even the surgery for the leg will have to wait."

"You have done all you can for tonight. He's in good hands now. It's time we go home."

"I don't want to leave until I know he's safely in ICU." Macie turned toward where the man still fought for his life.

"Okay, but the minute he's settled, we're going to get some rest." Landon gave her a firm look.

"You can go on home." A hopeful note entered her voice.

Was Macie trying to get rid of him? "Not going to happen. I too want to see him settled in ICU."

A few minutes later they helped push the patient's gurney to ICU. Landon listened to the ER doctor's report and added a couple of notes that he knew from the accident scene. While he did that, Macie stayed busy assisting the nurses as they hooked the patient to the monitors and organized the IV lines.

The patient had been settled in ICU, and finally there was nothing left for them to do but pray he remained alive until the airlift from Guam arrived. From there he would go to a hospital in Hawaii or if his family wanted to his home country for care.

They stopped by the on-call room long enough to bag up their wet clothing before they left the building.

"I'm starving," Landon said as they walked across the parking lot in the rain.

Macie stopped. "Where're we going? We don't have a car here."

Landon grinned. "I had a couple of guys who work in Maintenance go and pick up my car. Now, about food. We need some. Then bed."

"What?"

He spoke evenly. "We're going to have some breakfast before I take you home."

"Okay." Macie said nothing more as they climbed into the car. She must have been as dead on her feet as he was.

As he drove, she laid her head back and closed her eyes and only opened them when they arrived at his house.

"What are we doing here?" Her voice was higher than normal.

"Having breakfast. The one thing I do well in the kitchen is breakfast. Besides, nowhere's open this early. Even the hospital cafeteria doesn't open for staff for another thirty minutes."

Macie grunted as if she didn't care one way or the other. "All I want to do is sleep."

"Food first."

While he went to the kitchen, she wandered out onto the porch.

He called out, "Do you want vegetables in your omelet or not?" There was no answer. "Macie?" There was no answer. "Hello, Macie?" Still nothing.

Landon found her lying on the cushioned lounge on her side with her knees drawn up, her hands under her cheek, sound asleep. He smiled. Going to his bedroom, he pulled a light blanket off the end of the bed, then returned to the porch. He placed the cover over Macie and she sighed softly. His heart did too.

There were gray smudges under her eyes. His little heroine deserved a good rest. She'd done an amazing job that night, more than some would have dared. Landon gave her a light kiss on her forehead.

Sitting on the small couch beside her, he propped his feet on the coffee table, crossed his ankles, leaned back and overlapped his arms on his chest before closing his eyes. Food for him and his angel would have to wait after all.

CHAPTER SIX

MACIE WOKE TO the sound of rain tapping on tin. Opening her eyes, she recognized the porch at Landon's place and snuggled deeper into the blanket around her. The noise was comforting, and she watched the water dripping off the eaves for a moment.

What was that sound? Something clinked from far off. She knew that sound. It was whisking, and it was coming from the direction of the kitchen.

How long had she been here? With the grey day and no sun to judge by, she had no idea.

She pulled the blanket up around her face. Where had it come from? *Landon.*

"Hey there, sleepyhead."

He stood in the doorway between the porch and kitchen. His hair was damp and mussed as if he had just toweled it. She liked the look on him. His white T-shirt pulled tight across his chest, and she couldn't help but notice that he had a nice one. Well-worn jeans covered his lower half and his feet were bare. He was too sexy.

Last night he had been supportive, caring, professional. She couldn't have done what she had to rescue that man if she hadn't known Landon was there with her. When was the last time she'd had that type of security? It had been so long she couldn't remember. Maybe before the walls had come tumbling down on her father and their family? But even that had been false security. Last night she'd known Landon would do everything in his power to take care of her. That had been real. *He'd* been real.

"How about breakfast?" His focus remained on her as if he waited for her reaction.

She moved to get up.

Landon waved her down. "No, stay put. I was just checking to see if you were awake. Give me two minutes and I'll have it ready. You deserve breakfast in bed."

She didn't argue any further. He went back to the kitchen, and she slipped into the visitor's bathroom in the hall. She returned to the porch and found him waiting with two plates filled with toast, bacon and the most divine looking omelet she had ever seen.

Suddenly, she was ravenous. Her stomach punctuated it with a nice rumble of hunger. It seemed ages ago when they had eaten on the beach by the fire. "It smells wonderful. And looks just as good."

"Have a seat and let's eat." He picked up a plate and handed it to her.

She sat on the lounge and took it from him, then just as quickly put it down and jumped to her feet. "I forgot. I need to call the hospital to check on the man."

"I called half an hour ago. The weather has let up enough that the plane from Guam can get in. It's already on the way. He should be medevaced in the next hour. Now you need to eat. When you're done, I'll take you home. I'm sure you're ready to climb into a bed. I know that lounger wasn't the most comfortable thing for you to sleep on."

"I was too tired to notice." She took a bite of the eggs and savored the wonderful taste. Landon hadn't lied. He did make a fine omelet. "I bet you only feel that way after sleeping in your cushy bed while I was out here."

He patted the cushion next to him. "I slept right here beside you."

"You did. Why?" She tilted her head to the side and gave him a questioning look.

"I don't know. It just seemed like the right thing to do at the time. I sat down for a minute, and the next thing I knew I was sound asleep."

They ate for a few minutes in silence.

"You're a nice man, Landon Cochran."

"I appreciate that, coming from you. I know you haven't always believed that."

She shrugged and looked bashful. "Maybe that's true. But as time has gone by, you have proven yourself different."

Landon placed his empty plate on the table. "I know I've said it before, but I am sorry."

"I think I might have taken it harder because of what my father did. I felt like I had been lied to again and I was laying my anger at him on you." She hadn't realized that until this moment. Landon had made her no real promises. "I'm sorry I was so hard on you when you first came to the island. You really were great last night."

"I feel the same way about you." Picking up his coffee cup, he took a sip. "It certainly was an experience."

"Yeah, one I don't plan to repeat. I don't know what I was thinking when I said I'd go down."

"You weren't. You were just doing what had to be done."

"I don't even do climbing in general, much less narrow spaces." Her heart still beat faster at the thought of the danger she'd been in.

He grinned. "You didn't hesitate. I'd never have known you were afraid if you hadn't said so."

She fiddled with her fork. "An experience like that makes you feel lucky to be alive."

Landon's look met hers and held. His gaze dropped to her lips. He said softly, "Yeah, it does."

Macie's mouth went dry. She wanted to go to him, kiss him and then snuggle into his strong, reassuring body. To remind herself of why it was good to be alive. Instead, she stood with her plate in her hand and picked up his. "You cooked, so I should wash. Thank you for the meal— it was wonderful. Do you have other hidden talents?"

"No, just that one." The words had a solemn tone, as if he were disappointed in himself.

"I know that can't be true," she called over her shoulder as she went inside. Running water into the sink, she started washing the dishes.

A few minutes later Landon joined her. "I'll dry." He picked up a dish towel. "I had no idea you were so domestic."

She glanced at him. He was standing close, and she found that his warmth soothed her jumbled nerves. It felt too right to have him near. Her hand shook as she picked up a plate. "There's a lot you don't know about me."

"Is that so?" He watched her intently.

Something about his question challenged her. Made her feel daring. Or was that from the scare from the night before? Whatever it was, she wanted him. Wanted him to feel as out of sorts as she felt. Leaning her hip against the counter then turning toward him slightly, she grinned. "Yeah, that's so."

"Okay, let's play twenty questions." His voice held a dare.

"Twenty? That's too many. I've got to go."

"Okay. Make it ten. I'll start. What's your favorite color?" He sounded like a kid who had just gotten his way.

She returned to washing. "Blue. What's yours?"

"Green."

"All right. Favorite movie?" He stacked a plate in the cabinet.

She immediately came back with "Anything that ends in a happily-ever-after."

Landon pursed his lips in thought. "Really? That one I hadn't expected."

Macie placed their utensils in the holder to drain. "How about your favorite movie?"

"Any of the *Star Wars* films."

"Why am I not surprised?" She pointed to the stove. "Hand me that pan."

He picked it up. "Was that one of your questions?"

"No." She shook her head and took the pan from him. "I want to know…" She thought for a minute, then asked, "What was the name of your first dog?"

He grinned. "That one came out of left field. His name was Rufus. What was the name of your first boyfriend?"

She swung the washrag at him, sprinkling him with water. "Now you're getting personal."

His shoulders straightened with indignation. "And a guy's dog's name isn't?"

She huffed. "Steve. Satisfied? We were in the first grade. The baking pan, please. What's your favorite food?"

"I'll take a good juicy hamburger any day."

She laughed. "I should have known that. Nothing like a doctor who's heart smart!"

He bumped her with his hip. "I don't eat them all the time. They're more like my guilty pleasure."

"If you say so." Macie bet he ate more of them than he let on. This was too much fun. "What did you dream of being when you grew up?"

He shot right back. "A sheriff. I always liked Western movies."

"So, you have a hero complex? That came through clearly last night." She passed the pan to him to dry.

"You're one to be talking. You were the hero in my eyes. Do you think you'll always want to live in Saipan?"

She picked up the washrag, not looking at him. "I don't know. For right now it's the best place for me. Do you think you'll ever go back to just being a doctor?" She stopped what she was doing and looked at him. His back was to her as he hung the pan on a wall hook.

"Don't know. I've really gone a different direction now. The job in DC would be a desk job. If I get it."

"That's a shame. You're really good with the patients." Macie pulled the plug in the sink and watched as the water swirled down. She hated that his talent would be wasted. They sure could use him at the hospital. Would he ever consider staying in Saipan? Would she really want him around all the time? How could she possibly resist him then?

"What makes your heart flutter?" He folded the towel and neatly placed it on the counter.

She gulped. *Flutter?* "My heart flutter? What do you mean?"

His gaze met hers. "You know…pitty-pat." He put his hand over his heart and patted it with his palm. "You know…thump-thump."

Heat rose in her. She couldn't say it was him that made her heart flutter. "Puppies."

The look of astonishment on his face was comical before it turned piercing. Landon stepped closer. Her hand trembled as she placed the wet dishcloth over the divider of the sink.

"Really? That's the answer you want to go with?" His breath ruffled her hair.

He had her heart fluttering now. Turnabout was fair play. She faced him square on. "Hey, don't get ahead of yourself. It's my turn to ask a question."

"Shoot." His look didn't waver.

Did she dare ask? She felt more alive in the last few minutes than she had in years. She wanted more of that. If she asked the question, she'd have to accept the answer. Either way. She took a breath. "Would you like to kiss me and remind me of how wonderful it is to be alive?"

She didn't have to worry about the answer. Landon swept her into his arms, his mouth crushing hers. His lips were warm and firm. *Heaven.* She sank against him. Oh, yes, her heart was fluttering now.

Landon's mouth slanted across hers and then traveled off to follow the line of her jaw. She purred as she leaned her head to the side, giving him access to her neck. The soft, barely there brush of his lips made her shiver and heat pool low in her belly. When he kissed the hollow behind her ear she sucked in a breath and gripped his shoulders.

His mouth returned to hers. He demanded more. She moved closer, bringing her chest against his. Landon's hold tightened as his tongue caressed the seam of her lips in his request for entrance. With the skip of a heartbeat, she opened for him. His tongue joined hers, teasing, then insisted she join him in an erotic dance.

Landon turned her so that she stood between him and the counter. He pressed against her, his desire thick between them. Her arms circled his shoulders when her knees went weak so she wouldn't fall. His hands came to rest at her waist. Breaking their kiss, he stepped back and lifted her so that she sat on the counter.

She spread her legs and tugged him back to her. Once again, she'd stopped thinking about her actions and started living through his touch. Landon's lips found hers again as his hands slipped under the hem of the scrub shirt she still wore. Her skin quivered at the heat of his fingertips as they traveled across her skin.

"So soft. So perfect," Landon murmured against her cheek.

Macie's hands ran over his strong shoulders, following the muscles that had held her safe less than twenty-four hours ago. Her fingers moved on to his back. She nudged him closer. He resisted, taking her shirt and pushing it up to reveal her naked breasts. Macie squirmed, unsure about being so exposed.

"Please let me admire you. I've been thinking about you wearing no underwear the entire time we were eating." His words were almost a plea.

That knowledge sent heat rocketing through her. "Only if you remove your shirt so that I can do the same."

It took but seconds for him to jerk his shirt over his head and drop it to the floor. Placing a hand on his chest, she smoothed it over the hard plane, with its light dusting of hair.

Landon's finger touched her already extended nipple, making it harder. He circled it with his fingertip before cupping her breast in his palm. Lifting it, he took her breast into his hot, wet mouth.

Macie moaned. Molten desire pooled heavy at her center and throbbed forming a knot of aching need. When Landon sucked on her nipple, her fingers bit into his shoulders. She leaned her head back, closing her eyes as ripples of pleasure rolled through her. His other hand palmed her lonely breast. His tongue twirled around her nipple again, causing her hips to flex forward.

She wanted Landon with all that was in her.

He pulled slowly away, letting her nipple slide out between his lips, then he kissed the slope of her breast. "I've found something you like."

"Mmm…" Macie was in a sexual fog.

His mouth moved to her other breast and gave it the same attention as the first. Macie pulsed with want. She needed, needed…

Landon's mouth traveled up to her shoulder, where he dropped a kiss before continuing to her neck then finding her lips. "Put your legs around me."

She did and his hands cupped her bottom and he picked her up. He headed down a short hall and into the master bedroom. Her center rode along his hard length, teasing her heat as he walked. At that moment she would have gone anywhere with him.

Landon leaned down and pulled back what she guessed was the bedcover, then laid her on the soft mattress and settled himself over her. As his tongue ravished her mouth, one of his hands fondled her breasts. She pulled him closer, giving as good as she got.

Macie had been fighting her attraction to Landon since the moment she'd seen him again. It had all been building to this time and place. The life-and-death situation last night had only heightened her awareness. Being with Landon meant feeling alive.

His hand left her breasts and skimmed over her middle and lower half. Too soon, or not soon enough, he cupped her center. She lifted her hips, wanting more. Frustration built because the material of her pants prevented him from giving her what she desired. Her hands squeezed the muscles of his back, begging.

Landon's gaze met hers. His eyes had turned dark with desire. Seconds later his mouth found hers while his fingers went to the band of her pants. "These need to come off. I want to see all of you."

She lifted her hips, and Landon pushed the pants along her legs and down to her feet. She kicked them off.

He stepped far enough away that he could admire her. "You're beautiful. Amazing, in fact."

Macie couldn't help but blush. The few men she'd been with had never looked at her like Landon did now. Even during their first time he hadn't taken the time to look at her as he was now. It scared her and empowered her at the same time.

Quickly, he brought his body alongside hers again. She could feel his heat. He kissed her tenderly, and his hand cradled her breast and teased her nipple before his fingertips trailed a line over her belly and then lower, to where she craved his touch the most.

His mouth moved to one of her breasts as his hand ran long the top of her thigh to her knee, then followed the seam of her legs up again. He raised his head and looked at her. "Open for me, Macie. I want to touch you."

She relaxed her legs. His gaze didn't leave hers as his finger found her center, and she jumped as his touch sent a quiver through her. Still, his scrutiny didn't waver. He continued to tease her opening but didn't enter.

She moaned and lifted her hips. Offering. Begging. Her fingers dug into his shoulders. Anticipating.

Finally, Landon's finger slipped inside her. She closed her eyes, feeling the pleasure build, while Landon swept his mouth over hers again. Using her hips, she pushed into his hand. He continued to thrust and retreat, even finding her special spot.

The heat grew into a spiraling column of need that

burned within her. She pulled at Landon, grappling for something to end this delicious torture that was almost more than she could endure.

Landon flicked her nub. What was holding her to the earth sprung loose, and she flew into the heavens and a cloud of bliss carried her out of herself.

Landon raised his head and watched as Macie found her release. Had there ever been anything more beautiful? Not that he'd seen.

Now he truly regretted all the time they had lost over the years, though he wasn't sure what made him think they would have stayed together that long.

Macie's eyes opened and a dreamy looked filled them. There was a hint of wonder there as well. She smiled at him as she ran a hand along his forearm. Maybe the feeling of pure pleasure he still felt at giving her pleasure would have kept them together.

Easing down, he lay beside Macie and watched her. He wanted to be inside her, desperately. He ached with need, but he'd never experienced a moment like this before and he wanted to savor it. The throbbing in him turned to pain. He needed her.

Macie cupped the back of his neck and brought his mouth to hers. Her kiss was gentle, appreciative, but soon turned suggestive as her tongue caressed his. That strong will he so admired in Macie transferred to the bedroom.

With reluctance, Landon broke away from her. He stood and shucked off his jeans, leaving them in a pool on the floor. Reaching for the drawer in the bedside table, he pulled out a small square package. Opening it, he quickly covered himself.

Macie spread her arms wide, tempting him to rejoin her. He accepted the invitation and slid over her body, enjoying the connection between them. She cupped his jaw and directed his mouth to hers. Her kiss was warm and tender. Moments later her mouth left his to place tiny nips along his collarbone while his length strained between them.

Had he ever wanted a woman more? Only that once in Hawaii. Still, this was different somehow. More mature. More binding. More special.

Moving over her, he positioned himself between her legs until the tip of his manhood rested at her entrance. He broke their kiss. "Are you sure this is what you want?"

"I want you. Now."

With muscles straining to keep himself in check against his natural desire to go to the hilt, he slowly entered her. Inch by excruciatingly pleasurable inch he drove into her. Macie's fingers gripped his hips, encouraging him.

A soft sigh brushed his ear as he filled her. She was liquid fire, tight and oh, so sweet.

Landon held himself there a moment, just enjoying the connection. Soon, the need to move overcame him and Macie followed his lead. Need turned to heat, and heat turned to frenzy as he plunged into her.

Macie squirmed and gasped beneath him. Her legs circled his legs and pulled him more securely to her so she could match his rhythm.

He sensed her building release as her arms tightened around his neck and she tensed and arched her body. "Landon," she breathed.

Making a final deep thrust, he found his own release and joined her in ecstasy. Heaven help him, he wasn't sure he would ever be the same again.

Sometime later he woke from the daze of satisfaction to find he lay sprawled across the bed. He was spent like he never had been before. His hand brushed her silky hair, and lifting a handful, he let it flow over his fingers. The next time he picked up more.

Eyes still closed, he rolled toward Macie and inhaled deeply, committing her scent to memory.

"What're you doing?" Her voice held a curious note.

"Smelling you," he stated matter-of-factly.

"Why?"

"Because smell is the strongest sense for memory."

"And you want to remember my smell?" She rolled her head just enough to open one eye.

"I want to remember you."

Her hand trailed down his chest. "I rather like touch."

"I do too." Landon rose to rest his head on his hand. The other he grazed over her hip. "But I find sound rather rewarding as well. Especially when you call out my name."

Macie groaned and covered her face with her arm.

"Hey." He lifted her arm. "I want to see you. You're beautiful."

She grinned. "I think you're milking this for all it's worth."

"Maybe so, but just so I don't leave anything out..." The tip of his tongue licked the curve of her breast, and Macie rewarded him with a quick intake of breath. "You taste good too."

Pushing his shoulder, she pulled the sheet over her. "That tickles. I need to get up anyway. I need a bath and some clothes of my own."

"Do you really want to go?" He hated sounding pathetic, but he wanted her to stay.

She sat up, taking the sheet with her. He didn't bother to move, grinning when she looked her fill. His manhood flickered to life under her perusal.

A slight grin formed on his lips. "You know, if you keep that up, I'll hold you here and have my way with you again."

She looked down at him. For some reason, he had the idea she was trying to distance herself from him.

"You think so?"

"I know so." He took her hand in his, interlacing their fingers.

"I don't know that this continuing is such a good idea." She tugged on her hand. He let go of it, and she clasped her hands in her lap.

What? He already wanted her again. "What's wrong all of a sudden? Talk to me, Macie."

She looked everywhere but at him. "Nothing."

"Come on. A few minutes ago you were smiling, and now you're not. What gives?" Anger built in him, and it was starting to show.

"Do you think you could cover yourself if we're going to have this conversation?" She glanced down at his naked form.

He wiggled his eyebrows and gave her a wolfish grin. "Can't stop yourself from admiring me, can you?"

Macie huffed. "I can too."

"I saw you checking me out a minute ago."

She blushed. "Please."

Having compassion for her, he flipped the blanket over himself, leaving only his chest visible. "Okay. What's eating you?"

"I can't do this." She waved her hand around.

"What? Talk to me? Have sex with me?"

She avoided his gaze. "Yes. No. I mean, get involved with you."

"Are we involved?" He'd not thought that far ahead.

He knew only that he desired her. Admired her. Wanted to be around her.

She pierced him with a look. One he didn't like. "When I have sex with someone, I consider myself involved. I'm not very good at one-night stands. You of all people should know that."

"You asked me to take you to bed."

She dropped her head and covered her face with her hands. "I'm sorry. I know I suggested this. I was feeling vulnerable after that horrible rescue, and I have to be honest…" She looked at him. "I'm sorry, Landon. I was looking for an outlet for my emotions. I used you. I shouldn't have. Please take me home."

Now he was really angry, and he could tell it was about to boil over. Maybe it was best she did go home. He *felt* used, and he didn't like it one bit. Was this how she had felt all those years ago? Was she trying to get back at him? "You're right. I should take you home."

By the time they had gotten in the car it was dark. Thankfully, he had to concentrate on the winding road. Macie sat stiffly beside him, her hands firmly together. For the life of him he couldn't figure out what had gone so wrong so fast between them. Especially when it had been so perfect just minutes before.

He'd never had better sex, and from what he could tell, it had been no different for Macie. Even now he still wanted her. If she said the word, he'd turn around and carry her back to his bed.

But she wouldn't do that. The determined set to her jaw made that clear.

When they arrived at her house, she was out of the car and at her door before he could climb out. He sat watching the house until her light came on. Driving slowly, he returned home, suddenly feeling very lonely.

He would discuss this with her tomorrow after they'd both had a good night's sleep. Maybe they would be in a better frame of mind, be more able to talk this out. They had to work together for the next few weeks, and he didn't want animosity between them.

Somehow, he'd have to keep it all business. The problem was he didn't think about just business when he was around Macie. Too often his mind went to touching, kissing and the wonder he'd seen on her face. He wanted to give her that again, and again…

CHAPTER SEVEN

MACIE DIDN'T KNOW what had happened. The past—and all its pain—had come streaming back. Her father's betrayal. Landon's disappearance. She couldn't go through all that again. She was becoming too attached to Landon, and he would soon be gone.

It was all an illusion anyway. He wasn't offering her forever. He would be leaving and she would be staying. So how could she let things continue? Permanence, a solid foundation, was what she was looking for. Something more than sex. With Landon, wasn't sex all it would ever be? He'd made it clear he wasn't offering more.

The rescue had been so intense, and she'd just wanted someone to hold her. Landon had been available. Yet there was more to it than that—she'd come apart so completely in his arms. Even this morning as she'd admired his amazing body, hers had heated in response. That spark that they had once known had quickly turned into a flame.

Then reality had hit her. She didn't want or have time for heartache. She wanted her life to stay as it was. She had it under control. That had taken her years to achieve, and she couldn't let go now. The problem was, it had all changed when she'd made the decision to go to bed with Landon. Now she wasn't sure she could get it back to normal, but she would try. She had no plans to repeat what had happened between them.

She crawled into her cool, lonely bed and wished...

The next morning, she arrived at work early, making sure she had left her office for the wards before Landon got there. By the time she returned, Landon's door was closed and she could only assume he was busy inside. She was dodging him. She didn't want to ask Tatiana about him, fearing she would see the emotions Macie could barely conceal. Not very adult of her, but there it was.

By lunch she still hadn't seen Landon. Maybe she would get through the day without doing so. Yet she missed him. His grin, his teasing, the way he challenged her, had so quickly become an important part of her life.

Her phone buzzed. It was Tatiana. "Landon would like to see you when you have a minute."

"Okay. I'll go over in a few minutes."

"You do know he doesn't bite?" Tatiana asked.

That's what Tatiana thought. Macie's hand went to her neck where Landon had slowly and exquisitely nipped her skin the day before. "I know."

A few minutes later she stood at his office door, ready to knock. Even now, heat filled her at the thought of seeing him. She shook her head. *No, no, no.* She just couldn't do this.

Macie tapped on the door. At Landon's response, she opened it but remained in the entrance, unwilling to step too far into his space. "Tatiana said you needed to see me."

The look of expectancy on his face soon changed to coolness. Like her, he appeared to have slept poorly. Seconds later, his face became neutral and held only an expression of professional politeness.

Things had been so good between them two days ago,

and she had changed all of that with one simple question. Why had she let it get out of hand? She knew better. They had shared the most intimate interaction, and here they were back to being strangers, as much as they had been when he'd first arrived on the island. She didn't like it but would remain strong. Somehow, she'd survive the few weeks he would be there.

"Tatiana has made appointments with all three of the council members you introduced me to the other night. I'd like you to go with me to those meetings, if you would. I know it's inconvenient and you have your own work, but you're a good liaison and your presence will ease my way through the door. You put a face on the hospital that I cannot."

"I had suspected you would want me to go."

He leaned back in his chair and stretched. "There's one this afternoon. Another one tomorrow morning and the other on Thursday. Can you arrange your schedule to be available?"

It ran through her mind to go to him and massage his aching shoulders, and it took an iron will not to. Landon had really gotten under her skin. She feared he had snuck into her heart. "I'll make it work."

"Okay. Great. Today's is at two. I'll see you here at one thirty." His attention returned to the laptop in front of him.

"I'll be ready."

Landon nodded and returned to his work. Apparently, their meeting was over and she had been dismissed. Already she missed Landon's ready smile. What was wrong with her? She couldn't have it both ways. Wasn't he doing what she'd wanted him to do?

A few hours later she stood beside Tatiana's desk when Landon came out of his office with his sports coat hooked on one finger and slung over his shoulder. He wore a crisp light green shirt that made his eyes stand out and khaki pants. Everything about him said casual, confident, professional. He was so handsome it almost took her breath away.

He gave her a smile but his eyes remained cool. She'd hurt him. Deeply.

Macie tried to swallow the lump in her throat. She didn't want this bitterness between them. Somehow, she had to fix things. If only she could bring herself to explain.

What would she say? That she was afraid she was falling for him? That she didn't want to be left again? That she wanted forever not a fantasy. That she…loved him?

Loved him? Did she love him? She couldn't. Why couldn't she? He'd proved more than once that he was a good man. Whatever the reason, she wanted to see that light burning brightly in his eyes again when he looked at her. She would take that for as long as she could have it. When he left, she'd have that to hang on to. To bring out and enjoy whenever she wanted.

If she didn't do something soon, she'd miss out on what little happiness she might have with Landon.

"Macie?" he asked with a questioning expression.

"Yeah?"

"Are you ready?"

"Sure." She followed him out the door.

They walked in silence side by side along the hall and out into the parking lot to his car, and moments later they were headed up Capitol Hill.

"You remember where we're going?" She kept her tone light and friendly. She would talk to him after their meeting.

"Yes. I've driven around enough now that I can find my way, I believe."

Which was another way of saying he didn't need her anymore. She sat quietly the rest of the way.

Not soon enough for her, Landon pulled into a parking space in front of the Municipal Building. He retrieved his jacket from the back seat and shrugged into it. It made him look only more amazing. She had it bad.

Her fingers tingled with the urge to run them along his lapels and kiss him for luck. After the way she had acted, she was sure he wouldn't appreciate that. He'd treated her with tender care and she'd thrown it back at him. She would make it up to him. Somehow.

Since they were going to a business meeting, she'd gone home and put on a sundress and dressy sandals, which gave her some confidence. She looked more professional than she would have in her usual scrubs.

As Landon fixed his collar, he said, "By the way, you look nice."

"Thank you." Relief flowed through her. He had at least noticed she'd changed. Those few simple words made a spot in the middle of her chest glow. Maybe all wasn't lost.

Without further discussion, they entered the building. Landon spoke to the receptionist, and she escorted them into the mayor's office, where they were greeted warmly by Mayor Luc Ramos.

After a few minutes of small talk and questions about the accident, Landon presented his ideas for improvements at the hospital, spending a long time discussing the scholarship idea. He also explained his concerns for the hospital and how they would adversely affect the island if they weren't cleared up, and he finished with why she and Landon were there and what he would like the government to do to support the hospital, reminding Ramos of what quality medical care meant to the islands and the economy.

The mayor seemed to react positively to their ideas. Macie became concerned only when he questioned the hospital's ability to attract and hold on to consistent and appropriate leadership to see the plan through.

"We need new nurses and doctors, but if the leadership changes constantly, we can't offer anybody any incentives to live here. I see this as the largest need. Do you have any ideas in that direction?"

Landon spoke with authority, clearly having expected the question. "Not outside of offering financial incentives, which will be based on fulfilling a contract to stay for a minimum length of time."

The mayor nodded. "And I think we need someone who is not only committed to the hospital, the island and the surrounding islands in the senior role, but who also wants to make this their home, not just use it as a springboard for their next promotion." He gave Landon a pointed look. "Do you know someone who could fit the bill?"

Macie looked from one man to the other. Landon had all the right skills for the job, but his eyes were firmly on the job in Washington.

"I will make your concerns clear to my board and share your suggestions. With my organization's help, I believe you will find that person. We would evaluate every applicant carefully."

Mayor Ramos stood and offered his hand. "I know you will, and I offer my support for what I have heard so far. Thank you for coming."

Landon shook his hand. "Thank you, sir. You have my assurance that I'll see you get a quality administrator."

A few minutes later she and Landon were in the car.

"I think that went well." Landon wore a broad smile, the first real one she'd seen since she'd left his house.

"I do too."

For the first time that day, Landon truly looked at her. "Thank you for helping. I think having your seal of approval makes all the difference."

She returned his smile. "And I think you give me too much credit."

Landon started the car and drove back to the hospital. He had impressed her with his ability to concisely summarize a problem then offer a solution and project what things would look like if nothing was done and if his suggestions were implemented. It was an effective way of getting people on his side. She could understand why he was good at his job and was up for a promotion.

Everything about Landon appeared above reproach. Unlike her father. So why did she continue to have trouble accepting that? Landon wasn't a man who kept secrets or conducted business in an underhanded manner. Yet she had thought that about her father as well until she'd learned the truth.

"One down, two more to go," Landon said as they arrived at the hospital. "Tomorrow's meeting is at nine in the morning. Should I just pick you up at your house?" They got out of the car and headed inside.

"That'll be fine. It'll be nice to have a morning to sleep in."

"Okay. I'll see you at eight thirty."

"Landon, about yesterday—"

"Macie, you made yourself perfectly clear yesterday. Let's not rehash it. I have a job to do here and only a few more weeks to do it. If you don't mind, I'd like to concentrate on that."

His words were like a shot to her chest. She stood there, hoping her knees would remain stable. They'd made such a good team in the mayor's office, in the tanker, figuring out a plan for the hospital moving forward, and now he could hardly look at her. She'd messed up big-time. She'd let fear rule her. Her stomach roiled. There must be some way to get through to him. To get them back to the friendship they'd once had.

She watched Landon walk away and felt bereft. If she went after him, would he listen? She had to give him time, which left her standing there with her heart aching.

The next morning Landon picked her up, and they made the trip back up to Capitol Hill. Once again they had a fruitful discussion with another mayor who had already spoken to Mayor Ramos. This mayor was in agreement with Landon's plan , but also believed solid leadership would be necessary to make a difference.

As Landon drove down the hill, he commented as much to himself as to her, "Getting the correct administrator will be the key."

"I think I mentioned that was a problem the first day you were here."

He raised his brows. "Would that be an 'I told you so'?"

"Well, maybe, but an unintentional one. But a fact nonetheless."

"Point taken. I'll start compiling a list of requirements and let my boss know. He'll notify the board and see if they might have someone in mind."

At least they were being civil, she thought, though when he had picked her up that morning, he had greeted her with one of those smiles that didn't reach his eyes.

"Don't get too far ahead. We still have another mayor to see and the governor as well."

"I didn't have Tatiana make an appointment with the governor."

"Do you mind thinking outside of the box on that one?" She climbed out of the car.

"No. What do you have in mind?"

"Let me check on something and get back to you."

"Okay. Now I'm really curious." He walked beside her on the way inside. "I'm going to recommend to the hospital board that you be in on the vetting of a new administrator. Especially since you've been in on the ground floor with the new ideas."

"Thank you. That would be nice." At least he hadn't lost his professional respect for her.

They entered their office area together.

He stopped and looked at her. "Thank you for your help this morning. Your presence makes all the difference."

"I'm glad to help. This is something I believe in."

He continued to study her as if he were thinking, *But you can't believe in me?* Finally, he nodded and went into his office.

Even with Landon saying nothing she felt sick. What she'd had—could have had—she'd let slip through her fingers. When he'd left her in Hawaii, she'd not felt this miserable.

Macie wanted to scream.

Landon hadn't felt this ill since he was a child. His stomach was rolling like the giant waves that bashed the rocks at Banzai Cliff. His head pounded as if a jackhammer was running inside it and he was on fire. Somewhere he had picked up a virus. One that was kicking his butt.

He had called the hospital the day before and told Tatiana that he would be working at home that day. This morning he couldn't even get out of bed to call in because he was so weak. He'd spent most of the night going between his bed and the bathroom. He'd finally ended up just lying on the bathroom floor. More than once he'd tried to force some water down to keep from becoming dehydrated, but that hadn't gone well either. In his delirium, he'd thought if someone would just shoot him like they did horses when they went down, he'd be better off.

He groaned. To make matters worse, he was in the tropics, where it was steamy and hot half the time. He had just enough presence of mind to know that a storm was building. Having a fever didn't help. He dripped sweat.

What could be worse?

He could hear tapping. He closed his eyes. Maybe it would go away.

There it was again. He rolled to his side, putting his cheek against the cool tile of the bathroom floor.

"Oh, my heavens, Landon. Are you all right?"

Was it Macie? He had lost his mind. She didn't care about him. Didn't want his kisses, his loving. Why would she be here? He opened one eye enough to see a fuzzy version of her. The light hurt. He closed it again. "Go away."

"I can't do that."

She sounded so close. Worried. It had been a long time since someone had been concerned about him. He was the one who took care of people. His mother, his brother and sister, patients, hospitals.

"We have to get you to the bed." Macie pulled on his arm then tried to put hers under his back. "Landon, Landon. You're going to have to help me. You're too heavy for me to carry."

"Stay here." Why didn't she just leave?

"No! Now, help me get you up or I'll have to call for help." She pulled on him again.

Nope. He wasn't going to face that humiliation. Macie seeing him so sick was enough.

He moved to his hands and knees with more effort than he would ever admit to. Macie grabbed him around the waist as he pushed himself up to sit on the toilet. With great effort and Macie's help he managed to get to his feet. She grunted when he leaned heavily on her as they worked their way to the bed and fell on it. That was all he could do. His eyes closed and she lifted his legs and placed them on the mattress.

"Shift over. You don't want to roll off." Macie pushed at his hips.

He moved closer to the center but only because she did most of the work. "You can go now."

"Not going to happen" came her clipped return.

He didn't have the energy to argue with her, so he closed his eyes and drifted off into painless sleep.

The next time he woke it was to something cool on his head and somebody brushing his hair back from his forehead. Everything about it felt wonderful. He was still on fire, but the touch made it bearable. He moaned.

"Landon, you need to wake up. You need some medicine and to drink something."

He knew that voice coming down the tunnel. More than once he'd heard it in his dreams. *Macie.* Macie was here? Was he dreaming?

"Come on. You've got to sit up." She put an arm behind him, lifting him forward.

Something cool touched his lips.

"Drink."

He licked his lips.

"Good. Now I want you to swallow this pill." She pushed it into his mouth.

He shook his head. "Throat hurts."

"I know you're miserable, sweetheart, but you have to swallow this if you're going to get better." She gave him more water.

He coughed but forced it down.

"Take another swallow." The glass returned to his lips.

He didn't make any effort. It was just too hard.

"Just one more," Macie begged.

He did as she asked then dropped back on the bed and closed his eyes.

The next time when he woke it was to a cool, damp cloth moving across his chest. The hammer in his head had eased and his eyes no longer felt like salt had been poured into them. He still didn't think he could stand, but that didn't matter. He was happy right here with that cloth cooling his body. He sighed. Something pressed against his forehead. Lips, perhaps? Then sleep overtook him.

When he next became aware of anything it was someone shaking him awake. He'd been dreaming. He lay on the beach with Macie next to him. She held his hand as he listed to the waves. Rising over him, she leaned down and softly kissed him then moved away. He reached out to bring her back.

"Macie?"

"I'm right here."

Landon opened his eyes to see her above him. He made an effort to touch her, but his hand was too heavy and fell back to the bed.

"How're you feeling?" Her voice sounded so sweet and caring.

His eyes focused. "You're here."

"Yes."

His mind cleared. She was *here*. He was sick. "What are you doing here?"

"Nursing you. When you didn't show up for the meeting with the mayor, I knew something was very wrong. I came to check on you." She picked up a glass. "Here, you need to drink."

She held his head as he drank and swallowed half a glass. It tasted so good. "Thanks." The word sounded rusty.

"Lie back and go to sleep while I get you something to eat."

He looked beyond her to the window. It was dark. "What time is it?"

"Around nine o'clock."

He groaned.

"You've been asleep for hours."

"Last thing I remember was something cool moving over my chest."

Macie brushed a strand of hair out of her face. She looked tired. "I had to get your fever down. It broke a couple of hours ago. Now we need to get some food in you."

"Thank you." The words trailed off as he closed his eyes. He listened to the sound of Macie leaving him and going in the direction of the kitchen. He couldn't see her, but it was comforting to know she was there. She returned a few minutes later, and he opened his eyes to watch her. He liked the way she moved.

"Good. You're awake." She carried a bowl and a glass. Placing them on the bedside table, she stood above him. "Before you eat, do you need to go to the bathroom?"

He did but he didn't want her to help him, though he didn't think he could stand up by himself. "I can take care of that myself."

"I doubt that. Come on. I'll help you."

"I really—"

"No more arguments. You don't have anything I haven't already seen. Now, put your arm around my neck and let's go so we can get you fed."

She made it sound as if he was like any patient she'd ever had. He wasn't sure he liked being relegated to just anybody. Still, he did as she said.

Macie put her arm around his waist and they made it to the bathroom. In truth, he was glad of her help. "I can handle this part by myself."

"Since you're so squeamish, I'll just stand behind you and not look." Her hands remained firmly at his waist.

He'd been completely humbled in front of the very woman he wanted to impress. So much for his ego.

She helped him back to the bed.

"You do know I'll get you back for this," he grumbled.

"For what? Being the perfect nurse?" she asked sweetly.

"That and seeing me at my weakest."

She helped him to sit back against the pillows she'd piled behind him along the headboard. "Hey, we all have a time when we need help."

Had she ever really had one? She always seemed so self-sufficient, so self-assured.

"Seriously, you can go now. Just leave me alone and let me die in peace." Had she murmured something about men and their sickbed dramas?

"You're not going to die. You've just caught what we call the Pacific Grunge. Now, sit up and let me get something into you."

"What happened to the sweet nurse with the lovely bedside manner? Now you've turned into Nurse Iron Panties."

She chuckled. "It went out the door when I realized

how sick you were. Why didn't you call me and tell me you were so sick?"

He glared at her. Like he would have admitted that. Especially after the way she had left him on Sunday.

Macie's mouth formed a line and she nodded. "Got it. The great Dr. Cochran can't show weakness. I won't tell anyone."

It was more like he didn't what her to know just how hurt he had been after they'd made love. Or how badly he wanted her back in his arms. Or just how weak he was where she was concerned.

She perched on the side of the bed and picked up the bowl.

"I can feed myself."

She lowered her chin and gave him a doubtful look. "So you're willing to spill this lovely warm soup all over you to prove you're a man?"

Waiting a beat, she filled the spoon and put it to his lips. He slurped it in. The warmth felt good going down his raw throat. She offered him more and he gladly took it.

"I've not had someone feed me since I was a kid." He'd not thought of that in a long time. Most of his memories of his mother were negative or troubled ones. He'd been the caretaker for so long, he'd forgotten what it was like to be on the receiving end.

"My mother used to stop what she was doing—all her fund-raising duties and social obligations—when one of us was sick." Macie pinched her mouth closed as if she'd said something wrong.

"Us?"

"I have a brother and a sister too."

"Really? You've never mentioned them before. May I have a drink?"

She handed him the glass, but her hand hovered nearby in case.

"Where do they live?"

"Jean lives in California and Rob in New York. We couldn't stay in Chicago."

"Because of your dad?" He watched her closely.

Macie nodded as he studied the spoon she'd just filled so carefully.

"Do you ever talk to them? Your parents?"

She acted as if she had to think about that. "I talk to my mom pretty regularly. My brother and sister on holidays and birthdays."

"Your dad?"

The spoon clanked against the bowl. She put the bowl down and stood. "You need to finish all that water while I get some medicine. I'll be right back. I want all the water gone by the time I return." Nurse Iron Panties had returned.

Macie made it to the door before he said softly, "Your dad?"

She turned and faced him, her legs spread as if preparing to fight. "I haven't seen my dad since the trial. He's in jail anyway."

CHAPTER EIGHT

MACIE BRACED HER HANDS against the kitchen counter and hung her head. If she wasn't careful, she would be sick too. Why had she let Landon push her into saying that? Why did she need him to know? So he would realize what type of person she was? That she held a grudge. That when someone hurt her, it festered inside her. That he'd hurt her one time—unintentionally, but he'd hurt her nonetheless—and she just couldn't let it go. Couldn't easily give her trust. That she lived in fear of not seeing the true person behind their actions.

Taking a deep breath, she fortified herself to return to him. Shaking out a couple of pills into her palm, she went back into the bedroom. Landon had already slid down on the pillows and closed his eyes. The glass sat on the bedside table with most of the water gone. There was just enough left for him to take the medicine.

"Landon, don't go to sleep yet. You have to have this."

His eyelids lifted slowly. She picked up the glass and placed the pills in his open palm. Without complaint he swallowed them and handed the glass back to her.

His beautiful green eyes disappeared once again. "Thanks for taking care of me."

Macie looked down at him and saw he'd gotten some color back in his face. His hair went every which way, but she knew how soft it was. The stubble on his jaw gave him a dangerous appearance, the type that always made her heart beat just a little faster—flutter, as he would say. The man, even in his illness, did something to her.

He hadn't wanted her to see him vulnerable. Had it been necessary for him to hide any weaknesses for so long that he now couldn't? She had no doubt if she hadn't come to check on him, he wouldn't have called for help. What was it like to never open up to anyone? To always have to be the strong one?

She gave him a kiss on the forehead. "I'll never tell anyone how much you needed me."

She carried his bowl and glass into the kitchen and put them in the sink. She ate her own soup standing up at the counter. Finished, she washed the dishes and straightened up the kitchen before going to check on Landon. He slept peacefully.

Planning to stay the night to look after him, she needed something to sleep in. She rooted through his T-shirts in the chest of drawers, then pulled one out. She went to the bathroom to dress and slipped the shirt over her head, leaving her panties on beneath. It would be long enough on her to make her presentable if she had to get up in the middle of the night.

On the way to the living room she pulled Landon's door closed, leaving just enough space so she could hear him if he woke. Lying down, she tugged the blanket off the back of the sofa and covered herself. She had been busy and worried by the same measure, and she fell asleep right away.

Macie woke with a jerk. There had been a noise. Slinging the blanket off, she headed to Landon's bedroom. He wasn't there, but she could hear water running in the bathroom. He shouldn't be up without help. What if he had fallen? She hurried to the door and opened it.

"Landon, what are you doing?"

There was no response. She stepped inside. "Landon?"

"What?" He stuck his head outside the shower.

"What are you doing? You're too weak. You could fall. You should have called me." The man was trying to make her crazy.

"I needed a shower." His head returned inside the curtain.

She moved farther into room. "I know you did, but you should have let me help you in here."

"You're here now."

"How are you feeling?" She sat on the toilet seat, waiting impatiently.

"I'm fine. Better now that my fever has broken and I'm getting a shower."

Neither of them said anything for a few minutes.

"Landon, please get out. If you fall, I can't lift you." She stood, panic filling her at the possibilities of what could go wrong. Even a busted head was more than she could stand at this point.

He didn't answer her. Unable to endure it any longer, she pulled the curtain back. "Get out now."

Landon was leaning against the wall, and he had gone pale.

"For heaven's sake, Landon." She stepped in and turned off the water. Wrapping an arm around his waist, she led him out of the shower. "Sit." She helped him onto the toilet. Supporting him, she grabbed a towel off the rack and started drying him.

He shivered. She put a hand to his forehead. No fever. That was good, but he had the chills.

She finished drying him. Pulling the other towel from

the rack, she wrapped it over his shoulders. "Okay, Superman, let's get you back in bed."

"Not feeling all that super right now."

Macie helped him to stand, and he placed his arm over her shoulders. "I can believe it."

Slower than she would have liked, they made their way to the bed. Landon had become more dependent on her the farther they walked, and he dropped rather than sat on the bed.

She pushed his hair back. "No more getting out of bed without calling me for help."

"Yes, ma'am," he murmured as his eyelids lowered.

"You lie right here on this side of the bed. I need to change the sheets before you go to sleep." She pulled the blanket up over him and tucked it in close. "I'll be right back."

Once the bed had been changed and he had swallowed another pill, she tucked the blanket more securely around him. "In the morning you should feel a lot better. You just have the Pacific Grunge. You get it from not being used to the food, water or weather. Or all three."

He handed the glass back to her. "I'm cold. Keep me warm."

She wanted to lie next to him, to comfort him. She was tired too, and she thought how nice it would be to sleep on a bed instead of the sofa. Refusing to question her decision, she slipped under the covers and placed her head against his shoulder and an arm across his waist.

Landon exhaled and murmured, "I like you in one of my T-shirts. Especially when it's wet."

Macie sucked in a breath. The man had been ogling her. She grinned. He wasn't so sick he hadn't noticed her, which was good news. It would hurt when he left but she would deal; she'd just have to.

She snuggled closer and joined him in sleep.

* * *

Landon woke to the room bright with sunlight. From the direction of the beam he could tell it was late afternoon.

He felt better—weak, but better, though his stomach was rumbling fiercely. If he could get something to eat, there was a chance he would feel more alive.

A pleasant warmth lay against his back. *Macie.* Her arm was draped across his waist and one of her feet rested over his. His manhood reacted to the knowledge. This was a good way to wake, whether well or sick. She'd been the perfect caregiver, but was that professional nursing or because she had feelings for him?

Despite the reaction his body had to her, he had other issues to see about. He was still too wiped out to consider lovemaking, even were she to want it.

He could vaguely remember taking a shower and needing her help to get back to bed. And the soft wet material of his shirt outlining her breasts. That part of the night he'd like to revisit, but right now, he was going to have to wake her to get help to go to the bathroom. He wasn't going to make that mistake twice. The last time hadn't been his finest hour. Macie had made it clear in no uncertain terms he wasn't to get out of bed without her help.

Looking over his shoulder, he said, "Macie, I need to get up."

"Huh?" Macie jerked to a sitting position. "Okay."

She scrambled out of bed. Her hair was a wild mess around her face and the hem of his navy T-shirt hit her at midthigh and the sleeves covered her elbows. His shirt had never looked better. Macie was adorable. And now another part of his anatomy ached that had nothing to do with his stomach.

She hurried around the bed. "How are you feeling?"

"Better, and I want food. I hated to wake you, but I

was afraid Nurse Iron Panties would come out and I need to go to the bathroom."

She chuckled. "I'm not that bad, am I?"

"Only when I get in the shower without you."

"I believe you are feeling better." Happy notes filled her voice.

"You do remember I'm buck naked under here?" He referred to the sheets.

"I think I can control myself," she clipped.

"I was being a gentleman."

"I appreciate that, but I'll survive."

He pursed his lips. "Now I think my ego is damaged."

"I doubt that. Let me see you to the bathroom, and if you're steady enough, I'll leave you to get something for you to wear."

They made it across the room without mishap, Landon looking stronger than he felt. He didn't have to lean on her the entire way, yet she kept a hand on his arm all the same.

"Don't fall," she said as she left him to his business and went in search of something for him to pull on. She returned with a pair of his sport shorts. "Do you need help getting them on?"

He glared at her. "I do not."

She grinned and raised a brow. "You're getting feisty now."

He pulled on the shorts as she picked up the towel that lay on the floor and straightened the bathroom.

"I'll help you back to the bed." She took his arm.

"I've had enough of bed. I'd rather sit in the kitchen and watch you cook some eggs, bacon and toast."

"That's not going to happen. I think we should settle on something a little less aggressive. How about we start with some cheese toast? You can have something more substantial later."

He huffed. "Nurse Iron Panties is showing up again."

"Maybe so, but we need to make sure you don't have a relapse before we start filling your belly."

He took a seat at the dining table. To himself he had to admit he was glad to sit down again. Over the next few minutes he watched as Macie moved around the kitchen. She really was something. He wished he had the strength to show her how much he enjoyed watching the teasing sway of the hem of his T-shirt just below her temping backside.

She might have hurt his feelings, but he wasn't immune to her. Nothing had really changed about that. If anything, after the last few days, he was crazier about her than ever.

What if he let go and admitted his feelings for her? Both to himself and to Macie. What was the worst that could happen? He placed a hand on his stomach. It ached at the thought. He couldn't care that much; if he did, his life might be destroyed if she didn't feel the same. Everything he had worked for would be at risk. No, he couldn't allow that to happen. Landon had seen what that type of love could do to a person. He had no intention of letting another person destroy him like his father had his mother.

Macie turned to him. "How about a cup of hot tea?"

"I'd rather have coffee."

"Okay, but your stomach may not like it."

"I'll take my chances. Yesterday, I thought I was going to die. Nothing can make me feel worse than that." Except her not feeling the same about him as he did about her.

"A little dramatic, don't you think?" She placed bread on a baking sheet.

"I'm a doctor after all. I should know."

She went to the refrigerator and pulled out the cheese. "Isn't the saying that doctors make the worst patients?"

"There's old Iron Panties again. I prefer the warm, tender Macie curled up beside me." He needed to watch his thoughts and what he said.

Blushing, she went about making them some food. Soon, she placed a plate of toast in front of him and one in her spot. She brought over coffee and a glass of water for him and a mug of tea for herself. They ate in silence.

To his great relief, the toast settled in his stomach without any negative reaction. When he finished the second piece, he leaned back and held his coffee cup. "Thanks for coming to my rescue."

"You're welcome. No matter how strong you guys think you are, you still need support when things aren't going your way."

He took a sip of his drink. "That's an interesting way of putting it. I think there's something behind that."

Shadows filled her eyes.

"What happened?"

Macie blinked, surprise now in her eyes. Was she amazed he'd seen the shadows? She didn't say anything, just watched him. He recognized the second she made up her mind. "When my father was on trial, he wanted us to all be there. Standing behind him. Supporting him even though he'd taken all those people's money. The media followed us everywhere. They even came to the hospital when I was trying to work, yet my father showed us off like everything was all right."

Landon set his mug down. "That must have been difficult and more than a little humiliating."

"It was. Very. That's why I went to Hawaii. To get away." She wasn't looking at him. Instead, she twisted her napkin, something he'd learned she did when she was nervous. "About the other day—I know you must think I'm a tease."

"I don't think that. I understand now. It's probably for the best."

"Still, you deserved better. I tried to tell you that on Monday but you didn't want to hear it. I was scared."

"Scared?" That wasn't what he wanted her to feel. "I didn't hurt you, did I?"

"No, I'm not talking about physical hurt." She pointed to her chest. "I'm talking about me liking you too much."

There it was. Not what he wanted to hear, yet also what he wanted to hear so very much. His heart swelled. She did like him. "That's a bad thing? There has always been a spark between us."

"I know. It's just that I don't know where this is going."

Macie did sound scared. "I won't make you any promises. I've already told you I don't do forever. Never plan to. What I would like very much is to enjoy the here and now. Couldn't we just be good friends and make the most of that while I'm here?"

"I'm not very good at trusting people. Or taking them at their word. My father saw to that."

He reached across the table, placing his hand over hers. "I won't disappear on you ever again, Macie. I'm not your father. You *can* trust me."

She gave him a wry smile.

Landon had hoped for more than an unsure smile. Why? Didn't he just want a good time, nothing more? He'd let her think about whether or not she could trust him. He couldn't even imagine what it had been like for her to endure what her father had put her through. Then he'd come along and left her like he had in Hawaii. No wonder she was unsure about relationships. She'd been disappointed one too many times. He would make sure he never hurt her again.

"What time is it?" he asked, looking toward the clock on the kitchen wall.

"Four o'clock."

He started to stand. "I need to call the hospital. Check on things."

"I told Tatiana yesterday that we were working from home today. Everything is fine or someone would have called. What you need to do is go back to bed and get some rest."

He grinned. "And there's Nurse Iron Panties again."

"Maybe so, but the only way you're going to be well enough to meet with the governor by Sunday afternoon is to rest."

He sat straighter. "You got us an appointment?"

"Of sorts." She picked up the plates and started toward the kitchen.

"What does that mean?"

"It means I hope you like to fish." She put their dishes in the sink.

His lips pulled tight. "We're going fishing with him?"

She looked back over her shoulder. "We're going to his favorite fishing hole, where we'll 'accidentally' run into him."

"Macie Beck, I had no idea you were so sneaky."

She grinned and shrugged. "What can I say?"

"You can say you'll come watch a movie with me. I'm not sleepy." He picked up his water and drank it all. "See, I'm following the nurse's orders." He set the glass down with a thump.

Turning away from him, she stood beside the sink. "All right. Let me straighten up in here."

By the time Macie joined him, he had a movie queued

up and ready to go. She pulled the chair that sat in the corner over to the bed.

"Hey, what are you doing?"

"Getting a seat," she answered as if he had asked a stupid question.

"Come up here beside me. Be a friend." He patted the bed. "I promise not to attack you. I don't have the energy even if I wanted to."

Macie looked from the bed to the chair and back. "The bed does look more comfortable." Propping a couple of pillows against the headboard, she sat and leaned back against them, leaving as wide an expanse between them as possible.

"I hope you like suspense."

"I do. Very much."

"Then I think you'll like this one." He clicked the remote and the movie began playing.

They were into the film only a few minutes when he looked over to find Macie asleep, her chin resting on her chest. Smiling, he put his arm around her shoulders and brought her closer, letting her head rest on his shoulder. She rolled to her side, her hand coming to sit over his heart. With the movie droning on, he closed his eyes and drifted off to sleep. If he must be sick, this was the way to do it.

Macie woke to a late evening stream of light coming through Landon's bedroom window. The brush of a hand over the outside of her thigh shot a tingle of awareness to her center. The touch went farther up then slowly down again.

She lay curled against Landon's side, her hand on his chest. She nuzzled against him. He trailed kisses across her forehead. She looked up at him. His gaze met hers, a flame that had nothing to do with a fever or friendship flickering brightly in his eyes. Landon wanted her. He kissed her, his lips tender and questioning as if he were holding back, unsure of his welcome.

Macie had to make it clear that she wanted what he could give while she could have it. He'd made it clear where he stood and she believed him, and she still wanted him anyway.

She ran her hand up to circle his neck and opened her mouth. He might break her heart, but she wanted him and she wanted him to know it. She said against his lips, "Should we really be doing this? You've been sick. You're weak."

"I'm not that weak." He took her hand and ran it over the length of his arousal. He gave her a wicked grin. "But it might help if you did most of the work."

Her blood raced and pooled at her center. She smiled. "What do you have in mind?"

"Climb up here and I'll show you."

He pulled her leg over him and she shifted so that she straddled him. "Like this?" she asked.

"You're getting the idea." He reached out and cupped her breast. "So perfect."

She ran her hot center over his hard length. "You'll tell me if it's too much for you."

Landon groaned. "I don't think that's gonna happen."

She giggled.

His palms came to rest on top of her thighs, then slid along them before going under the hem of her shirt. His thumbs made little circles over her skin. She hissed as tingles zipped through her. Landon's look locked with hers and held. His hands moved higher and she lifted her hips. One of his hands moved closer to her center. A finger traced the line of her panties and teased her. He pulled it away.

She whimpered her disappointment.

"The panties have to go. I need to touch you."

Without breaking eye contact, she lowered her panties and kicked out of them. Landon licked his lips. She stepped to the bedside table, pulled out the drawer and removed a foil package.

Landon reached out a hand and cupped her backside, caressing it. She moved to climb over him again.

"Wait."

She stayed where she was.

Landon's hand left her bottom, and he rolled to the edge of the bed. Bending his arm, he rose up on an elbow and rested his head on it. "Now, come here please, and put your knees against the mattress."

Macie did as he requested.

Using his free hand, he drew a finger up her thigh, brushed her curls and drew it down the other leg. She quivered, thankful for the support of the bed.

"Let me touch you. I want to feel your heat so badly."

Her eyes met his. Desire filled and flickered in Landon's gaze. She throbbed for his attention.

"Please." His finger tracing down her leg was little more than a whisper of movement.

She shifted slightly, widening her stance.

With a lift to his lips, Landon leisurely ran his finger across her center.

Her legs shook. "Landon?"

"Shh. You're so responsive. I like how you answer my touch." His eyes moved to focus on his finger.

Placing her hand on his head, she gripped his hair, needing something to support her.

This time his hand went under the shirt to tease her

breast. She leaned into his touch. Goose bumps rippled over her skin as he brought his fingers down over her stomach and lower.

Macie bit her bottom lip. Wanting, needing, silently begging for more. For him.

Landon's hand found her center again, a finger entering her. Bending her knees, she pressed down on his hand. Her grip on his hair tightened. She wanted...

He pulled his hand back. She whimpered her displeasure and was rewarded with its return. Grinding against his hand, she wanted more.

"Look at me, Macie. I want you to know who's giving you pleasure. Who it is you can trust to be open and honest with you."

She studied his body for a moment. He might have been in a relaxed position, but every muscle was tense, as if coiled to spring. His manhood lay thick and extended, ready beneath his shorts. Her bright gaze met his smoky one. Landon moved his hand again, setting up a rhythm that she joined. Her knees sank into the mattress as she pulsed over his finger.

"Landon?" she whispered as her eyes widened, and that silver coil built and tightened within her.

He didn't blink. "Let it go, honey. I'll catch you."

She threw back her head, pressing hard into his hand, and soared into the power of her release. Landon caught her before her knees buckled, pulling her across him. Her heart pounded next to his.

Holding her, he rubbed her back and said soothing nothings against her ear. She was weak as a newborn kitten, and she'd thought he might not be strong enough to make love.

After a few minutes had passed, Landon said, "Honey, I need you."

Macie didn't move immediately, but soon she wiggled over him and drew down his shorts so that his length stood tall and proud between them. Finding the package she had dropped near his leg, she opened it and rolled it on him.

She rose onto her knees until his tip waited at her opening, then she slid her center over him. Her gaze found his. His eyelids were lowered halfway and his jaw was tight.

"Landon, look at me."

His eyes widened.

"I want you to see who's taking you." She glided down him.

Landon groaned. When she finally held him completely, he sighed, then began to move his hips. She placed a hand on his shoulder. "Nope. I promised to do all the work."

She raised herself onto her knees until she held only his tip, then plunged down again. She repeated the move until his hands gripped the sheet. Increasing the speed, her need grew. His hand circled her neck and brought her mouth to his. The kiss was so erotic she tightened around him and shook, but she never changed her rhythm.

Landon's hips rose in a hard lunge as he ended the kiss and grabbed her hips, holding her secure as he howled his release. With a wiggle of sweet pleasure, she joined him, then fell over his chest.

Macie smiled. As sure as the ocean waves hit the beach, she was in love with Landon Cochran.

Landon looked at Macie as she walked along the pier beside him on Sunday afternoon. She wore a baseball hat on her head, dark glasses and a tight-fitting T-shirt that hugged the curves of her breasts. The scoop neck of her shirt just covered one of his favorite spots to kiss, while her cutoffs allowed a beautiful view of her legs. Well-worn deck shoes protected her feet. The best part was that she wore a smile, one he was confident he'd placed there. He couldn't help but return it.

His recovery had been quick. He and Macie had spent all Saturday in bed watching movies, talking and making love. He had never shared a more fulfilling love life. Macie was everything he'd ever dreamed of.

He grinned.

She met his look. "What's that grin for?"

"I was just thinking, if I share my cure for Pacific Grunge, they might not believe me."

"That would be?"

He squeezed her hand. "Taking a lovely woman to bed."

Macie rewarded his teasing with a blush.

"I don't take care of all my patients in the same manner."

Landon raised his shoulders in a look of mock importance. "I certainly hope not. I like thinking I'm special."

It was her turn to grin. "Oh, you stand up and out… in a crowd."

His satisfaction grew at her innuendo. He appreciated the sassy Macie. "So exactly why are we going fishing?"

"Let's just say that the governor is a lot more approachable when he's outside with a rod and reel in his hand."

"He doesn't have his business meetings in his office?"

"Sure, he does. He's very official. But you're more likely to get his support and a yes by approaching him this way. You said we needed to have some tax breaks and an influx of money. He's the guy to give the hospital those, so we need him to agree. Fishing makes him agreeable."

"You're a devious person, Macie Beck. Remind me to stay on your good side."

"I like to think of it as being smart." She pulled her hat down a little.

"That too. So, what's the game plan?" He became more interested by the minute.

"Nothing special. Just sit down next to him and start fishing. Have a conversation."

He nodded. "Okay. That sounds reasonable."

She shifted the tackle box she carried to her other hand. "Do you fish?"

"Not often. It's been years." When he was a boy with his father. Those days were long gone. He'd not seen his father in a long time.

"Let's hope it's like riding a bicycle and you never forget how. Okay, focus now. See the man with the blue shirt up there on the left?"

"Yep."

"That's the governor," she whispered as if they were doing espionage.

Minutes later they sat on the pier with their feet hanging over the side. They had settled in and dropped their lines into the water.

Macie leaned forward, looking past him to the man sitting a few spaces farther beyond.

"Governor Nandos? Is that you?" she asked sweetly.

The stout middle-aged man looked at her. "Well, Macie. How are you doing?"

"Fine, sir. And you?"

His attention was on his line. "Great. Great. Any day is a good one when you get to fish."

Landon wasn't sure about that but he nodded his agreement anyway.

Macie waved a hand toward him. "Have you met our interim administrator, Dr. Landon Cochran?"

"No, I haven't." The governor looked at him.

"Nice to meet you, sir." Landon reached over and shook his hand briefly.

Macie looked at the governor again. "Are you catching anything?"

"A few. Not what I want them to be. But the day's young." The older man gave them a toothy grin.

The conversation tapered off for a few minutes.

Macie broke the silence once more. "Governor, I don't know if you know it, but Dr. Cochran has been doing an evaluation of the hospital. I've been assisting him in a number of areas. Together we've come up with a plan to build on what we already have."

"Is that so?" The governor started to pay attention to her.

"Yes, we have a couple of very inventive ideas."

"I don't usually talk business while I'm fishing, but I have to say you have pricked my interest. What are some of those ideas?"

Landon launched into their short but sweet preplanned speech.

The governor's face screwed up in thought. "I have to admit that sounds promising. Something that I could support. Put together your proposal and I'll give it a look."

"May I tell my board that you like the plan?" Landon dared.

"You may certainly tell them I'm giving it serious consideration. And if they agree to do their part, I'll do mine." His attention returned to his fishing.

Macie squeezed Landon's hand. He grinned at her.

Half an hour later, Macie stood. "At the rate we're catching fish we're going to starve. I think they're hiding from us today." She looked down at Landon. "How about buying me a burger?"

"Okay." He helped her gather up their equipment.

As they started to walk away, the governor said, "Giving up already?"

"Yep," Landon said. "Macie has decided on a burger instead of fish."

"Okay. I'll expect that proposal on my desk this week." The governor spoke more to the water than to them.

"It'll be there," Landon assured him.

As they walked back toward dry land, Macie grabbed his hand and swung it between them, taking a little skip. "We did it."

Landon grinned as a glow of pleasure grew in him. He could get used to this feeling, even though he knew it couldn't last.

CHAPTER NINE

ON MONDAY MORNING Macie and Landon returned to work. Tatiana had given her a questioning look when they'd entered the office area together, but Landon had immediately handed Tatiana a list of the information they needed.

After Macie saw to some nursing problems, she went to Landon's office to help him compile the proposal for the governor. They planned departmental meetings, staff meetings and changes that needed making. Positive ones. Landon had a knack for getting people to buy into a plan. Part of that was that he made them feel like they were partners instead of subordinates.

They rescheduled the visit to the mayor that they had missed while Landon was sick, and Landon apologized profusely for not being able to make the first one, bringing the mayor a bottle of the local drink to make up for it. The mayor was more than happy when they left.

Macie hadn't been this excited about life since before her father had destroyed her world. The only dark cloud in her happiness was that Landon would soon have to leave. His assignment had been for six weeks, and that was almost up. They didn't talk about it, yet they were both aware. More than once Landon had caught himself before he said something. By the look on his face, she'd known it had to do with him leaving.

A couple of times he'd taken calls in his office with the door closed. He said nothing to Macie, but she had been pretty sure they had been about the job he was trying to get. She wanted the best for him, but she didn't want him to leave. Landon didn't mention what was between them, and she didn't ask. He also never said anything about his feelings, but based on his actions he was as in love with her as she was with him. The question was whether he would allow himself to act on those feelings.

Her greatest worry was how they would ever survive a long-distance relationship. She had to accept that her heart would break. But she'd made a choice, and she would have to live with it. The even sadder thing would have been if she'd stood by her original plan and kept him at arm's length. The happiness she had so far would be worth all the heartache to come. This would always be the most precious time of her life.

On Tuesday afternoon, two days after they had talked to the governor, they were in his office working when Tatiana rushed in. "Macie, you're needed in Emergency right now."

"Why?"

"Something about the birthing clinic." Tatiana looked anxious. "The EMTs are bringing in a mother and baby."

"Let them know I'm on my way." Macie stood.

Tatiana left.

"Birthing clinic? I had no idea there was one." Landon had come to his feet as well.

"Can you come too? I may need your diplomatic skills. I'll fill you in on the way." She headed for the door.

Together they hurried toward Emergency.

Macie spoke as they went. "There's a birthing center

in part of one of the closed resorts. They've taken a few of the rooms and made them into birthing areas. Chinese women—I guess it would be more like their families— pay an exorbitant amount, upward of fifty thousand dollars, to have their babies here."

"Why?"

"Because Saipan is a US territory. The babies are American citizens. They get a US birth certificate and passport. Those babies are called ABC babies—American-born Chinese. The laws are changing to control this but we do have a few that slip through."

"I had no idea that was going on." Landon sounded as surprised as she thought he might be.

"I didn't either until I started working here. There are travel agencies in China who make a business out of selling to the mothers. They have brochures and offer packages."

"The mothers must be from families with a lot of money to afford that." Landon's strides lengthened.

"Yes, most are from well-to-do families. The ABC babies make up a large percentage of the babies born on Saipan currently."

He shook his head. "Unbelievable."

"I have a few issues with this clinic which is run by a representative of the tourism company in China. Despite what he says, I don't believe the clinic offers the standard of care they advertise. Another issue I have is that the clinic is only prepared for healthy births. If something goes wrong, they don't have the equipment or the ability to handle issues. They're quite arrogant about what they do and don't care to have any type of relationship with the hospital. And mostly I just don't like the concept of paying for US citizenship."

"Amazing."

"I've had dealings with this clinic before and they're uncooperative. They believe if the word gets out that we were involved, it will hurt business. One case that came in, the mother was in such bad shape that by the time they called us, she'd spent weeks in the hospital. I think they are more interested in the bottom line than they are their patients."

"So why am I coming along?" Landon held the door open for her to enter the ER.

"In traditional Chinese culture they recognize a man's authority more than a woman's. I think you might help the mother and baby get the care they need with less hassle."

"Got it."

Thankfully, Landon was in a suit instead of scrubs. That would add to his look of power.

The ambulance was just rolling to a stop at the door when they arrived. They picked up the pace and went out to meet it along with the ER doctor and nurse. A Chinese man hovered nearby.

Macie touched Landon's arm. "That's the medical tourism representative. He'll act as if he doesn't speak English well, but he does. Last time he spent most of the time on the phone."

Landon nodded as he seemed to size the thin young man up. The mother coming by them on a gurney drew their attention. She and Landon joined the other staff members in an exam room.

The EMT gave a report. "Twenty-three-year-old Chinese female. Postpartum hemorrhaging, low BP. Patient has a history of smoking."

Macie groaned.

Landon raised a brow in question.

"They're supposed to screen the mothers. They have to

be drug-free and have never smoked." What she didn't say was that they would take anyone willing to pay enough.

The ER doctor was busy doing a uterine massage in an effort to stop the bleeding. "We need whole blood here stat."

"Heart rate going down," the nurse called.

The monitor warning bells went off. The patient had no heartbeat.

Macie and Landon stepped into action then. Landon started hand compressions on the mother's chest while the nurse worked at pushing medicine into the IV that the EMTs had placed. Macie pulled the crash cart close and prepared the defibrillator paddles.

"Ready?" she called. She checked to see that the ER doctor had removed his hands from the patient before handing the paddles to Landon.

He quickly took them and placed them on the mother's chest.

Her body jumped as the electric current flowed through her body.

"Nothing," the nurse stated.

Landon said, "Again."

Macie reset the machine. "Ready?"

Landon placed the paddles once more. This time there was a small beep as the heart returned to beating. A look of relief came over his features as he handed the equipment back to her.

"Let's get this bleeding stopped and get this woman to ICU," the ER doctor said. "She's going to have a long recovery."

Half an hour later, Landon and Macie watched as members of staff pushed the mother up the hall toward the ICU.

Landon looked around. "I want to talk to the guy from the clinic."

Macie wasn't so sure that was a good idea, but from the determined look on his face, now wasn't the time to argue with him. He was a man on a mission.

"There he is." Landon headed toward the outside door.

Macie followed, wanting to make sure no one overstepped—she wasn't thinking so much about Landon, but about the other man. She'd had dealings with him before and was not impressed.

"May I speak to you a moment?" Landon asked the man.

He just looked blankly at Landon then back at his phone.

"I've been told that you speak English well. So please don't try to imply you don't." Macie recognized the tight notes in Landon's voice. He was controlling his anger.

The man shrugged and gave Landon a disinterested look. Landon told the man who he was but received no reaction from him.

"That mother back there—" Landon indicated with a thumb over his shoulder "—almost died from your company's negligence. I'm still not sure she won't, and she might have brain damage. And there's a baby that has no one currently to see about it. You get on your phone and you let your bosses know that I'll expect them to take care of her bill and see that she has the care that she requires at home, or I will make it my life's mission to shut you—and all the other agencies like yours—down."

Macie's chest filled with pride. With the World Health Organization behind him he just might have the clout to make his words a reality. The man's eyes widened as Landon spoke. His haughty look had disappeared.

Landon glared at the man. "Is that understood?"

The man nodded.

Landon turned and walked away. Macie followed him with a smile teasing her lips. They stepped out of earshot of anyone else. She leaned in close to him. "That might have been the sexist thing I've ever seen."

Landon's shoulders relaxed. He met her look, a smile forming on his mouth. "You think so?"

"I do."

"Maybe I should go talk to him again." He moved to turn.

She grabbed his arm and shook her head. "I don't want you to single-handedly ruin our tourist industry by making China mad at us."

"Okay. I'll keep it together. Let's go check on the baby."

They strolled to the nursery. There they received a report that the baby was doing fine but just a little small. She and Landon stood over the bassinet, looking down at the newborn.

When the nurse had walked away, Macie asked, "Have you ever wanted children?"

"I used to, but that was a long time ago. Before I understood how they could be hurt by their parents. Would you like to have children someday?"

"I used to dream of having a houseful." She glanced at him. What she didn't say was *with you*.

"I think you would be a great mom." His words were almost a soft caress.

"Thanks, that's nice to hear. I would certainly try. I bet you would be a wonderful father."

"I don't know about that. I don't have any real knowledge of how to be a good one. I had some really poor examples in my parents." He turned toward the door.

She joined him. "I would never lie to my children."

"I'm sure you wouldn't." He gave her a sly grin. "Back to you thinking I'm sexy—"

"I knew I shouldn't have said that."

He winked. "Now that you have, how about showing me just how sexy you think I am tonight?"

She raised her chin in thought. "Maybe I could be talked into doing that."

"I think I can do that." His hand brushed hers.

Macie lightly swatted his arm. "I'm not that easy."

"No, and I like it that way." He looked around and, not seeing anyone, gave her a quick kiss on the lips.

On Friday evening, they were in his office working on a presentation to his board when Landon looked up at the clock. "That's enough for today. I had no idea it was so late. I've got to go. I promised my girl we would do something special tonight."

"I bet she'll understand if you're running late."

He went around the desk to stand beside Macie. Running the back of his hand down her cheek, he said softly, "You think she's that understanding?"

"I think she'll think you're worth waiting on."

One of the nicest things about Macie was that she made him feel special. He had rarely felt that type of regard from a woman. "Do you, now?"

He liked playing word games with her. She had a quick wit. "I tell you what. I'll go home and see that she's all dressed and ready to go."

"Okay. Tell her I'll see her in an hour."

Macie giggled. "She'll be ready. Can I tell her where she's going?"

"Nope. It's a surprise."

His phone rang. He checked the screen and saw it was a Washington number. This might be the good news he'd been hoping for...but that would also be the news that takes him away from Macie. "I've got to take this."

She nodded and gave him a little wave before going out the door.

As he pulled up at Macie's, she came out of her door as if she had been standing at a window watching for him. The idea that he had planned a date and wouldn't tell her about it had made her restless. Yet she wore the dress he had requested, the flowing yellow one with the flowers. The slim straps left most of her beautiful tan shoulders bare, and the dress hugged her hips. Everything about her made him feel good from the inside out. His chest tightened.

He swept her up in his arms, and she kissed him as if she hadn't seen him in days, not just a few minutes. This he would miss most of all. But for tonight he would enjoy every minute they had and deal with the rest tomorrow.

"Now, tell me where we're going?"

Landon chuckled. "Not yet. You'll see." He went around the front of the car and opened the door for her.

He drove along the beach road, going well past the lights of the city, until he saw the pole with the orange ribbon, where Joe had told him to turn off. It was little more than a path, but when he could see the water he parked the car.

"How did you find this place?"

"I asked Joe. One of his family members owns this land. He gave me permission for us to come here."

"Why, Dr. Cochran, you're becoming a regular islander. Networking and all."

"Maybe a little bit. I do know a few more people than I did." Landon opened the door. "This is where we get out."

Landon helped her out then went to the trunk and retrieved the picnic basket. Taking her hand, he led her down to the beach. There he was pleased to see that the firepit he had expected had been prepared.

"Just when did you do this?" Amazement filled Macie's voice.

Landon shrugged. "I might have had a little help. You won't let me out of your sight."

"You do have a healthy ego. I might have overdone making you feel important."

Landon couldn't imagine that ever happening. He barked a laugh. "It's more like keeping me humble."

When they reached the pile of wood, he spread a blanket out and started the fire, then helped her to sit. She looked so feminine sitting elegantly with her legs to the side and her hair softly blowing in the breeze.

He joined her on the blanket and pulled the basket close. "Let's see what we have in here."

Macie watched as if he were a magician and she was expecting him to pull a rabbit out of a hat.

"We have champagne." He handed her a flute that he had filled from a bottle. "And there's shrimp cocktail."

"Where did this all come from?"

"Joe again. His uncle is a chef at one of the resorts."

"I'm going to have to thank Joe."

Landon grimaced. "It was my idea."

"Oh, I plan to thank you." She gave him a sexy smile.

"That's more like. I'm always better when I'm appreciated." He pulled another bowl out.

"I thought I had made it clear more than once that you are appreciated," she said softly.

He gave her a long look. "I believe I should see what else is for dinner, or we won't be eating if you keep looking at me that way."

Macie's giggle circled his heart. He focused on pulling more seafood, fruit and raw vegetables, and bread from the hamper.

"Goodness, this is a feast."

"Yeah, I had him pack it full." Landon was pleased that he'd impressed her.

Landon raised his glass. "I'd like to make a toast. To a beautiful night with a beautiful girl."

"Thank you."

He clinked his glass against hers. They each took a sip. "As much as I enjoy the champagne, I am hungry." Landon secured his glass in the basket and pulled out plates. "Would you like me to serve you?"

Macie smiled. "That sounds nice."

Landon filled her plate with a little of everything, then handed her the food and did the same with his plate. They ate for a few minutes as they watched the waves roll in.

Macie took a sip of her drink. "What gave you this nice idea? I didn't realize you were quite so..."

"Romantic? I actually had the idea while I was sick."

Her brows rose. "Really?"

"I dreamed of lying on the beach with you, holding your hand while we looked at the stars. I thought we should give it a try. I've never taken you on a real date, and I thought you might like to be wooed."

"Wooed. That's going back into the annals of time."

"Maybe so, but isn't that what a man does when he wants a woman?"

"What I do know is that I like it. Thank you." Macie leaned forward, and he met her for a tender kiss.

"You deserve it."

After they finished their meal, he cleaned things away and placed more wood on the fire. They stretched out on the blanket, and Landon took her hand and intertwined her fingers with his. She laid her head against his upper arm.

"Why did you decide to do this tonight?"

"You sure are full of questions. I heard there were supposed to be shooting stars tonight, and I thought this would be a perfect spot to watch them."

"I like your ideas."

They spent the next hour quietly looking at the stars. A few times one of them would point and call, "There's one."

Unable to stand having her so close but not in his arms, Landon rolled toward her. He kissed her bare shoulder before traveling over its ridge to nuzzle her neck on his way to her mouth. He was going to miss her more than he ever dreamed he would. "I really like you in this dress."

"I thought you might, since you asked me to wear it." There was such happiness in her voice.

"Always the smart mouth. But I'm thinking I might like you better without it." His lips took hers.

Macie smiled as she lounged on Landon's porch and drank her morning tea. He sat beside her on the small couch within touching distance. Last night had been wonderful. She was still floating with contentment.

They had made love on the beach and returned to his house to do so again in the middle of the night. He had been so tender and caring, and something about it had made her wonder if he'd been trying to tell her something. As if he wanted her to understand how special she was to him.

Now they were making a leisurely morning of it. She wished it could always be like this. Maybe she could talk Landon into staying. Get him to see that he could have a good life here with her.

"Macie?"

"Mmm?"

"That phone call yesterday when you were in my office was from DC."

Her stomach dropped. She turned to him. Was this the day she had been dreading? He would leave her once more. Only this time she'd known all along it would happen. She'd chosen this hurt and would have to deal with it. "When are you leaving?"

"In a couple of days."

A heaviness pressed down on her chest. She placed her mug on the coffee table and swung her legs round so she faced him. "That soon!"

He reached over and touched her arm. "We knew this was coming."

Yeah. But that didn't mean she had to like it. Or that she couldn't fight against it.

"Come with me," he said softly, almost as a plea. "I know you would be an asset to the World Health Organization."

She shook her head. "I can't do that."

"Why not? You haven't signed a contract here. You could stay behind long enough to train your replacement. We're great together. I don't want us to stop yet."

"I'm needed here. This is my home now."

Landon stood and glared down at her. "This is your hideout!"

"What?"

"You're here because you're afraid to go home. Afraid to face what you left behind."

She couldn't believe he was saying this to her. "That isn't true. And I don't even have a home to go to."

"You have a mother, brother and sister. Even a father. Who do you have here?" He waved his hand around.

"I have a lot of friends."

"Agreed, but they're not family. You live in a tiny rented house, and you work all the time. Every time someone needs something, you're there for them, but who's there for you?"

"You have been, but now you are leaving." She hadn't meant to sound so pitiful.

Landon eased back to the couch. "We both knew when I came that I wouldn't be staying long."

"I know." She looked at the floor. This was what she'd feared for weeks. What she'd chosen to ignore. "I told myself not to like you too much. But it didn't work."

He gave her a wry smile and reached for her hand. "If you come to Washington and don't want to work at World Health, with your skills you could work at one of the great hospitals around DC. You could still be making a difference but with me. Come on, Macie, think about it."

"I need to stay here and help the people of Saipan. One of us needs to stay to see that all those plans we've made happen." She saw him flinch. Her remark had hit home just as she'd hoped it would. He let go of her hand.

"I think you've already done your time." His words sounded like a judge giving his ruling. Firm and undeniable.

She lowered her chin and narrowed her eyes. "What're you talking about?"

"That you have been doing penitence for what your father did to all those people by being out here in the middle of nowhere, helping the forgotten."

"That's not true."

"Yeah, it is. Come on, Macie. You ran to Hawaii because of what your father did. You ran from Hawaii to here because of me, and now you're running from me again. There are only so many places you can go. All that *stuff*—" he tapped his chest "—is still with you. You can never outrun it because you carry it with you. Somewhere along the line you have to turn and face it. You're trying to make up for all your father's shortcomings by sacrificing your life."

"I'm not sacrificing anything." She glared at him.

"What about us?"

"What us? You don't really want an *us*. I've lived in a dreamworld before, and I refuse to do it again. What we've been doing here is playing house. What you have been offering me in Washington is more of the same. I don't want pretend. You said yourself that you could never give more, yet you are demanding I give up everything I have built to do just that."

"That's not true."

She looked at him for a moment. "For that matter, why can't you stay? Be the administrator. Better yet, practice medicine like you used to. We could use you here."

"I have a job waiting on me in DC that I've worked hard for years to get."

"Is it really what you want to do? To sit in an office pushing papers and telling people what's best to do for their patients, or would you rather be working with patients of your own? You've moved into what you're doing now because you needed the job to help your family, but is it really your dream? Haven't you left that behind?"

His mouth gaped as his stared at her. "I do important work."

"No one says you don't, but is it your dream? What you went into medicine to do?"

He just looked at her. She'd poked a tender spot. "A perfect world isn't possible."

"I'd be the first to agree with you on that. You took your job because it was a means to help your family, but your brother and sister are doing well—they even have families. But what about you? Isn't it time you get what you want? You could have a family that loves you if only you would let someone in. You don't have to be afraid of becoming your father."

"I'm not afraid."

"I think you are. You're better than him."

"It's not my father I'm afraid of becoming. It's my mother!" He all but shouted the words.

Macie couldn't have been more shocked. "Your mother?"

He stood again and paced the porch. "Yes! She loved my father so desperately that she destroyed her life and her children's lives when he left. I'm afraid that when I love, it will be so deeply that it could damage everyone around me if I lost it."

"So you're willing to keep me at arm's length for fear of loving me too much? That sounds like the perfect kind of love to me."

"That's not love. That's obsession."

"Landon, I think you need to figure out what you want." She stood as well.

"I want the job in Washington. I've worked for it and now is my chance. I can't just pass it up."

"You can't just pass it up *for me*. That's what you're not saying."

Landon gave her a stricken look. "I didn't say that."

"No, but that's what you mean. If you want me you have to stay here, which means that you have to give up the job and admit to loving me. Your attitude reminds me a lot of my father's. Whatever it takes for you to have what you want but not have to give anything back in return."

He jerked to a stop. "That's unfair. I would never hurt people the way your father did."

"I agree. You're a better person than him, but the principle is the same. Look, your work is in Washington and mine is here. Maybe we should just leave it at that. Say we had a good time while it lasted." She stood. Everything that needed saying had been said. "I'd like to go home now. We both need some space to think."

"Macie," he pleaded, stepping toward her.

"Please don't. I might fall apart if you touch me, and neither one of us needs that. The last thing I would want is for you to feel fenced in by me."

Landon sucked in a breath and backed away. "Macie, it isn't like that."

She pursed her lips. His inability to see the truth was a physical ache in her chest. "Isn't it?"

He had the good grace not to say anything.

This pain she carried was more than she had ever imagined. She wanted to run into his arms, hold him tight and have him say he would never let her go.

Landon turned toward the door. She quietly gathered her belongings, and then he took her home.

As she stepped out of the car, he asked, "Can I call you later today, or tomorrow?"

She shook her head. "No, I don't think that'll make anything easier, nor will it change our minds."

"I have the first flight out on Monday. Will you come see me off?"

She blinked a couple of times to control the moisture in her eyes. Shaking her head, she ran blindly for her front door, just managing to get inside before she burst into tears.

CHAPTER TEN

LANDON HAD BEEN in Washington, DC, for a week. Despite being busier than ever, he felt it had been the longest week of his life. He had left Saipan with a heavy heart when he should have been happy to be taking up the position he'd been working so hard to achieve.

He hadn't seen Macie—except once briefly at the hospital—since he had left her at her home. More than once he had picked up the phone to call her but had put it down again. She had needed space and he had given it to her. Still, it hurt that she hadn't wanted to spend what little time they had left together. He had hoped they would make plans to see each other, to maybe meet in Hawaii, but she had made no contact.

She hadn't come to the airport to see him off. He'd counted on her at least doing that. The chance to hold her one more time… But nothing. He had looked for her, but in the end he'd walked out to the plane with weighty steps. And then he'd become angry. He couldn't fathom why she wouldn't come with him. It had been years since she'd visited her family. Why couldn't she a least try? For him? For herself?

It wasn't until he had looked out the window as the plane took off that he saw her car parked on the side of the road, Macie standing beside it, looking up at the sky.

And at that moment, she had pulled his heart out and held it. He knew the love his mother had had for his father, the kind with the ability to take him to the highest high or the lowest low.

After a long flight and a night on the west coast, he had arrived in Washington, DC, to a hotel located a block from the World Health Organization office. He'd actually come home to nothing. He didn't own a house or a car. Because he was traveling all the time, he'd not seen a reason to buy either. He had nothing—emotionally or physically—in his life. How had he become such a loner? Had he been so busy protecting himself against being hurt that he had nothing to show for it?

He hadn't been alone in Saipan. He'd had Macie. What would it be like to come home to her every day? To their children? He'd never thought like that before. Right now, it sounded like bliss.

Over the past week he had spent a good deal of time urging board members to consider his suggestions for the hospital. He felt fairly positive about the proposal's chances, but the board needed an extra push for it to pass and he was going to suggest that they speak to both the Saipan representative to Congress and the governor to get a personal perspective.

Despite how busy he was, he couldn't get Macie out of his mind. During the day he survived, but it was the nights in his box of a room when he felt the loss in his life the most. He made a habit of working late so he didn't have to spend any more time there than necessary. Another week crept by, and the loneliness squeezed him like being crushed by a rock pile. Would he ever find that happiness again?

He had to make a trip to the Midwest to check on a project that he had worked on before going to Saipan.

That put him within hours of his sister's and brother's homes, which were in the same state.

He called Nancy and, as always, she made arrangements for the three of them to get together. Adam and his family would be coming to her house for dinner, and Landon would be the honored guest. He was looking forward to seeing his family again, but he also felt a twinge of nervousness. What would they think?

Both Nancy and Adam enveloped him in their arms. Finally, he felt a tiny amount of what he had experienced in Saipan, and the pressure in his chest eased some. This was love—the good, healthy type.

The evening meal was a rambunctious affair since his siblings both had small children. There were smiles all around and much laughter, and Landon enjoyed every bit of it. For the first time he was even envious. He wanted what they had.

The meal was at an end when Adam's wife announced she was putting the baby down for a nap. His brother-in-law took his child from Nancy's arms and mumbled something about watching a game on TV, leaving the siblings alone to catch up.

For a few moments, the three of them looked at each other, unsure, before they smiled and started talking at the same time. With the tension broken, they went back in time to when it was just the three of them against the world.

Adam said, "We need to do this more often."

Landon leaned back in his chair. "I couldn't agree more. It's great to see you both."

"So," Nancy asked as she studied Landon, "tell us, very important brother—" Adam huffed "—how have you been?"

"Fine."

Nancy's eyes narrowed. "You don't look fine."

When he had looked in the mirror that morning, he'd thought he looked the same as always. He just didn't feel the same.

"It must be jet lag. I've just gotten back from Saipan."

"That's right. I had to look that one up," she said.

"Yeah, me too," Adam added. "So what was in Saipan?"

Happiness. Macie. Everything. "A hospital that I was evaluating."

"And how did that go?" His sister refilled his glass.

"Overall, I think it was positive. There are still some decisions to make but I think it'll be very successful."

"And you'll be getting this new job?" Adam crossed his arms on the table, giving Landon his full attention.

"Yes, I'll be Director of the World Health Organization."

"Impressive." His brother nodded thoughtfully.

"And living in Washington?" Nancy asked.

"Yes. I'll be staying in one place finally." Somehow that idea had more appeal than ever before.

"Great. We'll get to see you more often. We won't have to chase you down all the time." She gave him a pointed look. "For a man who has a big new job, you sure don't look very happy about it."

He didn't feel it either. "It's a great job. I can make a difference."

"That's good." Nancy didn't sound like she really believed him.

Landon could always talk to his brother and sister. What they had lived through had brought them closer; they understood him. Despite the fact that they didn't see each other often, they knew each other well. They always slipped back to where they'd left off.

Nancy continued to give him an unwavering look. One that reminded him too much of their mother. Landon shifted in his chair.

"I've always known when something was bothering you."

She had. Landon looked at Adam, who just grinned at him.

"I know that look. You've met a woman!" Nancy said it like she'd just made a difficult puzzle piece fit in.

Landon groaned.

His brother slapped his hand on the table. "It's about damn time."

"So when do we meet her?" Nancy demanded.

His lips tightened and he looked away. "I don't think you will."

"What! Why?" His sister all but squealed.

Landon explained what had happened between him and Macie. He finished with "She wouldn't come with me."

"Did you mention to her that you're in love with her?"

As if a lock had sprung, his brain engaged. He was in love with Macie, and he'd left her halfway around the world. What had he been thinking? He hadn't been.

"You didn't know," Nancy said in disbelief. "Or if you did, you didn't tell her."

"Landon, I know that Mom and Dad's marriage nearly wrecked us," Adam offered, "but that's no reason not to have someone to love."

"I, uh…"

His sister placed her hand over his. "Landon, you had a harder time than we did because you were the oldest and you thought you had to take care of us, and everything you've done since—including your jobs—has been about what we needed. Have you ever thought about what *you* want? We appreciate everything you've done for us, but we're all settled now and we would never want you to give up your life for us."

"I haven't given up anything." Landon didn't like the turn the conversation had taken.

"Yes, you did," Adam insisted. "We weren't so young that we didn't know where the money was coming from."

"And you don't have to be like our parents. Just because they had a horrible marriage doesn't mean you have to. Or that you would be as uncaring as Dad or as needy as Mom. We can be our own people." Nancy nodded toward Adam. "If we took a chance, so can you."

Had he been doing those things? Projecting his parents' problems on to himself, on to the women he dated, on to Macie? If anything, she had proved herself to be nothing like his mother.

"We always knew, and we love you for it, but it's time for you to decide what you want and go after it. Time for you to live your life. Time to find happiness." His sister patted his hand.

Could he give up everything he had worked for and go back to Saipan? "It's too late."

"It's never too late to tell someone you love them," she assured him.

He looked at Adam then Nancy. "I love you guys."

Macie watched the plane disappear into the sky, taking Landon with it. The beautiful sunny day was in complete opposition to the gloomy tempest of emotions within her. The love of her life had left her again, and this time she'd known it was going to happen and still had been unable to prevent it.

She climbed into her car, placed her hands over her face and sobbed. Had she done the right thing? Or had she been doing exactly what he'd accused her of: hiding?

For the first time since she had come to Saipan, she called in and took a day off. She drove out to the place where she and Landon had gone on their beach picnic. It had been the best of nights and the worst of mornings. That had been only two days ago, but it felt like forever. She'd missed him the moment he'd left her at her house. She'd needed to think. He'd not called, and she'd not tried to get in contact with him. Was it going to change anything if she did? Hadn't they picked their corners and made their decisions?

She walked to the beach and sat down to watch the waves roll in. How had she come to this? Because she'd let her emotions take over. She'd opened her heart and Landon had walked in. From their time in Hawaii she'd known he had the power to make her love him and she was well aware of how it felt to have someone you loved disappoint you.

When the sun started setting and the hunger pains didn't pass, she went home. She prepared her supper but ate only a few bites. Deciding sleep would give her some relief from the pain, she went to bed. But she was disappointed. All she could think about was how she missed Landon's arms around her and his warm body next to hers. She tossed and turned until the sky turned pink, and then she dressed for work. Maybe there she could find some peace.

But she didn't, and the rest of the week went much as the first day had. She became even more sleep deprived, and her colleagues began to look at her oddly. She'd snapped at a number of them, and Tatiana gave her a wide berth. Even in the darkest days of her father's trial she'd never been this miserable.

Why had she let this happen? She should have protected herself better.

But what was done was done, and now she had to figure out how to survive. Was that really what she wanted, to just survive? Wasn't that what she'd been doing for the last eight years? Surviving by hiding. If she wanted to deserve Landon, she had to do better than that. When she went after him—which she planned to—she had to be worthy of him.

She'd accused Landon of needing to clear up stuff in his life. Didn't she need to address her past as well? She hadn't seen her family in years, and it was time for her to face what her father had done head-on.

With weeks of vacation time stored up, she could go get her life in order, and then she would find Landon and tell him how she felt. Even if he didn't want her, it was time she reenter the world.

She couldn't leave the hospital without making arrangements and finding a replacement. If Landon still wanted her, she would return to pack up and move to Washington so she could be with him.

It took her a little over a week to get her affairs in order at work and to make phone calls home. When she spoke to her mother and said she was coming for a visit, her mother broke down in tears.

"I'll be waiting for you at the airport," her mother said.

"You don't have to do that, Mom."

"I want to. I can't wait to see you."

In that moment Macie was confident she was doing the right thing, regardless of what happened with Landon.

"Your brother and sister will be so excited. I'll ask

them to come for the weekend. I can't believe I'll have all my children under one roof again."

Macie had to admit she was looking forward to seeing her family. If she'd been asked a few weeks ago if she would be seeing them, she wouldn't have thought it possible.

"How's Daddy?" It was the first time she'd ever asked about her father.

"He's fine. Just a little older and more tired."

Macie had to admire her mother. She had stayed by his side—that was true love. Would she do that if Landon were in prison? Love meant love in good times or bad. Thick or thin.

"Do you think he'd like to see me?"

There was quiet on her mother's end then a sniffle. "He would love that."

"Could you please make the arrangements?"

"I will," her mother assured her.

"I'll see you soon, Mom. I love you." Macie looked out the window of her house. She really had placed her life on hold when she'd come here.

Her visit with her family a few days later was wonderful—a little uncomfortable at first but heartwarming in the end. At the airport, her mother had pulled her into a hug so tight that Macie had found it difficult to breathe. As they'd approached her mom's small house in a subdivision, Macie could see a large sign across the front door that read Welcome Home Macie.

Her chest had tightened. She should have been better to her mother—she wasn't the one who had done anything wrong. All that fell on her father.

It had been wonderful to reconnect with her siblings and their families over the weekend, and she'd regretted the time she'd missed with them, especially her nieces and nephews.

After her visit with her family, her phone rang Monday morning. "Hello?"

"Macie Beck?"

"Yes."

"This is Dr. Larry Fitzgerald with the World Health Organization."

Her hand shook. Had something happened to Landon?

"We'd like to invite you to come to Washington to share with the board your view on the proposed changes to the hospital and what we can do to help."

Really? Why wasn't Landon calling her? "Did Dr. Cochran ask you to call me?"

"No. He's currently on assignment out of town."

Oh. A pain shot through her. She hadn't told him she was coming to the States, so there was no reason to expect he would be sitting in Washington waiting for her.

The man continued. "Will you come? We would certainly pay your expenses."

"Yes." She had to. It mattered to the hospital. It mattered to Landon's future for the project to go well.

"When could you be here?"

"Would the end of the week do?"

"So soon?" The shock was clear in the man's voice.

"I'm actually in the States currently, in the Chicago area."

"Good, good. I'll be back in touch to finalize arrangements. Please plan on Friday."

"I will. Thank you for this opportunity."

"Thank you, Ms. Beck."

The next day, she drove to the minimum-security prison outside Chicago to visit her father. Her stomach was a jumble of nerves. She had to grip the steering wheel to keep her hands from shaking. If she wasn't careful, she'd lose her lunch.

She had to wait in a large room with tables populated by other visitors meeting with their loved ones while two men stood guard on each side of the room. Her father came in wearing an orange jumpsuit and looking much older than she remembered. Life had beat him down.

He smiled, but it was an uncertain one as he approached. "Macie."

She thought to stand to greet him or to hug him, but she couldn't bring herself to do either. She didn't know how to respond, so she just nodded.

"You have grown into such a beautiful woman. I almost didn't recognize you." He took a seat across from her. "How have you been?"

"I've been fine." She twisted her fingers together.

"Working as a nurse in Saipan, your mother has proudly told me."

"Yes." This was her father and they were strangers. They stared at each other for a long moment before Macie blurted out, "Why did you do it? Why?"

He looked at the table then back at her. "Because I didn't think I would get caught."

"But all those people you hurt?"

"For that I am sorry."

At least he could say that, but it didn't bring their life savings back. "I have hated you."

"For that I'm sorry as well. Please keep your voice down."

One of the guards watched them with interest.

"You do know that I've been gone all these years because I couldn't face people. The press hounded me, made my life a misery." All the bitterness flowed out of her as she said all the things she had not articulated to him before.

"All I can say is that I'm sorry."

"That's not enough," Macie hissed.

"I know, but that's all I have to give."

Macie just looked at him. What more did she have to say to him?

"Look, honey—"

"Don't call me that!" Macie snapped. Now she knew why she had stayed away.

Her father sighed and reached a hand across the table. "I can't give you what you want. The best I can do is to tell you I love you and ask you for your forgiveness."

She studied his hand but didn't reach out to him. It was still too raw. "I love you too, Dad. I forgive you—not for you, but for me. I have to let it go so I can move on."

He nodded.

"I think I need to go," Macie said.

"I understand."

Macie couldn't get to the car fast enough. She wished Landon was there to hold her. Gripping the steering wheel, she leaned her head against it, inhaling deeply and then releasing her breath slowly. She'd had no idea what to expect from her father, but she felt better for visiting at least and she'd gotten some of her anger out. A weight she'd had no idea she'd been carrying was gone.

How she wanted to see Landon. Would he be in Washington when she got there? If he wasn't, she'd wait.

Landon entered the boardroom in the World Health Organization building. The space had been rearranged so that the board sat in a semicircle of desks with chairs in the front, a long table between them with a microphone on it. Behind them, on either side of an aisle, were rows of chairs for those who were attending the hearing. This was a public event, so it often drew interested parties and the media.

It had been only the afternoon before when he had checked his messages and learned that he was expected to appear before the board and that Macie would be testifying as well. Since he had been out of town longer than he had originally planned visiting family and had not picked up his messages in the last twenty-four hours he'd just learned of the arrangements. To say he'd been surprised would be an understatement.

Macie was here in Washington. He would see her! After his conversation with Adam and Nancy, he had been convinced he had to return to Saipan, had to go after Macie, had to try again. If she wouldn't come here, then he would go there. It was time to quit living in the past and start building his future, and Macie was his future.

Despite his efforts to arrive early, he had been waylaid by a couple of phone calls and then stopped in the hallway by a colleague who wanted to discuss a project they had worked on during the last year. By the time he reached the room, it was filling with people. He searched for Macie; his body sensed her and he imagined if he inhaled deeply, he would be able to pick up her unique scent. Seconds later he spotted her, speaking to someone at the front of the room.

His heart came close to thumping out of his chest. Macie had never looked lovelier, nor more desirable. Or was that because he'd missed her so much? She wore a simple pale pink dress with a black blazer. A gold necklace hung around her neck, and her hair swung freely about her face. His hands ached to touch its silkiness.

Another person stopped him, but even as his colleague spoke, his attention kept returning to Macie. He noticed she kept looking over her shoulder as if she were expecting someone. Was she looking for him? Warmth filled his chest at the idea. He hoped she was as anxious to see him as he was to see her.

The president of the board spoke into the microphone in front of his chair. "We need to get this meeting started. Please take your seats."

As Landon excused himself from the conversation and walked to the front of the room, he watched as the woman Macie had been speaking to escorted her to a chair at the table facing the board. Before she sat, Macie pulled a folder out of the bag she carried.

He had just slid into the seat beside her when the chairman called the meeting to order. This wasn't the way he'd wanted their reunion to go, but under the circumstances it couldn't be helped. They would talk afterward. He would see to that.

Macie's eyes widened with awareness, and a look of pleasure filled them.

"Hey," he said well away from the microphone. Instead of speaking to her, what he really wanted to do was grab her in his arms and kiss her until both of them couldn't breathe. He settled for looking deep into her eyes.

"Hi. I was told you might not be here."

"And you thought I wouldn't show up to see you?" Landon searched her face. He had missed her so much.

"I hoped you would." Her words were soft and unsure.

Landon inhaled her heavenly scent—fresh air and coconut—and he held her look until the chairman called the meeting to order.

The chairman introduced the board and Macie, and Landon as well. The chairman then spoke directly to Macie. "Ms. Beck, I hope you don't mind if we tape this hearing. We'd like to have it for review purposes." He indicated the camera in the corner.

The tension in Macie came off her in waves. She stared ahead. Landon wanted to reach for her, knowing how she felt about cameras, but he couldn't do that, so he pushed a piece of paper off the table and leaned over to pick it up. Coming close to her ear, he said, "You can do this. I'm right here beside you."

Her gaze met his and she blinked. "That's fine," she said into the microphone.

"I understand that you'd like to make a statement," the chairman said.

"I would." She opened the folder.

Macie proceeded to give a statement that clearly came from her heart—how she felt about Saipan, the people and the hospital was evident in her voice. She finished with "In conclusion, I believe this is a sound plan and could make a difference in people's lives."

"Dr. Cochran, before we start the questions, is there anything you would like to add?"

Landon leaned toward the microphone. "No, sir. I think Miss Beck has more than adequately covered the points."

Macie looked at him, and he gave her a reassuring nod.

"Now, if any of the board has any questions for Ms. Beck and Dr. Cochran, this is the time to ask," the chairman said.

Over the next hour, Landon and Macie fielded questions about the hospital, the plans, updates on equipment and, most important, how much funding would be required.

Landon believed the meeting was winding down when one of the board members said, "All of this sounds good, but I'm still not convinced. You have both expressed your belief that it's the leadership going forward that will make the difference. I'd be more likely to vote yes if a committed administrator was in place."

Another board member spoke up. "I agree. Before we commit to the funding, shouldn't we seek to secure an administrator who commits to staying at least five years and who will be responsible for seeing these projects through? Otherwise, I don't see these plans being carried out to their fullest potential."

A couple of the other board members nodded. Macie's dejected look clearly said she was afraid their work had been wasted, her dreams gone. Landon wanted to make her dreams come true. Always.

"Sir, if I were to take the position as administrator of the Saipan Hospital until one could be found who would sign a five-year contract and be trained on the long-term strategy, would the board consider supporting the changes immediately?"

Macie's quick inhale of breath plainly revealed her shock. She looked at him in disbelief, her mouth gaping. She pushed the microphone back. "What are you doing? What about your new position?"

He smiled. "I've decided that some things are more important."

"What things?" she whispered.

"You."

The chairman cleared his throat, bringing their attention back to the room.

"How would the board feel about that arrangement? Under Dr. Cochran's leadership I think it would be a workable plan." The chairman looked at the other board members who had voiced their concerns. They all nodded agreement.

"I think we have all we need for now. Ms. Beck, thank

you for making such a long journey. This hearing is adjourned."

There was a shuffling of feet as everyone stood.

Macie couldn't believe what Landon had just done. What type of man gave up his entire career just like that? One completely different from her father, that was for sure. If she hadn't already been in love with Landon, she was now.

She turned to him and grasped his hand. "You don't have to do this. You don't have to give up all you've been working for."

"I'm not giving up anything. I'm just postponing it."

A man placed his hand on Landon's shoulder, interrupting their conversation. "Landon, if you're serious about returning to Saipan, then we need to talk."

"I'm serious, sir. Macie, this is my boss and friend, Dr. Russell."

"Hello," Macie said.

The man glanced at their hands and smiled. "I think our discussion can wait until tomorrow morning. Why don't you take Ms. Beck out to lunch and show her some of DC while she's here?"

"Thank you, I will." Landon offered the man his hand. "Thank you, sir."

"Ms. Beck, thank you for coming. You are an impressive and persuasive woman."

As Dr. Russell walked off, Landon said, "Let's get out of here before we're interrupted again. We need to talk."

He led her outside into the bright spring sunlight. Taking her hand, Landon started down the sidewalk.

"Where are we going?" Macie walked beside him.

"To a little café I know where we won't be disturbed.

I'd rather take you to my hotel room, but we wouldn't get any talking done there."

"Landon?" She pulled on his hand and stopped.

He did as well and looked down at her. "What?"

"I love you. I shouldn't have let you leave Saipan without me."

He cupped her cheek and looked into her eyes. "I love you too, and I should have told you that."

Coming up onto her toes, she met Landon for a kiss more perfect than she could have ever imagined. It wasn't until someone honked their horn that they drew apart, laughing.

Landon took her hand again and turned back the way they had come.

"Where are we going now?" She had to hurry to keep up with him.

"To my hotel."

She grinned as she tightened her grip on his hand. "I thought you were hungry and wanted to talk."

"I am hungry. For you. And we've already said what needed to be said."

A heat filled her chest that flowed right to her center.

Landon whisked her inside a stately old hotel, through the lobby and into the elevator. There he pulled her into his arms and kissed her until her knees buckled. When the doors opened, he guided her down the hall to a door, unlocked it and pushed it open. She stepped inside, but Landon remained outside.

"Aren't you coming in?" Panic filled her. Had he changed his mind?

"In a sec." He took a deep breath.

She watched him, confused.

Landon looked shaken. "I love you so much and have

missed you so much that I'm afraid I might hurt you with how much I want you."

Macie's heart swelled. She tugged him to her. "I'll take my chances."

He scooped her into his arms, and she giggled as he tumbled her onto the bed.

Blissful, precious hours later, they sat in bed wearing plush hotel bathrobes while sharing a meal Landon had ordered from room service.

"Landon, I appreciate your offer to be the administrator, but I don't want you to feel like you have to."

"I might have said it in the heat of the moment, but I would have never done so unless I thought it was what I wanted. I was happy in Saipan. With you, with the people, with the work. I found—" he met her eyes "—more than one thing I had lost. I want to work with patients again, and I was coming back anyway. To you."

"When I got the call to come to DC, I was already in the States."

"You were?" He lifted a strawberry to her lips.

She bit it and swallowed. "Mmm... What you said about me hiding out got me to thinking that I couldn't always live my life that way. It had been too long since I had seen my family, so I came to visit them. I even went to see my father."

Landon ran his hand over her hair. "I should have been with you when you went to see your father."

She gave him a wry smile. "Thank you for that."

"How did it go?"

She bit her bottom lip for a moment. "I'm not sure. He seemed glad to see me. I confronted him about some things."

"And?"

"He said he was sorry, but I'm still not convinced he

means it." Landon gave her a look of sympathy. "Anyway, I was planning to come here to see you when the chairman called."

"I didn't know you were here until yesterday afternoon." He played with her fingertips.

She grinned. "Were you surprised?"

"Pleasantly." He moved the food out of the way and pulled her to him, kissing her. "Anxiously." He nipped at her neck. "Hungrily." He kissed her palm. "And happily."

She put a hand on his chest. "Seriously, Landon. I don't want you to give up your promotion for me and my wants."

"I'm not giving up anything. I'm gaining a life, a job I love and, best of all…you. I hope you didn't give up your job. You're going to need it when you return."

"You said something about postponing your job. What do you mean?"

"I'm going to ask Dr. Russell if I can continue to be paid through the organization. That will help the hospital financially, and it'll also leave the door open for me to be considered for promotions in the future."

"Oh, Landon, that's too much." She wrapped her arms around his neck and kissed him.

When they broke apart, he said, "There's more.

"When there's an administrator in place who can handle the day-to-day issues, I'm going back to patient care part-time. I've missed it. I'll start working immediately in the ER on weekends when you are there. That'll sharpen up my skills, and I'm also going to stipulate that the organization pay for two airline tickets home twice a year. We need to visit our families. Sometimes you have to leave paradise."

Joy filled Macie. It all sounded so wonderful. "Do you think Dr. Russell will agree to everything?"

"I do." Landon's look turned serious. "I have a question for you."

"What's that?"

"Will you marry me?"

"Oh, Landon." She gave him a questioning look.

"Well?" He sounded worried.

"Are you sure that's what you want? I know how you feel about that type of commitment."

"Married or not, you're still my life. I love you so much already it almost takes my breath away. Nothing you or I do will ever change that."

"Yes. Yes. I'll marry you." She threw herself into his arms. "With you I'll always be in paradise."

* * * * *

FIGHTING FOR THE TRAUMA DOC'S HEART

RACHEL DOVE

MILLS & BOON

This book is dedicated to
all the parents and carers out there
fighting for their child's place in the world,
and to my sons.
Thanks for sharing your neurodiverse world with me.
I love you to the moon and back,
and all the stars in between.

CHAPTER ONE

MICHELLE FORBES WAS barely out of her car when she saw the ambulance pull into the bay at the front of the hospital's main doors. St Marshall's had another entrance for trauma, but that was around the other side. This couldn't be good.

Slamming her car door, she threw her backpack over her shoulders and thrust her keys into her coat pocket, pulling out a bottle of hand sanitiser and running straight to the ambulance. Dousing her hands in the alcohol solution, she shoved the bottle back into her pocket and greeted the two men pulling the gurney out of the back of the ambulance doors.

'What've we got?' she demanded, reaching for a pair of gloves from one of the rig's shelves before following them in.

'Welcome back. Female, twenty-seven, found unconscious at the scene of an RTA.'

They rushed through the main doors, shouting at people to get out of the way as they ran the gauntlet of the main reception area, heading right to the trauma wing. A medic she knew—Bradley—did a double-take when he saw her, but then it was straight back to business.

'We have two other ambulances incoming: an elderly couple, both awake and responsive at the scene, and one unconscious pregnant woman. Thirty-two weeks along. Her ETA is approximately ten minutes; they were cutting her out of the car when we left. This one—' the paramedic pointed at the unconscious woman as they ran hell for leather towards the nearest bay '—is a cyclist. Her helmet was on but not fastened. It came off in the collision. Her breathing is stable. Possible fractured pelvis, right broken forearm. She hit her head on the tarmac as she landed. No consciousness since, but pupils are equal and reactive.'

'Right.' Michelle nodded, jabbing at the door button as they hit the bay.

She noticed her hands were shaking slightly, but when she clenched her fists tight and then unfurled them it stopped. Heads turned as she barrelled through, barking orders as she went. Michelle commanded any room she walked into, and she had long since forgotten to be sorry about that, even now.

'Check for any other bleeding and call for a CT scan immediately. We need to check on that head. Get Ortho up here to assess these fractures, and I'll come back to reset them myself once we have the scans. Page OB and Ortho—tell them we have incoming traumas.'

Bradley gave her a curt nod and got to work.

The whole trauma centre came to life as she spoke to the room. If Dr Forbes spoke, you damn well listened. Out of respect, mostly. She didn't work on fear; she had seen its effects too many times to value it as any sort of teaching aid.

'Clear the beds, people! Three traumas incoming. One thirty-two weeks pregnant and unconscious. Two elderly people, awake and responsive. Bed Two is stable, unconscious, and has multiple fractures. Check them in, people, and check them out!'

She headed for the on-call room, grabbing a pair of fresh scrubs from the pile kept in there. Within seconds she was dressed and ready to go. Talk about a gentle easing back in to the day job. *Sheesh.*

She went to open the door, but froze when she heard her name being mentioned. She held her hands out in front of her, grateful to see that they were as steady as a rock now.

It must have been the adrenaline, she thought to herself. *I'm back. I can do this. I want to be here. Here grounds me. Normality. Work. Friends. Just got to keep it together. Fake it till you make it, Doctor.*

'Shh—not the time!'

One of the nurses was trying to silence a porter Michelle recognised—Alan. He'd worked in trauma for years and was one of her favourite colleagues. Fast, quick, and he got the job done. Just the kind of person every head of trauma wanted to have working for her.

'We have trauma incoming—just leave it!'

Michelle opened the door just a crack more, giving herself half a second to listen in. Alan seemed rattled, and that made her Spidey senses tingle. One thing she had learned from her tours as a medic: you listened to your gut. Helping charitable organisations overseas and working with the army had taught her that staying alive meant being true to your own instincts and having the courage to see your plan through.

'It's not fair, though,' Alan hissed into the nurse's ear. 'She went to help her fellow countrymen and this is what she gets? We don't need any more change around here; I don't like it. I really don't like lying to her, either.'

The nurse didn't get the chance to reply as Michelle swept out through the door, shutting it firmly behind her, having stashed her backpack under one of the beds.

'Michelle!' Alan said smoothly, and any reservation that might have shown on his face was shrouded carefully by his friendly open smile. 'Glad you're back.'

She smiled, tapping him on the shoulder. She could hear the incoming ambulances and was already back to thinking about work. Whatever that was all about, it would come out in the wash soon enough. Even in a large hospital like this gossip never stayed secret for long. No need for her to get involved.

'Glad to be back. I hope you haven't wrecked the place!' she called over her shoulder as she ran to the trauma centre doors.

Two ambulances came screeching to a halt, one after the other, and medics were already scrambling to help. Michelle burst through the doors and was at the door to the first ambulance when she was almost hit by one of the doors flying open, with a shouting man behind it.

'Trauma, people! Female, Annie Weston, thirty-two weeks pregnant plus three, knocked unconscious at the scene of an RTA. Vitals stable. Foetal heartbeat strong, detected in the field and en route. No sign of labour, but we need to assess the injuries, stat.'

Michelle, furious at being sideswiped by both the door and the stranger, sprang up from her position and poked the guy right in the chest. Quite a firm chest, as chests went... Her short, neat little fingernail jabbed into his pectoral flesh, producing a wince from him. He looked down at what was causing the pain as Michelle's team, already called by her, got to work on the pregnant patient and the two casualties in the other rig. His piercing green eyes locked on to her angry baby blues and they sized each other up.

'You almost clipped me with the ambulance door, genius. I don't know who you are, but please step aside.' She gave him a pointed look, turning away to see to her patient.

Honestly. These mansplainers, she thought. *They see a few episodes of* Grey's Anatomy *and suddenly they're all McDreamy.*

Although, truth be told, he *was* quite easy on the eye. If you liked arrogant, haughty men with delusions of grandeur. Michelle for one, did not.

The team sped off after the patients, and she went to follow.

'You don't remember me, do you?' came an amused voice from behind her.

She turned, eyeing up the man once more.

'Comobos…a year or so back?'

For a second Michelle just shook her head. Surely she'd remember having seen him before? Or would she? These days she wasn't one hundred percent sure which way was up when she thought of that tour.

Then it came. The wave of nausea, the feeling of being tied to the earth with only a flimsy string, like a helium balloon. One little snip and she would be airborne, helpless.

Oh, God, not now. Please.

Michelle felt sick. *Comobos.* That had been the start of it all—of the way she was feeling now. All the emotions that were tied up in that place, that tour, came flooding back.

Looking down at her hands, she saw that she was clasping her hands together tightly, the white gloves she held making her skin look all the paler alongside them. She took out her hand gel and coated her gloves with it, relieved when her hands were still again. Tremors were certain death to surgical careers.

'I was there. I don't remember you, though.'

She didn't elaborate, but waited for him to explain himself.

He smiled easily. 'I had to go wheels down before the end of the tour—left in a bit of a rush.'

His jaw flexed, and she saw something akin to pain flashing across his features. It was only there a moment, and then he put his smug mask back on.

'Rebecca's your close friend there, right? The nurse?'

Rebecca. Michelle swayed a little on her feet as a memory of her friend's face, twisted in panic and pain, slapped her. She practically growled at the man, hating him for ruining her first day back. She wanted to be normal; how could she do that with all this around her?

'Yes, she—' *Was.* A simple word, but Michelle couldn't spit it out. 'Rebecca's a friend.'

Then it hit her. This was him. *The* him.

'You're the doctor, aren't you? The one with the crème brûlée?'

The man smiled wolfishly.

Michelle didn't respond.

Rebecca, on that tour, had had a 'friends with benefits' relationship with some flash doctor. They had worked together before, briefly, but she hadn't really registered him at the time. Michelle and Rebecca had nicknamed him Mr Sweet Tooth after he had once managed to produce just the dessert that Rebecca had been craving since arriving in the Army camp, where such things had been almost impossible to get.

She could see Rebecca now, sitting on her cot, laughing with Michelle about her sexploits with him, and the delicious puddings he had provided. It was a nice memory, and one she was glad to remember. Even if *he* was the one to evoke it within her.

'I see my reputation precedes me,' he quipped. 'That *was* a pretty nice dessert. How is dear Becks? Wheels up again?'

Michelle shook her head and he frowned, catching her sudden change in demeanour.

She's dead.

'Something like that. Forgive me—I have a trauma centre to run.'

She turned away before he could question her further. She did have work to do, and memories, good or bad, weren't going to save any lives today.

'Sure, I'll see you around,' he called after her.

'Yep,' she said in reply.

Doubt it, bucko. Relatives' lounge for you, dude. No work for you today.

Passing Alan, who was pushing a patient in a wheelchair into the foyer of Trauma, she beckoned him closer.

'Alan, we have a family member outside—a doctor. Can you show him to the lounge please? I don't want him wandering around.'

She didn't want him about when she was trying to work; she needed to focus. She put her hands by her sides, nipping at the skin of her thighs to ground herself. She felt better here. If she could see her hand on her scrubs, feel the slight pain her fingers produced, then she was fine. She was here. Safe. Alive and intact—for the most part. Once he was gone and forgotten about, she'd be just fine.

'When you get a minute.' She smiled at Alan, grateful to see him there.

Alan nodded, but then, looking back at the doors, he stopped, his face dropping.

'Er...*that* man?' he checked.

Michelle turned to see Dr Dessert heading over to the pregnant woman. Michelle nodded, groaning. 'Let him check on his loved one—then he goes to the lounge.'

She passed a glance over at them. He was checking the monitors, asking the nurse with the patient questions. She'd let him get some peace of mind, then off he needed to go. She didn't want him hanging around. The thought of him being there thrust the past into her present. She couldn't deal with that today. She was back, and she needed to work.

Alan was looking at her gormlessly.

'Problem, Alan?' she asked.

Alan looked down at the man in the wheelchair, who shrugged back up at him. 'Sorry, pal, I'm just along for the ride.'

Alan sighed, patting the man gently on the shoulder. 'You and me both, brother.'

His meaty hand almost dwarfed the man's whole shoulder, and his dark-tinted skin looked all the deeper against the whites and yellows of the hospital gowns and blankets.

'Michelle, you need to speak to Andrew.'

Andrew Chambers was just asking his secretary to hold all calls so he could have lunch, his hands wrapped around his favourite steak and cheese sub, when the door nearly came off its hinges with a determined knock. He dropped the sandwich in shock, heading to the door, and groaned slightly when he saw who was making her presence felt.

'Michelle, you scared me! What's wrong?'

He picked up his sandwich again, taking a huge bite

as his chief of trauma stood before him, her arms folded. His secretary, Rita, came running in on her little heels.

'Sorry, Andrew. I asked her to wait till I could announce her.'

Andrew smiled through his mouthful, waving her away.

'It's fine, Rita,' Michelle replied, increasing her glare level to singe, her eyes never leaving Andrew's pale blue ones. '*He's* the one who should be apologising.'

He swallowed, wiping his mouth with a paper napkin. 'Rita, you can take your lunch now; get the secretarial pool to field my calls till you get back.'

Rita nodded, taking her leave, and Michelle closed the door behind her, throwing her scrubs-clad body into one of the chairs. She grabbed the other half of Andrew's sandwich.

'Hey! *My* lunch! Michelle—come on!'

She took a huge bite, chewing and devouring it fast. 'Not bad—bit more pickle would have been nice.'

'I hate pickles.'

'I know!' she retorted, dropping the rest of the sandwich back onto his plate. 'I hate a few things too—like coming back to find you've hired some other doctor to take my job!'

Thinking about this job had kept her going all these months since she'd returned to British soil, bringing Rebecca's body with her. After Scott had left, when she hadn't been able to get out of bed... The thought of losing it was making her react, and she couldn't help it. She felt threatened—as if the ground beneath her feet was turning to sand, shifting...

There was a gentle tap on the door, but the pair of them ignored it. Andrew laughed softly—out of awkwardness, probably. Michelle didn't see any humour.

'I had to get some help in because you kept leaving! The trustees of the hospital have ring-fenced some additional funding for Trauma and they want a figurehead. We have all the state-of-the-art machines now, and staff morale is high, but we need more. We need leadership, Michelle. You can't run a trauma centre from the back of a Chinook, as much as you *think* you can.'

The tap on the door came again, and Andrew stood up from his desk.

'You should have discussed this with me,' Michelle insisted. 'I said I would be back, and I am. We both agreed to those deployments. It's a good programme that helps me to sharpen my skills and bring back knowledge to be used here, where we have more facilities. It's a win-win— *your* words! And I did it; now I'm back. I don't need some alpha male peeing all over my territory.'

And it feels like he's brought the ghost of Rebecca with him, too. I just can't lose this job. Not yet. I just can't lose anything else. I won't be able to handle it.

'I respect you as a boss, Andrew, but this was the wrong move. I thought we were friends, truth be told. And I'm angry.'

Andrew sighed heavily. 'We *are* friends, Michelle; you're my star employee and you know it. But I need stability. Would you honestly want anything less for this place?'

She wanted to argue, but he had her there. She did want the best for St Marshall's, for her patients. She just wasn't sure how she would feel if that ultimately meant she had to step aside for someone else. Especially *that* someone else.

Andrew went to open the door as the knocking came yet again, casting her a sheepish look on his way back.

'Hello,' he said to his visitor. 'You might as well come in.'

Lo and behold, that man was there again, with the same smug grin on his face.

'The traumas are all stable, head scans all clear. The pregnant woman—Annie—should be waking up shortly. Bang to the head but no permanent damage. Could have been a lot worse.'

Michelle couldn't help but agree with that—at least in her head. She knew they'd all seen far worse happen in much less of an incident. He seemed to know his stuff— not that she'd lower her guard around him any.

'You could have told me she wasn't your loved one down there.'

'Why did you assume that she was?' he fired back easily, leaning against the wall, one foot crossed over the other.

God, he was arrogant. He was wearing an expensive suit, a crisp white shirt, and a tie with swirls of green that brought out the colour of his eyes. His macho, mocking eyes.

'I came out of that ambulance as a doctor—*you* made the assumption. I was on my way in to work when I saw the accident and stopped to help. Made sense to catch a lift with the ambulance. How long are you back for?'

'For good now, actually. No more overseas plans in the pipeline… Andrew?'

Both doctors turned to Andrew, who was back behind his desk, quietly watching the pair of them as he ate the remainder of his lunch.

'Well, Michelle, that's kind of the problem…' He sat back in his chair, motioning for them both to take a seat. 'This is Jacob Peterson, and he's one of the best trauma surgeons there is, and with you flitting off—'

'"Flitting off"?' She jumped on his words. 'Hardly, Andrew—and *you* gave me permission to deploy with the team, remember? Good publicity and all that?'

Jacob sat down, opening his legs wide and slouching languidly.

She pointed down at him. 'Please, do make yourself and your junk at home.'

Andrew choked on his sandwich a little, but Jacob Peterson just looked at her, a smile dancing across his amused face, making his muscular jaw twitch.

She turned back to Andrew. 'Andrew, just what are you saying?'

Andrew sighed, savouring the last hunk of sandwich before swallowing and addressing the pair of them.

'Like I said, this new funding will make us one of the top two trauma centres in the UK, and I am not about to lose any of it by not having effective leadership. The trustees are concerned and, frankly, I've decided to test a theory. Our new trauma centre will be publicly unveiled in less than three months. I need a crack team to be ready for the challenge, and a new Head of Trauma. You want the job?'

Jacob tutted loudly, and Michelle could feel her cheeks burn red with frustration. They both knew what was coming.

'You want me to apply for a job I already have? I appreciate that cover was needed when I was away, but I'm back now, so surely this isn't necessary?'

'Hey,' Jacob countered. 'Technically, love, the job's mine as much as it is yours.'

She wanted to go with the first response that popped into her head: *Not likely, player. Move along, job-stealer. I need this more than you will ever know.*

Scott had always said that she put the job before any-thing else. Before him.

Good job he didn't stick around to see this, she thought to herself. She was actively hating a stranger now, for dar-ing to exist in the world when so many didn't any more.

'No offence, Jacob, but I hold the position. I know the job and the staff. I'm here, ready to work. I'm sure you have other opportunities to pursue.' Her lip twitched on the word 'pursue'. She knew his usual methods of occu-pying his time.

Rebecca told me all about them.

He laughed—a soft little relaxed sound—and stuck his tongue out at her. Well, he licked his lips, but it felt as if it was aimed at her. She felt a flash of something, but brushed it away in revulsion.

Down, sweet tooth.

She looked at her boss, but he was oblivious.

'So that's it?' she demanded of Andrew. 'I go abroad for four months, to help people who really need it, and then I come back and have to fight for my job, against *him*?' She hiked a thumb over her right shoulder at her rival. 'He's probably boffed half the nurses already.'

'The nice-looking half, sure,' Jacob quipped, and there was a challenging look evident in his expression.

Michelle didn't smile, thinking of Rebecca again. *Dear, sweet, funny Rebecca.*

'I'm not worried. I like it here, actually, so I say bring it on. What do you say, Mich?'

She stood up straight, drawing herself up to her full height. She tolerated 'Mich' from people she knew and trusted, but *his* use of it sent a wave of rage charging through her body. He mirrored her actions, straighten-ing his tie. She was five ten—more when she was out of her trainers and in a pair of heels—but she still had to look up at her suave rival.

'What do I say?' she said to both men, her arms folded to keep her from flailing them about like a child in the throes of a tantrum. She'd never give them the satisfaction. She couldn't be childish about this.

So she'd left, and the place hadn't been able to run on its own. They'd needed Jacob. But now she needed her job—her normality—back. She needed him to leave so she could burrow back into her comfortable life. That was her plan, and she didn't have a back-up. No matter what he had meant or hadn't meant to Rebecca, she had to be the victor in this fight. She wasn't sure she would be able to get up again if she got knocked down this time.

'Bring it on. May the best doctor win.'

'In six weeks I'll make my decision about who gets to lead the new trauma centre as head of department,' said Andrew. 'Don't let me down; I need you both at your best.'

'Six weeks of working together...' Jacob smiled, his pearly whites flashing as they caught the light. 'How ever will you resist me, let alone win?'

Michelle looked him up and down pointedly, ignoring the frisson that his sculpted body produced in the pit of her stomach.

'I'll survive, I'm sure.'

She held out her hand, and he shook it, holding it between them. The warmth from his hand pervaded her bare skin.

'We'll see, shall we? This is going to be fun.'

'You really said that?' Nurse Gabby's mouth formed a huge 'O' as she and Michelle waited in the queue at the canteen. It was quiet, being too early in the day for the lunchtime rush. 'I swear, dermatology never gets action like trauma. What did they say?'

Michelle rolled her eyes at her friend, who was reaching over the small child in front of her to get a carton of apple juice. The little girl looked at the juice, and then tried to reach for one of her own.

'They looked a bit like you do,' Michelle quipped, mirroring Gabby's shocked face back at her.

Gabby burst into laughter.

'I don't know...it is what it is. We'll just have to see what happens.'

Turning back to the line, Michelle saw the little girl still struggling and passed her a carton of juice. The girl, dressed in white trousers and an orange flowered top, eyed her warily.

'There you go,' Michelle said, smiling at her and leaning down to meet her eyeline.

'You got any germs?' the little girl asked, her adorable little voice quiet and timid.

'No,' Michelle said, in an effort to comfort her. Pulling out her sanitising gel, she showed it to the girl. 'I use a lot of this to keep my hands clean. You want some?'

The girl didn't move, so Michelle demonstrated with her own hands, then popped the juice onto the girl's tray. She could see a woman over the little girl's shoulder, watching. Must be the mother. The child held her hand out and Michelle popped a tiny blob on her palm.

'Now rub them together,' she said, and the two of them rubbed in unison. 'Better?'

The little girl sniffed her hands and smiled. 'Yes, thank you!'

The woman came to the counter, to pay for the girl's lunch. As Michelle neared the till the little girl waved at her, before turning away and chattering to her mother. Michelle waved back.

'Cute kid,' she said, looking at the two of them laughing over their meal. 'Hope she's not sick.' It often went with the territory around here.

'She's adorable,' Gabby agreed. 'Not for me, though.'

Michelle nodded absently, looking back at the little family. *One day that will be me*, she had thought once, but that was long gone now.

'Nah.' She pulled her gaze back to her friend, handing over her badge to be scanned. 'Me neither. Besides, I already work with a couple of man-children, so I'm all set!'

The two of them were still laughing as they finished eating, and when Michelle looked back, the girl and the woman had gone.

Once Michelle had left Andrew's office and gone back to work, hiding her obvious discomfort and downright anger about the current situation, the two men were alone. The truth was, they both understood why she was angry. Jacob felt the same—though he was still in shock and hadn't found his voice as quickly as she had.

He'd been rather blindsided by the feisty woman who appeared to have taken umbrage against him the second she'd set eyes on him. It wasn't helped by the fact that he'd once bedded her friend, though he knew Rebecca wouldn't have said anything to get her friend so riled; she'd always known the score. Wheels down, they wouldn't be ringing each other.

What goes on on tour, stays on tour.

They'd been colleagues first and bedfellows second. It was company—pure and simple.

He thought Michelle didn't seem the type to use dirty tricks, but when things got closer to the wire she might not stay as frostily civil. She didn't seem the type to baulk at a bit of consenting sex between two people either, and they were all adults here. Though some were more adult than others—or it felt that way at times.

He was still feeling rather like a pimply teen who'd been left to look after a baby, but work was his sure thing nowadays. It always delivered, and it paid well. It kept him getting up every morning, even when he didn't quite know where to start with his personal life. And, as hard as trauma was some days, he knew where he stood. It was always there for him—the precision, the speed, the certainty that had to come with saving lives.

On the wards and in the operating rooms Jacob Peterson was steadfast and solid as a rock. Back home, with the boxes and the blank expressions, the silent reproaches for not being there all the time, he felt lost. Overwhelmed. He could run a trauma centre, but when it came to his own affairs he needed time. Security. This job.

'So, that went well,' Andrew said.

Jacob looked at him in confusion. *'Well?'* He raised a dark brow in his boss's direction. 'Define "well".'

Andrew wiped his mouth on his napkin. 'She loves her job, and it's not been easy for her lately...' Andrew looked across at Jacob as his words tailed off. 'It's not been an easy time for both of you, obviously, and I know coming back to work here is an adjustment compared to being out there. I just need the right person for the job. That's what will bring in the money. Investors buy *people*, Jacob, not medicine. They like a face for their money. That's all this is about.'

Jacob clenched his jaw, knowing he couldn't dispute the truth. 'It doesn't make it any easier, though, that's for sure. Are you ready for this?'

He tried to sound playful, slipping back into the cocky,

confident persona he used to give him strength when he felt just the opposite. He was half out of the door, trying to quell his panic at the thought of losing his job, when Andrew replied.

'I think I should be the one asking you that. Michelle's not going to give in easily. I did think she might be off for longer, but...'

'It's fine,' Jacob said, leaning against the door frame and looking every inch the cool, calm, and collected bachelor doctor he embodied.

He just needed to keep it together a bit longer, see this through, and then maybe—hopefully—things would work out. Both here *and* at home. Although he was keeping them separate for now—out of convenience rather than by design.

When he'd gone for this job all he'd been concerned about was landing the gig, buying the house, getting on with it and bracing for impact. Now he had to fight again, and the two worlds had to stay separate for a little bit longer than he had planned, until he was chosen to run the new trauma centre. Then he would be able to see through the fog of disgruntled but rather attractive rivals, broken promises, and terrors in the night.

'Like I said when you hired me,' he said, flashing a passing nurse a grin that made her collide with the wall. 'I want to be here, so I'll make it work.'

CHAPTER TWO

WHEN JACOB HAD SAID it was going to be fun, Michelle hadn't thought he'd meant forced fun, nor that it would start quite so soon. But now she found herself standing there in a posh dress pulled from the back of her wardrobe—her emergency little black dress that she kept dry cleaned in case she was forced to 'network'.

The very word made her shudder, but these days healthcare was a business. You had to get investors to back you, to pay for the riskier treatments and advances, to bankroll the new frontiers of medicine. In trauma, it quite often meant the difference between life and death, and Michelle hated the fact that a person's health—life, even—could be determined by the cost of medication or whether they had the right machine or tool for the job.

But it was that simple. Money talked, and tonight so would she.

She slowly walked into the huge events room at one of the top hotels in Surrey, which was hosting this fundraiser. Michelle wondered what was going to happen now that alcohol had lubricated the inhabitants of the space. Usually at these things, when the champagne started to flow people loosened up in both tongue and wallet.

She was here to pimp herself out to the elite, to showcase how sexy and cutting-edge trauma medicine was, how dynamic the staff were, and how they were able to network and save lives whilst doing all they could to be cost-effective. Michelle knew she could do all this—she just didn't relish the prospect.

Why would she when she'd been in some operating rooms a lot worse off than theirs, depleted of supplies, equipment, even light? There the safety of a modern, sterile hospital had been hundreds of miles away... When you were saving a life, watching a person fade away before you, you raced the clock—not a spreadsheet or the bottom line.

She wondered what these investors would make of frontline medicine. Would they see it as sexy? As worthy of investment? She doubted it somehow. That kind of work was half a world away. Out of sight, out of mind for many.

The lucky many, she added in her head.

She had cradled dying men who would never make the front page but who deserved to. Who deserved a lot more. Her tights bunching up under her dress tonight was something she didn't have the right to moan about.

A waitress paused beside her, her tray laden with flutes of amber liquid, and she reached for one. The waitress, ignorant of her presence, chose that moment to walk away, leaving Michelle without a drink and looking foolish.

'Can I offer you a drink?' a voice asked from over her shoulder.

Andrew Chambers was standing there, two full champagne glasses in his hands. He looked smart, in a midnight-blue suit that highlighted his tall, lean frame. She recognised the tie he wore because she'd bought two of them last Christmas: one for Andrew from the team and one for her ex, Scott.

They'd gone out for a meal once, Scott and her, and Michelle had pulled on that tie a little as they'd walked to his car. He'd dropped a soft kiss onto her lips...

That had been before her work had required a choice, and Scott had become the thing she'd left behind. He'd never understood, and when she'd got back home they'd both known it was already over.

'Not again,' he'd said, looking at her in disbelief. 'You can't be serious. Can't someone else go? You have a life here, Michelle. A life with me. Can't that be enough?'

She'd taken him out to dinner to tell him, hoping against hope that the relaxed atmosphere and the tone of the night would take the edge off her bombshell. It hadn't. And the way he'd looked at her when she'd told him she was leaving again had haunted her for a long time.

They'd barely spoken when she was on tour, and her calls had often not been picked up. He'd taken advantage of her isolation to ghost her, and she'd known he was punishing her for leaving, for choosing work over him yet again. She'd even understood it—had been able to see where he was coming from. She'd already done her bit, sure, but she hadn't been able to make Scott see that a *bit* would never be enough. There would always be battles and people to save.

All she thought about when she was home was the people she was allowing to die, but she'd never been able to articulate those fears to Scott. Not in a way he had ever come to accept.

After Rebecca, when she'd touched down on home soil, she'd needed him. She'd needed her Scott, her safe harbour. Even if he was never really going to understand what she was going through.

How could he, after all? He worked in an office all day. The calls he made were high stakes, but not life and death. He knew that he would go home every night, safe and sound. That no matter how bad his day at work had been, it would soon be six o'clock. Time to clock off and leave his problems at the door. How could he ever have understood that the woman he loved feared the door every single minute?

They'd gone through the motions of being a couple for a while, but the Scott and Michelle who had fallen in love and moved in together had been no more. Michelle had barely even been a person when she'd got back. He'd stayed for as long as he could, she guessed. That whole time felt like fog to her—a bad dream that had its dark, black roots in reality and had twisted them into something unrecognisable.

She took the flute from Andrew gratefully, drinking the lot straight down.

'Whoa, Mich—it'll be a long night, you know.'

She glared at him as she placed the empty glass back into his still outstretched hand. 'Don't remind me,' she retorted, deadpan.

He grinned a little, nodding his head towards a small crowd that was forming in one corner near the bar. 'Well, your rival is managing just fine. You should try it. Loosen up a little.'

Just as the pair of them looked at Jacob, he looked back from the crowd to them. She turned her head away, catching her reflection in the window and taking in her appearance properly for the first time.

She had her favourite heels on—the black leather ones that made her legs look longer and didn't kill her feet after an hour. They were plain, but elegant, matching her LBD. She had washed her hair, curled it, and allowed it to fall down her back and cascade over her shoulders.

When she looked back at the crowd, as Andrew started

making small talk with a person nearby, she locked eyes with Jacob and realised he had been watching her. The thought of him looking at her made her cheeks flush, and she was glad she'd made the effort to look good this evening. Whether or not Jacob had felt the same flip of the tummy as he looked at her as she had on seeing him she couldn't tell, but his face showed that he wasn't entirely indifferent.

She allowed him to look at her for a little longer before he went back to entertaining the crowd. Before she went back to watching him. He was behind the bar now, mixing drinks and sliding them down the bar towards delighted men and women who were whooping and cheering him on, shouting out cocktail orders when he pointed in their direction.

He looked good—even Michelle would concede that point, if only to herself. A beautiful disaster. He was wearing a black tuxedo, his white shirt open at the neck, his black bow tie hanging haphazardly from one of his pockets. Michelle could see a sprinkling of chest hair peeking out from his open collar, and found herself wondering whether there was a happy trail of hair further down, under the layers of his formal attire...

'Good, isn't he? Apparently he's something of a charmer. He seems very much at home being the centre of attention.' Andrew was back by her side now.

Michelle nodded dumbly, her emotions flitting from horny to annoyed to being reluctantly impressed by his antics. He had the whole room in the palm of his hand, and everyone was lapping up his words as he made cocktails even as he discussed the attributes of the new trauma centre and how it would revolutionise trauma care at St Marshall's.

'You awake?' Andrew quipped.

Michelle broke her gaze away to address her boss. 'Sorry, still a little tired, I guess. I should get in there.'

She needed to make her presence felt, so the benefactors knew they had other options beside this Tom Cruise wannabe.

She strode over, placed her clutch on the bar and flicked back her auburn hair. Jacob's eyes flashed as he watched her approach, making them look like emeralds against his thick dark lashes. Giving her a nod that looked like approval, he addressed the crowd. Ever the showman.

'Ah, ladies and gents, we have a treat for you this evening. The very talented trauma surgeon and overseas medical veteran Michelle Forbes. Say hello, Michelle, and tell us what cocktail you'd like.'

He flashed her a broad grin and she smiled right back like a big cat, showing him she had teeth too.

'Thank you, Jacob,' she said confidently, stepping forward as the crowd parted for her and walking right behind the bar.

She looked around her, smiling and greeting everyone as they watched her pass by, her dress swishing.

'Good evening, everyone. I am indeed Dr Michelle Forbes, and I thank you all for taking time out of your busy lives to come and celebrate tonight. As ever, we at St Marshall's aim to be at the forefront of trauma medicine, and our new trauma centre will be second to none.'

She placed her hands on the bar, pointing behind Jacob to a bottle of her favourite whisky.

'My favourite cocktail is pretty obvious, given my background and my favourite drink. Any guesses?'

There was a delighted murmur from the crowd, and Michelle allowed a little wry smile to play across her lips as she locked eyes with Jacob. He smiled back—a slow, languid smile that made her stomach flip. The man was so good-looking it wasn't fair. He knew how to work a crowd too.

She found herself assessing him with her eyes, up and down, slowly, deliberately, in an obvious way. She felt bold, buoyed up by the hit of champagne and the smell of challenge in the air. The delighted guests around her were giggling away, whispering to each other and shouting out cocktail names like Slippery Nipple and Harvey Wallbanger.

Jacob said nothing, just listened to the people in the crowd building themselves into an excited frenzy around them.

'Nope, no one has guessed it yet,' Michelle said after a while, and then she turned her back to the bar and lifted herself onto the polished metal surface.

The crowd booed, making her laugh. She was just scrabbling to stand without flashing her underwear when she felt a hand on her shoulder. Turning, she saw Jacob, also standing on the bar now, his hand open and out-stretched. She looked at him, trying to decide whether to take it or not, and he winked at her. Her hand felt the coolness of his skin as his fingers wrapped around hers, pulling her to her feet.

Putting his hand momentarily on her hips to steady her, he took the opportunity to lean in and whisper, 'Any clues, Doc? You look amazing, by the way.'

'Really? I think *you* look a little casual,' she said, tapping a finger against the skin exposed by his open collar. 'And you should know I never give anything away I don't want to.'

She took a slight step back, away from him, barely noticeable to anyone else but them. Jacob looked down at their feet and then back up at her, his long lashes making his green eyes look all the more alluring.

'Noted, Doctor.' He spoke in a deep rumble, his voice husky. 'The floor is yours.'

They both stared at each other, and the crowd around them was just white noise. If they had been two strangers in a bar right now would she still be staring dumbly at him? Or would she be lost in the search for that happy trail?

It took everything she had in her to turn away from him, to snap back into the moment.

'So...' she said to the revellers, who were now well into their third, fourth or fifth free drink and thoroughly enjoying the entertainment.

Her body felt as though it was tingling from Jacob's touch, his lingering look, and she had to concentrate hard on what she was meant to be saying. She knitted her fingers together in front of her, keeping them close to her chest.

'Who wants to hear about what we do?'

The crowd, delighted by the showboating doctors, erupted into excited whoops and a chorus of 'Me!'

Jacob looked across at his rival, who was now answering a question about the crash team from one of the bigwigs. She was leaning down, right in his eyeline, and Jacob could see that the man and all those around him were enthralled by her answer.

Whatever the reason for the two of them being thrown together like this, he found himself not totally hating the idea right now.

He turned back to the crowd and got to work.

A glass broke, its shards scattering like tinkling bells across the polished floor. A cheer rose, and there was a chorus of 'Wahey!' and 'Ooh!' as the last of the stragglers left.

Andrew was standing like a bouncer on the steps down to the entrance, collecting business cards and cheek-kisses from the well-oiled grateful guests.

Michelle was at the bar, legs sideways as she sat atop a fancy stool. She had a pink gin in front of her, and the smell of it reminded her of her friend Rebecca once more. The ultimate girly girl, she'd loved the stuff.

A happy memory popped into her head and she smiled as she allowed it to wash over her. The alcohol in her system was numbing her from the sharp pang of pain, and she hoped this would happen more and more, with her grief healing to a more manageable level of mourning.

She was as proactive as ever with her own mental health. At least she was in her own head. They'd offered her counselling, but she felt fine. She knew the cure: *work*. Always had been. St Marshall's was her rehab. Her home.

The staff from the hotel were all busy around her, cleaning up the debris, putting away tables and chairs, collecting glasses to be washed and polished ready for the next big event.

'Well, that went well.'

Michelle turned to see Jacob taking a seat on the stool next to hers.

'I think Andrew will be getting some calls in the morning and some nice fat cheques.'

She nodded at him, reaching forward without thinking and taking a deep glug of her drink, wincing as she remembered the taste.

'Not a gin girl, eh?'

She shook her head. 'Nope, it was given to me—a guest ordered it.'

It had been one of the reps from some big pharmaceutical company she'd never heard of, trying to get her to buy into some wonder of the modern medical world. They came to these events, invited to court the bottom line, as ever. Cheaper, more effective, safer drugs meant more profit, and more turnover for the hospital. The juggernaut of defying death rumbled on, ever threatened by cuts and the fear of private companies getting a foothold.

'You had a good night then?' she said. She raised a freshly plucked brow at him.

He grinned goofily. 'I did my job, that's all. *You* were a turn-up, though, eh? I swear, once you started talking they all held their breath. You have a knack for this, you know…no matter what happens.'

There it was. A nod to their impending career battle. He was trying to handle her.

'I have a knack for my job because it's already mine, Jacob. I did this job before you came, remember? Why do you want it, anyway? I thought you would be getting itchy feet by now, eager to be off.'

She kept her tone neutral, but it was hard not to feel a little threatened. There were other jobs, sure, but she needed *this* one. He had no ties, no commitments. Maybe he would leave after the centre opened—once he'd lost the job. Then she wouldn't have to work with him at all, having him second-guess her decisions, silently resenting her for winning.

She would miss the banter, though. It seemed they shared a sense of humour and showmanship she hadn't foreseen. Tonight she had actually had fun with him—had a glimpse of what he would be like to work with. The fact that he was a bit of an Adonis was irrelevant.

'I need a job as any person does—to have a life. And I could say the same to you about itchy feet,' he fired back, walking around to the other side of the bar and pulling out a bottle of beer from one of the glass-fronted fridges. 'You don't seem the type to just stop. No plans for any more airport departures in your near future?'

Twisting the cap off the bottle, he took a long pull, and Michelle had to look away. She didn't trust herself not to space out over his tanned neck and visible chest. She wasn't about to become one of those simpering women—although a cold shower wouldn't go amiss right now… She lost the battle with her brain and her eyes were feasting on him just as he lowered the bottle and made a satisfied 'Ahh…' sound.

'I'm not the type to stop—you're right there,' she said. 'I just choose to stay here now…for a while at least.'

She knew it would be a long while indeed, given how she had been feeling. When he'd uttered the word 'airport' it had sent a shot of icy water down her spine, making her sit up straighter and reach for her glass once more.

'We shall see what happens in six weeks, won't we?'

He nodded slowly, suddenly distracted. Reaching into his inside pocket, he pulled out his mobile phone, frowning as he read the display. He didn't reply, just closed the message.

'Problem?' she asked. 'Not on call, are you?'

He shook his head. 'Nope, not tonight. You?'

She waggled the half-full glass of liquid at him. 'Nope. Which means I get to finish this before I leave. You're not answering that?'

He took another bottle out of the fridge, coming to sit behind her, draining the first one and tossing it into the large bin one of the waiters was pulling out to deal with the recycling.

'No, I don't think I am. Not tonight. It's just a check-in text. It can wait a little longer.'

He nudged her with his elbow, his arm barely touching hers but making its presence known to her senses. She could feel the warmth of it running up her arm. She wondered whether his hands would be cold to the touch, or as warm as the rest of him.

'That other kind of work we do... I need a break. I'm guessing you do too, or else my arrival wouldn't have ruffled you so much. Am I warm?' Another pull on his beer.

Michelle could feel her defensive shields coming up around her. 'I have no plans to go back as yet.'

'I know that's the party line—you say it whenever anyone at work asks. That the truth?'

He drank slowly from his bottle, his fingernails working at the gummed paper wrapper on the side of the frosted glass.

She took another sip of her own, playing for time. 'It's *my* truth,' she said finally. 'I need to be at St Marshall's.'

He nodded slowly, still concentrating on pulling at the gummed label. A little pile of paper was growing at the side of the bottle.

'I feel a little like that myself,' he murmured. 'I guess we're stuck with each other, then.' He lifted his bottle, now nearly empty and bare of labels. 'To the next six weeks?'

She lifted her glass to meet his and they clinked in silence.

'Comobos was fun compared to tonight and some of our generous benefactors, eh? I met Mrs Pritchett; she's a character.'

Michelle laughed, seeing Jacob's face light up as she joined in with his attempt at breaking the tension. 'You think Mrs Pritchett is bad...? Her husband is worse. He tried to recruit one of the staff nurses to bed bath him last year. He asked me to come along too…to check a couple of moles in sensitive areas.'

Jacob burst into laughter and she realised how tense he'd been before, how peaceful and calm he was now. Maybe he did need to be here, the same as her. A safe harbour in a stormy sea. Could she get on with him for the next six weeks? She still wasn't sure. He was a threat. Without her job, she'd have nothing to steady her.

'Mole-checking is small fry compared to what Mrs Pritchett was suggesting in my ear. I thought she was going to try and drag me off.'

He made a motion as though he was being dragged away, his muscular arms gripping the bar in faux panic.

Michelle played along, grabbing his hands tight in hers. 'Mrs Pritchett, let him go!' she called out teasingly, laughing her head off as he grabbed her and pulled them both off their stools.

He turned, his hands in hers, changing his grip till he was holding both her hands in between them.

'I've got you,' he said, the laughter dying away as he looked upon her once again. 'I won't let the Pritchetts bring you down.'

He took a step closer and she followed suit. Or her feet did. They didn't even ask her what she wanted them to do—they just gravitated towards him. They stood centimetres apart, arms linked together, laughing. She felt him run his thumb along hers, just once, and resisted the urge to move her fingers, to touch and explore more of him.

'So…' she said, trying to break the silence, to will her body out of this numb stupor.

'So…' he echoed, moving closer again, his body starting to coil around hers as he moved to bridge the gap. 'What now, Michelle? What's the next move?'

As he leaned forward she could see a napkin hanging

out of his pocket, curls of writing on it, words written in lipstick. A number, Written in a woman's hand.

She felt herself bristle at the thought and she clenched her jaw, gently removing her hands from his and turning back to the bar. She needed to be one person again—away from him. Her body felt as if it had been magnetised by his, as if the strength of the pull was increasing the closer she got. She couldn't think straight when he was so up close and personal.

Draining the rest of her drink so fast the ice slammed against her front teeth, and then turning on her heel, she yanked the napkin out of his pocket and laid it on the bar. The ring of moisture left by her glass immediately soaked into the paper, making 'Maria' and her number look like finger-painting, not the work of a woman trying to bag a dashing doctor at a swanky booze-filled do.

'My next move is home, to a nice bubble bath and a set of clean sheets. I'm sure you can entertain yourself.'

That was too close, too stupid. You can't get close to him, Michelle, you're not ready. And him? He's not what you need. Get moving, medic. On your feet, soldier.

'Hey,' he shouted after her. 'What's with the attitude?'

She didn't answer him, just kept walking towards the door. She wanted to go home and sleep.

'No attitude—just an aversion to walking horn dog egos and a need for some shut-eye. See you at zero seven hundred hours. Give Maria my regards.'

She heard him chuckle behind her, and cursed herself for feeling secretly thrilled at the sound.

'Michelle?' he called, causing her to almost stumble on her heels.

What *was* it with that man? Why did he make her feel like a newborn giraffe, all clumsy long limbs? She'd lived through bombs, helped people survive. But the thought of a booty call…? It was another sweaty palm moment she couldn't process in her fragile state.

The feel of him had stirred things within her, but she hadn't got where she was by mixing business with pleasure. She needed to keep her head clear, and she wasn't about to be a conquest on someone's trophy wall. Especially not his. Rebecca was on that wall, and she couldn't—wouldn't, shouldn't—forget that.

'Yeah?' she replied, only half turning to look at him over her shoulder.

'Blood and Sand,' he stated, with no hint of a smirk or a simper. 'That's your favourite cocktail. Right?'

She didn't answer. She let the soft swish of the closing doors do that for her.

Damn. The man had her pegged better than she'd thought. Blood and Sand *was* her favourite cocktail, bar none. Just her luck to find a man who ticked so many boxes, but stood in the way of everything she wanted and needed.

If Scott were a fly on the wall, he would consider it karma. He'd said the same to her so many times.

The doors swished closed, taking Michelle and her answer with it, but he'd seen the way her shoulders had risen when he'd spoken of her favourite drink. He'd got it right—he knew it. He knew *her*. Or he felt as though he did. Which was weird, given the short amount of time they'd spent together.

Stop it, Jacob. Think about the job.

Going back behind the bar, he uncapped another bottle of beer and reached for his phone. Ebony had called him now—at this time. What was going on at home? He would have thought she'd be in bed. He was seeing her in a few short hours, and he was already dreading the inquisition that he knew was coming.

Every time he walked into the place he felt as if he had to account for his whereabouts. It was nice to feel wanted, but this was a little too close for comfort. He didn't enjoy the look of distrust in her eyes, though it was one he guessed he'd earned on occasion. People always said that guilt went with the territory, but this wasn't quite what he'd expected to feel.

He felt drained at the thought, and he pushed his phone into his pocket without calling back. It wouldn't do any good at this time anyway.

He thought of how close he had just been to Michelle, the way she'd allowed him to take her hands, the little gasp she'd made in the back of her throat when he'd brushed his body against hers. She was a puzzle to him, and yet he wanted to know each individual piece, each smooth edge, every jagged facet.

He felt that some of the pieces might fit him too—might solve his puzzle. They were the same in many ways, and it was this that confused him. Did she see through him? Through the bravado? He'd felt they'd begun to bond until she'd seen the phone number in his pocket.

He looked at the wet napkin on the bar. The number was barely visible. He could call her right now—Maria—and have company for the night. For a few nights. A body to hold…someone to wake up to. Usually that was enough, but things were different now. He had to grow up. He had to…

'You about done here?' The manager appeared at his side. 'We're just closing up. Did you get any good leads?'

Jacob stood up, patting the man on the shoulder. 'I did, thanks—plenty of stuff I'm keen to follow up on.'

The manager smiled and said his goodbyes.

As Jacob left the venue, heading for his waiting taxi, his phone buzzed again. A text this time. Another faceless woman from his contacts, with an empty bed and a late-night itch that needed to be scratched.

He opened the reply screen, but after a beat he put the phone back into his pocket and slid onto the black leather seat of the taxi. When asked, he gave the driver his home address.

'Good night?' the affable driver asked. 'Looks like it was a big event.'

A flash of memory popped into his head, making him smile. Michelle, walking the length of the bar, explaining in great and gruesome detail the work they had done that day, detailing their slick operations and their Hail Mary moments of trauma, the audience watching her intently, the venue lit up by her energy.

'It was, yes—we did well. I'm ready for home now, though.'

The driver caught his eye in the rearview mirror. 'Hot date?' he asked, his smile teetering on the precipice of a leer and evident even in the dim glow of the streetlights.

'Something like that,' he said, thinking of Ebony, who should be fast asleep in bed, not waiting for him to come home. 'My daughter needs a bedtime kiss from her old pops.'

The driver grinned, the leer gone without a trace. He pointed to his console, where a photo of an attractive woman and two small blonde-haired girls sat.

'I can't fault you,' he said, his eyes back on the road. 'Nothing like having a daughter to warm your heart. My wife and I are so happy. You married?'

Jacob looked out of the window to where a couple were sitting on a bench in the street, utterly wrapped up in each other, laughing and joking. It made Jacob's fists curl.

'No, I was engaged once. My daughter's mother. It didn't work out and she left. The job, I guess. I work a lot.'

The driver flashed him a look of solidarity. 'I get you there, pal. The hours I work, our lass always has her hands full. I'm sorry though, mate, must be tough.'

Jacob didn't answer. Resting his head on the back of the seat, he had already drifted off to sleep.

CHAPTER THREE

'THIS IS GOING TO HURT.' Michelle gave her patient, a biker with more tattoos than visible skin, an encouraging nod. 'On three, okay?'

She moved closer, setting her feet hard on the floor and holding his dislocated shoulder in position as best she could, whilst avoiding causing the patient further pain by touching his broken ribs. Thank the Lord of Bikers for thick leathers and helmets. One thing that bikers did well was to protect themselves from the hard surface of the road.

She caught a whiff of blood and smoke and inhaled deep. What *was* it about her that liked the smell of danger in the air? Scott had used to say she had gasoline in her veins. But that had been back when he'd thought it cute, and not a relationship deal-breaker.

'One…'

She felt more alive today—being back here, being busy. Her shifts here grounded her, made her forget. Made her feel her usual strong self. She was starting to feel…

'Two…'

Crack!

'And three—there we go.'

She helped a nurse to strap up his shoulder, and the

relief on the burly biker's face on top of her own assessment told her that the bone was back in the socket. The closed reduction procedure had been effective.

'Good. But no riding for a while, okay? I'll leave you with the nurse, who will get you X-rayed again and then settled on the ward.'

She was just heading to the door when it opened in front of her. She was smacked square in the face by strong male cologne. Woodsy. Familiar.

That open collar...

'What've we got?' Jacob asked, looking straight past her to the patient.

She could feel her endorphins decrease just from his presence. Images of last night at the bar kept flicking through her head. She'd dreamt of him last night—of him closing the gap between them further, of his lips... Which would probably still have been warm from the touch of Maria, the napkin chick. Iced water couldn't have stopped *that* train of thought any quicker.

Snap out of it, Michelle. Work, remember? Routine, normality. That's how this works now. He is the obstacle and you need to get around him, not climb him...

'*I* was here on time,' she said pointedly, 'and *I* had this patient, who came off his motorbike. Bruising, mild concussion, four broken ribs, dislocated shoulder. Just reset.' She unpinched her face and turned back towards the patient. 'That sound about right, Mr...er...?' She glanced down at her notes again. 'Mr Throttle...'

'Lunch,' Jacob said.

'What?' Michelle asked, looking nervously back at him.

'Lunch. I forgot my lunchbox at home. Had to go back.'

'Right,' Michelle said, pulling a face that made Jacob laugh.

The biker smiled at his doctor as she left.

Jacob still loitered in the doorway.

'Dr Peterson,' Michelle said over her shoulder by way of dismissal, as she left the examination room. She headed to the nurses' station to update the biker's chart and move on to the next patient.

It was a foggy day, which had thrown the inhabitants of Surrey into confused chaos, and accidents were trickling into the trauma centre at a steady rate. Michelle and the staff knew that this would change—for better or for worse. If the fog lifted, the casualties would become minimal. If it worsened, it would bring more confusion and chaos with it. They could feel the crackle of nervous tension and adrenaline as it swirled and filled the air around them.

'Dr Forbes,' said Jacob in a faux professional voice from behind her in the corridor.

She kept walking—fast.

'A moment, please?'

'Are you looking for something in particular?'

Jacob fell into step beside her easily, and she couldn't help but be amused by the squeak of his expensive leather shoes as he strode along, matching her step for step. He looked so relaxed...carefree. If she could have plucked him out of the corridor and put him into a park his easy gait would have fitted in well.

She had never been one for taking dainty little lady steps, even as a teen. She always had somewhere to be and a sense of urgency to get there. Just like now. But now, instead to trying to get somewhere, she was finding herself strolling too...

'Not really—just wondering how you're settling in. I think you'll probably have seen by now that I've made a few changes. I *did* want to tell you last night, Cinderella.'

Was that a clumsy attempt to make conversation, or

was he nervous about the alterations he had made while she'd been overseas? The Cinderella barb reminded her of the napkin. She'd always hated the name Maria. Sounded too Von Trapp to her. Too perky.

'The new coffee in the doctors' lounge is terrible.' She frowned at him, pulling a face as they passed the lounge. 'That change wasn't needed or wanted. What else? The new colour-coded filing system? Anyone can stick a few coloured dots around, Jacob. My niece could have done a better job, even before her nap, and she's two.'

The truth was, the changes he'd made were minor, but irritatingly effective.

'Your niece? No kids of your own, then?'

She stopped and glanced at him. He stopped too, a fraction of an inch too close, and held up his hands in surrender.

'Sorry, I know. Inappropriate and personal. I was just asking because we have to work together and I want to find out more about you.'

His stance had changed; his shoulders were hunched over. They were both stationary in the corridor now, facing each other, hands on hips. People were walking around them, the odd rubbernecker showing interest in the intriguing pair.

'Andrew speaks highly of you, and you ran this department for a long time. I just thought that us getting along might be easier than all-out war.'

'Yes, I *did* run this department—and look what thanks I got: I was replaced by an ape.'

She jabbed her finger at him half-heartedly, and his lips twitched in amusement.

'A usurper.'

He pursed his lips and she puffed air out of her own.

'Listen, it's not you, okay? I wasn't expecting this

when I got home. I just wanted to get back to work. I have a niece who thinks her aunt is pretty cool. No kids yet—the job, I guess. Never the right time, is it? Don't exactly fit around our hours, do they?'

He nodded, a look of understanding crossing his rugged features. His mouth opened, but he hesitated.

He gets it, she thought to herself. *He's been there.*

She pushed the thought away and shrugged at him. 'Better get on.'

He nodded once, closing his mouth, and then stepped to one side as though to let her pass.

'I'll let you go,' he said softly. 'When you have time, I would like to talk, though.'

She dipped her head noncommittally and headed off down the corridor.

Isaac, one of her best nurses, was just finishing up a call when she got to the station and rested her head on the desk.

'Bad morning with Mr Man Candy?' he asked, nodding his perfectly coiffed hair in the direction of Jacob as he headed the other way. Probably to flash his perfect teeth at some unsuspecting female.

'Bad week in general. What do you make of him and Andrew? He's pitted us against each other for the Head of Trauma job.'

Isaac pulled a sympathetic face. 'You know Andrew— it's all for show. He's just mad that you went on tour again and made his job harder. He'll get over it. He's having a tantrum because he can't have his favourite toy all to himself. This hospital is his project; he likes all the pieces to stay where he puts them.' Isaac smiled and continued. 'Jacob's not bad, really. Bluster mainly, and a dash of arrogance, but his practice is sound. He's a good doctor,

Michelle. Just give him a chance, eh? Not everything is as it seems.'

'I will—and I know.'

She opened her mouth to ask what else Isaac knew about him but her beeper sounded.

'Trauma incoming!' she bellowed, everything else cast aside as she ran to receive the ambulance.

She ran the length of the corridor, brushing arms with a solid body as she rounded the corner, her trainers squeaking on the polished floors.

'Time to talk yet?' Jacob quipped, flashing her a wink as he ran alongside her.

The man looked as if he was out for a jog around the block on a lazy Sunday. What had he been doing? Hiding around the corner?

'Where did you come from?'

'I was almost at the canteen doors when I heard the call. What can I say? Instinct took over.'

He zoomed ahead easily, leaving Michelle's side before she could answer back. She picked up her own pace, feeling a burst of adrenaline running through her. She wanted to whoop out loud, but she stopped herself. She wasn't in the desert now.

A porter transporting a wheelchair patient loomed in front of her as she ran, cutting her path off and causing her to swerve in the corridor before catching up with Dr Show-Off and snapping at his heels. They both bounced into the ambulance bay at once, but Michelle managed to get a sly dig of her elbow into his ribs, causing him to crumple theatrically and making her want to laugh.

'What have we got?' they both barked, panting into the face of the stunned ambulance driver as he opened the rig's doors.

'Who's running this?' he countered, looking from Michelle to Jacob and back again.

'I am,' they said in unison.

Michelle felt like verbally slapping down the man standing next to her, showing him *she* still had authority here, but instead she nodded. 'Fine, he's the lead on this one. Run it.'

'Lucas Masterson, aged twelve. Was retrieving a ball from a neighbour's shed roof when he slipped down onto some steel railings. Impaled through the right arm. the steel was dealt with on the scene by fire and rescue, and he was cut down as best they could with the jaws. He's been given ten milligrams of morphine and has remained conscious throughout. Parents were at work, but they're on the way.'

'Thanks.'

Jacob took the lead instantly, walking backwards alongside the gurney as it was gently pushed into the trauma centre.

'Hey, Lucas, I'm Dr Peterson, but you can call me Jacob—or Jake for short. Dr Forbes, here, calls me "idiot" sometimes, so I'll answer to pretty much anything.'

Lucas gave a little smile in response at that, and Michelle felt her own lips curling in something akin to amusement.

'Football Sunday not going well, eh?' Jacob asked. 'What position do you play?'

Lucas, looking pale and drawn, turned to look at Jacob.

'I'm a goalie,' he said proudly. 'I play for the Jets. We won this morning. I saved a penalty.'

Jacob held up a hand to Lucas's left side and the boy high-fived it.

'Brilliant—we could use you on my team. We suck at the moment.' He made a face at Michelle, who was following at the other side. 'Brighton... Lost my shirt last weekend.'

'Lost your shirt?' Lucas echoed, looking confused. Jacob laughed.

'Yep, I threw it in the bin after the game.'

Lucas gave a laugh too—a little croaky and muted, but there. 'My dad would think that's well funny. We love Spurs.'

In the bay now, Jacob and Michelle pulled one cot-side down each and got to work.

'Spurs!' Jacob squeaked. 'Dr Forbes, we have a Spurs fan here. Watch him closely.'

Lucas giggled, and Michelle's heart clenched. Lucas's colour was returning a little, and she couldn't help but think that it wasn't just down to the pain relief kicking in. Jacob was a natural with the kid. Maybe he had a niece or two of his own tucked away somewhere.

Lucas winced as he tried to move. 'It hurts, Jacob.'

He had gone from brave boy to scared little child in an instant. Michelle found herself wishing his parents were here. Jacob's eyes kept flicking to the entrance, so perhaps she wasn't the only one.

'Right, here's the *not* nice bit,' he said, scrunching his nose up to show he wasn't a fan of what he was about to say. 'Lucas, this piece of railing that went and stuck itself in your arm needs to come out, and it probably has germs on it. Do you understand?'

Lucas nodded warily. 'Will you wait for Mum and Dad to come?'

Jacob nodded without hesitation. 'Yes, of course. We need them to sign some forms anyway, but we can give you a tetanus shot now. That will make sure that any rubbish from the railing won't get into your body. Then, when your parents say it's okay, we will give you some medicine to make you go to sleep, and when you wake up it will be gone and your arm will be all stitched up. Isn't that right, Dr Forbes?'

Michelle found herself nodding, watching the nervous patient relax before her eyes. Jacob had the knack, for sure. This side of him—this paternal side—was a revelation to her. Especially after his hot hands on her hips the night before and his napkin-stuffed pocket. What was in there now? Lollipops and stickers? And why, just when she thought she had a read on the guy, did he do a one-eighty in the other direction? Michelle felt as if her head was spinning.

Despite them being in a bay, she could tell the department was busy today. A nurse pulled the curtains around them, but seconds later they was swept back again by a worried-looking redhead.

'Lucas!'

A woman who had the same eyes as the boy in the bed took one look at her son and went white, but she didn't stop moving. She went straight to his good side, taking his hand and kissing him over and over on his left cheek. He grimaced a bit, pulling back but smiling at the same time. A man followed soon after, his trouser pockets stuffed with screwdrivers and other tools. He looked as white as the woman.

'Jesus, Lucas!' he exclaimed, his voice cracking just a little. 'You okay, buddy?' He went to stand behind the woman, both of them now cradling their son.

'I'm okay. It hurts, but Jacob is going to give me a shot and then fix my arm.'

His mum gave a little relieved sob and hugged him awkwardly to her, careful to avoid his injury. She didn't look at it, Michelle noticed, and nor did the dad. They focused on their son—on his needs, his wellbeing. They didn't talk about blame, or what might have happened. They just sat there, chatting to their son, taking every opportunity they could to kiss him, to touch him. They were looking at him as though he might disappear in front of them.

'Michelle?'

'Yeah?' She snapped back into the room.

Jacob narrowed his eyes, his brows knitted together. 'Sorry, Dr Forbes, I just asked if you might be available to assist me in the OR today?'

He flicked his eyes across to the parents, who were both looking at her hopefully. She turned to face them, hand outstretched. Luckily there was no sign of the shaking today. She could handle this in her sleep.

'Of course—happy to help. Do you want to come to the nurses' station with me, and I'll ask one of the team to go through the forms for you? We need to get Lucas into pre-op shortly—he's in good hands.'

The woman took her hand and shook it hard, gripping it tight while she thanked her breathlessly.

Thirty minutes later Jacob was standing in the scrub room when Michelle walked in, ready for surgery in her blue scrubs.

'Hi,' he said, scrubbing his forearms in a relaxed but determined way.

She was glad the lather hid his corded forearms. He was becoming more and more of a distraction to her, something she yearned to look at for some reason, like a painting—though as she got ever closer her keen eyes couldn't find a flaw, or a brush stroke that didn't quite look right. She needed something—some imperfection that would help her to reject him, to get him out of her head. Her life. Her job.

'You okay working with me?' he asked.

'I'm fine. I said you could run point. I play well in a team, Jacob. I'll survive an operation with you, I'm sure.'

'Well, you've got through worse, right?' His eyes narrowed as he looked across at her, both their hands moving under the water now, preparing. 'I heard about Comobos after my tour ended. Africa was a bad one, but you're still here in one piece.'

Michelle's hands stopped, stilled. Just for a fraction of a second she was lost, and then she was back. Back in control, scrubbing hard around her thumbs, allowing herself to pinch and nip her skin as she went. Every tiny tweak of pain helped focus her mind, helped keep her head in the room.

'What did you hear, exactly?'

Has he been digging around? He doesn't know about Rebecca, or he wouldn't have mentioned her in such a flippant way.

She knew that about him now. He wasn't cruel.

He looked away, focusing on his task before speaking in a low tone. 'I heard about what happened. I know you were lucky to make it out of there.'

He was good at understatement, though. 'Lucky' didn't even come into it. Some days she still felt as if she was there and couldn't get out. Maybe she never would—not really. Maybe part of her would never escape the heat and death of that day. But she found herself grateful to be here, and that centred her even more.

She was home and about to operate. Happy days.

'Lucky isn't how I would describe it.'

'I know, but what word would?'

She almost snapped at him, but she knew he spoke the

truth. 'You planning on going back?' she asked, finding that she desperately cared what his answer was.

Ready now, they hit the button on the wall and walked into the operating room, where a couple of ready and waiting scrub nurses started to glove and gown them up. They worked in silence till they were standing at the side of Lucas's anaesthetised body, where his arm was uncovered and ready to be operated on.

'Well?' she asked impatiently. 'Are you?'

His surgical mask hid his face now, but his eyes were those same glittering emeralds she couldn't stop staring into. They locked onto hers, and she saw his brow crease.

'Are you worrying about me, Doctor? I have to say, I quite like it...'

They were both working on the arm now, slowly pulling the piece of metal out of the flesh, bit by bit, repairing the arm as they went. If they yanked it out all at once they risked massive bleeding, and Lucas needed his arm. He was a keen goalie, a young boy on the cusp of life. He would need two good arms to go and embrace all the world had to offer.

'Not worried, per se, more curious,' she said. 'Bleeder!'

The word had barely left her lips and Jacob was there, stitching the bleeder up and saving the blood flow to the vein.

'Got it—thanks. My touring days are done now, so don't worry. Whatever happens, you won't be sending me off to the front line.'

His eyes pierced through her. She felt exposed, as though she was the one on the table, open and vulnerable.

'What about you?' he asked.

She had been reaching for a clamp on the instrument tray but she stopped dead. It felt cold in her hands as the nurse passed it to her. She looked around her, just for a second, and knew what her answer was. But to him she gave nothing away, and she was glad she could hide her face behind her mask.

Jacob's hands had never stopped moving. 'We have another bleeder, Doctor. I can't take the rest of the metal out without clamping it off first. You got it? Clamp in three, two...'

She assessed the bleeder and applied the clamp. 'One,' she finished for him. 'Bleeder clamped. Once the railing is out, I'll repair it with a stitch.'

Jacob's eyes flashed at her, the green made all the more vibrant by the lights around them. She couldn't be sure, but she thought he was smiling behind that mask. She pouted behind hers, and they each put a hand on the piece of metal. Their fingers brushed against each other's as they counted to three once more.

After that, they were like two parts of the same machine. They worked in unison, their shorthand and skills at speed and under pressure driving them on. He was good—every bit as good as she was, even. He anticipated her moves as she did his; his hands felt like extensions of her own.

'You see this?'

She heard one of the scrub nurses whispering to the other.

'Have they worked together before?'

The other shook her head, her eyebrows high in surprise, and Michelle looked to see if Jacob had heard. He gave her a sexy raised brow.

Yep, he heard. Geez.

'Nope, never before. Weird, eh?'

Jacob made an odd noise from his throat—a laugh disguised as a cough. She tried to give him her best angry stare, but that just made him 'cough' even louder.

'Ah, Lucas,' he said to the boy on the table. 'We are having a day, aren't we?' His eyes crinkling at the corners, he grinned unmistakably at all the ladies in the room.

Ever the charmer, she thought to herself.

'Come on—let's get this young man back defending that net.'

'The answer's no,' she said softly, after some more time had passed and they had finished closing him up.

Blood flow was looking good, the arm had pinkened up already, and all his muscles and reflexes were intact. Lucas was a lucky boy.

'No more tours for me either.'

She thought about mentioning Becks, but the thought of speaking about her to him just felt too strange. It reminded her of his past, with Becks and probably countless other women. It confused her already jumbled feelings about him. She couldn't bring those worlds together—not yet. It was all right for him—his world was one big party.

She could feel the adrenaline and excitement of the operation ebb away, leaving her feeling shaky, worn out.

'Your choice, or the therapist's?' he asked.

They were alone now. The scrub nurses had gone off to get more ORs ready, and Lucas was being wheeled into Recovery. They were back in the scrub room, at the sinks.

'I didn't have therapy. Didn't need it.'

Jacob gave her a sideways glance that lasted far longer than was comfortable.

'You're joking, right? Nothing? Not even here? Did Andrew sign off on that?'

Andrew doesn't know the half of it.

'Of course he did. It was a tour that ended badly— that's it. It's happened before and will happen again. I'm back, safe and well.'

Well, I'm pretty sure I'm taped together well enough. I get by. My work is still the same.

She kept her hands out of sight as best she could, till the shaking had stopped. As soon as they had finished operating, it had come back. The sick, shaky feeling of being out of control.

She clenched her hands and forced herself to pull herself together once more. When she unclenched, her hands were as steady as a rock.

What? Jacob couldn't believe his ears. Andrew had let her come back to work, fight for her own job, without not checking that her head was even in the game.

He'd heard about Comobos, all right—everyone had. The details were sketchy in places, but he knew it had been bad. They'd lost people—a lot of people. Michelle had made it home, sure, but how much of her had actually boarded that plane?

He already knew his previous tour had been his last. Even without his home situation changing he would have been done anyway. The call from home had just speeded things up. There were only so many times you could cheat death before the rules changed and it took you anyway.

He found himself at Michelle's side before he even knew what he was doing. His hands newly clean, he went to touch her shoulder, but stopped himself.

'Michelle, I saw you in there…in the OR. With the clamp. I *see* you. And I know what you're going through.'

'So?' She looked at him blankly. 'You've been on tours; you know how bad it is. I'm fine. I'm working, eating, sleeping—the lot. The clamp was a one-off.' Holding out her hands to demonstrate, she looked everywhere but at him. 'Steady.'

'No nightmares? No sign of anything bad?' He was in

full doctor mode now, peering at her closely as though
he wanted to strip her down and do a full examination.

'No, Dr Peterson, no scary monsters under my bed.
We help the people who kill the monsters, remember?'

She'd switched it off, he realised. Like a light going
out. She'd turned off her humanity—turned herself into
a walking, talking, functional doctor-bot.

It was a setting he'd defaulted to a lot over the years,
till he hadn't known how to function any more. Till
Ebony had come into his life, smashing it apart. Even
then, with a daughter at home, he'd still done the tours,
the hard stuff. And then Ebony had become the hard
stuff, and then he'd stopped. For her. For them both, he
realised now.

'I was supposed to join that tour not long after you
went out there. I didn't know who had gone—just that
they wanted extra bodies.'

She snorted darkly, and he winced at his choice of
words.

'The point is, Michelle, I didn't go. I wasn't there that
day, so I will never fully understand.' He touched her
shoulder now, turning her towards him as she finished
drying her hands. 'I do, however, have experience of a
lot of other bad days, and I know how it feels to come
home and feel guilty because others didn't. I get it. But
I didn't get through it alone.'

It was on the tip of his tongue to tell her about his
counselling, about the fact that his daughter had saved
him just by needing him home. He wanted to tell her
about his daughter. About how his heart, beaten and bat-
tered in his chest, could hear Michelle's broken heart
calling to him like a voice in the dark. How confused he
was now that she was here.

She might take his job, affect his life—*their* lives—

and he couldn't allow that. How could he make her see that he had pain too? Pain that ran like a ribbon through him, as it did her?

He couldn't tell her about his child.

She stepped a tiny bit closer, leaning infinitesimally towards him. He held his breath and waited for her to make a move.

If she kisses me I won't be able to stop myself from grabbing her and kissing her back. I need to.

'Jacob, I'm fine.'

She patted his cheek with an open hand, like a grandmother would. His ego and his hopes deflated like a balloon.

'Better get on. Give my love to Lucas.'

She walked by him, through the doors with a swish. He could still feel her touch on his cheek, and he rubbed at the area. He didn't know exactly what her deal was, but he *did* know a few things.

One, he wanted her so badly his skin prickled when her name was mentioned. Two, she wasn't fine but she was trying to be. And three, when it came to the crunch—her or the job,—he didn't have a clue which one he would fight for and which one he could bear to live without.

CHAPTER FOUR

MICHELLE STAYED INFORMED on the Lucas case from afar for a little while, getting the nursing staff to provide her with discreet updates on Jacob and his work.

The whole day had spiralled into a day of seeing Jacob's face everywhere and never having a minute to herself. Every minute meant a new case, a new patient, a new decision. The poor nurses didn't know where to put themselves as the day wore on and the workload became tougher.

Jacob was every bit a machine, as she was, and between them they managed all the work together, challenging each other, coming up with surgical plans, the shorthand between them soon becoming familiar to each other.

Just as they had in the OR, they'd developed a pattern of knowing each other's moves. Several times, the two of them had actively disagreed, warring with each other on points of medicine and treatment, but they always to put the patients first.

It was eight p.m. now, and Michelle could feel every second of her twelve-hour shift taking its toll on her still healing body. She did the hand-over, from which Jacob was conveniently missing for the first millisecond all day. Then she waved Isaac and the rest of the outgoing team off, pressing a bunch of banknotes into Isaac's hand as he left.

'For today. Buy yourselves a drink each—at least. Tell Bill I said hello, and to put Lucas on the board for tonight.'

Bill ran The Pub on the Corner—a local public house with a genius name. It *was* on the corner, and only a couple of streets away from St Marshall's, so it was often filled with hospital staff having a pint to take the edge off, or a few shots to celebrate saving a patient—pulling off the cheating of death for another broken and now mending body.

The board on the back wall was for the good ones. A photo or just a name was all that was needed—a chicken scratch on the wall to mark them. The ones the doctors and nurses wanted to remember.

Seeing Lucas settled in bed tonight, his parents watching over him as he slept, was a *good* memory. One to add to the board for sure. He would be a goalie again, with full hand and arm function, and he'd have a piece of metal and an impressive scar to show his teammates.

The fact that it was the first time she had operated with Jacob had nothing to do with her happiness. It was purely about the save.

Isaac went to give her the money back, protesting that there was no need, but she was steadfast in her decision. She closed her hands around his and pressed firmly.

'Don't forget Lucas,' she said, and pushed a photograph of Lucas saving a goal into his hand. His mother had had it in her purse, and had been only too happy to give it to the doctors who had saved her son's arm.

Michelle wanted to promise Isaac and the others that tomorrow would be better, that *she* would be better, but she kept quiet. She knew she'd not been at her best today.

She'd been being standoffish with everyone, keeping them at a good arm's length. But she couldn't risk them asking questions she didn't want to answer or noticing how changed she was in herself.

Her teeth set. Scott had noticed—had seen how different the woman in his life had become, how angry and shut off. He'd left, and she didn't want that again. Her colleagues wouldn't understand, so she kept it hidden.

'No excuses—I insist. You all earned it.'

She leaned in closer, touching Isaac's arm in gratitude. She appreciated the loyalty of her close friend, both professionally and personally.

'Well, if you *insist*, boss, I think I can twist a few arms into a bevvy or two.'

She wished him a good night, and he headed to the hospital doors to meet the rest of the tired workers. They all whooped and cheered when he fanned himself theatrically with the wad of notes.

'Drinks are on her!'

He pointed over his shoulder at Michelle, and she plastered a fake smile on her face and raised a hand in their direction. Feeling a little less guilty for her behaviour, she signed off the last few remaining charts and headed to the on-call room. She was on beeper rota for tonight, which was what they called 'on call' around here.

'On call' didn't really translate to working in a battle zone. There was no real rest there; you were always ready for the call, primed for action at a moment's notice. She didn't even change into nightwear at home any more—if she went home. She felt less anxious if she went to sleep ready to jump up in a split second.

After today, she couldn't summon the energy to go back to her empty flat just to stare at the boxes of trinkets and the pictures she hadn't got around to hanging up. Those empty walls mocked her whenever she walked in the door.

Isaac and some of the others had offered to help her move in all those months ago, when she and Scott had started to divide their lives, but she'd refused. Scott had had a flat-share organised already, with his brother, and she had thought that a new flat—a place that only she had lived in—would help her to nest.

But that hadn't quite happened either. She was still waiting to find out where she belonged. Still longing for somewhere to call home, a sanctuary from the days of battling death and disease.

She felt wretched, with a bone-deep lethargy that made her muscles ache and her head swim. She just wanted to get her head down for a while, switch off the world and rest.

'I know, darling, I know. It's not for ever, though, remember? I just need to prove myself in my new job, then we'll have more time. Please, just try. For me...'

Jacob's voice was coming from the on-call room, where the door stood slightly ajar. He sounded different. Softer. Less confident.

'I know, but I'll see you tomorrow. I promise. I love you.'

Michelle balked at his words. This guy had managed to fall in *love*? Everything she had seen and heard of him so far ran contrary to this little love chat. Including his smouldering looks and the way his fingers twitched when she was nearby—as though he couldn't help himself and *had* to touch her. *Especially* his smouldering looks, she thought, as a flash of the green beauty of his eyes behind a surgical mask swam into her memory.

She found herself wondering who was at the other

end of the line, being consoled by him now. What sort of person adored a man like this?

A person like me.

She didn't hear anything else, so she opened the door and closed it behind her, feigning surprise at seeing him standing there. His mobile phone was still in his lowered hand.

'Oh, sorry. I—'

'It's fine,' he replied quickly, shrugging her off and turning to one of the beds.

The room was essentially a small square, with a single bed at the left and right of the space, against the walls and facing the door. There was a bathroom off to the right. In the middle, on the far wall, there was a large window, showing the city outside the hospital lit up by streetlights and traffic. They twinkled in the night and she watched them absently.

'I was going to sleep anyway,' he said. He put his phone on charge, taking off his doctor's coat and his shirt before she could make sense of what her tired eyes were feasting on. He wore a white vest underneath. Very John McClane.

'You're staying here?' she asked, seeing her hopes for a few hours of peaceful sleep being dashed before her. Not very *yippee-ki-yay* of him. 'I'm on call, so there's no need for both of us to be here. I'm taking one for the team.'

Plus, it sounds like you have someone to get home to.

She took off her own doctor's coat and laid it on the bottom of the bed, shucking her trainers off and sticking them under the frame.

He didn't make a move, and she looked up at him pointedly. 'You've not moved.'

He looked down at her, before sitting down on the

other bed and sliding off his posh squeakers. 'You don't need to take one for the team. I kind of thought we *were* the team, after Lucas today. I thought I was on the rota, so I planned to be here. You can go, if you like—get some rest, acclimatise. Word is you have a new pad to settle into. Shouldn't you be shopping for knick-knacks or fluffy cushions or something?'

I think you'll find the word is 'ugh'. 'Acting head,' she said.

'What did you just say?' he asked, his eyes looking almost shark-like in the darkly lit room as he leaned infinitesimally closer.

She leaned in closer herself, till their knees were almost touching. She could feel a trace of heat from his body, and felt herself shudder in response. *Why* did she flop into a puddle of goo whenever he was near her?

She swallowed and locked eyes with her rival. 'Acting head—which is what you are.' It sounded weak, even to her, but she was trying to stand firm against him.

'What we *both* are, if you think of Andrew's plan. We're both auditioning for the job. I am on the on-call rota tonight, and I can't swap to another, so you can go home tonight, good Dr Forbes.'

'Fine,' she said. 'But the same goes for me, so you're stuck sharing.'

Jacob's eyes flicked from her face to the bed behind her. She knew he'd see the scrub cap sticking out of her white coat pocket, and that he might remember that he had seen it before, somewhere. She followed his gaze and folded her coat over, hiding the contents of her pocket.

'I'm going to turn in.'

She searched his features for any kind of reaction, but he was all business. She turned on her side, making her green khaki vest top ride up a little as she twisted her body to lie facing the wall. She pulled her lab coat up with her feet and wrapped her arm around it like a child would a security blanket.

She could hear Jacob shuffling about for a while, getting comfy, and then she lay there looking at the wall, listening to his breathing. When it became shallow, indicating that he was asleep, she reached into her coat pocket. Pulling out the scrub cap, she ran her fingernail along its stitching, thinking of her friend and settling her head down onto the soft pillow.

She remembered the day Rebecca had come running up to her from the village, eager to show off her purchases. She'd spent the day at one of the local clinics that had been offering drop-in appointments for healthcare: trauma injuries, dietary problems, vaccinations. They'd treated people as best they could there, offering them the basics that people back home wouldn't even think twice about. Tampons. Fresh water...

Rebecca had loved those days—had adored helping people, feeling useful. It had been one of the things about her that had made Michelle persuade her to come on that last tour with her. Scott had barely been speaking to her for signing up again, and she'd wanted her happy-go-lucky single friend there to make the trip better, more fun. They always had such a good time working together.

'Free Prick and Period Day was a success!' she'd screeched, barrelling into camp and leapfrogging over Smithy, who had been bent double, cleaning his boots. 'We rocked!'

'Becks, knock it off!' he'd said grumpily, but she'd just stuck her tongue out at him and kept running towards Michelle.

'You need to stop calling it that—especially so loudly!' Michelle, ever the professional, had chided her. But that stern talk had lasted all of two minutes, and then she'd been cracking up with Becks about her day and her stories of the patients they'd helped.

'I got this too—bought it from the market.' She'd pulled a small bundle of orange fabric out of her backpack, presenting it to her friend with a devilish glint in her eye. 'We are going to be the best-accessorised medical team this side of the border!'

Michelle felt a tear slip down her cheek as she remembered that day. The easy smile of her friend, the hope and the sheer joy she had put out there every single day, almost to the point of being annoying.

She'd always joked with Rebecca's mum, Kathryn, that her daughter hadn't been conceived—she'd been dropped off at the front door by a unicorn. Kathryn had reminded her of that at the funeral.

She tried to push the thought away, but other memories kept coming. Becks screaming at her to move. Smithy prone on the ground, his boots discarded on the sandy grit nearby. People running from all directions. The acrid smell of burning trucks mingled with the melting rubber of the tyres, the smell of flesh being seared off the bone in the heat…

'Becks!' she'd screamed, grabbing an abandoned gun and running for cover, searching for her friend in the chaos and panic.

The air had been thick with movement and death but she'd kept on pumping her arms and legs, desperate to evade the insurgents hot on their heels.

'Becks!'

She'd heard a voice behind her and, whirling around, she'd seen her. The orange cap had still been tied to her belt, where she'd always kept it. She remembered feeling comforted, seeing it. If they had their talisman caps they were both good…

'Nooooo!'

'Michelle?'

'Becks, no! Stand down!'

'Michelle!'

'You're not supposed to be here! Becks, I'm sorry!'

'Michelle! It's okay. I'm here… I'm here.'

Michelle was in a blind fury. She couldn't find Rebecca, but she could hear her. She was heading towards her voice when a bulky form stopped her. She felt strong arms encircle her, felt her head being pulled back. This was it. This was the time.

Fight, girl—now!

She brought back her head till it touched the tops of her shoulders and then thrust it forward with as much force as she could muster. A primal scream of pain and terror was ripped from her, taking her breath with it.

'Arrrgghhhh!'

The grip on her loosened, disappeared, and she took the opportunity to run. She got to her feet, banged into something. Her legs…she had to run…run and—

She was at the door of the on-call room, her hand on the doorknob, when she came to. The door before her was made of solid wood. There was no chaos. No death. No Becks.

She tried to release the door handle and realised that her hand was gripping on to it for dear life, her knuckles white and stretched taut to the point of pain.

A muffled sound came from behind her, and she turned, pale-faced, to look at the source. Jacob was sitting on the floor, his legs out in front of him, his hands covering his nose. He reached for a pillow from one of the beds, pulling the cover off awkwardly with one hand, his eyes never leaving her.

'Are you back?' he asked softly. 'Do you know where you are?'

She caught a glimpse of the pillowcase, a handprint of fresh red blood, and started to shake. 'Did I—?'

He folded up the pillowcase and pressed it against his nose, slowly standing up. He made no move to come closer, and she was grateful for that. She still felt as if she was standing there, in front of Becks. She looked down at her feet, registering that she was standing on a carpeted floor.

Her shaking hand reached down and started to pinch the skin on her thigh. *Pinch.* Safe. *Pinch.* Alive. *Pinch.* Out.

The shaking lessened a little, and she turned and left the room.

Jacob watched her leave, saying nothing. Once the door had clicked closed he lifted himself off the floor, sitting down on the bed. His nose was broken—he knew that. He'd felt the bone break when her head had connected with his. It wasn't the first time he had been headbutted, but it was the first time a woman had been the perpetrator.

He'd heard her shout 'Becks!' in her sleep, seen her thrashing, and one look at her had told him that she wasn't there. Michelle hadn't been in that on-call room—not really. She'd been standing in a war zone, unaware that she had got out.

Who was Becks? Was it a nickname for a soldier she'd met?

He felt his fists clench at the thought of her pining for a man. A man who was obviously still on her mind in some

way, good or bad. Was it the guy she'd lived with before?
He knew there'd been someone because the nurses chat-
tered in their down time.

He caught sight of himself in the mirror on the wall
and winced.

'Well...' he said out loud to himself.

Pulling away the pillowcase, he noted that the bleeding had slowed down a little, but he'd still need to get
his nose checked.

'This will take some explaining. Ebony is going to
freak.'

He went to stand, and the door flew open again. Michelle with an armful of supplies. She stopped dead when
she saw him there, the pillowcase growing redder and
redder by the moment.

'I'm sorry... I can ask someone else to do this if you'd
prefer.'

She was standing in the doorway of the still-dark on-
call room, the lights behind her illuminating her form.
She was biting at her lip, her eyes full of remorse, confusion and concern. She had never looked more beautiful to him.

It took all he had not to walk over to her and make
her forget every moment of the past hour with his lips.

He motioned with his free hand for her to close the
door. 'Mich...come in.'

She hesitated a moment, and then kicked the door
shut behind her. She knelt by him, gloved hands working fast to get everything ready. Then she shuffled along
the floor, positioning her body between his legs, and
slowly took hold of the hand holding the fabric. She put
the stained cloth into a plastic bag, and winced.

'It's broken...but the cut on top isn't too bad. I can
dress it. Are you ready?'

She was already holding his nose, her warm finger-tips slightly shaky till the moment they touched his skin. Then she was as steady as they came. Professional Michelle mode.

He nodded—the merest hint of agreement—and she had the cut dressed in mere seconds.

Jacob let her work. The truth was, he was in shock. Not at the headbutt. Hell, people had done worse to him before. At least she had spared the family jewels. The radiology nurse he had gone out with last year hadn't been so generous.

That wasn't it. That wasn't what made his heart beat faster, made his own memories and panic zing to the surface.

It was the lack of control, the fear—the sheer terror she had showed him in that room.

She wasn't well. And her brand of sickness didn't just go away. It didn't fade with time, and it didn't leave the sufferer with a moment's peace. She was in hell, and he had been her enemy back in that moment.

She wouldn't have stopped fighting if she hadn't come to, if her instincts for survival hadn't kicked in. How could he help her? Did he even want to? This was her Achilles' Heel. If he cut her down at the ankles the job would be his. His position would be safe. And he *needed* this job. He needed to be here—now more than ever. He had a child to raise, and that didn't come cheap.

If she were a man, would he even still be here right now? He'd already be in Andrew's office, ratting his rival out and taking the crown. So what was stopping him? The fact that she was suffering? That her suffering was something he wore too, like a favourite shirt he just couldn't get rid of? Was that it? Or was it because he wanted to know her better?

Right now, with her tending to him, it was hard for Jacob to know which part of his body was currently in control of his decision-making.

'That feel okay?'

She was staring at him now, her auburn hair hanging over one blue eye as she worked. He could smell her perfume, a light sweet scent that lingered in the short space between them. All traces of her panicked state were gone, aside from the fact that her skin was pale and drawn. She was in medic mode, and her hands were as sure and strong as ever.

She didn't look him square in the eyes, but he couldn't stop looking at her. His eyes were processing everything before him, trying to piece the puzzle of her together.

'Jacob, does that feel okay?'

He realised he hadn't answered her, but he wanted to ask so many questions of his own.

'It's good, thanks.'

'I've Steri-Stripped the cut, the wound is clean, and the break will heal itself. You might want to get an X-ray, just in case.'

He nodded slowly, both of them knowing full well that she didn't need to tell him any of this. It was basic training for them—a quick job. She was trying to fill the silence, but for whom he couldn't be sure.

She busied herself tidying away the kit she'd laid out on the mattress. He reached for her hand before his nerve-endings even registered the movement. He slipped his fingers under hers, trapping them lightly and running his thumb along the back of her hand.

She flinched, still sitting between his legs, pinned by their linked arms.

'What can I do?' he asked simply.

When he'd come back from a tour that had been all

he'd wanted someone to ask, but no one ever had. The stigma of poor mental health and the Alpha male tradition of manhood still lingered, silencing many in the throes of PTSD. He'd learnt the hard way just how many people suffered under the spectre of anxiety and depression. He'd been lucky to get out before his had got bad. His girl had saved him.

Now he was trying to help Michelle, but she kept taking his breath away, clouding the goal. 'Michelle, if you tell me what I can do, I'll do it.'

She pulled her hand away, slowly gathering the rest of the kit and moving to stand. Jacob stood with her, and as they looked at each other again Jacob saw that she was crying.

All thoughts of weakness disappeared and he took a step forward, encircling her with his arms. She made no move to stop him, but he felt her whole body tense, muscles and sinew turning to cold, hard steel in his embrace.

'Michelle, you don't have to do this alone.'

He had said the same thing to someone else only a short time ago, and he'd meant those words then too. Not that it had done any good. It had to be different this time; he had to work harder. Be better, do more. Fix things. Be there.

'I'm here for you.'

Another crying face popped into his head, and his heart squeezed for them both.

She sobbed then—just one short outlet for her pain before she locked it away again. He could feel her starting to pull away, so he released her, not wanting to push. Her cheek brushed against his, the salty silent tears rubbing off onto his stubbly cheek.

It made his whole body stir into life, and he felt a pang
of guilt and confusion.

You need to tell her.

CHAPTER FIVE

THE WORDS HE was whispering in her ear should have soothed her, but the situation was all wrong. He couldn't help her; no one could. Just as no one had been able to help Becks, or Smithy, or any of the other people she had tried and failed to save.

Sometimes life was just dark and broken and people suffered. She got that now.

She started to pull away from him and he let her go without pushing. It wasn't till she saw his face that she realised what was going on. Her whole body felt as if it was tingling; the thought of him being so close was lighting her up from the inside. He felt so good, so comforting, so warm.

She locked eyes with him and saw the same confused need on his face that she felt in the pit of her own stomach. Frowning, she dropped her kit onto the floor and, reaching forward, placed her left hand on his cheek. Leaning in, she dropped a kiss on his lips.

She had barely touched him when she felt him move closer, taking her face in his own hands and tilting his head to deepen the gentle exploration of her lips. She let him, moving in once more slowly, gently, taking care to protect his injury. The injury *she* had caused.

He should have complained, but he hadn't, and she

wondered just who *was* this man kissing her so passionately. He moaned, just a little, against her mouth, and her stomach flipped in response. She kissed him back, letting her tongue flick out to massage his, and felt him respond, pulling her down to the bed, wrapping her legs around his waist to hold her in place.

'This isn't a good idea,' he said.

She nodded against his mouth, kissing him back even as he dived back in.

'We shouldn't. We need to talk,' he said.

She felt him run his hands down her back before settling at the base of her spine, pulling her closer to him. She could feel the evidence of his attraction against her body, and he didn't try to hide it from her.

'Stop, then,' she said, running her hands through his thick black hair, giving it a playful pull that made him growl.

He stopped kissing her, pulling away and searching her face.

'Stop?' he checked, moving his hands away from her bottom to his own hips.

The loss of his lips and touch felt like having a comfort blanket ripped from her, but the cold realisation helped. She looked at his face, at his broken nose, his beautiful dark-lashed eyes, the already developing bruises beneath them, and she was lost to the moment.

She was so sorry—for him, for Becks, for everything—and only his touch numbed the pain.

She lowered her lips to brush them against his once more.

'Dr Forbes?'

Her name was being called through the door, and there was a strong knock against the wood.

'Andrew,' she whispered, her lips so close to his that

she tapped the word out on his skin, like Morse code for lovers. 'It's Andrew.'

Jacob's face registered annoyance, but he made no move to release her.

'I'm here—getting changed. What's up?' she shouted towards the door.

Her pager was silent. What did he want?

They both sat there in the dimly lit room, holding their breath, their arms still wrapped around each other.

'The door's not locked,' she whispered into Jacob's ear.

He nodded and lifted her off him. 'You go. I'll come out after.'

'Turn around,' she whispered, and he did as she asked.

She grabbed a pair of fresh scrubs from the pile kept under the bed and changed quickly. She gathered her things and then, waiting till Jacob was behind the door, stepped out, closing the door firmly behind her.

Andrew looked behind her, trying to see into the room.

'One of the A&E nurses has crashed out in there,' she told him smoothly, cutting off his question and holding up the used kit. 'Bit of an accident—all good now. Had to change.'

Andrew's all-seeing eyes landed on the bloodied pillowcase in the plastic bag. 'Nice. Report filed yet?'

Shit. Andrew never could let anything go. Excellent management skills, but a pain when you were trying your best to dig your way out of a hole.

'None needed. It was a minor thing.'

Andrew shook his head. 'Still need a report on my desk.'

She nodded, knowing it was impossible to argue. Since there *was* no nurse, she'd just have to hope he wouldn't follow it up later. For now, she needed to keep him busy, and away from the door.

The thought of Jacob in there, hiding, made her head spin. She'd been kissing him, straddling him, touching him.

The man who could take away her job, her career here. The same man she had hurt whilst in the throes of a flashback so vivid that she could still feel the dust and sweat on her skin. The man who had slept with her best friend. The man she was supposed to hate for trying to take her job, for being the type of man she had avoided her whole life—a player. And now he was a player with dirt on her that could cost her everything.

If she lost this job, she would be adrift.

'Did you want something?' she asked, walking away from the door towards Andrew's office.

Andrew fell into step beside her, rubbing the back of his neck. A sure sign he was about to say something awkward.

'I actually wanted to talk to you about the job. I feel as though things have been a little difficult since you got back and I just wanted to check in.'

A nurse sidled up to Andrew, holding a pen and clipboard. He took it from her, read through the notes and signed it with a flourish.

'Do you mean *things* have been difficult or *I* have been difficult?'

Don't bite, Michelle, you're being paranoid.

He hushed her, waiting till they were outside his office door, then leading her inside and answering her question.

'I didn't think I handled your return as well as I could have. I know you've made a lot of adjustments already, coming back to work.'

She smiled at her superior, not wanting to give anything away, and not wanting to talk either. 'It's fine, honestly. I—'

An insistent knock came on the door.

'Come in,' Andrew called. 'Sorry, won't take a minute.'

Jacob peeked in, most of his face obscured by a patient file.

'Sorry, boss, Dr Forbes is needed urgently on the floor.'

Michelle grabbed her beeper. 'But my pager di—'

'Network problem,' Jacob said smoothly. 'All fixed now. We need to go.'

Michelle opened the door and Jacob ducked out of sight, leaving the file flapping in his wake. Squeezing through, she shouted, 'Thanks, Andrew,' and half ran after the retreating file.

They walked deeper into the hospital and headed for the trauma bays. Jacob released the file, first checking down the corridor as though Andrew was hot on their heels.

'Thanks.' It was all she could think to say. 'Where's the patient?'

He turned to face her in the corridor, pointing at his nose and now even more black eyes.

'It's me. I think I need that X-ray now. You caved half my face in with your head.'

He crossed his eyes comically, making her laugh.

'The X-ray department is down on the first floor. Plenty of staff on.'

'Ah...' he mused, moving out of the way of a crash cart rolling towards A&E. 'If I speak to them, though, they'll need an explanation. Of how I came to break my nose, on shift, with no witnesses.'

Michelle pursed her lips. 'I *am* sorry—I didn't mean to. You surprised me. I feel awful.'

'Is that why Andrew was talking to you back there?'

What do I say? Yes? Mind your own business?

'No. I didn't tell him about your nose. I would have had to explain what happened.'

The penny dropped and realisation set in. Passing by a supply cupboard, she came to a halt, moved away from the people walking past.

'That's it, isn't it? You're going to tell him so you get the job.' She leaned against the wall, her head resting on the painted surface as she looked up at the strip lighting. 'I assaulted you, I'll have to resign, you get my job by default.'

'What?' His phone started to ring in his pocket, but he ignored the call. 'You think that's why I was there at Andrew's office? I was looking for *you*. I came to *help*.'

She snorted with derision. 'Help yourself to my career, sure…'

Jacob's eyes widened. Grabbing the door handle to the store cupboard, he pulled her inside after him.

It was basically a huge white room, fitted out with shelves of racking containing various medical supplies. As soon as they were through the door he closed it behind them and backed away. Sitting on the floor, his back resting against one of the shelves, he took out his phone and checked the display before tapping out a message and putting it back in his pocket.

'I need this job too, Michelle, but I am not out to damage another doctor's career to get it. I came to look for you because I was worried.'

'I'm fine,' Michelle countered, taking a seat on the floor next to him, careful to leave a gap between their bodies. 'I don't need looking after; I'm fine on my own. Have been for a while.'

She didn't elaborate on the car crash that had been

her last relationship, wincing at how much she had already admitted. But it was done, and now she was in self-preservation mode more than ever. Scott had once called her a robot, among other things. He'd told her he'd come home from work one day to find a stranger with his girlfriend's face, rattling around like a shell-shocked ghost.

'When I saw you outside his office I thought you were there to tell him what had happened,' she said now.

Jacob shook his head, brushing his hair back from his face. He looked across at her and she felt his eyes boring into her. 'I want the job—but what happened in that room…it's all forgotten. I'll never mention it again.'

Michelle felt a punch in her gut at his words. She didn't *want* to forget everything. She would remember some aspects of it for ever. She thought of Andrew, so concerned. Of Becks, standing there and screaming at her to move. That orange scrub cap lying on the floor, covered in blood.

Whenever she got close to anyone, pain was the only outcome. Today was a prime example.

Andrew probably blamed her for Becks. He knew, and he was holding it over her, trying to get her to talk. She wanted to tell him, but she couldn't. She couldn't tell anyone. She would rather curl up and die like her friend.

I'm sorry, Becks. I talked you into coming with me. I needed you there and it cost you your life.

'Start again? Clean slate?' said Jacob.

He was holding out his hand for her to shake, and she clasped it in hers. 'Deal. No more fighting.'

'Or head-butting,' Jacob added, and she couldn't help but laugh when she looked at his swollen face.

'No head-butting. I am *very* sorry,' she added, reaching out to stick down a tiny piece of dressing that had come undone.

He closed his eyes at her touch and she pulled away, moving to the door before he could open his lids again.

'Hey, not so fast, Zidane. I have one condition, for my silence.'

A condition? Play it cool, Mich.

'Zidane?' she queried, turning back to face him.

He grinned, his lips forming a perfect shape as he teased her. 'World Cup 2006. Zidane head-butted Materazzi. Keep up.'

She smiled despite herself. 'Nerd.'

'I prefer jock nerd, actually.' He pointed at his temple. 'I have brains *and* brawn.'

'Really?' She guffawed. 'Who told you that? Your mother? Mothers have to tell you that, you know, even if you turn out to be Billy Bragger.'

He looked affronted, giving an exaggerated snapping back of his head, a theatrical gasp. '*Someone's* deflecting!' he sang out in the space.

A faint echo sang back, taunting her in stereo.

'Go on   ask me what my condition is. I dare you.'

Michelle swallowed, the gulp ringing in her ears. She wouldn't back down though. Not. A. Chance. She made her body relax. Some days her stomach ached and her shoulders cramped with the effort of keeping herself looking 'normal' on the outside whilst wrestling her demons on the inside. Her whole body was suffering, coiled like a stress-filled spring.

'Go on then, Mr Perfect, what's your condition? Charity football match? Doing your charts for a week?'

He looked straight at her, his jaw tensing before he spoke. 'You won't like it.'

'Try me, Jacob. I'm a big girl.'

'You see a therapist here. Five sessions, then we're quits.'

Later that night she headed to the car park and threw her bags into the back seat. It was a very cool night for April, so she flicked on the heater to full blast. Turning on the ignition made her CD player spring into life once more, and she flicked it off. She'd been listening to her road trip mix that morning, but after the long day and night she couldn't bear to hear a single note.

The memories were just too heavy in the air tonight—like the ghosts of the departed, unseen and unfinished. The hospital stood before her, its hundreds of windows giving out light, containing loss and love and all the emotions in between. This place was her battlefield now, and she wanted to fight for it as much as she wanted to run away. She was broken, and St Marshall's was where people came to heal.

She could heal herself, stick herself back together within those walls. Every saved life was another Elastoplast applied to her own inner wounds. She would do it for Becks, for Smithy—for all of them. Therapy, though? Did she really need that? Why did everyone seem to be getting at her? Was she worse than she thought at hiding her pain?

As she pulled out of the car park she didn't see the man standing in one of the windows at the hospital, looking out at her. She drove on unaware. Her head full of broken soldiers, violent dreams and stolen kisses.

CHAPTER SIX

PICKING A CLUMP of sticky sugar off his elbow, Jacob came jogging down the plush carpeted staircase of his new house and sighed when he caught sight of the multitude of boxes piled up in the dining room.

He'd wanted to be ready for his early shift, and also fit in a jog on the way, but coming face to face with how much he had avoided unpacking was sobering to his good mood.

The truth was, not a lot of his bachelor lifestyle would transfer well to this new house. Framed art posters, trophies and awards from his marathons and surgical achievements...they were all so at odds with the person who had bought this place. He felt like a jumble of different people, all trying to get a hold on their new life.

He felt different. He'd woken up this morning happy, despite his lack of sleep. His nose was sore, and it had kept him awake last night, but the last few days had been interesting, to say the least. The more he learned about his co-worker—his rival for the top job—the more conflicted he was. And dare he say...aroused?

The thought of her all dressed up, out of her scrubs and without her usual guarded stance, stirred something deep within him. She had been a revelation that night of the party, and that night in the on-call room... He wanted to know more, to see more. He wanted to know what made her tick…why she was so adamant about getting the job.

Why did she want it? Was it just about winning? Ambition? Wouldn't she get bored eventually?

She struck him as the type of woman who would tire easily, work with the comfort zone of a role and then kick like hell against it. He was the same: living life to the full, hopping on planes at a moment's notice to save a life, helping the survivors of natural disasters.

They were cut from the same piece of adrenaline-soaked cloth, so her actions now were confusing to him. As confusing as his own must be to those who knew him in the profession. Was she that far gone?

She hadn't answered him yesterday, when he'd laid out his condition. His price for his silence. He'd braced himself for a kick-off, a battle with the fiery temptress who kept his thoughts jumbled and his head turned. She'd just left, though. Left him sitting there in the storeroom like an idiot.

The next time he'd seen her, it had been as though it had never happened. At one point Jacob had even wondered whether she had an evil twin. The two sides of her were so different that he couldn't reconcile them as being the same person.

Heading to the kitchen, he flicked on his coffee maker—one of the few things he had got around to unpacking from his old apartment. He'd mostly left his bachelor life boxed up. It was at odds with his new life with Ebony. The two worlds just didn't connect, but he was working on evolving. A lot faster than he'd expected to as well, thanks to Michelle. She had awoken something in him he hadn't known was there in the first place.

Nothing happened when he hit the button, and Jacob

frowned. Then he saw the nanny had left a note stuck to the front of the machine.

Out of filters. Have added to shopping list.

He flicked the note, grateful that she was on the ball at least, but that wouldn't get him coffee.

'Dad?'

His little girl was standing in the doorway of the kitchen, looking cute in her soft cotton onesie. She slept like an explorer, loving to wrap herself in soft fabrics that held her skin tight and gave her the sensory feedback that made her feel centred.

'Morning, munchkin,' he said, glaring once more at the coffee machine and then looking back at her. 'It's a little early. You want some breakfast?'

As soon as he spoke, he felt his panic rise.

'Toast, please,' she said, walking up to the breakfast nook and trying to pull herself onto a stool. He watched her, unsure whether to help or not, but she soon got herself up. Giving her a weak smile, he opened the bread bin and was relieved to find half a small loaf in there. Thank goodness for the nanny.

Making Ebony some toast, he started to rummage around in his cupboards for some jam. Everything was still alien to him here. Most nights by the time he got home he was too tired for much, and Ebony would already be asleep, adding to his guilt. At least before Steph had left she'd had a parent who knew where the jam lived, and her home hadn't been filled with boxes.

After the first few days of them being a family of two, Jacob had reeled. He was still reeling, frankly. He'd been summoned from the scene of a battle to face a different one back home. A mother who wanted her life and her freedom. A daughter who needed a home, a family. And the realisation that the disconnect between them was too wide to repair.

The first nanny he'd hired had quit. Probably due to the fact that she'd been dumped with the fractious autistic daughter of a surgeon who barely knew how much work being a full-time single parent was and seemed to dash off far too often.

Looking at Ebony now, eating toast and drinking juice while watching something on her tablet, he felt that twinge again. As soon as Susan arrived—the wonderful nanny who had dug her hands in deep and pulled their home into some sort of order—he'd have to go again. To fight for a job he needed, but didn't want to take from a woman he respected. A woman he craved a little. It was all very perplexing—and before coffee too.

He sat down next to his daughter and kissed the top of her head, avoiding her headphones.

'Daddy,' she said sweetly, 'it's bake sale day at school today. Did you get the things from the shop?'

Jesus. The text last night. He remembered now.

The kids were holding a bake sale after school, raising funds for more sensory equipment. So he'd called at the supermarket on the way home, throwing things from an online recipe into his trolley and heading home. Then Jacob had spent three hours in the kitchen, turning out crappy batch after crappy batch of cupcakes.

The first ones he'd burnt to a crisp; the second and third had turned out to have salt instead of sugar in them. The fourth batch were edible but looked like roadkill—leading to him downing a shot of tequila to recover.

'I did, honey, but Daddy's not a good baker.'

Turning to his little girl, he started to apologise, holding the plastic box of bashed buns in his hand. Ebony's little face was so innocent, he felt his heart squeeze once more.

You're failing, Jacob. Get it together. Do better.

He knelt down in front of her, putting the box to one side and pulling her onto his lap. 'I'm trying, sweetie. Maybe we should buy some cakes, or Daddy can donate some money?'

Ebony looked at him with her little blank face, leaning in and dropping a kiss on his cheek. 'It's okay, Daddy. Don't worry.'

The front door opened, startling them both, and Susan bustled in. Taking in the uncharacteristically calm morning scene before her, she recovered herself well and raised a carrier bag full of shopping.

'Baking day, Ebony, and we're all set! I made some buns for my Charlie, and I made too many! Do you want some for school?'

Ebony squealed, jumping off Jacob's lap and hugging Susan. Jacob tipped his buns into the trash before they noticed. *Phew.*

Susan pulled a bag of coffee filters out of the bag and pushed it into Jacob's arms. He cradled it like a newborn baby.

'Thanks, superhero,' he said to her, and she patted him on the shoulder.

Ebony was back with her headphones on now, and she dodged half of his goodbye kisses but laughed when he pulled one of his silly faces.

'I'll be back late.' He said this to Susan, but he looked straight at his daughter when he spoke. 'Have a good day.'

He'd take a coffee with him, walk to work, see his new neighbourhood…maybe shake off the residual daddy guilt that seemed to have come with the territory the moment the stick had turned blue.

The old Jacob hadn't exactly been the type to put down roots, that was for sure. He'd bought and sold apartments every couple of years, moving on to the next job, the next project. Now he had gone and bought a house, with a garden and a drive—white picket fence territory.

He hadn't even told anyone at work about Ebony, and he was feeling more terrified about that than ever. He had planned to start telling people once he'd settled in, sure that he'd be able to pull it off for the meantime, till they found some kind of groove back home. When Michelle had come, that idea had gone out of the window. Now he was waiting for the right moment.

At this time in his life he needed that job, needed to be here—but what about Michelle? Would he even *want* the job after the battle that lay ahead? Now he had worked with her, it wasn't so easy to see what it would be like without her. The whole thing was giving Jacob a headache—but this time he wasn't running. Those days were gone, replaced with mortgages and bedtimes and baking supplies.

For now, he would settle for taking in the scenery.

One of the docs at the hospital had signed his broken nose off and he was fit for work, as long as he was careful, and he found himself picking up his usual leisurely pace through the park, backpack swinging from his shoulders.

He wanted to get to the hospital and punch in—and see the girl who had punched him out in more ways than one.

Definitely a knockout.

Forty minutes later, freshly dressed and in his uniform of sharp suit and white coat, he headed for the nurses' station to see who was already clocked in. Looking at the trauma board, he saw that Michelle's name had been marked as offsite for the day and her OR schedule was empty. *What?* Was this because of the other night? Jacob felt a lurch in his stomach. Was that it? Had she been suspended?

'Is Dr Forbes off today?' He collared a passing nurse— Wendy something. 'There's nothing on the board?'

Wendy shrugged. 'I don't know what to tell you. Andrew has covered her shift today, cancelled all non-emergencies. She's out the whole day.' She stood a little straighter, pushing her chest out and giving him her best smile. 'Anything else you need?'

Distracted, Jacob muttered his thanks and turned on his heel towards Andrew's office.

'You're welcome,' Wendy said, and sighed, heading on her way.

Jacob, oblivious to her simpering, was just outside Andrew's office door, hand up ready to knock, when his boss opened the door and walked straight into him.

'Jacob,' he said smoothly. 'I was just coming to find you. Dr Forbes isn't in today, so I'm afraid it's up to you to step up.' He spotted Jacob's healing injury, a deep frown marring his features. He pointed towards Jacob's nose. 'Did you get that in A&E, by any chance?'

Jacob shook his head, but didn't elaborate. He felt a strong instinct to protect Michelle, to give her a chance to consider his request. He owed her that as a fellow combat medic.

It's nothing to do with the kiss—or her. I'm giving her a chance. She gets help, we fight for the job, and that's it.

He didn't want to push his brain into thinking any

more deeply about the issue because he feared he might be lying to himself.

Was he at a disadvantage too? Mentally? He sure felt that way.

He didn't know what the hell he was doing as a man, but as a doctor he was clear. He wanted this job—he wanted to win it fair and square. What happened after that was anyone's guess, and his heart started to pound at the thought.

Exiting the lift on the third floor felt like entering a bubble. The moment the lift doors opened Michelle was enveloped by the calm, almost numb energy that emanated from every facet of this department. The lights were warm and dim. There was no rushing around, no screams of pain, no blood on the floor from an arterial spray or a knife wound. Everything seemed to be slowed down—Michelle included.

She was already feeling odd, being dressed in her civilian clothes at her place of work, naked without her armour, but she had dressed in her favourite jeans and a cute top instead, slinging her running gear into a backpack, with a new pair of trainers she was going to break in.

By the time she had walked down the long corridor towards the man in a shirt and tie sitting behind the reception desk she felt as if she was having to really pull her feet off the floor with each step, as though she was wading through treacle to get there. Her jaw felt wobbly, breakable, and as the man turned to look at her with an easy open smile she stalled.

'Can I help?' he asked, giving her a broad, welcoming grin and his complete attention.

Okay, so he's definitely in the right job. Now I just need to get the words out.

'I have an appointment at eight a.m. Michelle Forbes.'

His face lit up in recognition and his smile widened.

Maybe they gave the staff free samples of happy pills here.

'Yes, Dr Forbes, I'll let Dr Colton know you're here. Do take a seat.'

She sat down on a comfortable-looking easy chair in the corner, away from any other people who might come in and wait. Her phone beeped in her pocket and she flashed the receptionist an apologetic look. He waved her away with another dentist-approved flash of teeth.

It was Wendy, messaging her to check if she was okay. She'd not told anyone where she was going. She tapped out a message saying that she was fine, and was in the building, but not on shift. She knew she'd been seen this morning, and that word would get around, but it wouldn't be from Wendy. She wasn't the type.

Michelle pressed 'send' and sat watching the dots flick across the bottom of the screen as Wendy replied.

Heads-up: Mr Trauma God has been looking for you.

She smiled to herself. Even when she was away, the others in her team had her back. She knew Jacob would never have an easy ride with them around, no matter the outcome of the job race. The hospital would be in good hands either way.

The happy receptionist's phone buzzed. 'You can go in now, Doctor.'

Michelle gulped, standing and nodding her thanks. She kept her head held high, her hands by her sides. Her fingers found a bruise-free piece of skin on her left leg, and before she walked towards the room she pinched herself. Hard.

Still here. Alive. You feel that pain? That's good. That's nerve-endings telling you you're alive, safe, and in pain. Pinch. Now, walk, soldier. Left. Pinch. Right. Pinch.

Taking a deep, shaky breath, she wrapped her free hand around the brushed steel door handle. It had taken her a long time to pluck up the courage to make the appointment, let alone get up this morning and drive here. Jacob's challenge had been the tipping point, though: she wouldn't welch on a bet, and that had given her the impetus she'd needed to finally pick up the phone. She hadn't told Jacob, and he'd never mentioned it.

They had worked together well since Lucas—watching over each other as they worked, pulling together when they needed to—and their working practice was tight and efficient now. They were equally tenacious about medicine, about saving lives, and Michelle had come to realise that there was no bigger turn-on than working with him when the chips were down. After a couple of stabbing victims had rolled in, leaving them both fighting to save people all day, it had taken everything she had not to jump him.

It was a welcome distraction from the perpetual gnaw of anxiety she carried deep in her gut. The way he made her feel involved different body parts altogether. It was frustrating, to say the least, but it had pulled her out of her fog just enough for her to lift her head towards fresh air. She needed to do this now—for her and for him. For her patients. For herself. For Becks.

She needed to stop blaming herself for Becks's death. She hadn't killed her, and she would have given anything to save her. She needed to put her friend to rest—but she didn't have the first clue how to do that. How to feel like herself again. Jacob had made her wake up, but his connection to Becks, their rivalry for the job… It was all a tangled ball of yarn in her head. She needed to find the end and start to unravel the mess. For everyone's sake.

'Everything okay?' the chirpy receptionist checked.

She had been staring at the door handle in her hand for the last few minutes, as though it would open the door to another world. Perhaps it would.

That thought got her moving.

'Not really,' she admitted finally, giving him a smile that she felt sure came across as a sad grimace. 'But I'm here. Gotta start somewhere.'

'No! Get off me!'

Little Benjamin Johnston wasn't having any of it. He didn't want to be tickled, he wouldn't let them lubricate his head, and he didn't even flicker so much as an eyelash in Jacob's direction now, as he produced a lollipop from the jar at the nurses' station.

'Don't want it!' he screamed, little fists clenched as he fully embraced his tantrum.

His mum was trying every trick she could—setting off the little siren on his favourite fire engine toy, pulling funny faces, threatening to call his nana...

Right, I'm going in.

'You don't want to be upsetting Nana, do you, Ben?' He kept his voice light, understated, but tinged with authority.

We do not negotiate with toddlers.

'If you let me have a look I'll only be a minute. Do you know how long a minute is? I bet you do, being such a big boy.'

Ben, clad in blue dungarees and a red-and-white-striped T-shirt, stopped his tight-fisted scream-fest just long enough to give Jacob a sideways glance. The potty-training toilet seat he was currently wearing as a hat didn't move as he turned his head. Jacob could see the tufts of hair sprouting up around the lodged plastic seat.

His mother whispered out of the corner of her mouth. 'Keep talking—that's the first time he's been quiet in four hours.'

Jude, the nurse standing behind Mrs Johnston, waggled her finger in her ear. 'Thank Christ for that; I thought I'd gone deaf.'

Jacob slowly moved closer to him, walking on bended knee to reach his eye level. The little lad was cute when he wasn't holding the trauma department hostage. A&E had sent him over, due to overcrowding and complaints from the other patients in the emergency waiting room.

'I tell you what, young Ben...'

Ben jerked a little at the sound of Jacob's voice, and his little fists clenched tighter, his mouth opening to show five little pearly-white teeth poking through his gums. He started to draw a breath...

'Oh, Lord, not again,' his mother wailed.

'Jesus, I am *never* having kids,' Jude muttered, patting Mrs Johnston on the back soothingly.

Ben straightened his back, taking a deep breath and using every bit of his two-foot-something stature to impress upon them his frustration. 'No!' he shouted. 'Potteeee!'

Then it clicked. Jacob had a vision pop up in his head: Ebony, sitting on a plush cream-and-yellow-striped runner, screaming because her favourite character-emblazoned shoes were dirty. He never knew what to do. He got it now—even if he hadn't then. His daughter's tantrums and meltdowns over the years had opened his eyes. Sometimes, you just had to think outside the box.

He looked over his shoulder at the nurses, talking to them out of the corner of his mouth. They all strained to hear him, leaning forward as he instructed them what to do.

Jude's eyes lit up. 'I have just the thing—wait there.'

She dashed out of the room whilst Ben screeched on, his big sad eyes looking at them the whole time, not letting anyone near him.

Jacob looked across at Mrs Johnston and sighed. She was sitting there, hugging her bag, talking softly to Ben, trying to console him, trying to distract him, to make him laugh. He was having none of it. And when she tried for a hug it only made him louder and more agitated. She looked exhausted, and embarrassed, and a little beaten down.

Not for the first time Jacob found himself wondering why people did it. The whole parenting thing. To him, it seemed like a lifetime of worry, of always being 'on call', of always having that gnawing fear.

Looking at Mrs Johnston now, he couldn't help but feel sorry for her. Maybe he was throwing a little pity party for himself too—not that he could ever speak out loud how he felt. It just wasn't done…

'Got it! You're lucky it's curry night Chez Jude.' Jude trotted back in, brandishing a big white pot of coconut oil.

Ben's mother's face was a picture. 'Will that work?' she asked, looking from medical professional to medical professional.

Jacob gave her an easy smile. 'Distraction is a powerful weapon,' he said, and it hit him how true that was in his own life.

He'd felt constantly distracted since he met the ball of chaos that was Michelle. He even found himself thinking of her now, but he pushed her out of his mind. Ben's screams and general hatred for everyone around him helped to quiet the noise of the woman in his head.

'Ladies, get ready. I'm going in...'

Taking the pot from Jude, Jacob sat down on the floor near to Ben and slowly unscrewed the cap. The other nurses left to attend to their patients, leaving the four of them alone. Slowly Jacob rubbed some of the coconut oil from the pot into his own hair, making it stick up at odd angles.

Ben side-eyed him, and the cacophony of shouts and moans slowly subsided, as though someone had found his remote control. Mrs Johnston sighed audibly with relief, and Jacob winked at her.

He dipped his finger into the pot again, pulling out more this time and rubbing it between his fingers before slapping it all over his hair. When he caught his reflection in the mirror on the wall he saw he looked like a mad professor—and he saw something else too: Michelle. She was standing—well, peeking—in the doorway, in civilian clothes, watching him.

He felt his heart thud in his chest and looked away quickly. Knowing she was watching him work felt like showcasing his skills, showing her that she could trust him, and that meant a lot to him.

He didn't want to probe the reasons why it mattered so much. Why his interaction with this child was something he wanted her to see. That was another thought for another sleepless night, with the sheets wrapped around his sweat-slicked body.

He'd used to sleep better out there, on tour, which was crazy, really. But many a night he had slept like a newborn babe, lulled into slumber by the sounds of unrest all around him. He'd felt part of something there; here, he'd just felt...lost. Powerless, even. Overwhelmed. Until her.

Ben padded over, his feet now bare after an earlier shoe and sock purge, and Jacob held the pot out to him.

Ben looked at him, then back at the pot, and then his little fingers were in the sweet-smelling waxy mixture. Pulling out a covered hand, he laughed, holding it up for them both to see.

'Yeah, that's it, little man—like this!'

Jacob rubbed oil into his hair again, following the rough shape of the potty seat that was stuck to Ben's head. After a moment Ben started to rub it into his own hair, and Jacob took that as a signal.

Getting another good handful ready, he shuffled forward, hands raised to warn Ben what was coming. 'Now, let's get that off, dude, and go get you a lollipop.'

Ben took the signal and, leaning forward, rubbed his little hands on Jacob's head. His hair was now almost crunchy with the mixture, but it was worth it. In return Jacob massaged oil into the little boy's head, gently pulling and testing the seat's level of tightness as he went. A few more rubs and the seat started to give. Ben shoed no sign of being distressed; in fact, he was beckoning his mother to come and play.

'One more little...' Jacob pulled again, and this time the seat came free.

Ben barely noticed; he was having too much sticky-fingered fun.

His mum burst into tears on the spot. 'Oh, my God, I can't believe you got it off! Thank you!'

She hugged Ben, laughing as he grabbed her face in coconut-scented hands, giving her a big kiss. His earlier bad mood was forgotten, and all was right in his little world.

'It's no bother,' Jacob said, smiling at them both broadly.

The feeling of having helped someone, changing

someone's day for the better, was always a high, and he basked in it now.

He waggled the potty seat at them. 'I'd recommend not using these again. I hate the things. Never worked for me.' *This was it. This was his chance.* 'My daughter hated them too—and potties.'

Ben's mum rolled her eyes conspiratorially at him. 'I can relate. What worked in the end?'

Jacob opened his mouth to answer but realised that he didn't know. The truth was, he'd gone away on tour, leaving a stubborn Ebony with her frustrated mother, Jenny—a nurse he'd been seeing on and off for a while… nothing serious.

Until she'd fallen pregnant and he had stepped up. Or tried to.

He and Jenny had had nothing in common other than a basic physical attraction and jobs with unsociable hours. Bringing a child up together, living together…it had been complicated. In the end Jenny had left—and he had come home and stepped up.

'Perseverance, I guess,' he said, as truthfully as he could. 'You're there, doing it, helping him learn. That's all he needs. He'll get there with your help.'

She nodded, the anxiety and stress visibly falling away from her as she held her son close.

'You're doing a great job, Mrs Johnston. Don't worry—he's thriving.'

He remembered Michelle then, his heart thumping faster at the thought. He looked to the doorway but she was gone.

Another missed opportunity to add to the others.

Thank God for en-suite bathrooms in on-call rooms. Far better than a tarp, a few poles, and a bucket of water.

Although even with cutting-edge bathroom facilities, it took Jacob a good twenty minutes of scrubbing and shampooing to get rid of the oil in his hair. He could still smell coconut in the air when he came out of the shower, throwing a towel around himself and grabbing another to dry his hair.

Heading out of the bathroom to the connected on-call room, he threw the second towel onto his head, drying his fragrant locks.

'You smell like the air after a tropical storm.'

The words came from nowhere, and Jacob jumped a foot and a half in the air, his head still encased in the towel, his limbs flailing against the intruder.

He spun around, wrestling wildly with the towel around his head. He managed to pull it off at the very same second as the bath sheet around his torso fell down, hitting the deck and leaving him standing there butt naked.

He looked for the voice and there she was. Michelle. Lying on her side on the far bed, propped up on one elbow, looking at him open-mouthed, her expression showing as much shock as he felt.

'I...er...' he began.

'Oh, I'm so...'

They both stopped, the ends of their sentences floating in the air around them like wisps of snaking smoke.

'I didn't think anyone was going to be in here...sorry,' he said, once he had the power of speech.

She nodded, a little smile playing on her features. 'That's okay, I sneaked in. I don't really feel like going home, to be honest.'

She looked him up and down, her eyes drinking him in. He let her—and then he realised he hadn't picked up the towel.

'Oh, God—still naked!' He cursed, scrabbling for the towel and wrapping himself up again.

'Aw...' Michelle said, surprising him. 'Show's over, eh?' She pulled a silly face, laughing again when he blushed furiously. She stood up, heading towards the door. 'I'll let you get changed.'

She reached for the door at the same time he did, and just as quickly as it had opened, it clicked shut.

'Don't go,' he found himself saying. 'Stay—just for a little while. I have something to tell you, actually. I tried to tell you earlier...in a way.'

He walked his fingers along the polished wood surface of the door, brushing his hand against hers and threading his fingers through hers. They stood just inches apart, each with one hand on the door, turned towards each other.

He wanted to tell her about his daughter, about how wrongly she had read him, but he couldn't articulate anything that was flashing through his brain into actual words. He felt as if his skin was on fire, and his chest was rising and falling rapidly from the shock of his sheer need for her. Looking at her, he knew she felt it too. Her pupils were dilated in the charged darkness of the room.

'I should let you get on,' she tried feebly, but she made no move to leave. 'Tell me later.'

'I have time,' he said, his voice thick with lust. Then he thought of her being MIA earlier, and felt his heart clench. 'Where were you today?'

A shadow crossed her features. 'Third floor. Head shrinkers.'

He saw then how pale she was, how drawn. She'd done it; she'd taken the first step. He felt a surge of pride swell in his chest, and a rush of something else not far behind.

'Why? Did you miss me?' she added, her lips pushing out into a little faux pout.

She's teasing me, he realised with a jolt. *Careful, Jacob, this is not the time to start anything. You need to tell her. Think of the job...think of...*

She closed the gap between them before he had a chance to react. Her lips closed on his in a soft, gentle kiss that was over before it began. *Blink and you'd miss it.* Jacob would have happily surgically removed his eyelids so as not to miss that moment again.

She pulled away, and it took every ounce of his self-control for him not to lunge for her, to take her into his arms, show her what was under that towel again.

'Well, I think *you* missed *me*,' he quipped, before his playful look could turn to want again. 'You okay?'

He looked into her eyes and could see that she was miles away again. Probably back in that room, having to lay out the bones of her past for a clinical stranger. It was a lot, but he knew she could take it. Getting a handle on it was the first priority.

He saw her free hand fall to her side, pinching the skin on her leg through her clothing. He turned to face her square-on, their toes kissing each other through her shoes. Taking the hand away from her thigh, he took it in his and, bringing it up to his face, kissed it.

'You're not alone, you know,' he told her.

Once upon a time that would have been his stock response—telling people that he was there, that there was a light at the other side, to hang on. No man left behind. Or woman. Especially not one he was rapidly falling for, head over heels.

She made him want to be better, to try harder, to push himself to go that extra mile. She challenged him, excited his senses, made him hard at the mere flash of her skin or the touch of her lips. He was standing in front of her and he couldn't think of any better place to be. He wanted to help her. He needed her to recover from this, to be whole again. He needed it because *she* did. Anything less than one hundred percent was just not good enough for people like them. They were cut from the same cloth.

'I'm here.'

'That's half the problem,' she muttered, a flash of humour rolling across her features.

'Now, now…' Jacob chided, pulling her closer. 'I think having me around isn't so bad after all. You just won't admit it because you're as stubborn as they come.' He saw her mouth drop, and he laughed softly. 'Gotcha!'

She smirked in response, making him want to kiss her again, to make her legs wobble. He liked the challenge she represented, but in a very different way from the way he'd liked his previous conquests. They had been a diversion, a way of scratching an itch, a moment of shared comfort in a tormented war zone, a distraction from playing unhappy family at home, where he'd co-parented a child as one of two people who had just been making the best of a one-night stand with consequences.

Michelle was more than that.

Jenny was off doing her own thing now, her daughter and her ex-lover firmly in her rear view mirror. Jenny was nothing like Michelle. Michelle was something to strive for—not a short-term crutch to see him through the night.

She opened her mouth to speak, and surprised him all over again. 'What did you mean earlier, when you were talking about the potty seat?'

She knows I saw her.

'You sounded like you had some experience in the matter.'

'You saw that?' he asked, feigning ignorance for just a minute longer. 'How much did you hear?'

She shrugged. 'Just that you hated those potty seats. I got called away. Cute kid, wasn't he? Hard work, though. I can't imagine having to cope with tantrums like that day in, day out. Makes our job look a little easier, doesn't it?' She laughed a little. 'My niece is gorgeous—don't get me wrong—but that kid was another level today.'

She giggled again, and Jacob's plan to tell her about Ebony clanged shut in his mind like a steel cell door.

'I've seen it happen before,' he said, his voice weak and flat. 'The best time was when a dad got one stuck on his head, trying to dance for his kid to get him to use the potty.'

And also another time. A screaming little girl going red in the face because she hadn't been able to cope with what was being asked of her.

He would hear those sobs till the last day he drew breath. That was the moment they'd known Ebony was different. Not worse—just different. They'd been told Ebony was autistic, and his impending tour had made things so much worse for all three of them.

'Do you want kids someday?' he asked, holding his breath for her answer.

'Sure,' she said, nodding at him. 'Someday when things settle down, maybe. I always thought I would— but this life, you know…?'

He nodded, trying to hide his swirling emotions of relief and worry. 'Yeah, I know. I actually—'

A laugh sounded at the other side of the door, followed by a crash and a cheer. The universal sound of someone with butterfingers. Michelle had turned her face towards the door, her work brain clicking on and assessing the noise. He watched her, saw the frown lines on her forehead deepening as she strained to listen for any danger.

'It's probably Wendy—that woman would never make a juggler,' he muttered, leaning closer till their foreheads touched.

He needed to touch her, to comfort her, and he couldn't stop himself any longer. She let him, and even pulled him closer, a soft laugh escaping her.

He snapped, unable to take any more. 'What are we *doing*, Mich?'

He felt like a teenager—all hormones and insecurities. How did she do it? She had him, an alpha male, wrapped around her surgical-gloved finger, and the best thing was she had no idea. For the first time in Jacob's rather daring life he felt vulnerable, exposed, and he didn't even care. Not when it came to her.

She was biting her lip now, her eyes on the floor, and he used his left index finger to raise her chin, to make her eyes meet his. He wanted her to *be* his, to know about Ebony, to understand what kind of man he was, what kind of father he was trying to be. He needed her to see him through the blood and the loss and the fear. The way he had seen her.

PTSD loves company—go figure.

'Michelle, what is this? What are we doing?' he asked again. He could feel his heart pounding in his chest, sounding the drums of love loud in the silent room. 'Do you feel this? Do you feel for me what I feel for you?'

It was out there. The question he had wanted to ask since that first night. She had broken his nose, and now he was terrified she would break his heart too. He held his breath.

'Yes,' she said, looking him straight in the eye.

She had never looked so sexy.

'I feel it too.'

He didn't wait a second longer. Reaching behind him, not moving his gaze from hers, he clicked the lock on the door. Slowly he ran his fingers up the sides of her cheeks, taking her face in his hands and touching his lips to hers. She tasted sweet, and he kissed her again, moving his mouth from her lips to the side of her neck, running his tongue along her clavicle, pulling her top out of the way and growling in his throat when he was rewarded with a peek of black lacy bra and pink skin.

He reached the end of her shoulder and nipped her, just once, with his teeth. The resulting moan from her spurred him on, and he put his broad arms around her, lifting her off the ground. She wrapped her legs around him readily, her back now pushed against the on-call room door, his body slotted against hers, till only the clothing they wore separated them.

She moved her arms around his shoulders, running her fingers through his hair, giving it a sharp tug and pulling his mouth against hers once more.

The kiss ignited as they both fully gave in to sensation. Mouth on mouth, tongue caressing tongue… They moaned and panted as they kissed each other passionately, exploring each other with everything they had. He tried to wrap his hands tighter around her and growled in frustration.

'The bed,' she muttered into his mouth, barely breaking the kiss.

He whirled her around, walking her in his arms, still locking lips with her, and laid her down on the bed, lying down alongside her. She moved position, pushing him till his back hit the mattress. He let her take the lead, not quite believing how things had gone from him being covered in coconut oil and keeping secrets to being here, kissing her in the on-call room, touching this woman who wanted the job he needed.

She looked at him, her lips swollen from their kiss, and put her hand on his chest, over the space where his heart lived. He covered it with his own hand, linking their fingers together and pulling her closer. She came easily, her legs astride him now, so she was sitting on him, her hair ruffled, sexy. She looked him straight in the eye and started to pull her top up.

Jacob leaned forward, resting on his elbows, kissing the skin that she uncovered. Her stomach—flat and still tanned—her ribs—one side and then the other. He left a trail of hot kisses all the way up her body, reaching up and cupping her through her black bra. She let him, moving her body closer to his touch, rubbing herself against him, those pieces of fabric the only barrier.

She moved to take the towel away, and he rose with her, helping her, giving her access to every inch of him. The towel dropped off the bed and Michelle drank him in. He lay there beneath her, letting her feast on him, enjoying the sensations evoked by having her this close. There wasn't a drug rep in the world who could sell him anything that would top this. It was pure, wild… And, whatever they were doing, if they went any further there would be no going back.

He moved slowly, bringing her with him till they were sitting up, her legs wrapped around him, his arms around her. Only her bra and her jeans to go now, but he wasn't going to make the first move. It had to be her, on *her* terms. For once Jacob found himself enjoying relinquishing control to someone else.

'This is a bad idea…' she said, running her fingers

along Jacob's bare chest, leaning forward to lick the glistening drops of water still left from the shower.

He flinched at her touch and his muscles tensed. She laughed, running her tongue along his side now, along the bumps of his abs, clearly enjoying the feeling of him bucking and writhing beneath her.

'Insanely bad...' he breathed, pulling her mouth back to his and kissing her. He could feel himself hard beneath her, and he couldn't take much more. 'Do that again.'

She laughed, pushing him gently, with a poke of her finger in his chest, and he flopped back, undoing her bra with a well-practised flick of his wrist. From his position he could see the swell of her breasts under the fabric and he slowly pulled it off, her bright eyes following his movements. The piece of lace followed his towel to the floor and there she was, laid out before him.

It was then that he saw it—a scar, running down one side of her left breast, puckering the skin slightly as she moved to cover herself.

'No,' he said, shaking his head and gently taking her hands away, resting them on his chest again. 'Let me look at you.'

He ran a finger along the scar, seeing where the surgeon had tried to repair the injury as best he could. He knew from his training that this was a patch-up job, done with speed and skill, minimum tools and medicine. It was a battle scar and she clearly hated it. He could see it in her eyes, which were now looking at anything and everything in the room apart from him.

'You are absolutely perfect,' he murmured.

He'd only said that to one girl before today—Ebony—and both times he'd meant it as earnestly as any man ever had.

'Don't ever feel the need to hide any part of yourself. Especially not from me.'

He moved his head to one side, exposing the small silvery scar that ran along his collarbone. She gasped a little, running her thumb along it and making him want to kill whoever was stupid enough to have invented denim. He needed her so much it was painful.

'Shrapnel?' she checked, and he nodded.

'Qatar. Those last few days were pretty bad in our camp.'

He ignored the flash of his memory, the thought of his pain as the home-made bomb had exploded, showering them all with shards of jagged metal, nuts, bolts, pieces of old buildings. Anything that would cause the most damage. It could have been a lot worse. Jacob was grateful that the bomb-maker had been an inexperienced small child. Imagine being grateful for such a thing in this world.

'Yours?' he asked.

She was still self-conscious—he could tell. She lifted her left arm, bent it at the elbow so her fist rested on the ball of her shoulder. Red lines like jagged cuts ran along her side, where the skin was raised, still healing.

'Ambush. One of the people we were treating was being hunted, and the hunters came to camp to try to get him back.'

A single tear escaped her eye and ran down her cheek before she had a chance to stop it. It dripped from her cheek onto his muscular chest and she rubbed it away.

'I raised my arms to protect myself...took a chunk. I thought I'd lost my arm for sure.'

Another tear dripped down and he rubbed it with his thumb, lifting himself up to meet her chest to chest and kissing her tears away. She kissed him back, wrapping her arms around him again. Slowly he moved them both till he was on top of her, pinning her gently to the bed with his naked body.

'You're okay,' he murmured between kisses. 'You're here. You made it.'

'So did you,' she deadpanned back. 'Does that mean we really are out, though? Does anyone really get out?'

What wasn't she telling him? What was hidden behind those cautious eyes?

He didn't answer her with words, because he didn't want her to hear him lie. He answered her with his hands, moving them over her, bringing her closer to him. He wanted to unzip himself from head to toe, to take her into him and keep her close, the two of them together against the world with all its struggle and enemies.

They moved together, healing each other with their touch, and he whispered things into her ear, letting her open up to him in her own time. He knew she needed to be in control, and he was a willing passenger on her journey to recovery, to becoming fully herself once more.

He had so much to tell her, but this wasn't the time. He would speak to her with his body for now...show her what he couldn't utter with his voice.

'Do you have anything?' she whispered in his ear, nibbling at his neck as she went.

'In my trouser pocket,' he replied, suddenly grateful that old habits died hard. 'A good soldier is always prepared.'

She raised a brow at him, and he wanted to take her there and then.

'On a promise?' she teased.

He laughed—a low rumble in his chest that made her body move with the movement. Her eyes rolled back a little and he grabbed her hips, moving her just once over his pelvis.

'A man needs to be ready for anything, but it's been a while.'

Arching a brow, she looked at him. 'How long?'

'Long enough. No more talking, Dr Forbes.'

She moaned, reaching across to the discarded clothes on the other bed and getting what she needed. Tearing open the packet, she took her time, with Jacob moaning about slow torture.

'You ready?' she asked, once he was sheathed and waiting.

'I was born ready, woman. Come here,' he growled, and reached for her.

CHAPTER SEVEN

A BUZZING NOISE woke Michelle from her slumber. For once her sleep hadn't been full of terrors, and she hadn't even dreamed. She lifted her head a little, listening to the noise. On the other bed Jacob's pager was lit up, just visible clipped to his white coat. It wasn't the emergency tone, but it made her very aware of her surroundings all the same.

A stirring came from the side of her, and she turned to see Jacob lying on his back, naked, one arm underneath her back, pulling her close, the other holding her hand tight. She made a move to leave him, but in sleep he tightened his grip, mumbling to himself and making it harder for her to pull away.

She'd slept with a colleague. In the same on-call room where she had head-butted him and broken his nose just a short time ago. They were nearing the halfway mark in their race for the job, and now things were more complicated than ever.

What the hell are you doing?

Rebecca was somewhere laughing at her, no doubt. It gave her a pang to think of her friend. Had he whispered the same things to her? Used the same moves? But it didn't feel as if it was just lust, and he'd said all the right things. Could a man be a player one day and a relationship man the next?

She gently peeled herself away from him, dressing quickly and quietly. She needed to get up, get out of there, go home.

What if Andrew found out? Would they both lose their jobs before they'd even had a chance to prove themselves to the investors?

He moved, and she turned in panic. He was still asleep, smiling at something. She grabbed her things and then knelt by the bed, watching his long dark lashes flutter against his skin.

What's in that handsome head of yours, Jacob? Can I really trust you? Do you really know how messed up I am? Do you know how messed up you are?

She stroked the thick dark hair back from his forehead, exposing a tiny scar in his hairline that she hadn't seen before. She bent down, running her lips along it like a whisper in the dark.

She knew it shouldn't work. He was her rival, a player who had slept with a friend she still mourned, but she just couldn't leave him alone. She was starting to think about him all the time, wondering how he was, how his day was going, what his home looked like.

A knock came at the door, and she flinched.

'Dr Peterson?'

Shit. The page must be urgent after all.

She checked, but Jacob was still asleep. The pager went off again, but it was unnoticed by him. The man was exhausted.

She smiled a little, feeling a dirty kind of satisfaction that she might be the cause.

We have a lot to talk about, she thought to herself. *But maybe we just need to go for it.*

She stood, checking her hair quickly in the mirror. She looked as if she had just been thoroughly seen to—which wouldn't do at all. She smoothed it down as best she could, opening the door a crack. One of the receptionists was standing there—a temp whose name Michelle could never remember.

'Yes?' she said, in her firm doctor voice.

'Oh, sorry, Doctor.' The woman blushed, trying and failing to peek behind Michelle into the room. 'I thought Dr Peterson was in here.'

'He left a while ago,' she lied. 'Canteen. Is there an emergency case?'

The woman, a nervous, mousy-haired twenty-something, shook her head vigorously. 'No, nothing like that. I just need him to call home—can you tell him if you see him?'

Call home? It was then that Michelle noticed the little pink message the receptionist was holding in her hand. She eyed the scrawl but couldn't make it out. A cleaner, maybe? A contractor? People who lived alone like she did didn't get calls from home.

'No problem,' she said brightly, grabbing the piece of paper from her in a flash. She had to see it. The woman balked, but said nothing. 'I'll pass the message on. Thank you.'

She waved the woman away, closing the door slowly. One look at Jacob and she knew he was still fast asleep, his breathing slow and deep. She read the message, then crumpled it into a ball, tight between her shaking fingers.

I can't believe I was so stupid.

She looked around the room. Sheets and clothes tossed everywhere. Pillows on the floor. The smell of sex in the air. It felt so cheap now—a sordid and tawdry bunk-up at work, not a passionate meeting of bodies and minds.

She felt a wave of shame—and then came the anger. She'd done it now. The epic cock-up that would end everything she'd been clinging to. She had to leave immediately. She was just another trophy on his wall and she hated herself for falling for it.

She knew better; she always had. When she got close to someone it was for a reason, and it didn't come easily.

What was she going to do now? Why, just when she'd been able to see a glimpse of a future, had it been taken away? She couldn't handle it. She was going to break down right here and right now, and she was terrified that once she went down that road it was be hard to come back.

A solitary sob erupted from her, and she slapped herself hard across the face.

'Stop it!' she whispered to herself angrily. 'Stop it. Now. Pull. Yourself. Together.'

She punctuated each word with a sharp slap, her other hand pinching her thigh over and over again, till she could barely stand the pain. *Better*, she thought as her nerve-endings screamed at her to stop.

Listening with one ear to the door for a moment, she checked the coast was clear. She slammed the door hard behind her and didn't stop until she was safely in her car, heading out of the car park with a screech of tyres.

She kept on pinching herself till she was safely locked behind her front door, and it was there, on the polished wood floor, that she finally fell apart and let the hot, salty tears flow freely.

I'm alone, she realised with a jolt, knowing that the reassuring solid presence of Jacob had been taken away in one pretty pink note. *I'm alone and I deserve to be. It's over. It's just all so...hopeless.*

* * *

'What?' Jacob blurted, flying out of bed and going from being fast asleep to standing there alert, arms out in a fighting stance, all in a few seconds. *'What?'* he barked again—before his vision and his brain caught up, processing the images.

A loud bang had woken him and now he was standing there in the buff, looking as if he was about to fight the door.

'Michelle?' he asked, but he knew she had left the room.

Her stuff was all gone...no note left. He rummaged in his clothing, throwing on his boxers and checking his pager. *Phew.* Nothing work-related. He frowned as he saw the group of messages so close together, frantic. He needed to call home.

He had been enjoying a dream—him at home with Ebony, and Michelle right there with them. But he felt bone-tired all of a sudden, and with a groan he headed back to the reality of the day.

The next day Michelle strode into a room on the third floor, slapping down the pink piece of paper in front of her very surprised therapist.

'Dr Forbes. I actually have a patient in—'

'Open up, you said. Trust someone, you said. Well, what do you say about *this*?'

She grabbed the note back from the coffee table, thrusting it into his face.

'Dr Colton, you suck at your job.'

She rolled the paper into a ball, throwing it into the wastepaper basket at the side of her with a huff of disgust before flouncing down onto the leather couch opposite him.

'Firstly, I only have a few minutes before my next patient, and secondly, the name's Greg. What seems to be upsetting you?'

She pounded the sofa cushions with her fists, trying to get a grip on her anger. Mostly at herself. She had taken her eye off the ball and look what had happened. She'd become a notch on Dr Love's bedpost—a bedpost already so notched that it looked more like a set of toothpicks than a trophy wall.

'I tried what you said. I tried reaching out.'

An image of Jacob's corded forearm, reaching down between their bodies, his hand pressing his thumb against her nub, sprang into her head.

Get out, Lust MD. Today is angry woman day. I hope you got the memo.

Greg Colton's face developed a slow, cautious smile. 'I see,' he said. 'And…?'

'Read the note, Doctor. I put myself out there and made a fool of myself. I failed—*again*.'

Greg said nothing as he unfolded the crumpled piece of paper, read it. His face remained the same, not changing expression.

Damn, what is it with shrinks and their poker faces?

He smoothed the paper out, tucking it into her client file and then sitting back down in his easy chair.

The note read.

Chinese tonight? Hurry home.
Love you.
Call me.
Ebony

'This is addressed to Dr Peterson. Is he the doctor who has your job?'

She nodded, wanting to disagree with him about the finer points of who had the job, but deciding against it. It *was* her job—although now the lines were even less clear.

'This is upsetting to you?'

State the obvious, Greg.

She rolled her eyes at him and he smiled, just a fraction, before those shutters came down again, disguising his thoughts.

'Yes,' she replied eventually. 'It does. He did this to Rebecca, you know.'

'Did what?' he asked.

'Slept with her…used her.'

Greg smiled kindly. 'From what you've told me about the situation, and your friend, it sounds to me like it was a mutual arrangement. Friends with benefits, as they call it. Do you *really* think he exploited her?'

She opened her mouth to say yes, but she knew it wasn't true. Rebecca had been a modern single woman; she'd known what she was doing the same as him.

'Still, he wasn't free like she was. He wasn't single and modern. He was just the same as half the men in the world. He went with his trouser brain. I should have known better.'

Greg's eyes narrowed, and he wrote something on a pad next to him just as the buzzer from Reception sounded.

'Dr Forbes, my patient is here, but I want to talk about this further. Are you available for a session tomorrow? It can start early if you need to work around a shift. Book in with Reception, okay?' He patted the note. 'We will start here tomorrow.' He sat back in his seat, making a steeple with his long fingers. 'The key point here is forgiveness, remember? You need to stop apologising for surviving, Michelle. It's hurting you.'

Michelle left, reluctantly making an appointment, and then heading to the lift to go down to the trauma floor. One floor lower and Andrew was standing there, waiting to get on.

'Hi,' he said jovially, waving his briefcase at her as they stood side by side, waiting for the lift doors to close. 'You okay?'

'Fine,' she said, giving him her best at-the-top-of-my-game smile. 'Ready to get going.'

Andrew beamed. 'Great! Jacob's clearly had the same idea. He's been like a man on a mission all morning.'

Michelle turned to look at him. She was an hour early for work, but Jacob was already here?

'What do you mean, on a mission…?'

Jacob Peterson was already walking on cloud nine when he spotted the lift doors opening and saw Andrew and Michelle standing there, deep in conversation. So deep that they didn't even realise the doors had opened.

What was the deal? Were they talking about him? About the job? Was she filling him in on their recent interactions?

The more they stood there talking, the more Jacob felt his hackles rising. His paranoia was so large it felt like a full-sized companion, a shadow on his back. He'd never been scared of losing things before, and he wasn't doing well at it. When Ebony had needed him—when Jenny had said she was done with him, with her, with them—he had fought for her. He'd stepped up—albeit far too late. If he lost Michelle now he knew he wouldn't take it well.

He looked down at his sides and saw his fists were clenched tight.

What was going on?

Michelle was smiling at Andrew now, and Jacob wanted to slap him for being the lucky receiver.

As though his thoughts had summoned her, Michelle turned in that moment, stepping out of the lift and looking straight at him. She looked him up and down, her face neutral, and then, turning on her heel, she was gone, leaving Jacob still wondering what the hell was going on.

She left you asleep in that room, naked. No note.

An uncomfortable notion entered his head. Maybe she regretted it altogether. He hadn't considered that. He hadn't been left in bed before. He was the one who did the leaving—or he had been. Was that the look in her eye? Regret?

After all, they barely knew each other and they were fighting for the same job. Could it end well for either of them? Just because Jacob was ploughing on ahead, despite these nagging issues, it didn't mean that Michelle was able to. She had her own demons and problems to face—just as he did.

The difference was that her pain was on show and she was letting him in…just a little. He knew he couldn't say the same about himself. Would she be okay with his baggage if she knew about it? What would that look like?

There were too many questions to be answered. And in their line of work that was a dangerous thing. In trauma, you were fighting fires constantly. Patching people up, making things work, improvising—anything to shovel the sands of time back into the timer, giving their patients more time, another day to live and to be loved.

Jacob thrived on it, and he knew Michelle did too, but, in real life was a relationship built on adrenaline and rivalry doomed from the start?

The feel of her moving with him yesterday had told him differently. They'd fitted each other perfectly, knitting their kind of damage together and healing it, turning it into something different. Was a foundation of that kind enough to sustain a relationship?

Jacob knew he wanted to try. They had almost three weeks left and he was going to give it his all, let the chips fall where they may.

He didn't answer the loudest question of all. At the end of that time would he want the job, or his rival?

As he walked away to see his next patient he realised that it was all a moot point anyway. The fact was that she'd left, and now she was talking in corners with Andrew. And that look she'd just given him didn't bode well. It might well be that the woman who ran through his mind fifty times an hour would break his heart as well as take the job he needed.

It ruined his good mood for the day.

Michelle looked at the OR board and cursed the light day. Then she cursed herself, for wishing for a bus crash or a small natural disaster to give her something to distract herself. She needed to have the feel of a scalpel in her hand as she worked to save a patient. She needed to get busy and bury her head in the sand.

Hell, the way she was feeling, she almost wished for the anonymity of the desert. Almost.

'Quiet day,' Jacob said, his deep voice making her body react.

Traitor libido! Lock it up, Medic.

He brushed his sleeves back from his wrists and loosened his tie. 'I've been wishing for a trauma. Is that bad?'

She laughed despite herself. 'It's pretty bad, yeah.'

He crossed his arms, showing off muscular forearms sprinkled with thick dark hair. She found herself wondering what his chest would look like if it was covered in hair…something to run her fingers through on a cold winter's night.

Geez, woman, get a grip. You are too badass to be a puddle at some man's feet. Especially his.

'I knew it. Where did you go yesterday?'

He lowered his voice, leaning in. She caught a whiff of his aftershave and felt her stomach flip.

'I had to get home; my place is a bit of a work in progress.'

She could have bitten her tongue off, but what else could she say? She couldn't exactly show him the telephone message, could she? Not only had she stolen it and not told him, she'd also tried to shame her therapist with it, and now it was hanging in her file like a big scarlet letter.

He pulled a business card out of his wallet, passing it to her as they both pretended to study the board. 'I didn't have your number, so here's mine.'

She looked at it in her hand, but didn't put it in her pocket right away. 'I have your pager number,' she said, and looked at him to judge his reaction.

He just looked confused. 'I know, but that's work stuff I'd like to have your home number…to call you and take you out, maybe? We could actually talk outside of these walls. I *need* to talk to you. Tomorrow? Eastgate Park?'

She was already shaking her head before he had finished speaking. 'I don't know what you think is going on here, Jacob, but we are still up for the same job. I think we should keep things professional from here on in.'

'What?' Jacob said, clearly aghast.

He went to touch her arm, to guide her away somewhere, but she pulled her hand away—hard. 'Dr Peterson,' she said, and her professional, detached voice sounded alien even to her. 'I have work to do, and I'm sure you do too. Let's just forget everything else, okay?'

She took a few steps back, folding her arms and fixing him with a stare she struggled to hold. He looked so upset, so confused. *Why* was this man such a puzzle? When they'd been together the day before she had never felt so cherished, so desired, so *seen* by anyone before. He'd made her feel alive, made her want to share her life with him. She cared what he thought about her even now, and she hated herself for being so weak around him.

'Michelle, I don't understand...'

He took a step closer to her and her fight-or-flight response kicked in. She pinched the skin around her left thumb-pad between her fingers, grabbing and twisting it till it seemed as if it was going to tear from her bones.

He saw and raised a hand. 'Michelle—stop. Look at me, okay? I'm here. I'm here for you, Mich.'

I'm here for you.

Those words. Of all the thousands of words in the world, they were too much.

Raising her head high, fixing Jacob with a hard look, she took the business card between her fingers and tore it in half, repeating the action till the card was a pile of paper confetti in her shaking fingers.

'I don't need anyone, Jacob. Have you not worked that out yet? I have my friends and my job. I had them before you, and I will have them after you've moved on to your next...challenge.' She turned her palm over, letting the pieces flutter to the floor. 'If you're feeling lonely from now on check your messages. I'm sure you'll find some company.'

She didn't hear his reply. She was already out of there—back to work. Jacob Peterson could jolly well please himself from now on. This job was what she needed, and she wasn't about to let it slip through her fingers like that business card of a total ding-dong.

She ignored the splintering pain in her heart as she strode away from the man she knew she was falling for.

'Michelle!' he called after her, and she closed her eyes against the sting of tears. 'What did I do? What messages?'

'Messages?' Jacob panted at the receptionist behind the desk. 'Messages…for…' He pointed at himself with a double thumb movement. He'd run all the way in a state of mild panic. 'I hear you have messages?'

The woman looked at him wide-eyed. 'I did, Doctor, but I put them in your pigeonhole.'

He nodded, still gasping for air, and half ran around the reception desk to the wall of staff pigeonholes. Thumbing through the pieces of paper, he frowned, brandishing them in his fist and waggling them at the poor woman.

'Is this all of them?' he asked, wondering what the hell was going on.

The woman winced, pointing down the corridor.

'I did give one of them to another doctor yesterday, to pass on to you. Was that wrong?'

She looked as if she was about to burst into tears and Jacob felt bad. He wasn't meaning to come across so bullish—he just needed to know what had changed Michelle's mind about him…what had turned her so cold. He'd tasted her now, and that couldn't be the last time. He wouldn't cope if it was.

He pushed the pieces of paper back into his pigeonhole and went over to the receptionist. 'I'm sorry…er…'

'Elaine.' The woman sniffed. 'I gave a message to Dr Forbes yesterday. I thought you were in the on-call room, but—'

Jacob's pager buzzed in his pocket and he checked it. Home—checking in. He read the message, feeling a second of relief. Ebony was fine and having a good day. She'd be heading to the park now with her nanny, if she hadn't already.

'Okay, so you gave it to Dr Forbes. What did it say?'

Elaine reached over her desk and grabbed a pink duplicate pad, flicking back through the entries to find her carbon copy of the message.

'Here we are,' she said shrilly.

She folded over the page and showed it to him in such a way that it told him she was by now terrified of him and his rather bizarre behaviour. To be fair, it was a little unlike him. He was the cool one—Mr Ice. Not lately, though. Not since Michelle had landed in his life.

Reading the notepad message, he felt his face drop. *Jesus Christ.*

'She read this?' he checked.

Elaine nodded. 'She said she would pass it on...that you weren't there but she would be seeing you.'

Something clicked in Jacob's memory. Like a piece that didn't quite fit till you turned it round and looked at it from a new angle. She'd got this message while they'd been together in the on-call room.

'That's why she left,' he muttered under his breath bleakly.

'Is something wrong, Doctor?' Elaine asked, her hands knitted together in front of her.

He smiled, passing the pad back to her. His pager went off again. Home? 'No problem, Elaine. Sorry for worrying you. It's my fault—nothing to worry about. Thank you.'

Elaine smiled, her panic subsiding. 'No problem, Doctor. Do you want to take your messages now?'

His pager went off again, and he waved Elaine away. 'No, thank you, Elaine, I'll grab them later. Next time only pass them to me, okay? Gotta go—trauma incoming!'

Half of his words were whipped into the air as he ran away from her to the ambulance doors.

His pager vibrated in his pocket again, and he saw Call home on the display.

Damn. He'd probably forgotten some trip slip or paperwork that needed signing for school, but he didn't have time now. Today was turning into a great day for annoying just about every female in his life, it seemed.

He winced at the thought and arrived at his destination to see a figure already there, briefing the trauma team while they gowned up in plastic aprons, gloves and headgear. Whatever it was, it clearly merited half the staff being here.

Michelle was gowned up too, and reading from a clipboard in her hand, using her pen to point people towards different areas to set up. He was almost at her side when she spotted him. A strange expression crossed her features for half a second, and then she was back to being Dr Forbes, trauma goddess. Tormentor of his very being.

'RTA, corner of St John's Road. School bus and a goods lorry. One confirmed fatality at the scene—the driver of the lorry. The other vehicles were a woman and a girl in a car—minor injuries. They were clipped by the bus as the truck hit it. They're on their way in. Second ambulance is still there. Some issue at the scene.'

She looked at him over her clipboard. People were flying in all directions around them, as the distant scream of sirens got nearer. Tannoy announcements echoed inside the walls, and people and equipment scrambled like a well-oiled machine.

For the pair of them the department might as well have been empty. They stood only inches apart, but a world away from each other. Jacob could see that she had deleted him from her memory, wiped out the few blissful moments they had enjoyed. He'd messed it all up, and he didn't know how to get out of it without causing further damage.

'How bad?' he asked.

'Bad,' she replied. 'Twelve kids are on their way in; the rest are being treated for cuts and shock at the scene, waiting for transfer here. We have the beds, thank God. No criticals yet, but the bus driver is still being cut out by the fire brigade.'

Jacob nodded, turning to face the throng of people in the trauma bay. 'Right, people. RTA incoming—three minutes! We need blood cross-checked and ready, we need blankets, bandages, and trauma trays set up for glass removal, cut-cleaning, stitching. Students—anyone mastered stitching, good suture techniques?'

A couple of hands went up from the pool of eager juniors who were hanging around in the corner of the department, hoping to get the chance to help.

He pointed at the two of them. 'You—go set up some suturing trays for the bays. Ask a nurse if you're not sure. You—number two—' he didn't have the time to look for a name tag or worry about hurt feelings here '—call Plastics. Get someone down here. They can assess the patients first, see what you can scoop up. Learn from them, people, and get moving!'

For a second nothing much happened, and Jacob noticed a few of the staff were looking at Michelle for direction. Too many cooks. *Goddamn it.* How could they work together if she hated him like this?

Michelle looked at Jacob and addressed the room.

'You heard the doctor! We run this trauma together—get moving, people!' She raised the clipboard towards the doors, like a warrior holding aloft a sword. 'Incoming—brace yourselves! No one else dies today, you hear me?'

Boom. Her words ignited the room, galvanising every person from the timid receptionist to the gaggle of student doctors who didn't know one end of a central line from the other. Everyone helped, everyone worked together, and Jacob and Michelle were like one entity, one brain.

The bus crash victims came in ones and twos, a fleet of ambulances bringing them through the doors. Their loved ones followed in tears, phones ringing in their bags and pockets. They came brandishing photos on their phone screens, gripping gilded silver photo frames they had ripped from sills and hearths and bedside tables to help identify their child.

Jacob couldn't bring himself to look at them, at their pain and utter terror. He'd seen that look on too many faces. So he focused on the people he could help—the ones needing medical attention.

The lorry driver's wife arrived a short time later, to see her husband, and Jacob took that second to escape. He couldn't bear to look her in the face, to feel her pain. That woman's life would be altered for ever after she'd walked through those doors, and he hated that part of his job. Hated seeing the ones they were too late for...the ones who'd never had a chance...never even saw it coming.

Heading to the on-call room, he tried the bathroom door but found it locked.

'Sorry,' he said, cursing the intruder. Then he heard it—the soft sound of someone weeping. 'Hello? Who's in there?' He banged on the door once and it opened.

'I'm in here. I just needed a minute,' Michelle said

gruffly, throwing a ball of rolled-up tissue into the waste-paper basket behind her and moving past him.

'You okay?' he asked, already knowing the answer.

Some shifts were much worse than others, and today was still happening.

'I'm okay.' She looked at him for the first time and her fingers flexed instinctively towards him at her sides, but she folded her arms, setting her face stubbornly.

'Me too,' he admitted. 'Did you see—?'

'The widow? Yeah, that's what set me off.'

Jacob's heart swelled. Here they were—not together, not even speaking, really—and they were so similar in so many ways.

He opened his mouth to tell her, but she beat him to it.

'I need you to leave me alone, Jacob. Please.'

She said it like *We need more pens in the nurses' station* or *Pass the butter.*

Jacob's words fell out of his head, jumbling into a pile in the pit of his stomach.

'I just need you to be my colleague today. The rest is done. Dead.'

Why me? Why him? Did he follow me? Sense my presence somehow?

When she'd opened the bathroom door to see him standing there, his lips tight with concern, she'd wanted to cry all over again, to run into his arms. But that wasn't her style. She'd needed a minute away from the pain and the sobs and the stricken faces of the relatives waiting for news of their loved ones, of their children—those same children they had kissed that morning before sending them off all excited for their school trip.

Sometimes life just seemed so unfair.

Before she'd known what was happening, she'd almost

blurted out the words that had been rattling around in her head for months, never fully forming, always lurking silently. But she'd grabbed those words and pushed them kicking and screaming back into her mouth.

She wanted to get it out there—to tell someone. To tell *him*. Despite herself, and that damn pink note, she couldn't help but still feel the attraction between them. Their shorthand in the trauma department was perfect; they worked together like a pair of limbs, each one knowing where the other was at all times.

She hadn't had that since Rebecca, and that crushing thought was the one thing that threatened to break the dam. She couldn't let it, though—not now. She had to get away from him, and she wasn't strong enough to do it alone. He had to stay away, to give her a chance of getting past this. Over him.

'I know you're going through hell, but I can help. I'm a mess too, Mich. I need to tell you something, but you won't listen!'

'Be my colleague today. Can you do that?' she asked again. 'Can you just be my colleague?'

Jacob took one step closer and both their pagers went off. He groaned in frustration when he read his.

'The occupants of the car are two minutes out,' he said flatly.

Nodding, Michelle pulled an errant strand of hair away from her face and, brushing herself down, followed him as he ran to the ambulance bay.

Two ambulances were coming in, and Jacob waited for the second.

Michelle already had her hand on the door of the first. The woman on the gurney was conscious, but very quiet, a wet slash of blood across her forehead and cheekbone.

Michelle checked her pupils, working carefully around the collar.

'How long has she been like this?' she asked.

The paramedic, Waseela, looked at her watch a millisecond before answering. 'Less than three minutes. Her pupils are equal and responsive. She's in a state of shock. She was on her phone earlier, trying to contact someone, but she wasn't making a lot of sense. She has a broken arm from the collision; she was trying to shield the passenger with her arm.'

The second ambulance screeched to a halt and Michelle saw Jacob go for the doors from the corner of her eye. He was on the case, and it felt good to have him there, at her side, even with her question still unanswered and his evident frustration.

She returned to her patient, asking for some more details, checking her vision as they walked her in—but then something stopped her in her tracks. The girl in the other ambulance was awake, and in a state of distress.

'Get off me! Don't touch me! It hurts…it hurts!'

Jacob froze—just for a moment, but Michelle noticed, and passed her patient to a nurse and headed over to help.

'Daddy!' The little girl said. 'Daddy!'

She had a plaster on her forehead and the skin on her face was cut, tiny little slits where the glass from the side windows of the car must have shattered with the impact.

Jacob had jumped into the back of the ambulance, and before anyone could object he sat himself behind the little girl on the gurney, her back resting against his front, and he slowly and gently wrapped his arms around her. The little girl stopped shouting and started whimpering, rocking back and forth. He rocked with her, whispering softly into her ear, words of encouragement, of love.

The crew brought her out, wheeling her off to the bay. Michelle followed.

'Daddy, I rang you!' the little girl sobbed.

Michelle looked around, but no one seemed to be racing to the youngster's side. Moving away a little, she beckoned to Jude, who was just updating the emergency board.

'Jude, can we call the family for this little girl? The driver she's with doesn't look as though she's the mother. Grandmother, maybe? I want to get her admitted, but Jacob's taken the lead.'

Looking back at the pair, she saw Jacob rubbing the girl's back while he held her tight on the gurney. The staff were keeping their distance from them and rushing to help other patients. Something felt odd. Jacob was good with kids, sure—she'd already seen that—but why wasn't he moving?

'Have a word, Jude, and get her details. I'll go and see to the driver.'

Michelle looked from the nurse to Jacob, and to the girl. She looked so familiar...

'Daddy, who's the lady?' a little voice asked, and Jacob's eyes flicked to where Michelle was standing, watching from the curtained doorway to a cubicle. He gave her an apologetic half-smile.

Softly, he spoke. 'I'm sorry. The park date was going to be an introduction.'

The park date she had refused to go on.

He looked at her with his big green eyes and it clicked in her head.

'I did try to tell you. This is my daughter.'

He turned back to the little girl while Michelle looked on. She'd seen her before—around the hospital, in the cafeteria, the gift shop. She was always with an older woman. She just looked like any other visitor—aside from the headphones and chewable jewellery.

The little girl with the juice… She'd spoken to her, said hi in the corridor, a few times since. The happy, polite little girl who had stolen her heart that day was his *daughter*. He'd not been hiding her, just biding his time, and she'd shut him down at every single opportunity.

'This is Daddy's friend, honey—Dr Forbes. She's here to make you all better.'

The little girl looked at her father with wide eyes that were a carbon copy of his own. Michelle saw it then. It was obvious. She was a mini-version of him—the same dark lashes, the eyes ever-searching, the bow of her lips, the turn of her cute little nose.

Him—all him.

He has a daughter?

Something else clicked in her—snippets of conversation they had shared over the weeks they had spent together.

'I have to tell you something.'

He'd tried to tell her. That had to be it.

'And Susan, too?' The little girl with dark brown hair, matted a little now from the accident, looked right at Michelle. 'Will you make my nanny better too? She fell asleep.'

The driver in shock was his daughter's nanny. The poor child must have been terrified.

Looking at Jacob's pale face, she could see that he was pretty shaken too, and her crushed heart still felt for him. Jacob Peterson: playboy doctor, player, battle-scarred hero… Father?

She was giving herself a headache, trying to make the pieces fit. There'd been more than love and rivalry between them in the on-call room. There had been secrets too—and not just the ones *she* kept. The women, the bravado, the tours—all with a daughter in tow? She couldn't reconcile the old parts of him with the new. It didn't make sense.

'Dr Forbes?'

A nurse from Orthopaedics sidled up to her, chart in hand. Michelle could have kissed her for providing a distraction when she needed one.

'The driver of the car is back with you. She's had her scans done and a half-slab put on till the swelling goes down. Jude is with her now.'

'Thank you, Nurse.' She pinned her face into an easy smile, despatching her and turning back to Jacob and the child. 'Lovely to meet you, Miss Peterson,' she said kindly, giving the girl a genuine smile.

The little girl didn't return it at first, but slowly a little smile crept across her features.

'I have a patient, but I'll be back soon.'

'But—'

She heard Jacob start to talk to her, but she wanted to be nowhere near either of them right now.

She checked on the driver; the woman was indeed the girl's nanny, but that was all they knew. As well as the broken arm she has a lot of soreness to contend with, so the last thing she needed was the staff who were meant to be caring for her asking inappropriate questions about her employer.

Michelle got back to work, checking each patient over, double and triple-checking everything. At one point, charting in one of the side rooms, she snapped a pencil in half with her hand. Her grip had been too tight and the pressure of her worry and anxiety had been too much to bear.

She needed help, and she needed it now.

* * *

The third floor welcomed her once more like a soft pink bubble. The carpet seemed to bounce underfoot when she hit the corridor and nodded to the receptionist. Today, after the bus crash trauma, she was glad that she had pre-booked this slot, and now she had something else to talk about: the fact that she was falling for her work rival—the man who was currently downstairs comforting his surprise child and no doubt waiting for her anguished and stunningly beautiful mother.

It was another complication to their lives, and they weren't even together. She thought she'd felt low when she saw that note, but now this—a child? It was too much even to try to wrap her head around. Surely even the strongest women in the world needed a bit of help from time to time. Sometimes a good push-up bra and a can-do attitude with a side of denial wouldn't cut the mustard.

The buzzer sounded the second after she sat down on the waiting couch, or so it felt. Nodding to the receptionist, she walked into the consulting room on shaky legs, not daring to look up till she was safely sitting down on the familiar leather chair.

Greg was in his usual seat, his manner gentle and calm as always. Michelle tucked her hands on her lap, the thumb and forefinger of one hand pinching and nipping at the thumb-pad of the other. They both looked at the clock—a matter of habit—and when the time signalled the top of the hour Greg clicked his pen.

'So, Michelle,' he said, 'where shall we start?'

The little girl in his arms sagged, and Jacob knew she had finally given in to her fatigue and fallen asleep. He moved as quickly and as smoothly as he could, placing her gently into bed and watching her sleep. She looked so pale and drawn Jacob couldn't stand it. He walked backwards out of the cubicle, heading to the nurses' station.

Jude was at the computer, and her look told him that people around here hadn't missed a trick.

'Yes, she's my daughter,' he said. 'The nanny was taking her out for the day. Is Susan okay?'

Jude pursed her lips, nodding. 'She's sleeping; her family is on the way.'

Jacob sighed, feeling guilty that one of his first thoughts was that he had no childcare, and no idea how to sort that out before it affected his job. But the whole accident could have been a hell of a lot worse, and he knew it, which made his thoughts seem all the more selfish.

'That's good. Page me when they get here? I'm going to stay tonight anyway.'

Jude nodded, her icy demeanour thawing just a fraction. 'No problem. Need a bed making up?'

He shook his head. 'I'll do it when I get back. I just want to go and get some things from home. Did they bring their belongings from the car?'

Jude nodded, pointing back to where his daughter was sleeping. 'I put her bag in her locker. Your nanny packs well.'

Jacob smiled, thinking of the bag of magic that was sitting in that wooden locker. 'She sure does. Thanks, Jude. Dr Forbes around?'

'She had an appointment,' the nurse told him. 'You could have told us, you know...about your daughter. We would have helped.'

'I was new in the job, Jude, and the single dad thing is rather new to me. I was going to tell people, but then—'

'But then Michelle came back and it got complicated.'

Jude's arched brow reminded him just how observant and astute nurses were.

'Got it in one. I *do* care, you know—about her. About both of them…'

Jude was already focused back on her screen now, and she didn't answer. Girl code or busy professional?

A bit of both, he thought wryly.

It spoke a lot about how loved Michelle was that people cared so much, closed ranks even against him, a superior. If only they knew how strongly he felt that protective instinct too—felt that fire in his belly that made him want to run to her, to seek her out.

They didn't need to shelter Michelle from him. He'd take a bullet to spare her an ounce of pain. She made him better just by being in his life. He had a passion for her, for the job, for life again, and now he'd gone and blown the lot apart.

What was it she had said before? *'Leave me alone. Please.'*

Just recalling her words made his gut drop to the soles of his shoes.

'Jude, where *is* Dr Forbes?' He changed his voice, back to the commanding professional.

Jude looked at him, jaw tight. 'She's off the trauma floor for a while; she won't be much longer.'

She gave him a sarky little smile and returned to tapping the keys—this time a little harder. She no doubt expected him to slink off, but he stayed firm.

'Well, page her, please. Call her back to the floor.'

He needed to see her *now*—had to. He had to explain, find out what was wrong.

Had she left the hospital? Who was she meeting ?

Jude huffed and, picking up the phone, sent a page out. Replacing the receiver, she nodded to him in a *I did it, now leave me alone* way and returned to her typing.

The page went unanswered, and Jacob grew more and

more frustrated. He glanced back at the cubicle, checking his daughter was still fast asleep, and then turned to walk away, pulling his car keys out of his pocket.

'Keep paging her till she answers; tell her I need to see her urgently. I'll be back soon.'

Jude barely acknowledged him and he narrowed his eyes at her, feeling his tongue loosening with stress.

'Jude, I do need to speak to Dr Forbes. It is important, and I expect you to do your job.'

She looked at him lazily over the top of her monitor. His threat hadn't even hit the board, let alone the bullseye.

'I am doing my job, Dr Peterson,' she said pointedly. 'My boss is off the floor, and will answer your page when she gets back, I'm sure. Anything else?'

She raised a brow at him, and he didn't know whether to report her to Andrew or to laugh.

The clock had kept on ticking all the same, even after she'd opened her mouth to speak and uttered those words to Greg. Three little words, she'd said to him, and then three little words she hadn't uttered to Jacob.

Rebecca is dead, Jacob's a father

She had been watching the clock the whole time while she spoke, the fingers of her left hand pinching the inner skin of her opposite forearm distractedly, twisting it to the point of pain because that felt less painful than the words she was pushing out of her mouth.

She'd said the words and the clock had ignored them. No reaction, no stalling. The machinery had kept going, the mechanism free of guilt and loss, free of pain.

Whatever happens in this room, the clock never stops ticking.

The thought entered her head and she focused on it,

grabbing on to it and marvelling that life could be so cruel and so bleak and no one truly acknowledged it.

Why did they even bother? Right now she would rather be a ticking clock. Machinery without emotion.

'Does it bother you?' Greg asked, and she realised that she had spoken out loud. 'The clock?'

She looked at the clock face again and nodded. He'd asked her to focus on her first three words.

'I hate it that Rebecca doesn't get to move on like the clock—to live like we do.'

She thought of Kathryn then—Rebecca's mother. She was still carrying on, still surviving. She was doing better than Michelle was, and she couldn't imagine what strength that took. If *she* had lost a daughter, would she still be here? Would she still be on this earth at all?

She thought of Jacob then, his pale, terrified face as he'd scrambled to comfort his daughter, to wrap her in his strong arms. She knew how it felt to be held like that, and she wanted to go to him—but how could she?

Everything was so linked together and such a mess. Jacob had slept with Becks and now she was dead, and now he was here, with a secret family in tow. A family he must have had back then. Had Becks known and not cared? It was all a mess, a jumble of faces and pain in her head, and she couldn't stand it.

'I hate it that Jacob knew her, had a history with her. It's all so entwined together—and that's before I knew about his child.'

Greg's eyebrows rose, which for him was a reaction. 'You hate that they had each other, or that he had a daughter back home?'

'Both,' she spat. 'I can't un-jumble them in my head. Everything is just so…so…'

'Linked?' Greg offered, and Michelle found herself

nodding. 'But we are *all* linked, Michelle. Karinthy talked about six degrees of separation, and I often see things like this occurring with my patients. Have you spoken to Jacob since?'

Michelle shook her head. 'He was with his daughter; it wasn't the time. I'm not sure he even took in what I was saying. I needed him to leave me be so I wouldn't tell him how I felt. Feel.'

She hoped he hadn't heard her at all. It didn't matter now. It was over, anyway, and she didn't want him to have ammunition against her for taking the job. She had to focus on the job now—that was what she needed to stay afloat. To be here and work, to talk to Greg, to try to get out from the deep fog in which she was constantly immersed.

She needed fifty degrees of separation, not six. She needed Jacob to leave so she could burrow into the hospital and hole up for the dark winter she was facing in her mind.

The worst part was, now she would have to bear the loss of him too.

'You have to process the events yourself if you have any hope of sharing your pain with others,' said Greg. 'I think it's time. This is the low point, Michelle; you can see the bottom. Let's start to look up. This is the time— right now.'

Michelle looked at him, digging into her skin even harder with her nails. Greg gazed at her clasped hands, expressionless, and she sat back on the couch, tucking her hands underneath her to stop herself.

'I don't know if I can,' she admitted, already fighting against the emotions she had suppressed for so long.

Greg thought for a moment and then went to get something from his desk drawer. Coming back to his chair, he passed her a small pile of elastic bands, putting one around his wrist and snapping it lightly against his skin.

'Let's try this and take it slow. We can stop whenever you want.' He sat back in his chair, adopting his usual open posture. 'You ready? Tell me about that day, Michelle. What do you remember about it?'

Michelle winced as an image of Becks on the ground screamed in her head.

'I can't.' She twanged a band against her own wrist and felt a flash of relief from the pain in her chest. All too soon, though, it was gone. 'I can't speak to you about this. I can't speak to anyone.'

'Anyone?' Greg said softly, kindly. 'There's no one in your life that you could share this with? Just telling someone is enough, Michelle. It's a start. You need to start talking about this—start letting people in. You can't do everything alone and you shouldn't have to.'

Michelle looked at him. 'And how do I do that, exactly? Let people in?'

He looked at her for a moment, before looking back at the ticking clock.

'One day at a time, Michelle. That's how. Next time we'll talk more.'

Jacob pulled into the car park with a back seat full of clothes and a rather ugly green crocodile. It was his daughter's favourite toy—the one that she'd drooled on as a baby and still wanted when she was scared or tired. She'd been so wiped out she had managed to fall asleep without it, but he wanted to see her face light up when she saw Crocky.

Or Crocky Six, he should say, since he had a closet full of the stuffed toys as back-ups. He'd caught on fast after Crocky One had met an ugly demise under the wheels of a street sweeper. He could still remember the cloud of fluff as poor original Crocky had been lost against the might of those powerful brushes. His daughter's heartbroken cries. Jenny's growing frustration with her daughter. It had been a sign of how things would end for them.

He grabbed Ebony's things, with his own overnight bag, and headed inside. After checking on his daughter and her nanny, and finding them both settled and asleep for the night, he took one look at the put-up bed in the corner of Ebony's room and walked the other way.

There was no chance of sleep—not yet. He needed to walk it off. His pager was quiet, and Jude had left for the day. He didn't have the heart to ask the other nurses to keep paging Michelle. If she'd wanted to answer him, she would have. It was too late.

The chapel was a hidden oasis of calm in a tucked-away corner of the hospital, with dark wooden pews and a large altar at the front, a metal candle rack for votive candles to one side. There were always candles lit, shining out to remember someone lost or to pray for someone hovering between life and death. It smelled of sandalwood and candle wax, the scent of a holy place, and there was a waft of lavender as she passed vases full of small bundles.

In whatever corner of the world a bolthole like this could be found, they all held the same reverent air, gave people the same sense of being in the presence of something far bigger than their problems. Michelle was far from religious, but she wanted to be alone and this had seemed as good a place as any.

She headed down the empty aisle, past the vacant pews, till she reached the front and felt the warmth from the candles. Taking a fresh one from the wooden box on an adjacent table, she lit it and placed it at the front.

Watching the flame flicker, she heard a swish of the doors behind her, and turned around to see Jacob standing there.

'I've been looking for you,' he said, looking at her pager, clearly visible and hanging from her belt clip. 'You okay?'

He took a step forward and she shook her head, stopping him in his tracks.

'No, not really. You?'

Jacob walked slowly towards her, his easy gait gone, his body tense and coiled. He was stressed, she realised, and she thought of his daughter—the little girl she'd been saying hello to for weeks.

'Has your wife arrived yet?'

She wanted to tell him how angry she was, how stupid she felt. How devastated she was that he wasn't free when she wanted him for her own, despite everything in her telling her to run.

A daughter wasn't a deal-breaker—far from it. Being the other woman was.

She wanted him to smart from her words, to feel the brunt of her disappointment and pain.

'I don't have a wife,' he said, his eyes fixed on hers, his feet moving slowly towards her, always moving. 'Or a girlfriend. Currently.'

'Ah, baby mama, then,' Michelle quipped, wondering why he was still coming towards her. She wanted to tell him to stop as much as she wanted to run into his arms and bawl like a baby. 'How very modern of you.'

His step faltered and he didn't take the next one. It was working. The grenades she was throwing at him were slowing him down. She wanted him to hurt like she did, and she couldn't stop the words coming from her mouth.

'I was engaged once. To Ebony's mother.'

Ebony. The note.

'The note was from your daughter?' she asked, giving herself away. 'The message?'

He nodded sheepishly. 'I'm a single dad, Mich, not a player. Maybe once upon a time...sure. But I was single then. We did try to stay together, but we both knew it was a mistake. We called off the engagement before the ink on the ring receipt had dried. We shared custody for a while, but it didn't go well. Ebony has autism, and Jenny wasn't able to cope. She did her best on her own, while I was working abroad, but then she got a new partner and things didn't go well. Ebony wasn't happy, and her health started to suffer. Jenny asked me to take over, so I came home and took Ebony with me. I hired a nanny, bought a house, and got the job here. I should have told you, Michelle, but I didn't know how. With everything else...and you. I never expected to meet you. I never expected to meet anyone like you.'

He stopped and smiled then, taking three steps towards her as though he just couldn't help himself.

'I didn't expect you. I know you hate me, but...'

'I don't hate you,' she said, going to sit down on the front pew and resting her head on the wooden back of the low seat. 'I've tried, believe me. I need you.'

She felt the low rumble of his laughter as he sat down near her, leaving a small gap between them.

'I've tried to hate you too, but I don't,' he said, his beautiful full lips curling into a half-smile. 'I like hearing that you need me, though. I feel the same. Do you want to tell me about what else is going on with you?'

She noted how he was careful not to push.

'What happened?' he asked.

She bit her lip till it hurt, then remembered the rubber band round her wrist and switched to that instead.

'I need to talk to someone. My therapist tells me it's the next step. But…'

Pain. Screams. Debris. Dust. Blades. Gunfire. Shouting. Running. The sound of my own blood pumping around my body.

She closed her eyes, her hand grabbing at the skin on her thigh.

Jacob's voice punched through the terrifying montage in her head, his words permeating her brain. 'I'm here, Michelle. It's okay. Talk to me.'

She reached for the elastic band, pulling it back and snapping it hard. She felt a sharp sting on the skin of her wrist and did it again. And again.

She looked at him, and mentally steeled herself. She was here, with him. Present. And her heart soared.

'Now, slowly, Michelle. Take it slow. Tell me.'

A flash of her friend's hair, matted with blood and dust, made her wince as though she had been stabbed in the side.

'I can't,' she said, her eyes welling up. 'I can't. I won't. It's too bad.'

'You can,' Jacob said, firm, confident, guiding. 'Tell me what you need to.'

She thought hard, her eyes still closed. She twanged the band again and then she was back there…on her old bunk. Transported into the memory as though it were tangible. The camp was quiet, the chaos something yet to occur. Rebecca was lying on her bunk, stitching a piece of orange cloth and laughing at Michelle.

'It's not like that! I'm not getting *married* to the man; it's just sex.'

Michelle had wrinkled her nose in disgust, making her friend laugh all the more.

'Give up being such a priss and making me laugh! I nearly stabbed myself with the needle.'

Michelle had thrown a sweet in her direction. Becks had caught it in her mouth with flair.

'I'm not a priss!' Michelle had said. 'I just don't see the point, to be honest. When are you ever going to see him again and why would you want to? Isn't he a player?'

Becks had snorted. 'Calm down, Jane Austen. I have no need or want of a husband, thank you. I just need to get laid and do my job. He's *fun*! It's no strings and he brings me pudding after—I mean, who wouldn't want pudding *and* dessert?'

She'd waggled her brows at Michelle, making her crack her sour face into a smile.

'He has his life, his own stuff going on back home, and I have you and my work. You don't fulfil *all* my needs, you know. You dragged me on this tour, but you didn't give me any toys to play with.'

She'd finished off her stitch, cutting the thread short and throwing the material at Michelle. Michelle had caught it and smiled.

'Sometimes you just need someone to hold you close and make you feel alive, like a woman should. He does that. We have fun. End of.'

'End *away*, more like.'

Michelle had tried and failed to be cross. She had known there was nothing wrong with a bit of fun. She had known she needed to lighten up.

A bit of company wouldn't go amiss for herself, if she was being honest, she'd thought. Scott had come to mind, and she'd realised that, although she missed him, she was dreading the next time they met. He'd been so cold on the phone last time they had managed to speak.

She'd unfolded the orange material and seen the delicate stitching, her initials stitched under the edge of one of the corners.

'A scrubs cap? This is gorgeous!' Michelle had put the hat on her head, tying it closed. It had fitted perfectly. 'For me?'

She'd looked back at her friend, who had been wearing an identical one, dying to laugh.

They'd both laughed for ages, dubbing themselves the scrubs cap twins, and had stayed up later than they should have, talking, but they hadn't cared. Those were the moments that kept them going when the firing started and the casualties started rolling in.

'That was our last night together,' Michelle said, finally holding up her head and looking Jacob in the eye. 'It happened the day after, and then she was gone. It was my fault, don't you see? I was right there. I tried to save her, but she died right in front of me.'

Jacob's eyes crinkled at the corners, but he kept his composure. 'Michelle, I read the reports. There was an ambush—a rebel band. You couldn't have foreseen that; no one could. Army personnel had no intel to suggest that your medical camp was under threat, and you two staying up a little late didn't cause any of that. You have survivor guilt, Michelle, and I suspect PTSD. It's important that you listen to me when I say this. It's not your fault, Michelle.'

She snapped the band on her wrist.

One. Two. It's not your fault. Three. Four. It's not your fault.

'Your friend died, and you were there with her at the end. You comforted her, you had her back, and you never left her side. Even when the world was falling down around you. You didn't panic, and you didn't make a false step or a wrong move. You saved people in a war zone and your friend didn't die alone. She left this life with you right there, showing her the love you showed her throughout your time together. You did nothing wrong, Michelle, and you need to stop feeling guilty for living. You need to say goodbye.'

Jacob pulled her into his side, hushing her cries and kissing her tears.

'I'm sorry... I had no idea... I came back home for Ebony. The news coming out of camp was sketchy, at best, and I couldn't go back. I had to ground myself. But I'm here now, Mich. Say your goodbyes. We're here, in this chapel. Speak to her.'

She snapped her band methodically, and slowly, very slowly, started to talk.

She spoke to Jacob and she spoke to Becks.

Him being there felt strange, but also... *right*.

She found herself telling him everything. How Becks had died, how lost she'd felt since. How the job, and then him, were the only things keeping her going. How she had been feeling so guilty, and how he had unknowingly helped her to work through things, challenging her and making her *feel* once more.

'So...' Jacob said eventually, when she had fallen silent. 'Do you think it helped?'

He was holding her hand tight in his, resting it on his lap. He was stroking her thumb slowly, tenderly, and the look he was giving her wasn't pity, but...

She didn't want to say it.

They were both such a mess, and in a few short days they would be in front of Andrew, fighting for a job that they both desperately needed. It wasn't a situation that Michelle could see any way out of, and she didn't want to think about it any more. She had done enough for today. She had exorcised as many demons as she could.

And as they both gazed at each other, happy in their silence, she couldn't help but think that without him she wouldn't have come this far. Not that she would tell him that…

CHAPTER EIGHT

'WHO WANTS PUDDING?' Jacob asked jovially, heading towards Ebony's room with a pack of her favourite chocolate dessert pots. He passed Wendy and waggled them at her. 'Wendy, do you fancy a teatime snack?'

He snapped one of the pots from its plastic housing and thrust it in the nurse's direction.

Wendy grinned and put it in her pocket. 'Thanks, Dr Peterson! Cute daughter, by the way.' She saluted him, heading off down the ward corridor, a spring in her step now.

The whole mood of the place had improved today. Michelle was working with Jacob on a double, and he was overjoyed to have twelve whole hours of working alongside her.

Andrew had grown noticeably more and more quiet as the time neared for the grand opening of the new trauma centre, and Jacob knew the decorators were scheduled to arrive in a day's time to start the cosmetic finessing. It was getting down to the wire now, but Jacob didn't find himself eager to get all the big cases today, to get himself noticed. He was, for once, just living in the moment.

'Dad, don't give all my pudding away!'

Ebony often acted as though she was twenty-seven years old, despite being only five, and when he walked into the room she was giving him her 'schoolmarm' look of reproach.

'Save some for Michelle!'

Jacob did a double-take as he clocked who was sitting in the chair by Ebony's bed. He saw Michelle tense, just for a second, and he gave her an easy smile. One that was appropriate in front of his only child and lacking his usual panty-dropping smoulder.

'I won't. I have plenty left for my favourite girls.'

Now it was Ebony's turn to beam at him. 'Daddy! Michelle's not a girl, she's a *lady.*'

'And I'm his boss.' Michelle winked at Ebony, making her giggle.

In such a short space of time she sure had won Ebony over fast, he thought. That girl didn't miss a trick, and she wasn't shy about speaking her mind either. Which probably meant they were two peas in a pod.

'Did you bring spoons, minion?' Michelle asked, standing up from the chair and coming to take the pudding pots from him.

Jacob waggled his hips at her as though he was trying to hula-hoop. 'Right here in my pocket.'

She smirked a little, seeing the plastic cutlery sticking out of his trousers and pulling them out with a flourish that made him go a little weak at the knees.

She skipped back over to Ebony's side, offering her a spoon and a pot of mousse. Ebony took them straight from her and Jacob's heart flipped. Ebony had issues with touch, as half the staff had found out when she'd been admitted. She didn't like to be touched by strangers, and yet taking that spoon from Michelle had looked as easy as breathing to Ebony. He found himself a little choked up and didn't trust himself to speak.

The two females in his new life ripped the tops off

their sweet treats and giggled together as they tucked in. Jacob wanted to get his phone out and take a photo, to remember this moment. He wanted the three of them to stay in this little bubble, away from jobs and battlefields and misunderstandings.

Looking at Michelle, who seemed brighter than he had ever seen her, he knew that she was feeling the same emotions.

Maybe it's not too late after all. Maybe I can still keep her for ever.

Ebony looked brighter today, and oddly relaxed around Michelle. What *was* it about her that put people at ease? He'd felt it as he'd watched her over the last few weeks—seeing how she dealt with patients and staff with the same care and respect. When no one was watching she even did some of the nurses' jobs—the ones that other doctors would never consider. She made this place feel like home—to the staff, to him. How could he go against her for the job with everything that had happened? He didn't want to think about it.

'You finished for the day?' Michelle asked him, licking her spoon clean and putting the empty pot down.

Ebony was just finishing hers and she eyed the two of them silently. She was a watcher, his girl. She didn't speak a hell of a lot but, boy, she never missed a trick. His daughter was as smart as a whip, and the way she was looking cautiously from face to face told him that she was picking up on every detail between them.

It made his stomach knot, to think that he might be bringing someone new into their family. Would she cope? Her mother was still in touch, but Jacob knew it was just a courtesy, really. He'd never even thought about the maternal instincts of the women he had slept with. But by the time he'd realised that he and Jenny were wholly unsuitable for each other, even as horizontal bed buddies, Ebony had been on the way and the die had been cast.

He felt two sets of eyes on him and shook himself out of his mood. 'I am. I was going to stay over, though, play a few games. Sound good, munchkin?'

Ebony wrinkled her nose at him, hiding her face a little. Michelle beckoned him, and he found himself kneeling before her. Ebony was already engrossed in the television that hung over the bed, mounted on a portable bracket, which was showing a wildlife programme.

'The other children are watching a film in the playroom after dinner,' Michelle told him. 'Ebony has signed up already.'

Wow, he thought to himself. *Ebony must feel comfortable here.*

Michelle must have caught his thought process, as she reached out and laid her hand on his, where it rested on the bed sheets. 'Jude's on later—she'll sit with them. She loves movie time; it's her thing.'

Jacob was nodding, willing himself to relax. She squeezed his hand again, and once more he wondered how she always seemed to be there for him, in his corner, and seemingly in Ebony's now too.

'Don't stress, Jacob, you look like the Hulk when you worry.' She made an over-exaggerated angry face, showing it to Ebony and making her laugh.

To Jacob's amazement, Ebony copied it, adding her own body-builder pose as she flexed imaginary green muscles at them both.

'Hulk smash!' she shouted, tittering into her little clenched fists.

Michelle giggled, holding up a hand that Ebony high-fived.

The sound of his daughter's laughter filled the room,

and he closed his eyes, just for a split second, to capture the soundbite in his head for ever. He knew now, no matter what, that he had made the right decision. Wheels down was the way to go—and, looking at his daughter, safe and happy after the events of the last few months, he realised that it was enough.

He just needed a couple more pieces of the jigsaw to fit, and that would be plenty for him. He would choose the sound of his daughter being happy over any siren, any scramble, over the sounds of chopper blades in the desert. He was done, and for the first time he wanted to be at home. A home that had both of them in it.

A couple of hours later he said goodnight to Ebony, watching her get wheeled into the TV room, sweets and drinks in her little excited hands, and then nodded to Jude, who gave him a mock salute and waved him away. Ebony didn't even look back, but he waved her off till the doors closed and the sounds of the hospital filled his senses once more.

Leaning against the corridor wall, he ran his hands down his face, trying to wake himself up.

'You going home?'

The voice to the side of him made him start. Andrew was walking up the corridor, his tie hanging from his partly open shirt, briefcase dangling from one hand.

'I was hoping to catch you, if you have the time?'

Jacob couldn't help but sigh, and Andrew winced.

'I know… I know. You've had it hard. It's just that we're less than two weeks from the new trauma centre opening, and both my star doctors are off their game.' He flicked his head in the direction of the TV room. 'How's your daughter and the nanny?'

He leaned against the wall too so they looked like a couple of sexy bookends to brighten up the stark white corridors.

'Fine,' Jacob replied, smiling at the relief he felt every time he thought of how lucky they had been. How much worse it could have been. 'Ebony can go home tomorrow, all being well, and her nanny is already home with her family. I don't think she'll be back any time soon, though; recovery will be a while with her injuries. No driving or working. Which means—'

'Which means,' Andrew said, preventing him from speaking any further with a nudge of his briefcase, 'that you need time. I get that. It's fine. But we need to make a plan, and soon. I have the refurbishment and rebranding of the trauma department to oversee, and I need a strong team. Have you and Michelle buried your issues?'

If only he knew. She'd buried *him*, truth be told. Planted him straight in a garden of lust and watched him grow into a song-singing, picket-fence-admiring man in love.

'We're rubbing along a little better,' he said. 'Has she left for the night?'

Andrew shrugged. 'I paged her, wanted the same talk with her, but I didn't get a reply. She's off-shift, so I'll catch up with her tomorrow. You get some rest, come see me tomorrow too. Even better, bring Michelle with you. We can make a plan together.'

You took the words right out of my mouth.

Jacob patted his boss on the shoulder, glad that Andrew had given him an out. He had plans, ideas, but every time he tried to put them to paper he stalled.

'I'll get my thinking cap on, Andrew. Goodnight.'

He was halfway down the corridor when Andrew's voice reached his ears.

'Whatever happens, Jacob, on the day I *will* have a trauma chief, ready to go. Trauma waits for no one, and I can't hold this back.'

Jacob, not even turning around, gave Andrew a thumbs-up. 'Not a problem, boss. One trauma centre god, coming right up.'

Scribbling away on her notepad, Michelle squinted her eyes, closing them against the small shaft of bright artificial light that had suddenly danced across her bed. The on-call room door closed again, leaving her in near darkness. The only light in the room now was a slit from the street lamp outside, casting lines across her paper. She was in bed, the covers wrapped loosely around her as she lay on her tummy, writing a long overdue letter.

She was about to ask whoever it was that had come in not to turn the light on when the bathroom light went on and she saw Jacob. He looked exhausted, the lines under his eyes even darker in the shadows of the room.

She wanted to speak, but what could she say? Would anything come out right? They were skirting around each other. She was watching him, hidden underneath her blanket like a child scared of a storm.

He was like a tempest, of sorts. He had come into her workplace, whipped everything up, damaged and broken apart her perfect existence. He had shown her what her lies and unspoken words had done to her seemingly idyllic life. He'd made her hold a mirror up to herself and her problems, just as she had his—or so she hoped.

But maybe his daughter had that honour. Maybe, Becks had been right about him. He had just about smashed every assumption she had made about him, and watching him with his daughter…so tender, so patient. She had seen love, fatherly love and concern, and it had made her fall for him all the more.

'Hi,' she said, finding her voice.

It pierced the silence of the room and he turned his head, his eyes finding hers in the dark.

'Hey, you,' he said back. 'You writing my reference?'

She laughed at his attempt to break the ice. They were both feeling the pressure of the upcoming opening, and it made her feel oddly better that he was struggling with it too.

'Nope. I've already written, *Don't employ this moronic imbecile.* That didn't take long, so I decided to work on the rotas.' She held the paperwork aloft, and Jacob kicked open the bathroom door to let in more light. 'You can check it, if you like.'

Jacob slowly slid the page from her fingers, touching it gently. Michelle rolled over, looking up at the ceiling as he came to sit beside her, his eyes focused on the page.

It was early evening outside. An occasional laugh or cough could be heard outside in the corridor, and the odd trolley trundling past. He read it for days, it seemed, before placing it back on the bed next to her.

'Fine with me. You know, this might be the most awkward thing I have ever said to a woman I've slept with, but I really did like your friend Becks. She was a really nice person and I can tell you were really important to each other. I'm so sorry it happened.'

'Me too,' she echoed.

After her sessions with Greg she'd come to the slow realisation that he was right. They all were. What had happened to Becks had been catastrophic, but not her fault.

'Losing my best friend like that… I just felt so desperately useless. She was right there in front of me. I couldn't do a thing but watch her die. I think I died too, a little. And I got so angry I shut everyone out. Her mum has tried to reach out to me so many times since the funeral, and I've just batted her away. I'm selfish, Jacob.'

She was already playing with her hands, pinching and nipping, twisting the skin on her wrist. The elastic band had broken an hour back and lay on the carpeted floor.

Jacob reached into his pocket and wrapped something around her wrist. 'Here...'

He raised her hand and kissed it, just once, on the back. His lips felt like warm velvet on her skin. She felt the new elastic band tickle as it brushed across her bare wrist and she smiled.

'Just happen to have one in your pocket, eh?'

His other hand reached back into his pocket, pulling out a small pile of different coloured elastic bands.

'Norma from General Office hooked me up. I had to bring her chocolate muffins, though.'

He put them back into his pocket, sitting down on the bed alongside her. Their hands found each other again; she was eager for his touch.

'Do they help?' he asked.

She paused long enough to make him concerned, but then slowly nodded her head.

'They do, actually. I like the green.'

She ran her finger along the band, flashing him her happy smile—one that he seldom saw but worked all the harder to get each day. It was a personal challenge to him now, to see that expression on her face. The one that told him she was healing and getting stronger each day. God help them all at St Marshalls when she was fully recovered. She ran rings around them all on her worst day.

'How's Ebony?'

He grinned at the mention of his daughter's name and lay back on the bed, taking Michelle's hand and her with him till they were lying side by side on the mattress.

'She's good. She likes you.'

He felt her shrug her shoulders beside him.

'She's gorgeous. I like her too.'

From her words, he could tell she was smiling.

'What are you going to do about childcare when she goes home?'

'That's pretty much all I've thought about, to be honest.'

Besides obsessing about you, wanting to help you, mooning over you...

'The agency has another nanny lined up; Ebony's due to meet her tomorrow, to see how they get on.'

Michelle didn't answer, and he squeezed her hand.

A fraction of a second later, she squeezed back.

'Andrew is getting pretty excited about the opening,' she said softly. 'He sent me an email today, with a dozen terrifying new names for the centre. He thinks we need to rebrand totally. He thinks it will help with the investors, who are apparently very impressed with his new drink-slinging and helicopter-hopping pair of doctors.'

Jacob laughed softly, turning on his side to face her. 'That was a pretty fun night.'

She laughed too, turning her head slightly to look him in the eye. 'I suppose it was, in the end. We *do* make a good team—when you listen to your boss.'

Jacob gasped theatrically, dropping her hands and tickling her. She squirmed and squealed, trying to get away from him.

'Okay, okay—I was joking!'

The single bed's frame kept her from getting away, and Jacob wasn't about to let her slip through his fingers.

'Stop, Jacob!'

He released her immediately, holding up his hands in surrender. Her eyes sparkled as she rose and hovered over him, her hands ready to tickle him back.

'Nope!' he said, taking the opportunity to wrap his leg over hers, pinning her to the bed.

She looked up at him, *so* sexy, and he couldn't take it any more.

'I think I'm falling, Michelle,' he said, wholly unable to stop the words from coming out of his mouth. 'I know that's scary, but I really do like you.'

Seeing her with his daughter today had been the icing on the cake. The first time he had laid eyes on her he'd thought her a threat—a danger to his precarious new life and a rival for the job he had fought to get. Now he saw everything that had happened as inevitable.

'We were meant to find each other, Mich. Why else would we have been thrown together on this job? We fit. Spending the last few weeks with you has been the best time, even though we've both been going through so much. You accepted Ebony, forgave me for being an idiot, and...'

'Broke your nose?' She leaned up on her elbows, dropping a kiss onto the bridge of his still healing nose. 'Where has all this come from? What about the job?'

He dropped a kiss onto her nose, right where she had kissed him. 'The job is beyond our control. Andrew will choose his person, and we will deal with it together. We'll deal with *everything* together.'

Jacob's body was shielding hers in the dimly lit on-call room. She could feel his heart beating, racing, even as he spoke. Words that she had never expected him to say. Words of feelings and emotion from the man she'd used to mock, the player with pudding.

If Rebecca had been here, they would have had a lot to discuss.

Thinking of her friend for once didn't feel like a stab to the heart, and she found herself feeling glad that he had known her. He got how funny she'd been, how much of a best-friend-shaped hole she had left behind after her death.

She couldn't quite see how it would work—what their life together would look like. But the only thing she knew for sure was that she felt the same, and she wanted to find out the answers to all those questions. With him.

It just seemed too big for the moment.

'Come here,' she said, instead of saying all the things she wanted to say. 'Shut up and kiss me, Jacob.' He tried to speak, but she silenced him with her index finger pushed against his lips. 'Kiss me *now*.'

He reached for her hands and raised both of them above her head on the bedspread. He kissed her then, just once, a small touch of his lips on her forehead, her cheeks, her chin...

'Like this?' he said, pulling down her top a little with his teeth and nibbling along her collarbone. 'Don't you don't want me to ask you how much you want this?'

He mouthed her breast through her clothes and she felt his hot breath blow on her nipple through the material.

'Or this? Don't you don't want me to talk about how this makes me feel?'

He ran a line across the length of her clavicle with his tongue, the two-day stubble on his tired face driving her crazy as he nuzzled against her skin.

'Jacob...' she tried, but he didn't give her a chance to answer.

He claimed her mouth, and all she could do was kiss him back while her head swam. He was all around her:

his touch, his scent, the feeling his fingers stirred in her as he slowly pulled off her clothing.

In moments they were naked on top of the covers, their bodies entwined together. She felt as if there was a huge question mark blinking above them, but as he moved inside her the only thing she could think about was saying yes and hang the consequences.

A frantic knocking at the door made them both freeze.

Jacob rolled over to grab the duvet and cover their modesty.

'Who knows you're here?' she whispered to him.

Their lips were almost touching. He'd wrapped himself around her tightly, and she was thrilled by his protective instinct—not that she would let on.

He shook his head. 'I'm not sure. What about you?'

She shrugged. The knock came again.

'Dr Peterson? Dr Peterson?'

It was Francis, a nurse from the ward. He had been looking after Ebony at night.

They both reacted simultaneously.

Michelle grabbed her clothes and ran to the bathroom.

'Ebony. You go. I'll follow.'

As she dressed she heard Jacob answer the door. She couldn't make out the voices, but she knew by instinct that trouble was coming. She shoved her feet into her shoes just as Jacob opened the bathroom door, the duvet only just protecting his modesty.

'Ebony's missing,' he panted. 'She wasn't in the TV room after the movie. She's gone.'

CHAPTER NINE

MICHELLE WALKED ON to the trauma floor and, sticking two fingers in her mouth, whistled hard. The cacophony of noise from the staff stopped and they all focused on her.

'Listen up! Ebony Peterson is missing. Security have locked down the building and Andrew is going over CCTV footage with the police. Ebony is five years old; she came in with the bus crash. Restrained passenger. Minor injuries. Due to be discharged tomorrow.'

She looked across at Jacob, who was going through the visitors' log with a fine-tooth comb, his phone in his hand. He'd already ruled out Jenny, who was away for the weekend with one of her friends. He had told her she wouldn't have come to take her anyway—she showed little interest in her as it was.

From the look Michelle had seen on Jacob's face when he'd spoken to her on the phone, she thought there wouldn't be any frantic mother-daughter reunion any time soon. She wasn't coming to help.

'Ebony has autism,' she added. 'She isn't good with strangers or unfamiliar surroundings. If you find her, do *not* put hands on. Do not chase her; only take steps to protect where absolutely necessary. You all have Jacob—Dr Peterson's pager. He'll be here in case she returns.'

She checked her watch.

'It's twenty-one seventeen. Ebony was last seen fifteen minutes ago, in the TV room. She wasn't there when staff came to take her back to her bed, and we believe that she's still in the grounds.' She looked at the sea of familiar faces in front of her—people she loved, admired, trusted. 'Ebony is vulnerable, guys. Let's find her—and fast. Move out!'

Jude came over. 'Nice speech, boss. Good to have you here. How can I help?'

Michelle passed her a soft toy—apparently one of Ebony's favourites from home. 'Check the children's ward. She could have gone down there, or if someone has found her they might take her there.'

Jude nodded, glancing back to where Jacob was sitting on a nurses' station chair with his head in his hands. 'He's in a bad way. You looking after him?'

Something in the tone of her comment made Michelle look at her.

Jude winked. 'It's not the time, but we need to talk, girl. I need details.'

Michelle looked at her open-mouthed. 'How...?'

Jude laughed, just once, before her expression turned back to concerned and professional. 'I've got eyes,' she said. She looked at Jacob, making Michelle turn her head too. 'It can work, Michelle. Don't question it. I'll let you know if I find Ebony.'

Michelle nodded, feeling numb, but Jude was already gone. Her team had scrambled and the place was crawling with medical personnel, all looking for the little girl.

Heading over to Jacob, she pulled up a seat, placing her hand over his. 'We'll find her,' she said, with absolute conviction.

She knew that every single member of staff at St Marshall's would turn over every bedpan and operating room looking for Ebony, and with the hospital on lockdown no one was getting in or out till she was safely back in her father's arms.

'Jacob, did you hear me? We'll find her.'

He didn't say anything, just sat there staring into space. Michelle had never seen him so lost before.

Over his shoulder, she saw Andrew hovering. 'I won't be long. You go and check on the CCTV again—see if you spot anything, okay?'

She beckoned Big Al from Security, who came over to Jacob. She reluctantly let go of his hand and it just fell into his lap. She wanted to throw her arms around him, to kiss his unshed tears away, but it wasn't the time.

'What's wrong?' she said as she reached Andrew. He pulled her to one side.

'We're all locked down, and CCTV doesn't show anyone fitting her description leaving in the last thirty minutes. The police and our security team are going floor to floor. She's here, and we will find her.' Andrew looked over to where Jacob was now pointing to designs of the hospital layout with Big Al and his crew. 'How's he doing?'

Michelle looked at Jacob, so pale, alert but distracted. In another life she might have gone for the jugular right about now. 'He's fine—or as fine as he can be. We have everything in hand. All new traumas have been diverted to other hospitals for now, but discharges are still happening—just taking a bit longer with security at the main doors having to be stepped up.'

Andrew didn't look convinced. He opened and closed his mouth, and she knew he wanted to say something else.

'Andrew, just say it. We don't have time to pussyfoot around.'

'No, you're right.' He gave her one of his trademark

thumbs-up, which made him look slightly goofy. 'It's not the time at all. We can speak later. Are you two friends now, or something?'

Michelle couldn't help but think he had more to say, but she had no time to digest it. His 'friends' comment had made her think of something and had given her an idea.

She patted Andrew on the shoulder. 'Something like that, boss…yeah. I gotta go.'

Heading straight over to Jacob, she put her arm on his shoulder, bending close and whispering something in his ear. He looked at her with a spark of hope in his eyes and then the pair of them headed down the corridor, delivering orders to staff on their way.

They were all heading elsewhere, but Michelle hoped with every fibre of her being that her hunch was right. The alternative didn't bear thinking about.

Just past the TV room there was another corridor, sectioned off from patients, which housed the offices, locker rooms and staff rooms for the adjacent departments nearby. Michelle and Jacob headed slowly down this corridor, looking in every room just in case. Nothing.

Soon they reached a locker room, and Michelle paused with her hands on the wooden surface of the door, wanting to give them both a second to catch their breath and offer up a silent prayer. She even spoke to Becks, asking her to give the Big Man Upstairs a nudge in their direction.

Pushing the door open, she held her breath. Jacob pushed past her, shouting his daughter's name, and as Michelle followed him in she hoped to God she hadn't got it wrong.

'Ebony!'

Jacob's joyous voice rang out and he ran to the corner of the room, where Ebony was sitting on a beanbag, her face full of chocolate pudding, a half-eaten pot on her lap.

'Ebony, honey!'

Jacob didn't tell her off, just sat down beside her and pulled her onto his lap. She squirmed a little, freeing her hand enough from her father's embrace to dip her spoon back into the mousse. He checked her over, looking for bruises, injuries, but there was nothing. She was absolutely fine—not a scratch on her.

Michelle felt something on her face, wet and dripping, and when she went to wipe her cheeks she realised she was crying.

'Michelle?'

Jacob was looking at her now, his face full of concern, and Ebony's eyes were tracking her movements as she half ran across the room and threw her arms around them both. Jacob moved till they were all sitting on the over-sized beanbag, a huddle of limbs and chocolate pudding.

'You're a good dad, you know?' she said, wiping away her tears of relief. 'I know it must have been hard, but she's adorable. Don't blame yourself for this; you know more than most that things just happen sometimes. She's in good hands with Susan. You were working…saving lives. I'm sure Ebony is proud of her old pops.'

She felt the same sense of pride, looking at him with fresh eyes now that she had all the pieces of the puzzle. She'd been so worried when Ebony had gone missing, and she'd felt something she'd not felt for a while. A rush of protective instinct, a bloom of love.

She cared about Ebony—had got used to seeing the little inquisitive lass around the place. The girl's health and happiness mattered to her, as it obviously did to Jacob. He'd been lost himself, but he'd still found the time to care for her, to be there when she needed him. He and his daughter were partners, in every single sense of the word.

'I get it now,' she said, giving him a look of adoration that made him blush a little.

'Get what?' he asked, dropping kisses on both their heads as though he couldn't quite believe his luck at having the two of them in his arms, safe.

'The pudding. It was all for Ebony, wasn't it? The whole "pudding man" thing?'

Jacob laughed then, and Ebony laughed with him.

Pointing at her dad, she said, as clear as a bell, 'Pudding man Daddy!' She squealed, belly-laughing this time, and touching Michelle's cheek, bringing her in on the joke.

Michelle took her little hand in hers and kissed it. 'Oh, Ebony, that laugh!'

Ebony laughed again, waggling her ears with her hands in response. Jacob followed suit.

And as Michelle grabbed her phone, to call off the alert, they all sat and waggled their ears together, waiting for the others to descend on their little moment. Right now, the three of them were enjoying just being together.

CHAPTER TEN

WAKING UP ALONE in the on-call room the next morning, Michelle felt she had never slept better. She had fallen asleep feeling content, the demons silent. The elastic band sat on her pile of clothes; her wrists were bare. The sun was low in the sky, peeking through the blinds and warming her skin as the day got started.

She saw from her watch that it was just before morning shift. She had half an hour—and less than two till her meeting with Andrew. For once, though, she found that she didn't want to scramble to her feet and hit the day with a fast pace. Not when the bathroom door had opened and Jacob had come through.

He shuffled into the bed behind her, his body flush against her back. 'What time is it?'

His low, rumbling voice vibrated around her, and he rubbed his stubble on her cheek, making her squirm and feel turned on at the same time.

'Half an hour till hand-over. Ebony okay? You're on all day, aren't you?'

Jacob groaned before answering her question. 'She's fine. The nurses have her—and it looks like Gok Wan came to dress her, judging by the outfit choices and accessories. Why do I do this again?'

He sat up a little as he spoke, his hair in tufts around

his head. He looked like a baby monkey, and it made her giggle.

'What?'

He ran a hand through his hair when he caught her looking and she pulled it away, placing it on her breast and moulding his fingers around it. He made a throaty growling sound and squeezed, running his finger over her bare nipple.

'Good morning, Dr Peterson.' She kissed him on the top of his head. He turned his head to claim her mouth, but she blocked him with her finger. 'Morning breath,' she quipped, pretending to cross her eyes.

He raised his brows, wordlessly reaching over to where his lab coat was thrown over the spare bed. Pulling out a pack of mints, he popped one in his mouth, waggling his eyebrows at her suggestively.

'Now, kiss me, woman. That's an order.'

The kisses turned to caresses in record time—even for two world-class trauma medics.

Later, sitting outside Andrew's office, Jacob knew they were both too wound up and worried even to acknowledge anyone who passed them, wishing them good luck. Looking across at Michelle, who looked confident, but was plucking her elastic band like a guitar string, he didn't even want to think about what would happen once the decision was made.

After the last few weeks, it felt so cruel that one little decision could hold so much power over their lives.

Ebony was settled, but fragile still, so much in need of someone to keep the home fires burning safely.

Michelle was in therapy, and it was working, but PTSD was no easy fix. She'd never be the same again. Love was a battlefield, they said, and loving and losing someone right in front of you brought the worst kind of grief. She was a trauma doctor and she'd been right there, and still helpless. Jacob knew from experience that Michelle would never forget that day, and that the memory of it would shape her future career whether she wanted it to or not.

He leaned in to her, whispering into her ear urgently, trying to get his words out before Andrew opened that door. 'You okay? You ready?'

Michelle flicked the band once more and, closing her eyes for a long moment, took a deep breath. 'I hope this works Jacob; it's a risk.'

He smiled at her, hiding his anxiety, showing her he had her back. 'What isn't a risk these days? You took me on, and that's worked out pretty well.'

She rolled her eyes, hiding the elastic band under her sleeve. 'Jury's still out on that one.'

He narrowed his eyes at her. 'You know me, honey. I'm a sure thing when it comes to what I want.'

The door opened. It was show time.

'So…' Andrew started, clearly trying and failing to be a detached professional in this situation.

He looked as if he had been made chief executioner and this was his first day on the job. If he'd been on a lower floor, he might even have done a bunk out of the office window. Jacob, for one, wouldn't have blamed him. It was a tough time.

'So?' Michelle echoed, leaning forward and picking up one of the iced Danish pastries from a platter on his desk. 'Any coffee?'

Andrew's shoulders dropped a little and he smiled at her. 'It's on the way. I want to talk to you both about the job. I've made a decision.'

Jacob was still standing, leaning against the wall behind her chair. She looked at him. 'Do you want to tell him, or shall I?' she asked.

They were interrupted by Andrew's secretary, bringing in a tray of coffee. They were all left to stare and glare at each other, setting their faces to happy whenever the secretary looked their way.

Jacob felt as if his heart was going to explode out of his chest. Michelle was so damn cool about it, the elastic band hanging loose from her wrist as she ripped into another pastry like a bear with a fresh salmon.

She gave him a look that helped him to find his voice.

She's in my corner and I'm firmly camped in hers. Stick an I-heart-Michelle flag in me, because I'm home.

'Andrew, we both want to take the job, so we humbly accept.' He kept his jaw tight, his look professional, steely. 'We do have a few conditions, though.'

'But— But— But...' Andrew started to say. 'You—? Both?'

Jacob could see pound signs and panic flashing up in Andrew's eyes.

'Part-time,' he said, to put him out of his misery. 'I have Ebony, and Michelle is in therapy—as you know.'

He didn't insult Andrew's intelligence; of course he knew the situation. Michelle was far too good a medic to put her patients at risk—intentionally or otherwise.

'We both love this place and we want it to run right. We think if we speak to the investors, show them our plans for the centre, they'll be on board. A once-in-a-lifetime, two-for-one deal.'

The fact that they had acted like a dream duo of medics on that fundraising night had helped them stand out in the crowd, and their investors were all about the 'faces' of the hospital. A short chat with them this morning and now everything was in motion. The investors were interested. They just needed Andrew to sign off.

Even the staff, who had been firmly in two camps—Peterson or Forbes—had come together over the last few days, cemented by Ebony's disappearance and the need to pull together as one.

Andrew, looking once more like a fish out of water, sat back in his swivel chair and poured himself a coffee, slugging it back like a shot.

Michelle winked at Jacob, and he winked right back.

'Go on, then,' Andrew sighed, half laughing, half crying at the thought of the impending paperwork. 'Hit me with it.'

Michelle had poured her own coffee, clearly brought to life with excitement now.

'We want to turn the job into a two-person role,' she said. 'It will mean we can both get the time off that we need and we can run the department better.'

She looked Jacob in the eye, and once more his heart swelled with love.

This woman, Becks... I can't help but think that you brought us together somehow. So, thank you. This pudding man is ever grateful.

Clearing his throat, he stood tall and began to speak.

Here goes. Stay with me, Michelle.

'We have run our proposal by the investors—a skeleton plan—and not only have they agreed to having us both run the centre, they want to offer us additional funding to run another project.'

Michelle's face dropped, and in a second Jacob knew her shields had gone whizzing back up. He went and stood behind her chair, placing both hands on her shoulders. She reached up and took his hands without thinking.

Andrew's eyes bulged. 'And how did you do *that* in one meeting?'

'A telephone call, actually. Right after the one we made to the Royal.'

Andrew's nostrils flared at Jacob's words. They had always been the rival hospital to St Marshall's, and Andrew's main goal in life was to stay ahead of the opposition.

'The investors didn't realise that both of their potential trauma doctors might be wanting to work elsewhere. They didn't seem keen on us working for the Royal, though, did they, Mich?'

Michelle was enjoying this now—he could tell by her look. It made him stir into life.

Not now.

'They weren't exactly doing cartwheels, no,' she replied. 'I think they might just want to keep us here.'

Andrew shook his head slowly, a disbelieving look of realisation spreading across his face. 'Well played. Wish I'd thought of it myself. And the project?' he asked.

Jacob squeezed Michelle's shoulders, once, twice.

I'm here. No more are you alone.

'Michelle and I both have overseas trauma experience. We want to help our veterans when they come back home, and since healthcare has suffered so many cuts we plan to run a privately funded post-service clinic for veterans of war. We have half the department heads already clamouring to help, and the nurses are all on board too. We can run it on the site of the old trauma centre, which was earmarked—'

'For storage.' Andrew nodded. 'I get it. Using that space makes sense. But can you do both? Even with the two of you it will mean long hours, and juggling your personal lives. Can you really work as partners to that extreme?'

Michelle, who had obviously been prepared to fight Andrew on every little point, looked a little blindsided by his easy acceptance. Jacob was ready for it, though, and he recited the words that had been seared on his brain for days.

'Andrew, we *are* partners. In every sense. We can do this—we just need you to give us the chance.'

He half expected Michelle to pull away, to withdraw her hands from his, but she stood up with him.

'He's right, Andrew. I know we didn't get on at first, but things have changed so much.' She looked at her old friend and he smiled at her. 'I've changed. Trauma needs to change too. We're cutting edge here, so why not reach out? Do more? Link our trauma department with helping our armed forces like they help us, going out there every day.' She thought of Kathryn, left without a daughter, herself without a best friend. 'We owe them that, at the very least.'

Andrew leaned forward, resting his elbows on his desk and forming a steeple with his fingers.

A classic playing for time move, Jacob thought. *We have him.*

Standing up, Andrew offered his hand to them both. 'Doctors, you have yourself a deal. I'll call the investors now.'

CHAPTER ELEVEN

'COMING, READY OR NOT!' Jude shouted, sending giggling children scattering in all directions over the grassy sun-lit fields around them.

Ebony was one of the loudest, screaming, 'No, Jude, don't find me!' as she grabbed Jacob's hand and took off running.

Jacob was howling with laughter himself, a relaxed figure in jeans and a crisp white shirt.

The opening of the new trauma centre was shaping up to be a day to remember. They had been able to utilise the fields near the hospital grounds, and now a square of beautiful white marquees stood proudly on the green grass that flowed like a carpet beyond them. Music was playing—a local band that Jacob had organised—family-friendly hits that everyone, young and old could enjoy together, and the children were busy playing hide and seek with Jude, but there were other activities dotted around too—most of them down to the genius of Ebony and her dear old dad.

When she was settled and happy Ebony uncurled, going from being a nervous little scrap of a girl to a very clever, happy little brainbox. Michelle was surprised by her every time she saw her, and seeing Jacob with her was showing her a whole other side to her former rival.

'Everything running smoothly, I assume?' Andrew came to her side as she watched the children, passing her a glass of Bucks Fizz. 'The investors are loving this fun day for the opening. How did you know they all had kids?'

She nodded towards Jacob with a smile. He was lying on the grass, getting tickled by half a dozen very excited kids. 'Jacob did some research. Worked out well, didn't it?'

Looking around at the milling crowd, all enjoying being together, she knew Andrew had to agree. All the patients who were well enough to leave the wards were sitting in the sun, spending time with their loved ones, and people had come from far and wide to mark this special occasion.

Michelle spotted someone she recognised in the crowd. Excusing herself from Andrew, she headed over, self-consciously smoothing down the maxi-dress and jewelled sandals Jacob had helped her pick out for the day. She didn't feel quite herself, dressed like this, but she wanted to look nice and make an effort for the special day.

A woman on her own had come from the hospital and was walking towards the refreshment tent, her head turning this way and that. She was looking for *her*.

Michelle took a deep breath, using the clasped hands and deep breathing exercises her therapist had been teaching her. She had a few elastic bands in her bag—just in case. Plus, she had a hot surgeon boyfriend who had a pile of them in his pocket at all times. She loved him for that, even though she pretended not to notice. Jacob had surprised her in so many ways...

'Hello,' she said, stopping a short distance away from the woman. 'Thank you for coming.'

Kathryn Hughes looked like a carbon copy of her daughter—right down to the eyes and the easy smile. It was a shock to Michelle's system, but she recovered well.

'Thank you for inviting me,' Kathryn said in her usual warm way. 'How are you? You look well.'

Michelle had a million replies in her head.

Thanks, so do you. I picked my outfit especially to meet you. I miss your daughter. Thanks for bringing such an amazing person into the world.

Nothing seemed right—or enough. So Michelle drew her into a tight hug instead, and the two of them clung to each other, lost in their own world together.

'I'm sorry I wasn't there after the funeral,' Michelle whispered to her. 'I wanted to be—I really did.'

Kathryn squeezed her tighter, stroking her long flowing hair with her hand. A mother for ever, but now her arms were empty.

'You did what you could, my darling I know it's been hard for you too.' She pulled away a little, smoothing the wavy auburn hair away from Michelle's face and taking her in. 'Are you getting help?'

'Straight to the point, as always,' Michelle replied. 'I am getting help—I promise.'

Kathryn's face relaxed a little, her smile a bit brighter.

'Don't worry about me, Kathryn. I'm good. And I have someone for you to meet.'

Jacob, whom she knew had been watching the whole exchange, came walking over with Ebony holding his hand. Ebony was wearing a cream tulle dress, now streaked with grass stains, and Jacob had bright green patches on his jeans from diving onto the grass.

'Look at you two!' Michelle said, laughing. 'I don't envy your dry cleaner.'

Jacob grinned, flashing her one of his sexy looks. 'It's totally worth it. Right, Ebs?'

Ebony giggled. 'Totally! Who's this lady?'

Michelle had been working out how to introduce the pair, but Kathryn was already kneeling.

'My name is Kathryn. I'm a friend of Michelle's.' She held out her hand, and Ebony high-fived her.

Kathryn laughed—a carefree, happy laugh that startled Michelle. She hadn't heard it in so long.

'Sorry,' Jacob said, taking Kathryn's hand and shaking it himself. 'We're working on greeting people. I'm Jacob, one of the doctors here, and this is Ebony, my daughter.'

'I love a good high-five,' Kathryn said to Ebony kindly. 'Makes saying hello fun. Do you like the new hospital?' she asked.

Ebony nodded, looking around her, already distracted by the stalls.

Jacob pulled a coin out of his pocket, giving it to her. 'See Jude over there?' he asked.

Jude was standing with a group of children near the ice-cream van they had hired, and she spotted them, waving at Ebony.

'You go get an ice cream. I'll come in a minute.'

Ebony seized the coin and took off, her cream dress billowing behind her like a cape as she ran to the others.

'She's beautiful,' Kathryn said as the three of them watched the little girl leave.

'Oh, she's a handful, believe me,' said Jacob.

She had her moments, Michelle thought. But she had recovered from the accident. Riding in the car had become a bit of an experience, but with headphones and the latest Disney soundtrack they'd managed to get her mobile again.

'So, Jacob, I hear you knew my daughter?' Kathryn said.

As Jacob looked in panic at a very amused Michelle, Andrew's voice rang out over the lawn.

'It's time,' Michelle said, and gathering her whole crew together, Kathryn at her side, she walked across the grass to the main marquee, which was positioned right near the entrance to the new trauma centre, and the building that housed the secret project they planned to break ground on in a few short weeks' time.

Just as they were entering the tent Michelle felt a little hand brush against her fingers, gripping them tightly. Little Ebony looked up at her before returning to her ice cream, and Michelle winked. Ebony did it back, with both eyes, making her laugh.

The guests were all taking their seats in the white wooden chairs that had been put into rows, facing a stage with a podium, which Andrew was now standing at. He was dressed in a lightweight linen suit, and the trustees of the hospital were sitting behind him, chatting amongst themselves.

Michelle and her party sat in the reserved back row. Everything had been planned to the last detail, and they had put oo much work into today. Now it was here, Michelle couldn't help but worry about it not going well.

'Hey,' Jacob said, looking at Ebony, who was talking to Jude and Kathryn as they waited. His dark hair looked so deep and rich against the white backdrop of the marquee. 'Stop worrying. We've covered everything. We've rocked it, and today's going to be amazing.'

Michelle's heart fluttered at his words, but she didn't tell him that. Not this time. She had to have *some* mystique left—despite the fact that since Ebony had arrived at the hospital they had barely spent a moment apart.

'I know, but—'

'But nothing. Just enjoy it.' He patted his pocket. 'You need a band?'

She shook her head. 'No, I'll be fine.'

Everyone was assembled, and the crowd fell silent as Andrew started speaking.

'I am very happy to see so many people here at St. Marshall's today, to celebrate the opening of our new trauma centre. Surrey, as you know, has a fantastic community spirit, and seeing you all here today, getting involved, has been amazing. We are now officially a top trauma centre—and, thanks to the generosity of our trustees and investors, we are delighted to announce that on the site of the old trauma ward we will be developing a veterans' treatment centre, specialising in trauma aftercare, orthopaedics and prosthetics, as well as bespoke mental health services to help with the after-effects of close combat and PTSD.'

His eyes locked with Michelle's and she nodded, spurring him on. The flashes of cameras all around him told her that the press were lapping it up. All good publicity—which meant more awareness, more people they could help. She looked across at Kathryn nervously, but she was paying attention to Andrew, unaware of Michelle's panic.

'And it is down to two doctors—two magnificent former frontline medics—that this centre is going to happen. So huge thanks to Dr Michelle Forbes and Dr Jacob Peterson, who will be around today to answer any questions you might have. They know their stuff, so do say hello, look around our new trauma centre, see the plans for the old site. Have fun with your families today, here at St Marshall's. And Mayor Atkinson will now open the centre.'

The Mayor of the county stepped forward. 'Thank you, Dr Chambers, and thank you, everyone, for coming out to support our hospital today. Without further ado, I officially declare the Rebecca Hughes Trauma Centre…' He reached for the rope which had been set up to pull a tarp from the side of the building. It fell away, revealing Rebecca's name up there on the wall. *'Open!'*

The crowd all gasped and cheered, clapping and standing up as they saw the building unveiled for the first time.

Michelle closed her eyes. *Goodbye, my dearest friend. I love you and I will never forget you.* When she opened her eyes Kathryn was standing there, tears in her eyes.

'Kathryn, I—'

Michelle's words were crushed in Kathryn's embrace as the woman threw her arms around Michelle, holding her tight.

'I can't believe you did this—not only getting in touch, but—' Kathryn's voice broke as she looked at her daughter's name, standing out clear and proud for all to see.

'I loved her too,' Michelle said, trying not to break down herself. 'I feel like she's always with me, and now everyone will know her name.'

Kathryn nodded, too choked up from crying to speak. She mouthed *Thank you,* and Michelle kissed her cheek as she took out a tissue and wiped at her eyes.

'It was down to Jacob,' Michelle admitted, when they had both managed to stop crying enough to speak properly. 'It was his idea—the centre name, I mean.'

Both women looked across the lawn to where Jacob was now playing aeroplanes with some of the children. Ebony was on his back, like a baby monkey, his arms were outstretched, and he was twisting and turning his body around, chasing the kids and making them all laugh.

Ebony laughed the loudest, and she looked so happy, her little face quite recovered from the cuts from the crash.

Kathryn smiled wistfully as she watched them, and Michelle saw her emotions change as she observed.

'He's a good man,' Kathryn said after a time. 'He's a good influence on you too.'

Michelle blushed.

'Oh, I see you. missy. Don't be shy. You never looked like this around Scott. He was nice, and everything, but I have a feeling you've met your match here. Life's too short not to grab a bit of happiness now and again. God knows, I wish I'd grabbed a little more.'

Michelle was about to ask what she was talking about when Andrew headed over.

'Michelle, I'm sorry but we have incoming trauma.' He smiled politely at Kathryn and she waved Michelle away.

'You go, pet. I'm fine here. Andrew, do you fancy getting a drink with me?'

Andrew, ever the host, bowed theatrically, holding out his arm for his new companion. 'I would be delighted, Kathryn. Let's go.'

Andrew nodded to Michelle and the pair headed slowly over to the refreshment tent.

Michelle looked for Jacob, but he and the children had gone.

Heading into the trauma centre, she looked above her head at the new sign and marvelled at how at home Rebecca's name looked up there. She would come through these doors every day now, and she couldn't think of a better way to remember her beautiful friend.

'Hey, no slacking now you're a part-timer.' Jacob came up beside her, discarding his tie on the nearest planter as they walked through the main doors of their new domain. 'Where's the fire?'

'Incoming. You get a page?'

He shook his head. 'Nope. Andrew mentioned it and I

just came to help. He's with Ebony and Kathryn—she's taken a real shine to our girl.'

Our girl.

Michelle didn't react, but her heart felt as though it was lit up like a glow-worm in her chest.

They both went in and Wendy and Imogen, the two trauma nurses on duty that day, galvanised themselves as soon as they set eyes on the doctors, heading straight for them and giving them the lowdown on the casualties.

'Okay,' Jacob said, after hearing about the injuries of the five patients who were en route. 'Cross-check bloods, set up crash carts in Beds Two and Three, get Ortho and Paediatrics down here, and we'll go and change.'

'What about the party?' Wendy asked.

'The party's here!' Michelle said, slipping off her sandals as she walked. 'We'll let them get on with that while we show them why this trauma centre is worth all that cash!'

CHAPTER TWELVE

Two years later...

MICHELLE WALKED INTO the hospital chapel, her dress swishing as she stepped up to the altar slowly. Her legs felt shaky, unsure. *Damn heels.* She never did quite feel herself in them, but needs must...

Heading to the candles, she lit one and looked up to the ceiling. 'Well?' she said, laughing even as she wiped a tear away from her face with a gloved hand. 'Here we are. What do you think?'

She walked in a slow circle, showing off her outfit.

'Not bad for a former desert-dweller, eh?' She sat down carefully on the front pew, watching the candle-light flicker in the room. 'I know you think I need a minute, but I don't. I'm absolutely fine. Honestly.'

The room stayed silent, and Michelle rolled her eyes.

'Okay, so maybe just a minute. It's a lot, you know?' She cocked her head to one side, as though she was listening. 'Yeah, yeah, I'm going.'

'You about done?' a voice said from behind her.

Turning, she saw Jude and Andrew standing there, arm in arm. Jude did not look happy.

'You've ruined my make-up job!'

She came running at her, grabbing cosmetics from

her tiny purse and getting to work on her face as Andrew looked on.

'Talking to Becks?' he said softly, nodding his head towards the candles.

'I gave her your love,' Michelle replied, squeezing his arm. 'How is he?' she asked nervously.

Andrew, ever the diplomat, shrugged easily. 'He's fine. Everything's good.'

Jude turned to glare at him. 'Andrew, don't lie to the girl.' She turned and gave Michelle a conspiratorial look. 'He's vomited twice—once in the nurses' station bin. It ain't pretty. We'd better not keep him waiting.'

Michelle nodded. 'Lead the way.'

Heading out of the hospital, arm in arm with her friends, colleagues who had borne witness to her past, her present and her future, she was grateful. Grateful that they'd stuck by her, been stubborn enough to hang on in there with her, even when she had tried to drive them away.

Heading to The Pub on the Corner, on Andrew's arm, she took a deep breath and started to walk inside. The pub had been transformed, with white organza and satin draped over the walls, the chair-backs trimmed with gold ribbon, the tables all moved to form a makeshift aisle.

Michelle didn't see the congregation there—she only saw him. Dressed in a grey suit, his collar constricted by a blue cravat. She locked eyes with him and floated the rest of the way.

Ebony was standing off to one side, and she stopped in front of her. 'Here you go, darling,' she said, passing over her tied bouquet of calla lilies.

'You look beautiful, Mummy.' Ebony beamed.

Her dress was a smaller version of Michelle's, her sparkling green eyes a present from the man she was about to marry—her daddy.

Michelle pulled her close and Ebony flinched. 'Your make-up!' she whispered. She cupped a hand around her mouth and whispered in her new mother's ear. 'Auntie Jude says she'll paint you like Bobo the clown if you mess it up again.'

Michelle made a little *'whoops'* noise, and the pair of them laughed.

'Love you,' Michelle said to Ebony, the daughter she had taken on as her own, whom she loved to the ends of the earth.

Her real mother had stepped aside long ago, giving them her blessing, and Michelle couldn't help but think that she *was* her mother now. The one who would be there, no matter what. Even a top-class surgeon knew that it wasn't all about blood. Ebony had people who put her first, people who cared. That bonded them as parents. Their love for Ebony and their care for her needs and wants.

'Love you too,' Ebony whispered back, dropping a little kiss on Michelle's nose before heading back to stand with Jude.

She walked over to Jacob, Andrew dropping a kiss on her cheek before going to sit with Wendy and the others.

Jacob looked across at her, as the pair of them stood toe to toe once more.

'You look utterly beautiful,' he said, a hint of wonder in his voice. 'I love you so much.'

She beamed at him, feeling the sting of tears in her eyes but not caring who saw them this time. She was happy—truly happy for the first time in such a long time.

She saw Kathryn, sitting with the rest of their friends and giving her a watery smile before dabbing at her eyes. The friends comforted her, making her laugh. Friends who were all family now. Ride or die.

Looking out across the little pub, she saw the board. Lucas smiled out from the wall of faces, right next to a new addition or two. The faces of some of the veterans who had come to their centre for help and found new purpose in their lives, children they had saved, families they had helped repair, one kind word and dedicated treatment plan at a time.

In the centre of the board another picture was pinned up. A photo from last month—one that they had hoped for but hadn't expected. The picture had been taken at home—Jacob's home. *Their* home now. They were sitting on the sofa.

She remembered Ebony calling Jacob to sit down and open his present.

'A frame! Wow, cool!' he'd exclaimed, opening the box face down in his excitement, spurred on by Ebony's loud and excited cries.

'Open it, Daddy, open it quick! I can't wait any more!'

Ebony had squashed into Michelle's side on the couch and they had both sat and watched his face as he'd turned the frame over. It was then that they'd taken the photo.

It showed his surprised expression as he held the frame up, saw the monochrome sonogram picture filling the glass. Ebony's fists were in the air, her face scrunched up in happiness, and Michelle was gazing at her growing family with a serene expression. Her favourite photo and it was here. Here to witness the final piece of the puzzle.

'Where did you go?' Jacob leaned in as the registrar started speaking, his brows knitted in concern. 'You okay?'

He put his hand on her stomach instinctively, and she covered it with her own.

'I'm fine. Happy. I love you.'

He squeezed her fingers between his. 'Kinda glad to hear that—not going to lie. I even threw up earlier.'

The registrar was looking at them a little quizzically now, but they smiled at him, and Jacob lowered his voice when he started to speak again.

'I have to warn you, though. I have a hot date later.'

He looked at her with his emerald eyes, and she had to concentrate for a second to stop her legs from buckling beneath her.

'That's fine,' she said nonchalantly. 'I have a hot doctor waiting for me in the on-call room anyway.'

His eyes flashed with challenge and her heart and her libido soared. Even here, preparing to commit to each other for life, they were still *them*. Messy. Hot-headed. Unconventional. Perfectly imperfect and blissfully happy.

'You won't get far in that dress, I can tell you,' he growled.

The registrar rolled his eyes, not missing a syllable.

'Anything can happen in Trauma—you know the risks.'

She did, she thought. She knew the risks—and the lows.

Looking at her husband-to-be, the father of her unborn child and of her daughter who looked just like him, she smiled.

'Bring it on, player,' she said, wrinkling her nose at him.

The nod to his old life held no barb for them now. It was a love token, an acknowledgement of their shared past, their entwined future.

'Woman,' he said, ignoring the registrar's pleading eyes. 'Bring. It. On.'

* * * * *

COMING SOON!

We really hope you enjoyed reading this book.
If you're looking for more romance, be sure to
head to the shops when new books are
available on

Thursday 20th August

To see which titles are coming soon, please visit
millsandboon.co.uk/nextmonth

MILLS & BOON

MILLS & BOON

Coming next month

THE VET'S SECRET SON
Annie O'Neil

Lucas threw Ellie a confused look and caught a flare of guilt lance through her green eyes. She looked pale, her hands shaking as she feebly tried to wave away her white lie. He looked back at the little boy, registered his hair colour, his eye colour, the way they sloped a bit, like his mother's…and his. Almond shaped, he called them. Sleepy sexy, Ellie had called them. He had the strangest feeling of déjà vu. As if he was looking at a photo of himself from when he had been a little boy.

He tried to estimate the little boy's age and then, with the power of a lightning strike, he got it.

Maverick was his son.

His heart crashed against his ribcage with a ferocity he wouldn't have believed possible.

One look at Ellie, eyes bright with a sheen of tears, and he knew he was right.

Trying his best not to frighten the boy, who quite clearly did not know Lucas was his father, he knelt down in front of him, took the paper and signed it, drawing in his signature pawprint at the end of the 's' in Williams.

This was not the way he'd expected to meet his son. Not even close.

He felt Ellie's eye boring into him throughout the short interlude.

When he looked up at her, she was shaking her head, No, no, no—don't you dare tell him.

So what was he meant to do? Leave?

Not a chance.

Emotions assaulted him like knife wounds. Elation. Pride. Loss at having missed so many precious moments. His birth. His first word. His first tooth. Disbelief that Ellie had kept Maverick a secret all these years.

He knew things hadn't ended with any sort of grace between them but hiding a child? His child? What the hell had she been thinking? This gorgeous little boy was his flesh and blood. More than any of their shared hopes and dreams, Ellie knew he'd wanted a family of his own. With her! But life had ripped that possibility away from him.

And now, thanks to her, he'd missed the first five years of his son's life.

He forced his raging thoughts into a cage as he reminded himself, thanks to Ellie, he had a son. A beautiful, healthy, happy little boy. But at this moment? The gratitude ended there. She should have told him.

He rose and looked her straight in the eye. 'You and I need to talk.'

Continue reading
THE VET'S SECRET SON
Annie O'Neil

Available next month
www.millsandboon.co.uk

Copyright © 2020 Annie O'Neil

WE'RE LOOKING FOR NEW AUTHORS FOR THE MILLS & BOON MEDICAL SERIES!

Whether you're a published author or an aspiring one, our editors would love to read your story.

You can submit the synopsis and first three chapters of your novel online, and find out more about the series, at **harlequin.submittable.com/submit**

We read all submissions and you do not need to have an agent to submit.

IF YOU'RE INTERESTED, WHY NOT HAVE A GO?

Submit your story at:
harlequin.submittable.com/submit

MILLS & BOON

LET'S TALK
Romance

For exclusive extracts, competitions
and special offers, find us online:

- **f** facebook.com/millsandboon
- **𝕏** @MillsandBoon
- **◎** @MillsandBoonUK

Get in touch on 01413 063232

For all the latest titles coming soon, visit
millsandboon.co.uk/nextmonth

WANT EVEN MORE
ROMANCE?
SUBSCRIBE AND SAVE TODAY!

'Mills & Boon books, the perfect way to escape for an hour or so.'

MISS W. DYER

'Excellent service, promptly delivered and very good subscription choices.'

MISS A. PEARSON

'You get fantastic special offers and the chance to get books before they hit the shops.'

MRS V. HALL

Visit millsandboon.co.uk/Subscribe
and save on brand new books.